AFRICAN RHAPSODY

AFRICAN RHAPSODY

SHORT STORIES OF THE CONTEMPORARY AFRICAN EXPERIENCE

Edited by Nadežda Obradović
With a Foreword by
Chinua Achebe

ANCHOR BOOKS
NEW YORK LONDON TORONTO SYDNEY AUCKLAND

An Anchor Book

PUBLISHED BY DOUBLEDAY

a division of Bantam Doubleday Dell Publishing Group, Inc.

1540 Broadway, New York, NY 10036

ANCHOR BOOKS, DOUBLEDAY, *and the portrayal of an anchor*
are trademarks of Doubleday, a division of Bantam Doubleday
Dell Publishing Group, Inc.

Acknowledgments for individual works appear on pages 350–53.

Book Design by Gretchen Achilles

Library of Congress Cataloging-in-Publication Data

African rhapsody: short stories of the contemporary African experience /
edited by Nadežda Obradović; with a foreword by Chinua Achebe.
    p.   cm.
   1. Short stories, African (English) 2. Short stories, African—
Translations into English. 3. Africa—Fiction. I. Obradović, Nadežda.
PR9348.A33 1994
823'.0108896—dc20   93-21132
                                                      CIP

CONTENTS

FOREWORD

Literary historians tell us that the English novel preceded the short story by a hundred years or thereabouts. In modern African literature events happened differently. The short story came first—a far more logical development, if one may presume to say so. And we did not, of course, have centuries but decades to play with.

In 1951 F. J. Pedler, a respected British civil servant with considerable experience of West African affairs, published a little book titled, simply, *West Africa* in Home Study Books, a prestigious series which enlisted the expertise of Britain's leaders in science, the arts, and public affairs to present in a lucid, nontechnical style recent advances in knowledge in their various fields. I suppose West Africa earned a position in the company of such topics as Russian literature, modern psychology, and organic chemistry, etc., on account of its accelerating pace of change from colonial dependency toward self-rule, a process which would change the face of the whole continent in one short decade and even encourage Prime Minister Harold Macmillan to tell South Africans of all people about "a wind of change."

Although Pedler's book was not altogether free of the stereotypes of European colonial literature, it was in some ways remarkably advanced for its time. For example, he told his readers the startling news that African men did not buy their wives. "It is misleading," he wrote, "when Europeans talk of Africans buying a wife,"* and thus assailed a pet notion which Europeans had invented and cherished and recycled again and again in popular as well as serious literature. The well-known British writer Joyce Cary had exploited this very notion in the crudest manner imaginable a few years earlier in one of the "great" novels of African denigration called *Mister Johnson*.

* F. J. Pedler, *West Africa* (London: Methuen & Co., Ltd., 1951), p. 32.

I am recalling Pedler's book, however, for a different reason. It offered, as it were in passing, one literary comment which I find extraordinarily shrewd and even prophetic:

> A country's novels reveal its social condition. West Africa has no full length novels, but a few short stories may serve the purpose. We quote from two recent publications which show how educated West Africans themselves describe some of the features of social life in their own country.

Pedler then proceeded to quote from and to summarize two stories published in 1945 in the Gold Coast. Having taken almost three pages to deal with this matter he concluded as follows:

> Here is a dramatic treatment of a contemporary social phenomenon which leaves one with the hope that more West Africans may enter the field of authorship and give us authentic stories of the lives of their own people.★

These brief quotations from Pedler speak volumes on the issue of people and their stories. Note his phrases: *West Africans themselves; their own country; authentic stories; of their own people.* Without saying so in so many words he seemed to be engaged in a running argument against the age-old practice of the colonization of a people's story by others.

It is inconceivable that Pedler was unaware of Joyce Cary's *Mister Johnson,* which was celebrated in England and America then as now, to say nothing of British expatriate circles in Africa. He must also have been aware of Cary's three earlier "African

★ Ibid., p. 51.

novels." And yet he sidestepped them and scores of others of their kind and went to two unassuming short stories written by two completely unknown West Africans whose names did not, and do not, ring any bells. He sought out these lowly witnesses for authenticity about "the lives of their own people."

Pedler was certainly ahead of his time, and probably of ours as well. But be that as it may, one year after his book, Amos Tutuola startled the literary world with a strange "novel" called *Palm Wine Drunkard* which sent Dylan Thomas into raptures. Two years after that Cyprian Ekwensi published *People of the City*. Then followed Camara Laye's *L'Enfant Noir* in 1956 and my *Things Fall Apart* in 1958. For good or ill nobody could say thereafter that West Africa had no full-length novels. Indeed, a major literary development of the twentieth century was under way.

Short stories gave us a convenient bridge from oral to written literature. Amos Tutuola's episodic "novels" attest to this as does the fact that Cyprian Ekwensi preceded his novel with short fiction in traditional settings. But short stories are not choosy about who writes them or how. They are versatile and will consort with all manner of people especially with those caught in tight and nervous conditions and desiring to unburden themselves. I recall one of my colleagues from South Africa saying some time in the sixties that their political situation did not permit them the luxury of novels like us West Africans but had pressed them into the guerrilla, hit-and-run practice of the short story. At the time, I thought to myself: Yeah, right! Later, when I was embroiled in the Biafran catastrophe, I began slowly to understand the predicament I had been so smug about. My next novel took twenty years to come. And we are not out of the woods yet.

In the 1980s the early hopes for Africa which Nkrumah's Ghana had launched in 1957 had been throttled everywhere by a grim combination of causes: military regimes, corrupt leadership, debt bondage to Western banks, drought, and famine. If we are not pushed into despair by all of this we may earn a harvest of stories.

Last year the British newspaper *The Guardian,* as its own contribution to the thirtieth anniversary of the African Writers Series, announced a short-story contest with a one thousand-pound prize. They were literally deluged by stories from all over the world. Apparently even in China African nationals will write short stories in English! Which reminded me of the copious response I received when, at the end of the Biafran War, I had decided to edit and publish a literary magazine called *Okike* in the war-torn territory. The journal's success as a magnet for short stories is exemplified by this present anthology where I was flattered to see that as many as six of its twenty-five stories were originally published in *Okike*. And these six stories came to us not only from Nigeria, but also Tanzania, Zimbabwe, and the French-speaking Benin Republic. Clearly African writers seem to find the short story form quite appealing.

There may be many reasons for this appeal. But one of them surely must be the ease of recreation it affords for movement from different varieties of story-telling found in oral traditions. I believe I actually saw this process taking place in the smithy of an Igbo epic recital just over a decade ago. A seventy-five-year-old epic poet from the culturally fertile Anambra River basin was performing on the invitation of *"Okike* magazine" and its associated Igbo journal *Uwa ndi Igbo,* on the campus of the University of Nigeria. In his rendering of an old epic, "Emeka Okoye," the poet inserted what must surely have been a new dimension in telling an ancient tale of tyranny. In this version the sky-dwelling tyrant, Enunyilimba, rains down on the world below a decree written on flying sheets of paper declaring a feast in the sky and prohibiting any food or water for twenty-eight days in the world.

The license the poet takes with his material which is actually an infringement no less of traditional canon can be the despair of museum-minded purists. But artists have never allowed that to trouble them unduly in Africa. We only need to take a look at the *mbari* display which the Igbo people put on in appeasement of an offended divinity to see how immemorial motifs, say the royal python, could jostle for space with the white district officer, a new icon, smoking his pipe. You might even find Amadioha, god of thunder himself, wearing a hat and tie! This is art celebrating the total world of its community, the probable and the incongruous. What the old, illiterate poet did on our university campus was to recognize and acknowledge the presence of paper and literacy in our new world. And in doing so he also challenged us to apply our new gifts and talents to the enrichment of our ancient celebration.

The short stories assembled here resemble the art of an *mbari* display in the great variety and frank energy of their styles and practices. We are not expected, or indeed intended, to experience every offering with impartial, even-handed enthusiasm. But we will do well as we embark on the journey they promise through the African terrain and cultural panorama to leave at home our baggage of pet notions and stereotypes. And we will encounter new forms and new contents and new relationships between them. If we refuse to make our journey, or if we travel lugging along heavy loads of excess baggage, we will be like the young man whom the Igbo say never left home and went on thinking his mother made the best soup in the world.

We seem to have more problem accepting unfamiliar forms than content. The reason perhaps is that the raw material of human experience does not vary that much while the forms our art can impose on it are infinite. Which should make us happy but doesn't seem to do so. When I began thinking of this foreword my mind went back to my first romance with short-story writing. It happened during that euphoric decade of the fifties when F. J. Pedler was expressing his thoughts and hopes about novels and short stories in West Africa. I was a student at the newly founded University College, Ibadan, preparing for an arts degree of London University. The department of English had just announced a short-story competition and prize. We were given the whole long vacation to think it over. A short story; I decided to write one. In due course the results were published on the departmental notice board. No story, alas, was up to the standard for a departmental prize. But wait, my story was given honorable mention! And there was the helpful information that its weakness was that of form.

I was madly excited by my partial success. The English department at Ibadan was a stern and severe place that did not encourage you to believe too much in your chances. One fellow student who later became an outstanding novelist took one look at the department and fled into the warm embrace of Latin and Greek. No, our English department was not, as my people might say, a dance you got into carrying snuff in one hand. So I was elated to be mentioned in dispatches. And then there were the prospects for learning about form, for the future!

I approached the lecturer whose name was on the notice and asked if she could enlighten me on form. *Yes, of course,* she said, *but not today. Sometime.* And she went away to play tennis. I went to her a couple of times more with no greater success. And then one day, after a whole term had passed, she said to me: *I looked at that story of yours again, and actually I don't think there is much wrong with its form.*

And so I never learned the secret about short-story forms

that I could pass on to anybody today. Except perhaps what Duke Ellington taught us: If it sounds good, it *is* good!

This anthology is not a happy recital any more than Africa today is a happy continent. In a prefatory essay Joyce Cary wrote for a new edition of *Mister Johnson* in 1952 he speaks about "the warmheartedness of the African; his readiness for friendship on the smallest encouragement" and a little later adds: "I can't forget their grins (and laughter—an African will laugh loudly with pleasure at any surprise)."

Stereotypes are not necessarily malicious. They may be well meaning and even friendly. But in every case they show a carelessness or laziness or indifference of attitude which implies that the object of your categorization is not worth the trouble of individual assessment.

In any event you will not encounter the famed African laughter in these pages. The twenty-five authors gathered under one roof here did not hold a meeting beforehand to banish laughter from their recital. They are responding to an overwhelming reality of their lives. Together they seem to be saying to us that the person who is laughing has not heard the news.

The decision of the editor to arrange the stories in order from birth to death is a good one. It reveals with painful poignancy how young we do hear the news. "The Advance" by Henri Lopès of the Congo is a heartrending story of a little boy who dies from disease, hunger, and neglect trapped in his mother's hovel while she must spend the whole day in faraway suburbia minding the children of the well-to-do, coaxing food into them and then singing them to sleep.

Tayeb Salih from Sudan is a well-known writer. His story, "A Handful of Dates," is the work of a master craftsman; no fuss, no tool marks.

I must have been very young at the time. While I don't remember exactly how old I was, I do remember that when people saw me with my grandfather they would pat me on the head and give my cheek a pinch—things they didn't do to my grandfather. The strange thing was that I never used to go out with my father, rather it was my grandfather who would take me with him wherever he went, except for the mornings when I would go to the mosque to learn the Koran. The mosque, the river and the fields—these were the landmarks in our life.

In this lucid and compact tale we see how a sensitive little boy's love and admiration for his impressive grandfather crumbles quickly in revulsion as the old man reveals callous self-righteousness and lack of humanity.

This anthology brings together names already widely recognized—such as the Senegalese filmmaker and writer Sembène Ousmane, and Njabulo Ndebele, Charles Mungoshi, Alifa Rifaat, Luis Honwana, and Bloke Modisane—with others not so well known and with some new discoveries, especially the writers from North Africa whose work in Arabic was specially translated for this book.

Sindiwe Magona is one of the new voices. Her very powerful story of the blighted life of a mere fourteen-year-old on whom the cruelties of apartheid on a victim who is black and female are embellished further by the terror of incest.

There are many good things in this anthology. The betrayal of innocence comes up again and again in different configurations and circumstances. Ossie Enekwe's "The Last Battle," a story of the Biafran War, presents in stark and simple lines how a hero is betrayed by the very cause he fights for and turns him into a traitor.

The common factor in all the stories is a pervasive atmosphere of pain and life's injustice—an atmosphere so powerful that even when the actors think they are having a good time with alcohol and sex and card games in Charles Mungoshi's Zimbabwean story, "The Brother," they could just as well be at a funeral.

Chinua Achebe
Bard College
Annandale-on-Hudson, NY

PREFACE

We have gone beyond the era when the African writer stated, much as Chinua Achebe did, "I would be perfectly satisfied if my work, particularly when I speak of the past, was to teach my readers—at least my compatriots—that their past, with all its imperfections, was not a long dark night for society, from which the Europeans delivered them." Or as Bernth Lindfors later wrote, "Instead of representing Africa as a barbarous wilderness where savages lived in a permanent state of anarchy until the white man came bringing peace, law, order, religion, and a "higher" form of civilization, Achebe showed how Africans led decent, moral lives in well-regulated societies that placed strict legal and religious constraints on human behavior. Indeed, according to Achebe, things did not fall apart in Africa until Europe intruded and set everything off balance by introducing alien codes which Africans were then told to live by. Europe did not bring light and peace to the Dark Continent: it brought chaos and confusion."*

The new generation of writers is more determined, theirs is a loftier goal.

"The African writer cannot and must not take pen in hand merely to offer pretty expressions and phrases. As the product of a society that has its problems, he can and must help in their presentation so that each person becomes completely aware of them, so that people think of them, and look for their solution. If that is what it means to be a committed writer, then that is what I am," said Aminata Sow Fall, the prominent Senegalese author in an interview, adding, "Our literature must raise issues that summon men to devise solutions to problems that are specifically ours, problems which, although existing in other places, take on a special dimension in our country."

* Bernth Lindfors, "New Trends in West and East African Fiction," *Black Africa* 15 (1971).

These specific problems, related to their inherited past or to conflicts brought by the new era, are reflected in almost all the works originating in this large, heterogeneous continent with its countless different peoples, religions, languages, and customs. These shared situations of conflict include making the transition from childhood to maturity, moving from a rural to an urban environment, the encounter and collision with foreign or Western cultures, rebellion against colonial exploitation, and—themes that often prevail in the most recent works—disappointment with the new movement and merciless criticism of corruption, unemployment and dishonor, exploitation, and adopting others' (western) values. All these conflicts rightfully find their place in African prose.

Achieving national independence brought with it liberation from the linguistic domination of the colonizer, and a retreat from Western writing models in order to reach original solutions, regardless of the fact that the colonizer's language is often still used. The problem of which language to write in is a frequent dilemma of African authors and has been ever-present since the Negritude movement (1934) when Senghor wondered whether the "music, melody and rhythm comprising the essence of poetry could be written in another's language." After fifty years, these words still resound in the statement by Congolese Labou Tansi, "We must attempt to shatter the frigid French language . . . trying to lend it the opulence, the twinkle of our tropic temperament, the breathiness of our languages." This dilemma has still not been resolved. Writing in one's own language means a small reading public—due to the enormous number of languages spoken in Africa and due to illiteracy. Writing in another language means a large international reading public and the possibility of world fame. Each writer finds his own answer; some write in their own language and then translate their own works into English (Ngugi Wa Thiong'o) and French, or try the new African English (Gabriel Okara) or French (A. Kourouma), while others turn to film (Sembène Ousmane), considering the silver screen to have replaced the traditional African tree where villagers used to gather to hear the griot—the oral storyteller.

The emphasis in this collection, apart from literary merit, is on the diversity of topics from the variety of countries involved—ranging from the north African areas, Algeria, Morocco, Tunisia, Egypt, to the southern, Mozambique and South Africa. The everyday ways of life, culture, tradition, superstition, religion, marital customs, politics, interpersonal and interfamily relations, and the behavior of men and women in crisis situations such as war all permeate the pages of these twenty-five stories from sixteen countries. Their plots span the colonial period (Henri Lopès's story "The Advance," L. Honwana's "Papa, Snake & I") to the troubled years of the Biafran War (O. O. Enekwe's "The Last Battle" and A. Maja-Pearce's "Civil War I–VII") and religious riots (A. R. Gurnah's "Bossy").

The greatest number of stories are from Nigeria. No wonder: Nigeria is not only a mammoth country with over 100 million inhabitants, it is also the country which produced *The Palm Wine Drunkard* by Amos Tutuola in 1952, the first book to earn worldwide acclaim and hint to the large international public something of the unknown creativity of this continent. An entire galaxy of talented writers followed. Chinua Achebe's books sold millions of copies and became mandatory texts in African schools and European, American, and Australian universities. Wole Soyinka received the Nobel Prize; Ben Okri was recently awarded the Booker Prize. Such greatness nurtured other creators of similar merit.

Many of the stories in this collection were originally written in English; others were translated from French, Arabic, and Portuguese. This fact further contributes to the variety of plots and literary expressions.

The wellsprings of these stories include the collections of individual writers and anthologies of African stories published by European publishing houses, such as Heinemann Educational Books, Longman, (Great Britain); Malawi Writers Series, (Malawi); Mambo Press, Zimbabwe Publishing House, (Zimbabwe); Enterprise Nationale du Livre, (Algeria); literary journals such as the Nigerian periodicals *Okike* and *Lotus,* the journal of the Association of African and Asian Writers; South African publisher David Philip; and Saros International, Nigeria. Several tales were translated especially for this collection and appear for the first time in English ("The Wicked Tongue" by Mohammed Moulessehoul from Algeria, for example).

My desire to include more women writers fell short of expectations since new literary names such as Tsitsi Dangarembga (from Zimbabwe) have not cultivated the short story as a genre. Therefore, the appearance of South African woman writer Sindiwe Magona is all the greater, as it is the first time that her work has appeared outside of South Africa.

The stories could have been arranged in several ways: alphabetically by author for example, or by geographical region. I have adopted another approach, however, arranging the stories by plot. The beginning of the collection presents stories with children as protagonists ("The Prophetess," "A Handful of Dates"), and the end stories of war, destruction, and death ("The Last Battle," "Civil War," "At the Time of the Jasmine"). The middle presents tales of everyday life and customs. Thus, I have attempted to portray a large spectrum of African life.

This collection mosaic may serve as a window on the present and future development and abundance of literary creations on

African soil, where new literary names emerge almost daily and continue to provide their valuable contributions to the body of African literature.

Nadežda Obradović
February 1994

AFRICAN
RHAPSODY

TAYEB SALIH

was born in 1929 in the northern part of the Sudan. He was the chief of drama in the Arabian department of BBC and at present he is working in UNESCO in Paris. A short novel and several short stories were published under the title Wedding of Zeine and Other Stories *in 1968. In 1969 Salih published his novel* The Season of Migration to the North.

A HANDFUL OF DATES

TAYEB SALIH

Translated by Denys Johnson-Davies

I MUST HAVE BEEN VERY YOUNG AT THE TIME. WHILE I don't remember exactly how old I was, I do remember that when people saw me with my grandfather they would pat me on the head and give my cheek a pinch—things they didn't do to my grandfather. The strange thing was that I never used to go out with my father, rather it was my grandfather who would take me with him wherever he went, except for the mornings when I would go to the mosque to learn the Koran. The mosque, the river and the fields—these were the landmarks in our life. While most of the children of my age grumbled at having to go to the mosque to learn the Koran, I used to love it. The reason was, no doubt, that I was quick at learning by heart and the Sheikh always asked me to stand up and recite the *Chapter of the Merciful* whenever we had visitors, who would pat me on my head and cheek just as people did when they saw me with my grandfather.

Yes, I used to love the mosque, and I loved the river too. Directly we finished our Koran reading in the morning I would throw down my wooden slate and dart off, quick as a genie, to my mother, hurriedly swallow down my breakfast, and run off for a plunge in the river. When tired of swimming about I would sit on the bank and gaze at the strip of water that wound away eastward and hid behind a thick wood of acacia trees. I

loved to give rein to my imagination and picture to myself a
tribe of giants living behind that wood, a people tall and thin
with white beards and sharp noses, like my grandfather. Before
my grandfather ever replied to my many questions he would rub
the tip of his nose with his forefinger; as for his beard, it was soft
and luxuriant and as white as cotton-wool—never in my life
have I seen anything of a purer whiteness or greater beauty. My
grandfather must also have been extremely tall, for I never saw
anyone in the whole area address him without having to look up
at him, nor did I see him enter a house without having to bend
so low that I was put in mind of the way the river wound round
behind the wood of acacia trees. I loved him and would imagine
myself, when I grew to be a man, tall and slender like him,
walking along with great strides.

I believe I was his favorite grandchild: no wonder, for my
cousins were a stupid bunch and I—so they say—was an intelligent child. I used to know when my grandfather wanted me to
laugh, when to be silent; also I would remember the times for
his prayers and would bring him his prayer rug and fill the ewer
for his ablutions without his having to ask me. When he had
nothing else to do he enjoyed listening to me reciting to him
from the Koran in a lilting voice, and I could tell from his face
that he was moved.

One day I asked him about our neighbor Masood. I said to my
grandfather: "I fancy you don't like our neighbor Masood?"

To which he answered, having rubbed the tip of his nose:
"He's an indolent man and I don't like such people."

I said to him: "What's an indolent man?"

My grandfather lowered his head for a moment, then looking across at the wide expanse of field, he said: "Do you see it
stretching out from the edge of the desert up to the Nile bank?
A hundred feddans. Do you see all those date palms? And those

trees—sant, acacia and sayal? All this fell into Masood's lap, was inherited by him from his father."

Taking advantage of the silence that had descended upon my grandfather, I turned my gaze from him to the vast area defined by his words. "I don't care," I told myself, "who owns those date palms, those trees or this black, cracked earth—all I know is that it's the arena for my dreams and my playground."

My grandfather then continued: "Yes, my boy, forty years ago all this belonged to Masood—two thirds of it is now mine."

This was news to me for I had imagined that the land had belonged to my grandfather ever since God's Creation.

"I didn't own a single feddan when I first set foot in this village. Masood was then the owner of all these riches. The position has changed now, though, and I think that before Allah calls to him I shall have bought the remaining third as well."

I do not know why it was I felt fear at my grandfather's words—and pity for our neighbor Masood. How I wished my grandfather wouldn't do what he'd said! I remembered Masood's singing, his beautiful voice and powerful laugh that resembled the gurgling of water. My grandfather never used to laugh.

I asked my grandfather why Masood had sold his land.

"Women," and from the way my grandfather pronounced the word I felt that "women" was something terrible. "Masood, my boy, was a much-married man. Each time he married he sold me a feddan or two." I made the quick calculation that Masood must have married some ninety women. Then I remembered his three wives, his shabby appearance, his lame donkey and its dilapidated saddle, his djellaba with the torn sleeves. I had all but rid my mind of the thoughts that jostled in it when I saw the man approaching us, and my grandfather and I exchanged glances.

"We'll be harvesting the dates today," said Masood. "Don't you want to be there?"

I felt, though, that he did not really want my grandfather to attend. My grandfather, however, jumped to his feet and I saw that his eyes sparkled momentarily with an intense brightness. He pulled me by the hand and we went off to the harvesting of Masood's dates.

Someone brought my grandfather a stool covered with an ox hide, while I remained standing. There was a vast number of people there, but though I knew them all, I found myself for some reason watching Masood: aloof from the great gathering of people he stood as though it were no concern of his, despite the fact that the date palms to be harvested were his own. Sometimes his attention would be caught by the sound of a huge clump of dates crashing down from on high. Once he shouted up at the boy perched on the very summit of the date palm who had begun hacking at a clump with his long, sharp sickle: "Be careful you don't cut the heart of the palm."

No one paid any attention to what he said and the boy seated at the very summit of the date palm continued, quickly and energetically, to work away at the branch with his sickle till the clump of dates began to drop like something descending from the heavens.

I, however, had begun to think about Masood's phrase "the heart of the palm." I pictured the palm tree as something with feeling, something possessed of a heart that throbbed. I remembered Masood's remark to me when he had once seen me playing about with the branch of a young palm tree: "Palm trees, my boy, like humans, experience joy and suffering." And I had felt an inward and unreasoned embarrassment.

When I again looked at the expanse of ground stretching before me I saw my young companions swarming like ants around the trunks of the palm trees, gathering up dates and eating most of them. The dates were collected into high mounds. I saw people coming along and weighing them into measuring bins and pouring them into sacks, of which I counted thirty. The crowd of people broke up, except for Hussein the merchant, Mousa the owner of the field next to ours on the east and two men I'd never seen before.

I heard a low whistling sound and saw that my grandfather had fallen asleep. Then I noticed that Masood had not changed his stance, except that he had placed a stalk in his mouth and was munching at it like someone surfeited with food who doesn't know what to do with the mouthful he still has.

Suddenly my grandfather woke up, jumped to his feet and walked toward the sacks of dates. He was followed by Hussein the merchant, Mousa the owner of the field next to ours and the two strangers. I glanced at Masood and saw that he was making his way toward us with extreme slowness, like a man who wants to retreat but whose feet insist on going forward. They formed a circle round the sacks of dates and began examining them, some taking a date or two to eat. My grandfather gave me a fistful, which I began munching. I saw Masood filling the palms of both hands with dates and bringing them up close to his nose, then returning them.

Then I saw them dividing up the sacks between them. Hussein the merchant took ten; each of the strangers took five. Mousa the owner of the field next to ours on the eastern side took five, and my grandfather took five. Understanding nothing, I looked at Masood and saw that his eyes were darting about to left and right like two mice that have lost their way home.

"You're still fifty pounds in debt to me," said my grandfather to Masood. "We'll talk about it later."

Hussein called his assistants and they brought along donkeys, the two strangers produced camels, and the sacks of dates were loaded on to them. One of the donkeys let out a braying which set the camels frothing at the mouth and complaining noisily. I felt myself drawing close to Masood, felt my hand stretch out toward him as though I wanted to touch the hem of his garment. I heard him make a noise in his throat like the rasping of a lamb being slaughtered. For some unknown reason, I experienced a sharp sensation of pain in my chest.

I ran off into the distance. Hearing my grandfather call after me, I hesitated a little, then continued on my way. I felt at that moment that I hated him. Quickening my pace, it was as though I carried within me a secret I wanted to rid myself of. I reached the riverbank near the bend it made behind the wood of acacia trees. Then, without knowing why, I put my finger into my throat and spewed up the dates I'd eaten.

HENRI LOPÈS

was born in the Congo in 1937. In 1981 he published his first collection of stories entitled **Tribaliques,** *translated into English as* **Tribaliks—Contemporary Congolese Stories.** *This book has the distinction of winning the Grand Prix Littéraire d'Afrique Noire for 1972 (the great literary prize of Black Africa). His novels* **La Nouvelle Romance** *(1976) and* **Sans Tam-Tam** *(1977) were acclaimed by readers and critics. His latest novel,* **Le Pleurer-Rire,** *was brought out in 1982 (The Laughing Cry, 1987).*

Henri Lopès has been very active in political life. He was Minister of Education in the Congo, Prime Minister, Minister of Finances. At present Mr. Lopès is with UNESCO in Paris, as Assistant Director General for Culture and Communication.

THE ADVANCE

HENRI LOPÈS

Translated by Andrea Leskes

"NO GOOD," THE LITTLE GIRL SAID, SCREWING UP HER face.

"Yes it is, Francoise. Look." Carmen herself swallowed a mandarin section, then closed her eyes. The little girl looked at her, impassively.

"Eat it all up."

Like a priest proffering the host, Carmen offered her the orange quarter. Haughtily, the little girl turned her head away. It was already seven o'clock. Carmen was eager to finish up her work, especially since she had not yet asked the mistress . . .

She spoke more sharply and looked stern.

"If you don't eat, Francoise, I'm going to tell your mother." Still the little girl did not relent.

The mistress of the house was in the living room, together with her husband, entertaining friends they had invited over for bridge. She had already warned Carmen several times not to bother her when she was, as she said, "with company." Did Carmen dare to interrupt the happy group anyway? She did not fear being yelled at. People raise their voices mostly to relieve their own tensions. And since, according to Ferdinand the watchman, Madam's husband beat her, she took her revenge out on the servants. Why feel resentful? It was far better to just accept it philosophically. But to be taken to task in front of others, strangers, that was worse than being slapped. So Carmen preferred to wait.

Also, Madam had the annoying habit of speaking to her daughter as if she were an adult.

"Francoise, sweetheart, what did you have to eat?" And little Francoise, while reciting for her mother, would delight in explaining that she had not eaten any dessert because the mandarins Carmen wanted to give her were rotten. And Madam would admonish Carmen for not having told her about it. Especially since she had already explained that without dessert the child might not get a well-balanced meal, and so on and so forth. Carmen would usually listen to it all, seriously. In her village, and over in Makélékélé, what mattered was that a child had a full belly and did not go hungry. If, in addition, they had to worry about a balanced diet, there would never be an end to it. Besides, Carmen must not forget to ask her mistress . . .

There was only one solution. Do as her own mother had done to get her to eat. With one hand she opened the child's mouth and with the other shoved in the piece of fruit. As expected, Francoise howled. She cried and choked with rage. From the hallway came hammerlike sounds on the tile floor—the footsteps of Madam who came running. Carmen had won.

"What's going on in here?"

"She doesn't want to eat, Madam."

"Oh, don't force her, poor little thing. Get her some grapes from the refrigerator. She likes grapes."

Madam took the little girl's head in her hands and kissed her several times. Carmen went to get the European-style dessert. As she was returning, she crossed Madam in the hall and almost broached the subject that was on her mind. But it did not seem like quite the right moment.

Francoise ate the grapes with relish. They must be good because instead of being her usual, talkative self, she remained calm and quiet as she ate the fruit. One day Carmen would have to swipe some of them and see what they tasted like.

While the little girl ate, Carmen wiped the tears from her cheeks. In her heart she cared a great deal for this child. Carmen had been with her since she was two months old and had practically brought her up. Francoise was as much her daughter as Madam's. Even if she quit her job, or Madam fired her, she would not be able to resist returning from time to time to see how Francoise had grown.

Then Carmen took the little girl to spend a penny, changed her, and put her to bed. By then it was 7:30. Night had fallen and she would still have an hour's walk to reach Makélékélé. But Francoise did not want her maid to leave. She clung to her annoying routine of wanting Carmen to sing her to sleep with a song.

> *"Nguè kélé mwana ya mboté,*
> Sleep baby sleep,
> Sleep baby sleep."

After that she had to sing another. Usually the child would fall asleep during the second song but that evening it took three. While Carmen sang, her thoughts were elsewhere. She thought about Francoise whom she loved as much as her son, a child of the same age yet so different. Francoise was the picture of health, while her son had come close to death several times already. Nothing intimidated Francoise, she was comfortable speaking with grown-ups, ordered about the servants and already showed a certain fussiness in her choice of clothes. Her Hector did not dare to speak. He was shy and withdrawn with strangers. His unhappiness already showed in his eyes. Yet both children were of the same generation. They spoke the same language but would they be able to understand each other? Carmen did not think this jealously. No, she would like Hector to be "well brought up," but how could that possibly be? Society and human nature would have to change.

That morning she had been very tempted to stay home from work. All night long the poor little fellow had cried. He complained of a stomachache. He had diarrhea and vomited at least three times. The first time seemed to relieve him, but the last brought something greenish up from his little stomach. Then his stomach continued to contract spasmodically and nothing more came up. The child was clearly in pain. His breathing was labored, his forehead covered with sweat. She was very frightened and thought of the two children she had already lost. She even panicked. She had almost awakened her mother, asleep in the same compound. But she restrained herself. Her mother would have taken him immediately to the fetishist. That was how it happened with the other two. And they died. Yet each time she paid the equivalent of her own earnings. And after their deaths it was worse. The fetishist concluded she kept losing her children because for five years she had been refusing to marry the man her parents had chosen for her. And, in addition to her grief, she was obliged to suffer the nonsense of a relentless succession of old hags who harped on the subject, and tried to pressure her into yielding and giving in to either the will of God, the ancestors, the spirits or her poor children. She should marry Kitonga Flavien and then everything would be all right again. Wasn't he a good catch? Besides his job as a government chauffeur, he was his own boss after work. He owned four taxis, a shop and a bar in Ouenze-Indochina. Kitonga would support her, she wouldn't have to work any longer. Besides, he already had two wives. One at Bacongo and the other who ran the bar at Ouenze.

While she contemplated all this, her son called. He wanted to sleep on her mat. He was afraid to be alone. Would he last until morning? When some children are sick their parents can immediately pick up the phone, dial a number and go straight to the doctor who does whatever is needed, or reassures them. But not poor people! The closest dispensaries are closed at night. And at the hospital we are received by a nurse who is rude and makes a fuss because we dared to wake him. As for going to a doctor, well, folks who live in the better parts of town won't open their doors at night to just anyone. Besides, she is letting her imagination run wild. A visit to a private doctor costs money.

Finally, at dawn, the child fell asleep. As for Carmen, she had to get up and go to work. Every day she must walk two hours from Makélékélé to Mipla. Since her mistress wants her to be there before 7:30, it's easy to calculate . . .

Despite her exhaustion she did not want to stay in bed. But neither did she want to go to work that morning. She would have preferred to go to the hospital and find out exactly what was wrong with Hector. Whenever he was ill, Carmen did not like to leave him alone. Her heart was not at ease. Once she tried to take him along to work, but Madam had made it plain that she was not being paid to care for her own son but for Francoise. Carmen knew that her mother and the other female relatives would take him to see a doctor. The tribal family is large and a child, no matter what happens, is never alone. But nonetheless, she believed that a child is best off being brought up by its mother. And those we have brought into the world need us most of all when they are sick.

But if she had devoted the day to her son, she would have been fired and then how would they manage? She had already missed work twice that month. The first time she really had been sick and had spent two feverish days on her mat. The second time was for a funeral. Madam was very angry.

"Carmen, I have had just about enough! Each time I need you, you aren't here. It almost seems as if you do it on purpose. You choose to stay home the very days I've made plans. My dear woman, I'm warning you now. If you miss one more day this month, you'll have to look for work elsewhere."

How could she explain? Carmen tried her best. But white people, they think that whenever we don't come to work, it's because we're lazy.

And today she came to work despite Hector being so ill. At noon her sister sent word that the doctor had prescribed some medicine. It was always the same old story. How would she pay for it? Yet Hector must be cured.

And that evening, there she was, singing for a little girl who had everything, and whose parents were playing cards with other ladies and gentlemen.

When Francoise had fallen asleep, Carmen went to wait in the kitchen until the guests had finished their game of bridge. She spent the time talking to Ferdinand, the old watchman. Those were moments she generally enjoyed. It lightened her spirits, eased her worry. They exchanged gossip on the short-comings of their employers. Usually when Ferdinand described things he had seen, he would mimic them and Carmen would laugh. That evening, however, she remained serious and Ferdinand remarked on it.

Finally Madam came into the kitchen.

"Haven't you left yet, Carmen?"

It was the most difficult moment. "Madam, I need some money."

"Again? But I paid you only ten days ago."

"My son is sick. He needs medicine."

"Listen to that, just listen to that! So I am now the public welfare fund. They have children without a husband and then they can't manage to take care of them!"

"Madam, white people say that . . ."

"So your child is sick? Well, it's because you don't listen to me. I've told you again and again that you must feed him properly. Did you do it?"

"No, Madam."

"No, of course not. It's easier to fill his stomach with your rotten old *manioc.*"

What could Carmen answer? That she had tried the diet Madam suggested but it was beyond her means. It seemed that Madam did not realize how in one week she spent three times Carmen's monthly salary just to feed her husband, her daughter, herself and their cat. If the maid had reminded her of that, she would have been fired for insolence.

"But anyway, I don't have any cash at home this evening. When will you natives understand that money doesn't grow on trees? When will you learn to put money aside and save?"

And Madam continued speaking like that for a long time. Carmen did not understand all she said. When people speak French too rapidly, she doesn't have time to translate it all in her mind, so she just tunes out and nods her head, as she did at that moment. Had that perhaps softened Madam? In any case, she gave her some aspirin and promised her 500 francs the following day.

So finally black Carmen left. She walked all the way back to Makélékélé. It was far from Mipla to Makélékélé. As far as from her native village to where she was sent to school. It left plenty of time for thought.

Carmen wanted to run, she felt so strongly that Hector needed her. But after not having slept the whole night, and eating nothing but a slice of manioc for lunch, she could not run. Suddenly she felt that Hector was calling her.

Poor little thing. "When he grows up, will he love me? To support us both I must leave him alone all day long. Maybe he'll resent it. I regret having left him without medical care so long. But I had faith in the white man's medicine and in his goodwill. If Mamma suggests I take him to the fetishist tonight, I won't be able to refuse any longer."

And she thought about all Madam had said. They would never really understand each other. Carmen spent more time with her mistress than with her own son. Madam entrusted her daughter to Carmen in complete confidence. And yet Carmen could not understand Madam's reactions nor could Madam imagine what was going on in her maid's head, or the difficulties of her world. She considered Carmen an irresponsible and frivolous girl.

How does she expect me to save money on 5000 francs a month. Last month she only paid me 4000. For six months now she has been keeping back 500 francs a month to help repay the cost of the watch I bought. It was my only extravagance. Then I had to give 1000 francs to the *tontine** of our community, 1000 francs to my mother, 1000 francs to pay for the trip home of my aunt and cousins who had moved in with us for a month. I had only 1000 francs left. And what is 1000 francs? Madam spends that much on food every day.

Cars passed by in the poorly lit streets. Those that came toward Carmen blinded her with their headlights. Those that arrived from behind barely missed hitting her. And no one stopped to give her a lift. Yet she knew that at least half of the cars were driven by blacks like herself. In today's world, each to his own.

Oh, if only Madam would remember to give her money for the medicine tomorrow.

As she approached Biza Street, the cry of women's voices raised in the night reached her:

---

* Community-based method of saving. Every month, each participant contributes a fixed sum. The entire amount is handed over monthly, in turns, to one of the members.

> *"Mwana mounou mê kouenda hé!*
> *Hector hé,*
> *Mwana mounou mê kouenda hé."*

She understood that medicine or fetishist, it was too late.

> "Oh, my son has gone away!
> Oh, my Hector,
> Oh, my son has gone away."

LUIS BERNARDO HONWANA

was born in 1942 in Maputo, Mozambique. Very early he started his literary and political activities. In 1967 he was released from a political prison sentence, and then lived in various countries—Portugal, Algeria, Switzerland, Tanzania. At present Honwana is a chief of staff to the President of Mozambique.

Honwana has made several documentary films and was awarded the Leipzig Film Festival prize in 1978. Another hobby is photography.

The book We Killed Mangy Dog and Other Mozambique Stories, *translated from the Portuguese, consists of seven stories, each set in Mozambique. It was published in English in 1967 and had many editions.*

PAPA, SNAKE & I

LUIS BERNARDO HONWANA

Translated by Dorothy Guedes

AS SOON AS PAPA LEFT THE TABLE TO READ THE NEWS-
paper in the sitting room, I got up as well. I knew that Mama
and the others would take a while longer, but I didn't feel like
staying with them at all.

When I stood up, Mama looked at me and said, "Come
here, let me look at your eyes."

I went toward her slowly, because when Mama calls us we
never know whether she's cross or not. After she had lifted my
lids with the index finger of her left hand to make a thorough
examination, she looked down at her plate and I stood waiting
for her to send me away or to say something. She finished chewing, swallowed, and picked up the bone in her fingers to peep
through the cavity, shutting one eye. Then she turned to me
suddenly with a bewildered look on her face.

"Your eyes are bloodshot; you're weak and you've lost your
appetite."

The way she spoke made me feel obliged to say that none of
this was my fault or else that I didn't do it on purpose. All the
others looked on very curiously to see what was going to happen.

Mama peered down the middle of the bone again. Then she
began to suck it, shutting her eyes, and only stopped for a moment to say, "Tomorrow you're going to take a laxative."

As soon as the others heard this, they began eating again very quickly and noisily. Mama didn't seem to have anything else to say, so I went out into the yard.

It was hot everywhere, and I could see no one on the road. Over the back wall three oxen gazed at me. They must have come back from the water trough at the Administration and stayed to rest in the shade. Far away, over the oxen's horns, the gray tufts of the dusty thorn trees trembled like flames. Everything vibrated in the distance, and heat waves could even be seen rising from the stones in the road. Sartina was sitting on a straw mat in the shade of the house, eating her lunch. Chewing slowly, she looked around, and from time to time, with a careless gesture, she shooed away the fowls who came close to her hoping for crumbs. Even so, every now and then one of the bolder ones would jump on to the edge of the plate and run off with a lump of mealie meal in its beak, only to be pursued by the others. In their wild dispute, the lump would become so broken up that in the end even the smallest chicken would get its bit to peck.

When she saw me coming near, Sartina pulled her *capulana* down over her legs, and even then kept her hand spread out in front of her knees, firmly convinced that I wanted to peep at something. When I looked away she still didn't move her hand.

Toto came walking along slowly with his tongue hanging out, and went to the place where Sartina was sitting. He sniffed the plate from afar and turned away, taking himself off to the shade of the wall where he looked for a soft place to lie down. When he found one, he curled round with his nose almost on his tail, and only lay still when his stomach touched the ground. He gave a long yawn, and dropped his head between his paws. He wriggled a little, making sure that he was in the most comfortable position, then covered his ears with his paws.

When she had finished eating, Sartina looked at me insistently before removing her hand which covered the space between her knees, and only when she was sure I was not looking did she spring to her feet with a jump. The plate was so clean that it shone, but after darting a last suspicious glance at me, she took it to the trough. She moved languidly, swaying from the waist as her hips rose and fell under her *capulana*. She bent over the trough, but the back of her legs was exposed in this position, so she went to the other side for me not to see.

Mama appeared at the kitchen door, still holding the bone in her hand, and before calling Sartina to clear the table, she looked around to see if everything was in order. "Don't forget to give Toto his food," she said in Ronga.

Sartina went inside, drying her hands on her *capulana,* and afterward came out with a huge pile of plates. When she came out the second time she brought the tablecloth and shook it on the stairs. While the fowls were skirmishing for the crumbs, pecking and squawking at each other, she folded it in two, four, and eight, and then went back inside. When she came out again she brought the aluminum plate with Toto's food, and put it on the cement cover of the water meter. Toto didn't have to be called to eat and even before the plate was put down, he threw himself on his food. He burrowed into the pile of rice with his nose, searching for the bits of meat which he gulped up greedily as he found them. When no meat was left, he pushed the bones aside and ate some rice. The fowls were all around him, but they didn't dare to come nearer because they knew very well what Toto was like when he was eating.

When he had swallowed the rice, Toto pretended he didn't want any more and went to sit in the shade of the sugarcane, waiting to see what the fowls would do. They came nervously toward his food, and risked a peck or two, very apprehensively. Toto watched this without making a single movement. Encouraged by the passivity of the dog, the fowls converged on the rice with great enthusiasm, creating an awful uproar. It was then that Toto threw himself on the heap, pawing wildly in all directions and growling like an angry lion. When the fowls disappeared, fleeing to all corners of the yard, Toto went back to the shade of the sugarcane, waiting for them to gather together again.

Before going to work Papa went to look at the chicken run with Mama. They both appeared at the kitchen door, Mama already wearing her apron and Papa with a toothpick in his mouth and his newspaper under his arm. When they passed me Papa was saying, "It's impossible, it's impossible, things can't go on like this."

I went after them, and when we entered the chicken run Mama turned to me as if she wanted to say something, but then she changed her mind and went toward the wire netting. There were all sorts of things piled up behind the chicken run: pipes left over from the building of the windmill on the farm, blocks which were bought when Papa was still thinking of making outhouses of cement, boxes, pieces of wood, and who knows what else. The fowls sometimes crept in among these things and laid their eggs where Mama couldn't reach them. On one side of the run lay a dead fowl, and Mama pointed to it and said, "Now there's this one, and I don't know how many others have just died from one day to the next. The chickens simply disappear, and the eggs too. I had this one left here for you to see. I'm tired of talking to you about this, and you still don't take any notice."

"All right, all right, but what do you want me to do about it?"

"Listen, the fowls die suddenly, and the chickens disappear. No one goes into the chicken run at night, and we've never heard any strange noise. You must find out what's killing the fowls and chickens."

"What do you think it is?"

"The fowls are bitten and the chickens are eaten. It can only be the one thing you think it is—if there are any thoughts in your head."

"All right, tomorrow I'll get the snake killed. It's Sunday, and it will be easy to get people to do it. Tomorrow."

Papa was already going out of the chicken run when Mama said, now in Portuguese, "But tomorrow without fail, because I don't want any of my children bitten by a snake."

Papa had already disappeared behind the corner of the house on his way to work when Mama turned to me and said, "Haven't you ever been taught that when your father and mother are talking you shouldn't stay and listen! My children aren't usually so bad-mannered. Who do you take after?"

She turned to Sartina, who was leaning against the wire netting and listening. "What do you want? Did anyone call you? I'm talking to my son and it's none of your business."

Sartina couldn't have grasped all that because she didn't understand Portuguese very well, but she drew away from the netting, looking very embarrassed, and went to the trough again. Mama went on talking to me, "If you think you'll fool me and take the gun to go hunting you're making a big mistake. Heaven help you if you try to do a thing like that! I'll tan your backside for you! And if you think you'll stay here in the chicken run you're also mistaken. I don't feel like putting up with any of your nonsense, d'you hear?"

Mama must have been very cross, because for the whole day I hadn't heard her laugh as she usually did. After talking to me she went out of the chicken run and I followed her. When she passed Sartina, she asked her in Ronga, "Is it very hot under your *capulana?* Who told you to come here and show your legs to everybody?"

Sartina said nothing, walked round the trough, and went on washing the plates, bending over the other side.

Mama went away and I went to sit where I had been before. When Sartina saw me she turned on me resentfully, threw me a furious glance, and went round the trough again. She began to sing a monotonous song, one of those songs of hers that she sometimes spent the whole afternoon singing over and over again when she was angry.

Toto was bored with playing with the fowls, and had already finished eating his rice. He was sleeping again with his paws over his ears. Now and then he rolled himself in the dust and lay on his back with his legs folded in the air.

It was stiflingly hot, and I didn't know whether I'd go hunting as I usually did every Saturday, or if I'd go to the chicken run to see the snake.

Madunana came into the yard with a pile of firewood on his back, and went to put it away in the corner where Sartina was washing the plates. When she saw him, she stopped singing and tried to manage an awkward smile.

After looking all around, Madunana pinched Sartina's bottom, and she gave an embarrassed giggle and responded with a sonorous slap on his arm. The two of them laughed happily together without looking at each other.

Just then, Nandito, Joãozinho, Nelita, and Gita ran out after a ball, and started kicking it around the yard with great enjoyment.

Mama came to the kitchen door, dressed up to go out. As soon as she appeared, Madunana bent down quickly to the ground, pretending to look for something, and Sartina bent over the trough.

"Sartina, see if you can manage not to break any plates before you finish. Hurry up. You, Madunana, leave Sartina alone and mind your own business. I don't want any of that nonsense here. If you carry on like this I'll tell the boss.

"You, Ginho," (now she spoke in Portuguese) "look after the house and remember you're not a child anymore. Don't hit anybody and don't let the children go out of the yard. Tina and Lolota are inside clearing up—don't let them get up to mischief.

"Sartina," (in Ronga) "when you've finished with that put the kettle on for the children's tea and tell Madunana to go and buy bread. Don't let the children finish the whole packet of butter.

"Ginho," (now in Portuguese) "look after everything—I'm coming back just now. I'm going along to Aunty Lucia's for a little chat."

Mama straightened her dress and looked around to see if everything was in order, then went away.

Senhor Castro's dog, Wolf, was watching Toto from the street. As soon as he saw Wolf, Toto ran toward him and they started to bark at each other.

All the dogs of the village were frightened of Toto, and even the biggest of them ran away when he showed his temper. Toto was small, but he had long white hair which bristled up like a cat's when he was angry, and this is what must have terrified the other dogs.

Usually he kept away from them, preferring to entertain himself with the fowls—even bitches he only tolerated at certain times. For me he was a dog with a "pedigree," or at least "pedigree" could only mean the qualities he possessed. He had an air of authority, and the only person he feared was Mama, although she had never hit him. Just to take him off a chair we had to call her because he snarled and showed his teeth even at Papa.

The two dogs were face-to-face, and Wolf had already started to retreat, full of fear. At this moment Dr. Reis's dog, Kiss, passed by, and Toto started to bark at him too. Kiss fled at once, and Wolf pursued him, snapping at his hindquarters, only leaving him when he was whining with pain. When Wolf came back to Toto they immediately made friends and began playing together.

Nandito came and sat down next to me, and told me, without my asking, that he was tired of playing ball.

"So why have you come here?"

"Don't you want me to?"

"I didn't say that."

"Then I'll stay."

"Stay if you like."

I got up and he followed me. "Where are you going? Are you going hunting?"

"No."

"Well, then?"

"Stop pestering me. I don't like talking to kids."

"You're also a kid. Mama still hits you."

"Say that again and I'll bash your face in."

"All right, I won't say it again."

I went into the chicken run, and he came after me. The pipes were hot, and I had to move them with a cloth. The dust that rose was dense and suffocating.

"What are you looking for? Shall I help you?"

I began to move the blocks one by one and Nandito did the same. "Get away!"

He went to the other end of the run and began to cry.

When I had removed the last block of the pile I saw the snake. It was a mamba, very dark in color. When it realized it had been discovered it wound itself up more tightly and lifted its triangular head. Its eyes shone vigilantly and its black forked tongue quivered menacingly.

I drew back against the fence, then sat down on the ground. "Don't cry, Nandito."

"You're nasty. You don't want to play with me."

"Don't cry anymore. I'll play with you just now. Don't cry."

We both sat quietly. The little head of the snake came slowly to rest on the topmost coil, and the rest of its body stopped trembling. But it continued to watch me attentively.

"Nandito, say something, talk to me."

"What do you want me to say?"

"Anything you like."

"I don't feel like saying anything."

Nandito was still rubbing his eyes and feeling resentful toward me.

"Have you ever seen a snake? Do you like snakes? Are you scared of them? Answer me!"

"Where are the snakes?" Nandito jumped up in terror, and looked around.

"In the bush. Sit down and talk."

"Aren't there any snakes here?"

"No. Talk. Talk to me about snakes."

Nandito sat down very close to me.

"I'm very frightened of snakes. Mama says it's dangerous to go out in the bush because of them. When we're walking in the grass we can step on one by mistake and get bitten. When a snake bites us we die. Sartina says that if a snake bites us and we don't want to die we must kill it, burn it till it's dry, then eat it. She says she's already eaten a snake, so she won't die even if she gets bitten."

"Have you ever seen a snake?"

"Yes, in Chico's house. The servant killed it in the chicken run."

"What was it like?"

"It was big and red, and it had a mouth like a frog."

"Would you like to see a snake now?"

Nandito got up and leaned against me fearfully. "Is there a snake in the chicken run? I'm scared—let's get out."

"If you want to get out, go away. I didn't call you to come in here."

"I'm frightened to go alone."

"Then sit here until I feel like going out."

The two of us stayed very quietly for a while.

Toto and Wolf were playing outside the fence. They were running from one post to another, going all the way round and starting again. At every post they raised a leg and urinated.

Then they came inside the chicken run and lay on their stomachs to rest. Wolf saw the snake immediately and began to bark. Toto barked as well, although he had his back turned toward it.

"Brother, are there always snakes in every chicken run?"

"No."

"Is there one in here?"

"Yes."

"Well then, why don't we go out. I'm scared!"

"Go out if you want to—go on!"

Wolf advanced toward the snake, barking more and more frenziedly. Toto turned his head, but still did not realize what was wrong.

Wolf's legs were trembling and he pawed the ground in anguish. Now and again he looked at me uncomprehendingly, unable to understand why I did not react to his hysterical alarm. His almost human eyes were filled with panic.

"Why is he barking like that?"

"Because he's seen the snake."

The mamba was curled up in the hollow between some blocks, and it unwound its body to give itself the most solid support possible. Its head and the raised neck remained poised in the air, unaffected by the movement of the rest of its body. Its eyes shone like fires.

Wolf's appeals were now horribly piercing, and his hair was standing up around his neck.

Leaning against the fence, Tina and Lolota and Madunana looked on curiously.

"Why don't you kill the snake?" Nandito's voice was very tearful and he was clutching me around the neck.

"Because I don't feel like it."

The distance between the snake and the dog was about five feet. However, the snake had inserted its tail in the angle formed between a block and the ground, and had raised its coils one by one, preparing for the strike. The triangular head drew back imperceptibly, and the base of the lifted neck came forward. Seeming to be aware of the proximity of his end, the dog began to bark even more frantically, without, however, trying to get away from the snake. From a little way behind, Toto, now on his feet as well, joined in the barking.

For a fraction of a second the neck of the snake curved while the head leaned back. Then, as if the tension of its pliant body had snapped a cord that fastened its head to the ground, it shot forward in a lightning movement impossible to follow. Although the dog had raised himself on his hind legs like a goat, the snake struck him full on the chest. Free of support, the tail of the snake whipped through the air, reverberating with the movement of the last coil.

Wolf fell on his back with a suppressed whine, pawing convulsively. The mamba abandoned him immediately, and with a spring disappeared between the pipes.

"A *nhoka!*"* screamed Sartina.

* A snake

Nandito threw me aside and ran out of the chicken run with a yell, collapsing into the arms of Madunana. As soon as he felt free of the snake, Wolf vanished in half a dozen leaps in the direction of Senhor Castro's house.

The children all started to cry without having understood what had happened. Sartina took Nandito to the house, carrying him in her arms. Only when the children disappeared behind Sartina did I call Madunana to help me kill the snake.

Madunana waited with a cloth held up high while I moved the pipes with the aid of a broomstick. As soon as the snake appeared Madunana threw the cloth over it, and I set to beating the heap with my stick.

When Papa came back from work Nandito had come round from the shock, and was weeping copiously. Mama, who had not yet been to see the snake, went with Papa to the chicken run. When I went there as well, I saw Papa turn the snake over on to its back with a stick.

"I don't like to think of what a snake like this could have done to one of my children." Papa smiled. "Or to anyone else. It was better this way. What hurts me is to think that these six feet of snake were attained at the expense of my chickens. . . ."

At this point Senhor Castro's car drew up in front of our house. Papa walked up to him, and Mama went to talk to Sartina. I followed after Papa.

"Good afternoon, Senhor Castro. . . ."

"Listen, Tchembene, I've just found out that my pointer is dead, and his chest's all swollen. My natives tell me that he came howling from your house before he died. I don't want any back chat, and I'm just telling you—either you pay compensation or I'll make a complaint at the Administration. He was the best pointer I ever had."

"I've just come back from work—I don't know any thing. . . ."

"I don't care a damn about that. Don't argue. Are you going to pay or aren't you?"

"But, Senhor Castro. . . ."

"Senhor Castro nothing. It's 700 paus.* And it's better if the matter rests here."

"As you like, Senhor Castro, but I don't have the money now. . . ."

"We'll see about that later. I'll wait until the end of the month, and if you don't pay then there'll be a row."

"Senhor Castro, we've known each other such a long time, and there's never . . ."

"Don't try that with me. I know what you all need—a bloody good hiding is the only thing. . . ."

Senhor Castro climbed into his car and pulled away. Papa stayed watching while the car drove off. "Son of a bitch. . . ."

I went up to him and tugged at the sleeve of his coat.

"Papa, why didn't you say that to his face?"

He didn't answer.

We had hardly finished supper when Papa said, "Mother, tell Sartina to clear the table quickly. My children, let us pray. Today we are not going to read the Bible. We will simply pray."

Papa talked in Ronga, and for this reason I regretted having asked him that question a while ago.

When Sartina finished clearing away the plates and folded the cloth, Papa began, *"Tatana, ha ku dumba hosi ya tilo misaba. . . ."†*

When he finished, his eyes were red.

---

* 700 "paus"—slang for 700 shillings (about 8 pounds).

† Father, we put our trust in Thee, Lord of Heaven and earth.

"Amen!"

"Amen!"

Mama got up, and asked, as if it meant nothing, "But what did Senhor Castro want, after all?"

"It's nothing important."

"All right, tell me about it in our room. I'll go and set out the children's things. You, Ginho, wake up early tomorrow and take a laxative. . . ."

When they had all gone away, I asked Papa, "Papa, why do you always pray when you are very angry?"

"Because He is the best counsellor."

"And what counsel does He give you?"

"He gives me no counsel. He gives me strength to continue."

"Papa, do you believe a lot in Him?"

Papa looked at me as if he were seeing me for the first time, and then exploded. "My son, one must have a hope. When one comes to the end of a day, and one knows that tomorrow will be another day just like it, and that things will always be the same, we have got to find the strength to keep on smiling, and keep on saying, 'This is not important!' We ourselves have to allot our own reward for the heroism of every day. We have to establish a date for this reward, even if it's the day of our death! Even today you saw Senhor Castro humiliate me: this formed only part of today's portion, because there were many things that happened that you didn't see. No, my son, there must be a hope! It must exist! Even if all this only denies Him, He must exist!"

Papa stopped suddenly, and forced himself to smile. Then he added, "Even a poor man has to have something. Even if it is only a hope! Even if it's a false hope!"

"Papa, I could have prevented the snake from biting Senhor Castro's dog. . . ."

Papa looked at me with his eyes full of tenderness, and said under his breath, "It doesn't matter. It's a good thing that he got bitten."

Mama appeared at the door. "Are you going to let the child go to sleep or not?"

I looked at Papa, and we remembered Senhor Castro and both of us burst out laughing. Mama didn't understand.

"Are you two going crazy?!"

"Yes, and it's about time we went crazy," said Papa with a smile.

Papa was already on the way to his room, but I must have talked too loudly. Anyway, it was better that he heard, "Papa, I sometimes . . . I don't really know . . . but for some time . . . I have been thinking that I didn't love you all. I'm sorry. . . ."

Mama didn't understand what we had been saying, so she became angry. "Stop all this, or else. . . ."

"Do you know, my son," Papa spoke ponderously, and gesticulated a lot before every word. "The most difficult thing to bear is that feeling of complete emptiness . . . and one suffers very much . . . very, very, very much. One grows with so much bottled up inside, but afterward it is difficult to scream, you know."

"Papa, and when Senhor Castro comes? . . ."

Mama was going to object, but Papa clutched her shoulder firmly. "It's nothing, Mother, but, you know, our son believes that people don't mount wild horses, and that they only make use of the hungry, docile ones. Yet when a horse goes wild it gets shot down, and it's all finished. But tame horses die every day. Every day, d'you hear? Day after day, after day—as long as they can stand on their feet."

Mama looked at him with her eyes popping out.

"Do you know, Mother, I'm afraid to believe that this is true, but I also can't bring myself to tell him that it's a lie. . . .

He sees, even today he saw. . . . I only wish for the strength to make sure that my children know how to recognize other things. . . ."

Papa and Mama were already in their room, so I couldn't hear anymore, but even from there Mama yelled, "Tomorrow you'll take a laxative, that'll show you. I'm not like your father who lets himself get taken in. . . ."

My bed was flooded in yellow moonlight, and it was pleasant to feel my naked skin quiver with its cold caress. For some unknown reason the warm sensation of Sartina's body flowed through my senses. I managed to cling to her almost physical presence for a few minutes, and I wanted to fall asleep with her so as not to dream of dogs and snakes.

NJABULO S. NDEBELE

was born in Johannesburg in 1948. He graduated with a double degree in English and Philosophy. He received his doctorate from the University of Denver. Ndebele is currently head of the Department of English at the University of Lesotho.

In the late 1960s Ndebele, as a result of his poems being published in many South African literary journals, became quite known.

His collection of short stories entitled Fools and Other Stories *was published in 1985. He was given the prestigious Noma Award for it. The collection consists of a long story "Fools" and four shorter ones.*

THE PROPHETESS

NJABULO S. NDEBELE

THE BOY KNOCKED TIMIDLY ON THE DOOR, WHILE A BIG fluffy dog sniffed at his ankles. That dog made him uneasy; he was afraid of strange dogs and this fear made him anxious to go into the house as soon as possible. But there was no answer to his knock. Should he simply turn the doorknob and get in? What would the prophetess say? Would she curse him? He was not sure now which he feared more: the prophetess or the dog. If he stood longer there at the door, the dog might soon decide that he was up to some mischief after all. If he left, the dog might decide he was running away. And the prophetess! What would she say when she eventually opened the door to find no one there? She might decide someone had been fooling, and would surely send lightning after the boy. But then, leaving would also bring the boy another problem: he would have to leave without the holy water for which his sick mother had sent him to the prophetess.

There was something strangely intriguing about the prophetess and holy water. All that one was to do, the boy had so many times heard in the streets of the township, was fill a bottle with water and take it to the prophetess. She would then lay her hands on the bottle and pray. And the water would be holy. And the water would have curing powers. That's what his mother had said too.

The boy knocked again, this time with more urgency. But

he had to be careful not to annoy the prophetess. It was getting darker and the dog continued to sniff at his ankles. The boy tightened his grip round the neck of the bottle he had just filled with water from the street tap on the other side of the street, just opposite the prophetess's house. He would hit the dog with this bottle. What's more, if the bottle broke he would stab the dog with the sharp glass. But what would the prophetess say? She would probably curse him. The boy knocked again, but this time he heard the faint voice of a woman.

"Kena!" the voice said.

The boy quickly turned the knob and pushed. The door did not yield. And the dog growled. The boy turned the knob again and pushed. This time the dog gave a sharp bark, and the boy knocked frantically. Then he heard the bolt shoot back, and saw the door open to reveal darkness. Half the door seemed to have disappeared into the dark. The boy felt fur brush past his leg as the dog scurried into the house.

"Voetsek!" the woman cursed suddenly.

The boy wondered whether the woman was the prophetess. But as he was wondering, the dog brushed past him again, slowly this time. In spite of himself, the boy felt a pleasant, tickling sensation and a slight warmth where the fur of the dog had touched him. The warmth did not last, but the tickling sensation lingered, going up to the back of his neck and seeming to caress it. Then he shivered and the sensation disappeared, shaken off in the brief involuntary tremor.

"Dogs stay out!" shouted the woman, adding, "This is not at the white man's."

The boy heard a slow shuffle of soft leather shoes receding into the dark room. The woman must be moving away from the door, the boy thought. He followed into the house.

"Close the door," ordered the woman who was still moving somewhere in the dark. But the boy had already done so.

Although it was getting dark outside, the room was much darker and the fading day threw some of its waning light into the room through the windows. The curtains had not yet been drawn. Was it an effort to save candles, the boy wondered. His mother had scolded him many times for lighting up before it was completely dark.

The boy looked instinctively toward the dull light coming in through the window. He was anxious, though, about where the woman was now, in the dark. Would she think he was afraid when she caught him looking out to the light? But the thick, dark green leaves of vine outside, lapping lazily against the window, attracted and held him like a spell. There was no comfort in that light; it merely reminded the boy of his fear, only a few minutes ago, when he walked under that dark tunnel of vine which arched over the path from the gate to the door. He had dared not touch that vine and its countless velvety, black, and juicy grapes that hung temptingly within reach, or rested lusciously on forked branches. Silhouetted against the darkening summer sky, the bunches of grapes had each looked like a cluster of small cones narrowing down to a point.

"Don't touch that vine!" was the warning almost everyone in Charterston township knew. It was said that the vine was all coated with thick, invisible glue. And that was how the prophetess caught all those who stole out in the night to steal her grapes. They would be glued there to the vine, and would be moaning for forgiveness throughout the cold night, until the morning, when the prophetess would come out of the house with the first rays of the sun, raise her arms into the sky, and say: "Away, away, sinful man; go and sin no more!" Suddenly, the thief would be free, and would walk away feeling a great release that turned him into a new man. That vine; it was on the lips of everyone in the township every summer.

• • •

One day when the boy had played truant with three of his friends, and they were coming back from town by bus, some grown-ups in the bus were arguing about the prophetess's vine. The bus was so full that it was hard for anyone to move. The three truant friends, having given their seats to grown-ups, pressed against each other in a line in the middle of the bus and could see most of the passengers.

"Not even a cow can tear away from that glue," said a tall, dark man who had high cheekbones. His balaclava was a careless heap on his head. His mustache, which had been finely rolled into two semicircular horns, made him look fierce. And when he gesticulated with his tin lunch box, he looked fiercer still.

"My question is only one," said a big woman whose big arms rested thickly on a bundle of washing on her lap. "Have you ever seen a person caught there? Just answer that one question." She spoke with finality, and threw her defiant skepticism outside at the receding scene of men cycling home from work in single file. The bus moved so close to them that the boy had feared the men might get hit.

"I have heard of one silly chap that got caught!" declared a young man. He was sitting with others on the long seat at the rear of the bus. They had all along been laughing and exchanging ribald jokes. The young man had thick lips and red eyes. As he spoke he applied the final touches of saliva with his tongue to brown paper rolled up with tobacco.

"When?" asked the big woman. "Exactly when, I say? Who was that person?"

"These things really happen!" said a general chorus of women.

"That's what I know," endorsed the man with the balaclava, and then added, "You see, the problem with some women is that they will not listen; they have to oppose a man. They just have to."

"What is that man saying now?" asked another woman. "This matter started off very well, but this road you are now taking will get us lost."

"That's what I'm saying too," said the big woman, adjusting her bundle of washing somewhat unnecessarily. She continued: "A person shouldn't look this way or that, or take a corner here or there. Just face me straight: I asked a question."

"These things really happen," said the chorus again.

"That's it, good ladies, make your point: push very strongly," shouted the young man at the back. "Love is having women like you," he added, much to the enjoyment of his friends. He was now smoking, and his rolled-up cigarette looked small between his thick fingers.

"Although you have no respect," said the big woman, "I will let you know that this matter is no joke."

"Of course this is not a joke!" shouted a new contributor. He spoke firmly and in English. His eyes seemed to burn with anger. He was young and immaculately dressed, his white shirt collar resting neatly on the collar of his jacket. A young nurse in a white uniform sat next to him. "The mother there," he continued, "asks you very clearly whether you have ever seen a person caught by the supposed prophetess's supposed trap. Have you?"

"She didn't say that, man," said the young man at the back, passing the roll to one of his friends. "She only asked when this person was caught and who it was." The boys at the back laughed. There was a lot of smoke now at the back of the bus.

"My question was," said the big woman, turning her head to glare at the young man, "have you ever seen a person caught there? That's all." Then she looked outside. She seemed angry now.

"Don't be angry, mother," said the young man at the back.

There was more laughter. "I was only trying to understand," he added.

"And that's our problem," said the immaculately dressed man, addressing the bus. His voice was sure and strong. "We laugh at everything; just stopping short of seriousness. Is it any wonder that the white man is still sitting on us? The mother there asked a very straightforward question, but she is answered vaguely about things happening. Then there is disrespectful laughter at the back there. The truth is you have no proof. None of you. Have you ever seen anybody caught by this prophetess? Never. It's all superstition. And so much about this prophetess also. Some of us are tired of her stories."

There was a stunned silence in the bus. Only the heavy drone of an engine struggling with an overloaded bus could be heard. It was the man with the balaclava who broke the silence.

"Young man," he said, "by the look of things you must be a clever, educated person, but you just note one thing. The prophetess might just be hearing all this, so don't be surprised when a bolt of lightning strikes you on a hot sunny day. And we shall be there at your funeral, young man, to say how you brought misfortune upon your head."

Thus had the discussion ended. But the boy had remembered how, every summer, bottles of all sizes filled with liquids of all kinds of colors would dangle from vines and peach and apricot trees in many yards in the township. No one dared steal fruit from those trees. Who wanted to be glued in shame to a fruit tree? Strangely, though, only the prophetess's trees had no bottles hanging from their branches.

The boy turned his eyes away from the window and focused into the dark room. His eyes had adjusted slowly to the darkness, and he saw the dark form of the woman shuffling away from him. She probably wore those slippers that had a fluff on top. Old women seem to love them. Then a white receding object came into focus. The woman wore a white *doek* on her head. The boy's eyes followed the *doek*. It took a right-angled turn—probably round the table. And then the dark form of the table came into focus. The *doek* stopped, and the boy heard the screech of a chair being pulled; and the *doek* descended somewhat and was still. There was silence in the room. The boy wondered what to do. Should he grope for a chair? Or should he squat on the floor respectfully? Should he greet or wait to be greeted? One never knew with the prophetess. Why did his mother have to send him to this place? The fascinating stories about the prophetess, to which the boy would add graphic details as if he had also met her, were one thing; but being in her actual presence was another. The boy then became conscious of the smell of camphor. His mother always used camphor whenever she complained of pains in her joints. Was the prophetess ill then? Did she pray for her own water? Suddenly, the boy felt at ease, as if the discovery that a prophetess could also feel pain somehow made her explainable.

"*Lumela 'me,*" he greeted. Then he cleared his throat.

"*Eea ngoanaka,*" she responded. After a little while she asked: "Is there something you want, little man?" It was a very thin voice. It would have been completely detached had it not been for a hint of tiredness in it. She breathed somewhat heavily. Then she coughed, cleared her throat, and coughed again. A mixture of rough discordant sounds filled the dark room as if everything was coming out of her insides, for she seemed to breathe out her cough from deep within her. And the boy wondered: If she coughed too long, what would happen? Would something come out? A lung? The boy saw the form of the woman clearly now: she had bent forward somewhat. Did anything come out of her on to the floor? The cough subsided. The woman sat up and her hands fumbled with something around her breasts. A white cloth emerged. She leaned forward again, cupped her hands, and spat into the cloth. Then she stood up and shuffled away into further darkness away from the boy. A door creaked, and the white *doek* disappeared. The boy wondered what to do because the prophetess had disappeared before he could say what he had come for. He waited.

More objects came into focus. Three white spots on the table emerged. They were placed diagonally across the table. Table mats. There was a small round black patch on the middle one. Because the prophetess was not in the room, the boy was bold enough to move near the table and touch the mats. They were crocheted mats. The boy remembered the huge lacing that his mother had crocheted for the church altar. ALL SAINTS CHURCH was crocheted all over the lacing. There were a number of designs of chalices that carried the Blood of Our Lord.

Then the boy heard the sound of a match being struck. There were many attempts before the match finally caught fire. Soon, the dull orange light of a candle came into the living room where the boy was, through a half-closed door. More light flushed the living room as the woman came in carrying a candle. She looked round as if she was wondering where to put the candle. Then she saw the ashtray on the middle mat, pulled it toward her, sat down, and turned the candle over into the ashtray. Hot wax dropped onto the ashtray. Then the prophetess turned the candle upright and pressed its bottom onto the wax. The candle held.

The prophetess now peered through the light of the candle at the boy. Her thick lips protruded, pulling the wrinkled skin and caving in the cheeks to form a kind of lip circle. She seemed always ready to kiss. There was a line tattooed from the forehead to the ridge of a nose that separated small eyes that were half closed by large, drooping eyelids. The white *doek* on her head was so huge that it made her face look small. She wore a green dress and a starched green cape that had many white crosses embroidered on it. Behind her, leaning against the wall, was a long bamboo cross.

The prophetess stood up again, and shuffled toward the window which was behind the boy. She closed the curtains and walked back to her chair. The boy saw another big cross embroidered on the back of her cape. Before she sat down she picked up the bamboo cross and held it in front of her.

"What did you say you wanted, little man?" she asked slowly.

"My mother sent me to ask for water," said the boy, putting the bottle of water on the table.

"To ask for water?" she asked with mild exclamation, looking up at the bamboo cross. "That is very strange. You came all the way from home to ask for water?"

"I mean," said the boy, "holy water."

"Ahh!" exclaimed the prophetess, "you did not say what you meant, little man." She coughed, just once. "Sit down, little man," she said, and continued, "You see, you should learn to say what you mean. Words, little man, are a gift from the Almighty, the Eternal Wisdom. He gave us all a little pinch of his mind and called on us to think. That is why it is folly to misuse words or not to know how to use them well. Now, who is your mother?"

"My mother?" asked the boy, confused by the sudden transition. "My mother is staff nurse Masemola."

"Ao!" exclaimed the prophetess, "you are the son of the nurse? Does she have such a big man now?" She smiled a little and the lip circle opened. She smiled like a pretty woman who did not want to expose her cavities.

The boy relaxed somewhat, vaguely feeling safe because the prophetess knew his mother. This made him look away from the prophetess for a while, and he saw that there was a huge mask on the wall just opposite her. It was shining and black. It grinned all the time showing two canine teeth pointing upward. About ten feet away at the other side of the wall was a picture of Jesus in which His chest was open, revealing His heart which had many shafts of light radiating from it.

"Your mother has a heart of gold, my son," continued the prophetess. "You are very fortunate, indeed, to have such a parent. Remember, when she says, 'My boy, take this message to that house,' go. When she says, 'My boy, let me send you to the shop,' go. And when she says, 'My boy, pick up a book and read,' pick up a book and read. In all this she is actually saying to you, learn and serve. Those two things, little man, are the greatest inheritance."

Then the prophetess looked up at the bamboo cross as if she saw something in it that the boy could not see. She seemed to lose her breath for a while. She coughed deeply again, after which she went silent, her cheeks moving as if she was chewing.

"Bring the bottle nearer," she said finally. She put one hand on the bottle while with the other she held the bamboo cross. Her eyes closed, she turned her face toward the ceiling. The boy saw that her face seemed to have contracted into an intense concentration in such a way that the wrinkles seemed to have become deep gorges. Then she began to speak.

"You will not know this hymn, boy, so listen. Always listen to new things. Then try to create too. Just as I have learned never to page through the dead leaves of hymn books." And she began to sing.

> *"If the fish in a river*
> *boiled by the midday sun*
> *can wait for the coming of evening,*
> *we too can wait*
> *in this wind-frosted land,*

the spring will come,
the spring will come.
If the reeds in winter
can dry up and seem dead
and then rise
in the spring,
we too will survive the fire that is coming
the fire that is coming,
we too will survive the fire that is coming.''

It was a long, slow song. Slowly, the prophetess began to pray.

"God, the All Powerful! When called upon, You always listen. We direct our hearts and thoughts to You. How else could it be? There is so much evil in the world; so much emptiness in our hearts; so much debasement of the mind. But You, God of all power, are the wind that sweeps away evil and fills our hearts and minds with renewed strength and hope. Remember Samson? Of course You do, O Lord. You created him, You, maker of all things. You brought him out of a barren woman's womb, and since then, we have known that out of the desert things will grow, and that what grows out of the barren wastes has a strength that can never be destroyed.''

Suddenly, the candle flame went down. The light seemed to have gone into retreat as the darkness loomed out, seemingly out of the very light itself, and bore down upon it, until there was a tiny blue flame on the table looking so vulnerable and so strong at the same time. The boy shuddered and felt the coldness of the floor going up his bare feet.

Then out of the dark came the prophetess's laugh. It began as a giggle, the kind the girls would make when the boy and his friends chased them down the street for a little kiss. The giggle broke into the kind of laughter that produced tears when one was very happy. There was a kind of strange pleasurable rhythm to it that gave the boy a momentary enjoyment of the dark, but the laugh gave way to a long shriek. The boy wanted to rush out of the house. But something strong, yet intangible, held him fast to where he was. It was probably the shriek itself that had filled the dark room and now seemed to come out of the mask on the wall. The boy felt like throwing himself on the floor to wriggle and roll like a snake until he became tired and fell into a long sleep at the end of which would be the kind of bliss the boy would feel when he was happy and his mother was happy and she embraced him, so closely.

But the giggle, the laugh, the shriek, all ended as abruptly as they had started as the darkness swiftly receded from the candle like the way ripples run away from where a stone has been thrown in the water. And there was light. On the wall, the mask smiled silently, and the heart of Jesus sent out yellow light.

"Lord, Lord, Lord," said the prophetess slowly in a quiet, surprisingly full voice which carried the same kind of contentment that had been in the voice of the boy's mother when one day he had come home from playing in the street, and she was seated on the chair close to the kitchen door, just opposite the warm stove. And as soon as she saw him come in, she embraced him all the while saying: "I've been so ill; for so long, but I've got you. You're my son. You're my son. You're my son."

And the boy had smelled the faint smell of camphor on her, and he too embraced her, holding her firmly although his arms could not go beyond his mother's armpits. He remembered how warm his hands had become in her armpits.

"Lord, Lord, Lord," continued the prophetess, "have mercy on the desert in our hearts and in our thoughts. Have mercy. Bless this water; fill it with your power; and may it bring rebirth. Let her and all others who will drink of it feel the flower of newness spring alive in them; let those who drink it, break the chains of despair, and may they realize that the desert wastes are really not barren, but that the vast sands that stretch into the horizon are the measure of the seed in us."

As the prophetess stopped speaking, she slowly lowered the bamboo cross until it rested on the floor. The boy wondered if it was all over now. Should he stand up and get the blessed water and leave? But the prophetess soon gave him direction.

"Come here, my son," she said, "and kneel before me here." The boy stood up and walked slowly toward the prophetess. He knelt on the floor, his hands hanging at his sides. The prophetess placed her hands on his head. They were warm, and the warmth seemed to go through his hair, penetrating deep through his scalp into the very center of his head. Perhaps, he thought, that was the soul of the prophetess going into him. Wasn't it said that when the prophetess placed her hands on a person's head, she was seeing with her soul deep into that person; that, as a result, the prophetess could never be deceived? And the boy wondered how his lungs looked to her. Did she see the water that he had drunk from the tap just across the street? Where was the water now? In the stomach? In the kidneys?

Then the hands of the prophetess moved all over the boy's head, seeming to feel for something. They went down the neck. They seemed cooler now, and the coolness seemed to tickle the boy for his neck was colder than those hands. Now they covered his face, and he saw, just before he closed his eyes, the skin folds on the hands so close to his eyes that they looked like many mountains. Those hands smelled of blue soap and candle wax. But there was no smell of snuff. The boy wondered. Perhaps the prophetess did not use snuff after all. But the boy's grandmother did, and her hands always smelled of snuff. Then the prophetess spoke.

"My son," she said, "we are made of all that is in the world. Go. Go and heal your mother." When she removed her hands from the boy's face, he felt his face grow cold, and there was a slight sensation of his skin shrinking. He rose from the floor, lifted the bottle with its snout, and backed away from the prophetess. He then turned and walked toward the door. As he closed it, he saw the prophetess shuffling away to the bedroom carrying the candle with her. He wondered when she would return the ashtray to the table. When he finally closed the door, the living room was dark, and there was light in the bedroom.

It was night outside. The boy stood on the veranda for a while, wanting his eyes to adjust to the darkness. He wondered also about the dog. But it did not seem to be around. And there was that vine archway with its forbidden fruit and the multicolored worms that always crawled all over the vine. As the boy walked under the tunnel of vine, he tensed his neck, lowering his head as people do when walking in the rain. He was anticipating the reflex action of shaking off a falling worm. Those worms were disgustingly huge, he thought. And there was also something terrifying about their bright colors.

In the middle of the tunnel, the boy broke into a run and was out of the gate: free. He thought of his mother waiting for the holy water; and he broke into a sprint, running west up Thipe Street toward home. As he got to the end of the street, he heard the hum of the noise that came from the ever-crowded barbershops and the huge beer hall just behind those shops. After the brief retreat in the house of the prophetess, the noise, the people, the shops, the streetlights, the buses, and the taxis all seemed new. Yet, somehow, he wanted to avoid any contact with all this activity. If he turned left at the corner, he would have to go past the shops into the lit Moshoeshoe Street and its Friday night crowds. If he went right, he would have to go past the now dark, ghostly Bantu-Batho post office, and then down through the huge gum trees behind the Charterston Clinic, and then past the quiet golf course. The latter way would be faster, but too dark and dangerous for a mere boy, even with the spirit of the prophetess in him. And were not dead bodies found there sometimes? The boy turned left.

At the shops, the boy slowed down to maneuver through the crowds. He lifted the bottle to his chest and supported it from below with the other hand. He must hold on to that bottle. He was going to heal his mother. He tightened the bottle cap. Not a drop was to be lost. The boy passed the shops.

Under a street lamp just a few feet from the gate into the beer hall was a gang of boys standing in a tight circle. The boy slowed down to an anxious stroll. Who were they, he wondered. He would have to run past them quickly. No, there would be no need. He recognized Timi and Bubu. They were with the rest of the gang from the boy's neighborhood. Those were the bigger boys who were either in Standard Six or were already in secondary school or were now working in town.

Timi recognized the boy.

"Ja, sonny boy," greeted Timi. "What's a picaninny like you doing alone in the streets at night?"

"*Heit,* bra Timi," said the boy, returning the greeting. "Just from the shops, bra Timi," he lied, not wanting to reveal his real mission. Somehow that would not have been appropriate.

"Come on, you!" yelled another member of the gang, glaring at Timi. It was Biza. Most of the times when the boy had seen Biza, the latter was stopping a girl and talking to her. Sometimes the girl would laugh. Sometimes Biza would twist her arm until she "agreed." In broad daylight!

"You don't believe me," continued Biza to Timi, "and when I try to show you some proof you turn away to greet an ant."

"Okay then," said another, "what proof do you have? Everybody knows that Sonto is a hard girl to get."

"Come closer then," said Biza, "and I'll show you." The boy was closed out of the circle as the gang closed in toward

Biza, who was at the center. The boy became curious and got closer. The wall was impenetrable. But he could clearly hear Biza.

"You see? You can all see. I've just come from that girl. Look! See? The liquid? See? When I touch it with my finger and then leave it, it follows like a spider's web."

"Well, my man," said someone, "you can't deceive anybody with that. It's the usual trick. A fellow just blows his nose and then applies the mucus there, and then emerges out of the dark saying he has just had a girl."

"Let's look again closely," said another, "before we decide one way or the other." And the gang pressed close again.

"You see? You see?" Biza kept saying.

"I think Biza has had that girl," said someone.

"It's mucus, man, and nothing else," said another.

"But you know Biza's record in these matters, gents."

"Another thing, how do we know it's Sonto and not some other girl. Where is it written on Biza's cigar that he has just had Sonto? Show me where it's written 'Sonto' there."

"You're jealous, you guys, that's your problem," said Biza. The circle went loose and there was just enough time for the boy to see Biza's penis disappear into his trousers. A thick little thing, thought the boy. It looked sad. It had first been squeezed in retreat against the fly like a concertina, before it finally disappeared. Then Biza, with a twitch of alarm across his face, saw the boy.

"What did you see, you?" screamed Biza. "Fuck off!"

The boy took to his heels wondering what Biza could have been doing with his penis under the street lamp. It was funny, whatever it was. It was silly too. Sinful. The boy was glad that he had got the holy water away from those boys and that none of them had touched the bottle.

And the teachers were right, thought the boy. Silliness was

all those boys knew. And then they would go to school and fail test after test. Silliness and school did not go together.

The boy felt strangely superior. He had the power of the prophetess in him. And he was going to pass that power to his mother, and heal her. Those boys were not healing their mothers. They just left their mothers alone at home. The boy increased his speed. He had to get home quickly. He turned right at the charge office and sped toward the clinic. He crossed the road that went to town and entered Mayaba Street. Mayaba Street was dark and the boy could not see. But he did not lower his speed. Home was near now, instinct would take him there. His eyes would adjust to the darkness as he raced along. He lowered the bottle from his chest and let it hang at his side, like a pendulum that was not moving. He looked up at the sky as if light would come from the stars high up to lead him home. But when he lowered his face, he saw something suddenly loom before him, and, almost simultaneously, felt a dull yet painful impact against his thigh. Then there was a grating of metal seeming to scoop up sand from the street. The boy did not remember how he fell but, on the ground, he lay clutching at his painful thigh. A few feet away, a man groaned and cursed.

"Blasted child!" he shouted. "Shouldn't I kick you? Just running in the street as if you owned it. Shit of a child, you don't even pay tax. Fuck off home before I do more damage to you!" The man lifted his bicycle, and the boy saw him straightening the handles. And the man rode away.

The boy raised himself from the ground and began to limp home, conscious of nothing but the pain in his thigh. But it was not long before he felt a jab of pain at the center of his chest and his heart beating faster. He was thinking of the broken bottle and the spilt holy water and his mother waiting for him and the water that would help to cure her. What would his mother say?

If only he had not stopped to see those silly boys he might not have been run over by a bicycle. Should he go back to the prophetess? No. There was the dog, there was the vine, there were the worms. There was the prophetess herself. She would not let anyone who wasted her prayers get away without punishment. Would it be lightning? Would it be the fire of hell? What would it be? The boy limped home to face his mother. He would walk in to his doom. He would walk into his mother's bedroom, carrying no cure, and face the pain in her sad eyes.

But as the boy entered the yard of his home, he heard the sound of bottles coming from where his dog had its kennel. Rex had jumped over the bottles, knocking some stones against them in his rush to meet the boy. And the boy remembered the pile of bottles next to the kennel. He felt grateful as he embraced the dog. He selected a bottle from the heap. Calmly, as if he had known all the time what he would do in such a situation, the boy walked out of the yard again, toward the street tap on Mayaba Street. And there, almost mechanically, he cleaned the bottle, shaking it many times with clean water. Finally, he filled it with water and wiped its outside clean against his trousers. He tightened the cap, and limped home.

As soon as he opened the door, he heard his mother's voice in the bedroom. It seemed some visitors had come while he was away.

"I'm telling you, *Sisi,*" his mother was saying, "and take it from me, a trained nurse. Pills, medicines, and all those injections are not enough. I take herbs too, and then think of the wonders of the universe as our people have always done. Son, is that you?"

"Yes, Ma," said the boy who had just closed the door with a deliberate bang.

"And did you bring the water?"

"Yes, Ma."

"Good. I knew you would. Bring the water and three cups. MaShange and MaMokoena are here."

The boy's eyes misted with tears. His mother's trust in him: would he repay it with such dishonesty? He would have to be calm. He wiped his eyes with the back of his hand, and then put the bottle and three cups on a tray. He would have to walk straight. He would have to hide the pain in his thigh. He would have to smile at his mother. He would have to smile at the visitors. He picked up the tray; but just before he entered the passage leading to the bedroom, he stopped, trying to muster courage. The voices of the women in the bedroom reached him clearly.

"I hear you very well, Nurse," said one of the women. "It is that kind of sense I was trying to spread before the minds of these people. You see, the two children are first cousins. The same blood runs through them."

"That close!" exclaimed the boy's mother.

"Yes, that close. MaMokoena here can bear me out; I told them in her presence. Tell the nurse, you were there."

"I have never seen such people in all my life," affirmed MaMokoena.

"So I say to them, my voice reaching up to the ceiling, 'Hey, you people, I have seen many years. If these two children really want to marry each other, then a beast *has* to be slaughtered to cancel the ties of blood. . . .'"

"And do you want to hear what they said?" interrupted MaMokoena.

"I'm listening with both ears," said the boy's mother.

"Tell her, child of Shange," said MaMokoena.

"They said that was old, crusted foolishness. So I said to myself, 'Daughter of Shange, shut your mouth, sit back, open your eyes, and watch.' And that's what I did."

"Two weeks before the marriage, the ancestors struck. Just as I had thought. The girl had to be rushed to hospital, her legs swollen like trousers full of air on the washing line. Then I got my chance, and opened my mouth, pointing my finger at them, and said, 'Did you ask the ancestors' permission for this unacceptable marriage?' You should have seen their necks becoming as flexible as a goose's. They looked this way, and looked that way, but never at me. But my words had sunk. And before the sun went down, we were eating the insides of a goat. A week later, the children walked up to the altar. And the priest said to them, 'You are such beautiful children!'"

"Isn't it terrible that some people just let misfortune fall upon them?" remarked the boy's mother.

"Only those who ignore the words of the world speaking to them," said MaShange.

"Where is this boy now?" said the boy's mother. "Son! Is the water coming?"

Instinctively the boy looked down at his legs. Would the pain in his thigh lead to the swelling of his legs? Or would it be because of his deception? A tremor of fear went through him; but he had to control it, and be steady, or the bottle of water would topple over. He stepped forward into the passage. There was his mother! Her bed faced the passage, and he had seen her as soon as he turned into the passage. She had propped herself up with many pillows. Their eyes met, and she smiled, showing the gap in her upper front teeth that she liked to poke her tongue into. She wore a fawn chiffon *doek* which had slanted into a careless heap on one side of her head. This exposed her undone hair on the other side of her head.

As the boy entered the bedroom, he smelled camphor. He greeted the two visitors and noticed that, although it was warm in the bedroom, MaShange, whom he knew, wore her huge, heavy, black, and shining overcoat. MaMokoena had a blanket over her shoulders. Their *doeks* were more orderly than the boy's mother's. The boy placed the tray on the dressing chest close to his mother's bed. He stepped back and watched his mother, not sure whether he should go back to the kitchen, or wait to meet his doom.

"I don't know what I would do without this boy," said the mother as she leaned on an elbow, lifted the bottle with the other hand, and turned the cap rather laboriously with the hand on whose elbow she was resting. The boy wanted to help, but he felt he couldn't move. The mother poured water into one cup, drank from it briefly, turned her face toward the ceiling, and closed her eyes. "Such cool water!" she sighed deeply, and added, "Now I can pour for you," as she poured water into the other two cups.

There was such a glow of warmth in the boy as he watched his mother, so much gladness in him that he forgave himself. What had the prophetess seen in him? Did she still feel him in her hands? Did she know what he had just done? Did holy water taste any differently from ordinary water? His mother didn't seem to find any difference. Would she be healed?

"As we drink the prophetess's water," said MaShange, "we want to say how grateful we are that we came to see for ourselves how you are."

"I think I feel better already. This water, and you . . . I can feel a soothing coolness deep down."

As the boy slowly went out of the bedroom, he felt the pain in his leg, and felt grateful. He had healed his mother. He would heal her tomorrow, and always with all the water in the world. He had healed her.

OLYMPE BHELY-QUENUM,

*a Beninian writer, was born in 1928. He was schooled
in France and worked as a journalist. He published a
novel* Un Piège sans Fin (Snares Without End,
1960, 1978), *which was followed by* Le Chant du Lac
(The Song of the Lake, *1965) and* L'Initié (Initi-
ated, *1979). For his novel* Le Chant du Lac *Quenum
was awarded the Grand Prize for Literature for Black
Africa in 1966. His collection of short stories is entitled*
Liaison d'un Été et Autres Récits (One Summer
Love Affair and Other Stories, *1968). The new collection of stories is entitled* Les Mille Haches (Thousand Axes, *1981).*

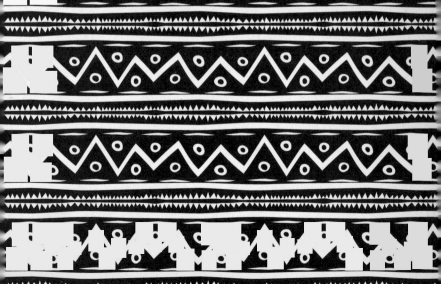

A CHILD
IN THE BUSH OF GHOSTS*

OLYMPE BHELY-QUENUM

Translated by Willifried F. Feuser

WHEN I WAS ELEVEN YEARS OLD, ONE OF MY UNCLES ONE
day took me along with him to his farm. His name was Akpoto.
He was a handsome man with large black eyes, sturdy and distin-
guished-looking.

We had set out early, and yet the African morning sun had
beaten us to it. We had covered more than thirteen kilometers
on the district council road; then we had taken the pathway that
led to Houêto. A small river, fordable at any time of the day, cut
across the path of fine golden sand which meandered through a
high and dense forest.

We had crossed the river and continued walking on sand. I
loved the softness of that sandy earth; its velvety surface pleas-
antly caressed the soles of my bare feet. But the joy I felt in
walking on that path gradually gave way to fear as we penetrated
ever more deeply into the forest.

When we left the path for a sodden trail, I suddenly had the
feeling that the humidity pervaded my whole body, and the
sense of fear became intolerable.

I therefore started pestering my uncle with little questions
which were as irritating as they were foolish. I kept knocking

---

* To Andre Breton to whom I first told this story; to the College Littre in Avranches and
my former schoolmates in that establishment where I wrote this story; but also to the city of
Avranches where I learned a great deal.

against him, clung to his hand, or moved clumsily in front of him and thus almost succeeded several times in making him fall . . .

We were crossing a kind of clearing where the sky above remained invisible as in most of our forests. We had already walked too much. For how long? I can't say. I was not yet going to school and, naturally, did not know any French, to the utter indignation of my father, the respectable primary schoolteacher who always saw me sickly and unable to stand the hustle and bustle of a school in session. As far as my uncle was concerned, he was able to determine the time of day from the position of the sun through a special kind of sensory perception, or other intuition. Therefore, after having raised his eyes in vain toward the arches of the towering trees hiding the sky from our eyes, he said to me in his gentle voice which I can still hear: "Wait for me here, I'll be back in a short while."

He left me, plunging with big steps into the bush that stretched out as far as the eye could see. He had put a big orange and four guavas into my hands.

Suddenly I felt dead tired. I was gripped by the urge to cry but controlled myself. I've never had much use for crybabies. There is nothing I detest so much as giving unbridled expression to our sorrows. And I waited. Oh, I certainly waited more than I shall ever be able to wait again, but my uncle did not return. There was plenty of time for me to eat two guavas, then my orange, and then I waited again a very long time before munching my remaining two guavas.

Worn out by the anxiety brought about by seeing nothing but the bush with its frightening calm around me, I sat down on the black forest earth and buried my face in my hands as if I never wanted to see any more of the place where I was. But as the humidity caught hold of me I had to rise again and started walking without really having any idea of where I was going.

I ought to have searched for the path we had followed until then but all my senses were gripped by panic and I marched like an automaton. I would have wished to be able to give out a single scream, to whistle, sing or talk loudly, or only just to mutter something—anything to assuage the effect of the fear in me, anything to make me feel aware of my person or simply to give me the illusion that I still was myself a human being, alive, finding myself there by chance, but I could not say anything . . . True to God, it is the only time I remember ever having felt fear.

I walked on relentlessly, unable to rediscover the path covered with sand; neither did I see the river again, its waters rolling with a sweet music, but I suddenly noticed in front of me a big woman wrapped in a white lappa that concealed her face and covered her feet. She advanced toward me; my heart started pounding precipitately; I felt as if I were receiving heavy blows from a ram inside me that did not quite succeed in splitting my chest wide open. I started shouting, no, I would have liked to shout; I felt I was shouting but did not hear myself shouting.

I wished to see the earth opening under my feet but the humus refused to do my bidding. Only then did I concede defeat and stretched out my arms to the lady like a baby to its mother.

To my surprise the woman passed me by in mute indifference. I looked backward. She too had turned her head and before I found the time to avert my eyes, she had already uncovered her face. I then saw something frightful: an emaciated face, the face of a fleshless skull, which made a horrid and repugnant grimace at me.

I started running head over heels but glanced backward from time to time. It was to no avail, for I constantly saw the person at a distance of twenty paces behind me, although she was not running. But my mad gallop did not last very long, for a few moments after that encounter I found myself right in front of the railway tracks. My heart was thumping so violently that it seemed to be about to burst my chest. I looked back again and saw my uncle.

"Where have you been? Why did you forsake me in the forest?" I asked, staring at him in bleak reproach.

He looked at me with pity because he read the anguish in my eyes; he told me, however, that he had not wasted any time at Houêto:

"I ordered my farm laborers at once to catch the chickens you see here, and I went to dig out cassava tubers for your grandmother and grand-aunt myself. As soon as the job was finished, I returned to the clearing and was greatly surprised not to find you. I then continued my return journey, looking everywhere. All of a sudden I heard a rustle in the bush to my left; first I thought it was a deer but I changed my mind afterward when I saw a human shape running helter-skelter; it was you. I could have called you but I preferred to follow you with my eyes, for we were moving along parallel lines. A single step, but a big one, separated me from you, my boy. And then, I had nothing to fear for you, for the bush is not dangerous."

I felt sad at having brought him to the point where he thought he owed me an explanation. But on the other hand, my heart was still throbbing with anger and subdued sobs when I asked him in a trembling voice whether he had seen the river again.

"Yes, of course. It was there even before our ancestors were born, and will certainly remain after we're dead and gone."

"You may be right, but I did not recross it."

"What are you telling me there? You must have forded it without noticing."

"But it's true, uncle! I didn't see the slightest trace of the river; just look at my legs and feet, they aren't soaked like yours."

"You surprise me, Codjo!"

"Let's return to the clearing by the path that has brought me here, if you don't believe me!" I said with an assurance that today I find astounding on the part of the child I was.

My uncle tucked his baskets with cassava and chickens under a thicket, put me astraddle his shoulders and we took the path on which I had come, or rather the trail which perhaps would never have come into existence if I had not been the first human being who in his terrorized gallop had savagely flattened the grass along that line.

We had arrived at the clearing, then at the farm much more quickly than we could have managed by walking on the sand-covered pathway.

Akpoto was dumbfounded not to be compelled to pass the river he had been crossing for more than thirty-five years, the source of which he imagined to be somewhat in the forest.

He put me down, my mouth felt dry. I quenched my thirst by drinking from a gourd, and this made me feel the freshness of the water and the pleasure of drinking it more keenly. Then we set out on the return journey, taking once more the kind of game track I had discovered and which had become the fastest way to go to Houêto and back.

"A walking skeleton, that sort of thing doesn't exist. No dead man comes back to stay among the living: my paternal grandmother and great-grandfather followed one another into death at a month's interval; nobody ever told me that he has met them during the three years since they stopped coddling me." So went my train of thought, and I was convinced that my encounter with the skeleton was merely the result of a hallucination.

Still I wanted to make sure it was only an illusion, and taking advantage of a moment when my parents' watchfulness had flagged, I fled from our compound where I was getting bored. I liked the open air, the solitude at the seaside or in the bush, and likewise the company of human beings who made no impositions on me but allowed me to make myself useful without feeling duty-bound to do so.

In my parents' house everything was offered to me on a golden platter; I was pampered and idle and felt my uselessness to the full.

I reached the clearing again through the game track and started searching for the source of the river. My mind was totally absorbed in the operation, perhaps, because I was what my parents called "a self-willed child," or perhaps also because I had an ulterior motive: to surprise my uncle by discovering the truth I wanted to find out.

I therefore headed into the bush, slipping over pebbles, sinking into the spongy suction of the soft ground; skipping over creepers, crawling among thorns. In front of me appeared a big chameleon. We looked at each other for a good second and its skin visibly, and gradually, took on the color of the indigo cloth tied around my neck, which I was wearing over my khaki shorts. At that moment I thought of my revered great-grandfather who in telling tales did not hide his predilection for the chameleon: *"It rarely misses its destination because it knows how to adjust itself to its surroundings and never looks backward."*

What did that mean? I hadn't the slightest idea. I was a spoiled, demanding child whom a too indulgent grandfather had perhaps wanted to convert to patience and gentleness by lecturing him on moral philosophy. But he had reasoned through the use of symbols that remained a mystery to the child. Still, it was of that venerable aged man that I thought on that day, and seeing the chameleon take on the color of my cloth, I not only decided not to look back but also to adapt myself to the bush, to understand its language, to bow to its laws, without however forgetting that I was a human being, the only creature who would not be forgiven voluntary subservience. I was born to grow big and to live even beyond death . . .

A small noise startled me; I did not pay any heed and continued slinking through the thorns that tore my cloth. A long snake carelessly passed between my legs, a boa rolled itself around a tree toward which I was heading. I was unafraid, beyond caring. My only concern was to discover the source of the river. I had met the chameleon that perhaps still retained the color of my garment in memory of our chance encounter or had swapped it for that of some of the distinctly green or red leaves I remembered seeing.

From among creepers and thorns I emerged into another clearing. In its immobility, the canopy of leaves above my head sealed off the place in tragic solitude. I felt the void within me as if I were nothing thenceforth but a wretched carcass draped with black skin. At that moment, the skeleton appeared a few steps away from me, wrapped in its big white *lappa* which covered its head. I felt no emotion, or more precisely, I was not afraid since I considered it like something I was used to. Still I rubbed my eyes as if to rid myself of an optical illusion, to make sure of what I was seeing. It drew closer; I did not rush toward it as in our first encounter, for I had to preserve my dignity. In my view, it represented nothing. It was nothingness in motion, and I was a man. This certainty, due to the realization of the difference between us, fortified me not with courage—that I didn't care about—but with cockiness, and I saw my body rising to its level. This was not the time for any more concessions. I felt that the bush was not supposed to be the abode of the dead but of the living. Wasn't I one of them? We converged as on a one-way track where no provision has been made for people to cross each other. I did nothing to let it pass when we were face-to-face. Then it stretched out its hand to me. At that moment I would have liked to cross my arms, to sport a scornful countenance since last time it too had snubbed me; but I decided to let bygones be bygones and gathered its bony hand in mine.

Instead of forcing me to retrace my steps it did the opposite, still holding my hand. I thus followed it, eager to discover where it was taking me. We wended our way side by side without my feeling the slightest apprehension. After all, what was there to be afraid of? Holding in my hand that of a human skeleton? Human. That was just the word I needed. Was I not with something human? Was I not sure now that my first encounter was not simply the effect of a delusion?

No, really, I was no longer afraid. I was eight years old when my grandmother and great-grandfather stopped living. I remember having cried a great deal by their bodies seated beside the mortal remains of these old people in their barely gnarled tallness during my vigil, despite my parents' vain effort to spare me what they called too violent shocks. Yes, I still remember: I hurled myself on my grandmother when they wanted to put her in the bier; I took her hand and squeezed it very hard so as to communicate all my warmth to her. Oh, the piercing coldness she left in my hands and which is still there, evermore! It was her that I felt again all along, while the skeleton kept my hand in its own. It did not hold it in a tight grip, did not apply any pressure, and we just wandered like two friends.

Still I did not forget that I was a man, a human being, a child barely twelve years old, while it was a skeleton. Had it been a man or a woman? I never found out. Besides, this was of no importance. With wide open eyes I stared at the bush in front of me. Not a single time did it occur to me to have a look at my fellow traveler. And why should I have looked at its skeletal visage since I was feeling its hand in mine? Had it suddenly vanished I would most assuredly not have worried about its disappearance but would have continued on my way amid the trees, the thorns and the beasts.

But I have to admit today that I had realized that from the moment we walked together the thorns no longer tore my cloth; everything slipped smoothly off me as it did off the skeleton. A wild boar and his mate emerging from their lair took to flight on seeing us. My uncle had told me that the bush was not dangerous; all the same, we saw more than one pair of lions and panthers; they had passed us by with something approaching indifference. To be precise they had invariably passed on my side; they had all sniffed at me and then walked away in haughty grandeur. Why? I wouldn't know. I may have appeared vile-smelling and undesirable to them, unless they just happened not to be hungry just then.

We had been walking like that for a time that seemed reasonably long to me but I was not tired. I did not feel any sign of fatigue. I paid attention to everything. Then, to my great surprise, I stopped seeing the bush around me and realized that we were in an underground tunnel hung with tree roots. The walls were oozing moisture but the ground was dry. The ear perceived the gentle distant murmur of a stream. I thought of the river while striding along with my queer companion.

At certain places the walls of the long gallery through which we were proceeding had been discreetly adorned with symbolic graffiti: snakes biting their own tails; arms cut off and placed on top of each other in the form of an X; sexual organs; copulation scenes; skin-bones; human skulls; mouths that were either laughing or distorted in an agony of suffering; horses without heads but galloping at full speed, tails and manes flying in the wind; fire shaped like an open lily blossom flaring from a pit;

coffins; people performing a ritual dance; a clumsily drawn rectangle representing a mirror.

We turned to the left and I had the impression that we were changing our direction from north to sunrise. A light entering the place from heaven knows where gently lit up the underground passage sloping downward in front of me. We walked unceasingly descending the slope, and arrived at a kind of crypt where human skeletons without the tiniest bone missing were stretched out side by side.

My guide stopped in front of one of them, uncovering his cavity-riddled face. I looked straight at him. He bowed slightly to one of the skeletons which sat up, crossed its legs, then its arms; he continued his homage and each one of his fellow skeletons took the same posture as the preceding one. And I saw seventy-seven skeletons thus sitting up and leaning their backs against the wall of the crypt.

Did they want to impress me? I had experienced fear before but fear held no more meaning for me. I had heard people talk a lot about death, but since the death of my grandparents I no longer feared it. Death had become for me such a familiar companion that I gave it no more thought. But looking at the skeletons attentively, I had a feeling that each one of them represented a human being I had known, and to which I had perhaps been close. It was good to see them again but I had not come here for them.

"Where is the source of the river?" I suddenly cried in a tragic voice which struck the walls in a zigzag line, provoking a long and sonorous echo.

And again I perceived murmurings of the water, then a groan followed by the sound of a torrent rushing away.

The skulls all seemed to have been raised again to look me straight in the face.

"You see that I have come to visit you without misgivings. I'm not afraid of you because you used to be men; for me you still are, and I don't believe in death!"

I heard my voice reecho. It ricocheted away from me along the underground passage.

"Why don't you answer? Should you really be so useless?" All I received for an answer was my own voice and its echo which gabbled any utterance.

"You hear me?"

"You hear me?"

"—ear me?"

"—me?"

"—e?"

"Why did you bring me here?"

"—bring me here?"

"—me here?"

"—'ere?"

I looked around me and noticed that my guide had disappeared; maybe he had quietly slipped back to his little niche among his peers. So I thought of setting out on my return journey but as the passage stretched out farther before me, I preferred not to retrace my steps; hence I moved ahead. Thus I continued marching at a normal walking pace, looking all the while at the walls covered with graffiti fraught with symbolism. Despite my casual and almost leisurely gait I was feeling tired. I later realized that the way was sloping upward. Moreover, the certainty that I was advancing toward the sun became more and more acute.

As if in a fog I saw a shadow passing before my eyes; then the shadow became a reality: a majestic skeleton without any garment, his right hand clutched to his heart and his left holding a shinbone with a skull on top.

I stopped short in front of him. He made to let me pass and

the moment I was going to continue on my way he slightly stroked my head with the skull resting on the shinbone. I did not react, did not look back. The light entering the cavern was becoming more and more intense, I inhaled the air charged with a thousand smells from the fields . . . Abruptly I felt carried off into a long sleep and saw myself in a place, the name of which someone seemed to murmur into my ear.

"Wassai"

O Wassai! Wassai! disturbing, exciting paradise of entwined bodies. Here was a pathway sundered into five branches, each leading to clearly defined places. On the one side of the main path stood a hedge of hibiscus, bougainvillea and campeachy separating the path from a vast ground planted with kola-nut trees dwarfed by iroko and silk-cotton trees. In the hollows of those giant trees nested birds; their lugubrious shrieks did not frighten me. Wisps of white smoke rose from the foot of the trees. Little did I care about their origin and meaning! Let the sorcerers abandon themselves to their orgies, let them devour the souls of their victims. I was in Wassai.

On the other side of the road was Wassai, little house of joy without a keeper. I entered. Ravishing young beauties with sturdy breasts, black skin, athletic bodies. And their nimble legs with prettily proportioned muscles, readily intertwining, pushed me gently into voluptuous depths. At Wassai I experienced unforgettable little tremors brought about by girls I did not know; their names have remained unspoken, I've forgotten their seductive faces; but the form of their lithe and supple bodies remains in my arms, the freshness of their jet-black skin still vibrates through my nerves. In their midst I underwent my sexual initiation till all the flowers of the world blossomed within me, till the hard egg was hatched whose unwonted presence I had felt deep within. No outburst of rebellious sex will ever surprise me. I have explored all its domains in Wassai, fearsome black slowly unfolding in the deep nights of a dwelling without a master.

When I came to myself, I went my way without slowing down my pace and thus came out into the open air.

Let it be said in passing that I did not for a single moment feel like a prisoner in that underground gallery. But instead of finding myself on even ground, at the skirt of the forest as I expected, perhaps because I had scented the wind and the sun, I realized that I was perched high up on a mountainside studded with shrubbery.

A little farther down, beneath my feet, a spring, gushing out from this imposing height I had not known before, flowed into the plain before me with a murmur. And the glittering reflections of light, a vast imaginary ocean, seemed to undulate on the surface of the stream.

I climbed on all fours up to the summit, stood erect and saw the top of the forest covering the villages all around.

Far away thin columns of smoke rose above the trees. Coming from another world I discovered the immensity of space above the earth; then I descended from the mountain as if gently impelled and held back at the same time by a protecting hand.

I had not succeeded in seeing what I was searching for: the source of the river. Disappointed, I had to rest content with following the stream which flowed into a natural canal, the banks of which were hemmed in by aquatic plants; and I saw the river again which here to my great surprise almost flowed alongside the railway line.

My cloth was in shreds. I followed the railway line, then the habitual way to go to town. I arrived there at nightfall. In front of the door of my parents' house, I was stunned to see on either side an earthenware pot containing a decoction such as our custom prescribes for funeral ceremonies; I also heard a dirge gently syncopated by calabash rattles.

I entered and saw a gathering of sad people. The women, including my mother, had untied their hair as a token of mourning. The gathering noticed my presence and started up. Some took to their heels, others, paralyzed by fear, just looked at me. I stepped forward to my mother who had been quickly joined by my father.

"What happened? Who has died?"

Dead silence.

"You have to forgive me for leaving without telling you about it."

"Where are you coming from? Are you a dead or a living person in our midst?" my father asked.

"I'm alive."

"What, alive?" my mother said, weeping.

"Nobody's dead. Death doesn't exist and if it does, no dead man will ever return," I replied firmly but with my most casual expression.

The people had come back, more numerous now than when I first had set foot in the house.

"Where are you coming from?"

"Where've you been?"

"For us you were dead."

"For the past three days we've been sure about it."

"The diviners have confirmed it."

I was somewhat depressed by these comments and asked if the funeral ceremonies had anything to do with me. They said yes.

"The diviners have all been telling you lies. I went for a walk, and I've come back with flesh and blood, body and soul, cured from the fear of death. I apologize for having given you so much worry."

"My son, tell me honestly where you're coming from," my father said.

"From a simple walk. I didn't realize that it lasted three days."

"What did you eat?" asked my mother.

"Nothing."

"Whom did you stay with?"

"Nobody."

"I don't understand you."

"I've nothing to explain."

"Why?"

"Such things can't be explained. I am alive and life goes on."

"Oh, this child!" my mother murmured.

"I'm hungry, Mother. You see I'm alive and kicking since I'm hungry and thirsty."

"May you never again disappear like that."

"I promise, but don't you ever ask me for an explanation," I said. And everything was all right again.

How long did this dream last? I shall never know.

SINDIWE MAGONA

*was born and educated in South Africa. In 1984 she went
to live and work in the USA, where she got her master
and doctorate degrees.*

*In 1990 Mrs. Magona published her first book with
David Philip, South Africa, entitled* To My Children's Children—*which is the first part of a two-vol-
ume autobiography. The second part,* Forced to Grow,
was published in 1992.

The collection of seventeen short stories entitled Living, Loving and Lying Awake at Night, *printed by
David Philip, South Africa, appeared in 1991.*

For the book To My Children's Children *Mrs.
Magona got an Honorable Mention in the 1991 Noma
Award for Publishing in Africa.*

IT WAS EASTER SUNDAY THE DAY I WENT TO NETREG

SINDIWE MAGONA

BRAKES GRINDING IN PROTEST, THE BLOODRED VOLKS-
wagen lurched to an uncertain, shuddering stop outside our
gate. All cars lurch drunkenly in Guguletu, for what passes for
streets are nothing but pitted, dirt-covered trails pockmarked
with ditches, and potholes so big a full-grown man could drown
in one. Stock-still I stood, looking out of the window opening
of the one-room shack I shared with Makhulu, my mother's
mother.

A full five minutes I'd been waiting for the car; alerted of its
arrival by the chorus "Imoto! Imoto!" Shouts that painted a
clear picture in my mind: barefooted children panting alongside
the car; galloping as I had done so many times. And not that
long ago.

Until the car leapt right into my eyes, I'd been standing on
the coir mattress on the floor staring out unseeingly. In the harsh
glare of the unafraid, early afternoon autumn sun the opening
was not unlike a gouged eye. Blindly, it stared out. And I, behind it, like some deadened nerve, mimicked. Now, the smell of
the old blanket with which we stuffed the window opening at
night assaulted my nose and its weight glued my feet onto the
mattress.

A small, compact woman, not yet thirty, scrambled out of

the car: Mother; a bright yellow-and-black plastic shopping bag suspended from each hand. Food and clothing. The invariable badge of her *medem*'s bounty; things Mrs. Wilkins had given her out of the kindness of her big heart. Too bad she had the body of an elephant in the family way; only Makhulu wore the clothes Mrs. Wilkins gave Mama. Makhulu didn't mind folding, pleating, and wrapping the voluminous garments around her own far from substantial frame. Mother, stooped under the weight of her employer's goodness, walked slowly from the car toward our shack. I watched her, and knew that the fact that today Mrs. Wilkins's beneficence stretched to include even me, personally, weighed heavily on my mother's heart. The same knowledge paralyzed me.

'Khulu, who had as usual been hovering around it, opened the door for Mother.

It was Easter Sunday. Three days before, Mother had said, "Mrs. Wilkins will come with me on my next day off; Sunday." I was ready long before they came. They were taking me to Netreg. Netreg (which means just right) is a colored residential area not far from Guguletu where I live. Guguletu is an African township.

"Are you ready, Linda?" I knew she had not put the bags down. I would have heard the "table," a plank nearly a meter long, sighing. The "table" sighed each time it had to find a new way of balancing itself on the empty paraffin tins on which it rested. I understood its disgust. I, too, had my sighs; but I kept them to myself.

"Is that how you greet these days?" asked Makhulu, clearly piqued.

First, the rustle of plastic as bags exchanged hands hit me. A few seconds later, the smell of fried fish enveloped me; blocking my air passage, I gagged.

"Oh, I'm in such a hurry. I'm sorry, Mama," replied

Mother. She had come nearer where I stood, I could tell from her voice. The linoleum on bare sand floor did not make much noise. But I knew she had come closer. I froze.

She lifted the "curtain," a tired, discolored damask tablecloth sporting interesting tears in varying shapes and sizes. It was, no doubt, bequeathed to us by some white family for whom Mother of 'Khulu (for she used to be in the same line of work in her younger days) worked. Behind this was my place: the mattress on the floor, a cardboard box with all my worldly possessions, mainly schoolbooks. A thin, bare wire hanger drew a dull gray outline on the newspaper-plastered wall where it hung forlornly from a crooked, rusty nail.

"Come." And, ffwhissh! I heard the curtain fall and sensed her stalking away. I turned and looked at the spot where, I fancied, she'd stood a second ago. The dumb "curtain" stared back; and I pictured her stalking back to the car. Once more, my eyes flew to the window opening; but my feet were still cemented onto the mattress on the floor.

I did not move. But my heart jumped forsaking its seat and went and plonked itself up my throat making breathing difficult. A cold blanket wrapped itself tightly around all of me as it coated every inch of me inside. I was turning into Lot's wife, in ice.

There was Mother getting back into the car. Come. One word. And all the fear I had ever felt since I was born collected itself into a ball of writhing worms at the pit of my stomach. COME, said the ball turning and turning in my stomach.

I was not surprised she had said no more to me. I did not expect her to be fussing over me. But Mother's one-word command stabbed my heart and jellied my already wobbly legs. I do not know how my feet managed it, but they must have done so because I was saying "Good Afternoon, *Me'm*" to Mrs. Wilkins as I slid onto the seat behind her.

"Linda," scolded Mrs. Wilkins, "when will you stop calling me *Medem?*" She was smiling her brown teeth smile to show me she was not angry. She wanted me to call her by her name, Sue. But, to this day, I don't know how to call any white person by their name. It is not done. Besides, she was older than my mother. So, I mumbled, "I'm sorry," and just in the nick of time, stapled my tongue to the roof of my mouth. I'd nearly said "I'm sorry, *Me'm.*"

Me'm Sue started the car and we were on our way. Unconcerned, the car grunted and tottered while a group of children, in varying states of nakedness, sprinted alongside it. Lithe mahogany limbs glistened announcing some mothers had had the Vaseline and time to scrub their offspring. One little fellow caught my eye. He was shaven so blindingly clean the sun bounced off his head as if it were a mirror or a miniature glass dome. He was clad in a torn, once-upon-a-time-white vest. Absentmindedly, I noticed that he'd grow to be a fine-membered man one day; for beneath the torn, scant garment dangled definite promise. That, or he badly needed to wet the grass.

I forgot . . . As the wonder of the ride filled me, I swelled: I was a passenger in a real car, a moving car. Then, glonk! went my heart as I remembered why I was in that car and where it was taking me.

Netreg is about ten minutes from Guguletu, by car. On those few occasions I had traveled to Langa or Cape Town I had seen the houses of Netreg, for the train passes through the township. But I had never set foot in Netreg (or, for that matter, any colored township).

It's strange how ten minutes can be such a long time. That was easily the longest ten minutes of my life. What would it be like? Netreg itself as well as the reason I was being taken there? How could I be doing what I was about to do? And Mama?

What was Mama thinking of me right now? Would things ever be right between us, ever? What would Mrs. Wilkins think of me? What would she think of poor Mama? All these questions raced through my mind robbing me of the joy that should have been mine on the occasion of my first real car ride.

Briefly, once more, the thrill of the ride seduced me. Oh, I had been inside an uncountable number of cars: that is, the broken bodies of cars cast off by their owners or stolen and stripped to nothing anyone in their right mind would attempt to salvage. Wrecks were a penny a dozen throughout Guguletu. But this was different. This was a living car. And not only was I in it, it was moving; going; VRROOHM! Actually taking me somewhere. My first car ride!

I was a Standard Three pupil at St. Monica's Primary School, the only Catholic school in Guguletu. The uniform—a badly cut dress the color of bile, a sickly yellow-green—was the only decent article of clothing I owned. Hence the unclad hanger I'd left behind, a grotesque shape blotting out part of a large smiling face belonging to an African woman hanging clothes washed "WHITER than WHITE—in OMO—OF COURSE!"

Any hopes of a few additions to my wardrobe had long been quashed: "That woman I work for does not only pay me better. She is a person. She knows I am a person." What did it matter to Mother that the woman she worked for had no children? That I would never get any hand-me-downs from her? Who can blame me for being so angry at Mrs. Wilkins? All the possible castoffs she had deprived me off: dolls, shoes, dresses, jerseys, to name a few. And then she wanted to tell me we were friends, equals, "Call me Sue!" Not me; she wouldn't get any Sue from me.

During the short journey, I sat behind Mrs. Wilkins driving

her red Beetle while Mama sat kitty-corner to her and the empty seat between us yawned, a *donga* neither she nor I would ever be able to ford; for that was the last day I would be a child.

It was also the day, although I didn't know that at the time, that would affect my whole life as a woman. Looking back, I am amazed at how normal a day it looked: gay, even.

Three weeks before, St. Monica's had played a game of netball with their arch rivals, Bulelani Higher Primary School. Bulelani is in Langa. And, for us therefore, this was an away from home match on two accounts: Langa was hostile territory.

For me, however, that match was to be the beginning of the new me. Or should I say the old me? The new me, whatever else she is or isn't, is very, very old: older than any living person I know.

And the day I went to Netreg is part of the birth of the me who became that day. Although, on second thoughts, perhaps it is not fair to blame it all on that one day.

Perhaps it all started when I was born. Or in Langa that day we played Bulelani and they clobbered us ten–zip; an unprecedented wounding. Or, perhaps it is all a bad dream.

At Netreg we had a little problem finding the address Mrs. Wilkins had been given by one of the women in her rap group, feminists. Thanks to her smattering of Afrikaans, Mrs. Wilkins was able to ask for directions and we finally made it to our destination. As we trooped out of the car, my last netball game flashed through my mind.

I played center. And, usually, I played a game both defensive and offensive: feeding my shooters and blocking the ball from getting to the wings of the opposition. I was an enthusiastic, energetic player who threw herself completely into a game. And early on in the match that was to change my life I'd done exactly that.

Now, as we walked uncertainly to the house whose number was written on a scrap of paper *Me'm* Sue held in her hand, the sickening feeling born in me the day of that match returned.

Fifteen minutes or so into the game, the Bulelani center shot the ball toward the wing nearest her posts. From the wing, I knew the ball could only come back to her or, with luck and skill, go straight to one of their shooters. Aiming at reinforcing our defenses, I went for the shooter positioned under the post; she had stepped out of the circle where I could not go.

Sure enough, the wing sent the ball flying to the shooter: a high, slow curve. I crouched, waiting. Then, like a spring, uncoiled as the ball began its descent; timing myself to grab it above the outstretched hands I knew would materialize. Grab it before they reached it, or bounce it right out of their fingers. That was my plan.

Three clear feet from the ground and, WHAAM! I'd made contact with a flying rhinoceros. At least, that is how I felt.

BOOM! I hit the ground. Flat on my face. I lay sprawled; certain that never again would I be able to move even a finger. Total paralysis.

Then, movement. A tumultuous, agitating protest. Inside my belly. A frightened, turbulent fluttering.

For a moment I thought the ground under me was heaving. And then, beyond doubt, suddenly and with utter searing clarity, I knew.

I was pregnant.

No one had ever told me babies move before they are born; move in their mothers' wombs. But that stirring told me all I did not want to know. After all, I was only nearly fourteen.

That was three weeks before Easter Sunday. I thought Gran would kill me. You see, she raised me from the age five when I became too old to stay with Mother at her place of employment.

Mother has always worked sleep-in. That helps a little bit with accommodation.

Till every hair on my head has turned snow white, I will never forget the look Gran gave me when I told her. Naked contempt stared at me as at a monster. If a look in the mirror had shown me I'd sprouted a second head, I would not have been surprised. And then when she started wailing: the frail but piercing wail women make when someone has died. And then the insults had rained.

That day I finally learned something of the father not frequently mentioned.

"What am I crying for? Yhoo! Ma Tolo! What am I crying for?" The anguished call to her ancestors brought a swift, brutal answer through her miserable lips: "What did I expect from a she-dog's illegitimate child?"

What had happened to the hero who was felled by the heartless Boers during the 1960 riots? But the kindly old woman who had been love itself to me was not quite done. Like a venomous snake, she hissed: "Doesn't a she-dog beget another she-dog? Hee-eh?" Her face was contorted with . . . grief?

As if my own revelation had not caused enough pain, my grandmother could not seem to stop herself from dishing out further enlightenment. For my benefit: my death. Or, hers? Her face was a hideous mask of moving emotions. Hate, fear, and dire misery chased one another; flitting across the kaleidoscopic landscape. Her eyes, florets of pain that had looked into her grave and seen the bones of the fruit of her womb, generations to come. In a voice I did not recognize she went on: "Your mother was a child herself when she went and spread herself at the zones. I never even got any payment for damages from that man. Indeed, I do not know his face because as soon as he knew that the she-dog was riding with his pup, he did what all these men from the zones do. Went back to his village and made sure he never again took a contract to Cape Town."

The zones, euphemistically called Single Men's Quarters, are barracks used to house African men forced to leave their wives and children in the village when they get "permission" to come and work in the cities. That most of these "migrant" laborers were very much married bothered government policy makers not at all. It could not. The white, highly specialized, and learned officials had yet to grasp the simple fact of these men's being human too.

The father of the child I was carrying was such a man. But that did not worry me. He had assured me that he wanted to meet my parents and not only pay damages but pay *lobola,* the bride price. When I'd told him about my father he was all concern. "Your poor mother," he said, "all alone, bringing you up by herself." He wanted to make me his wife. We had talked about this the night of the netball match. But, with Gran's ranting, I decided to wait until Mother's next day off.

That Sunday, my world did a crazy higgledy-piggledy and has not righted itself since. I doubt it ever will.

Mother had arrived a little after lunch. The kettle had not boiled before Gran gave her the bad news. But, although I knew I had done wrong and hurt Mother a lot, I was convinced when I told her of the willingness of my man to shoulder full responsibility she would feel a little less hurt; grateful I would not become an unmarried mother.

As is the custom when things of this nature happen, several male relatives were summoned. These would be men of the Tolo and Bhele clans; Makhulu's and Mama's clans. The clan ensures our survival. Everyone belongs to a clan and because of that, no one can ever be without kin. When we introduce ourselves, the clan name is of more importance to us than the surname for marriage within the clan is taboo. A complete stranger becomes a brother or sister when it is found that he or she is of the same clan. I was being brought up as a Bhele since my own father had died before I was born and I had had no connection with his people. Now, our relatives had come to assist kin in distress. It was decided to waste no time but go, that very same day, to discuss *lobola* with the culprit. I would accompany the party, for that too is the custom.

Mother, either not trusting these men to represent her capably or at Gran's instigation, I never found out which, decided to come too. Up to this point, everything seemed to be going according to plan.

"And these white people don't listen to us when we tell them it is not right to put all these 'single men' so close to our families." This came from the most senior of the men on realizing that the zones were where we were headed for. Fearing repercussions, I had not volunteered this information earlier on: there is a name for women who frequent the zones.

I had warned Mteteleli we were coming; so he was expecting us. He was not a boy by any reckoning. But he was also not old. We had never discussed things like age but I knew he was "proud to be with such a young, unspoilt, sweet thing." And I liked his being proud of my tender age. It meant he would never leave me, I thought. Oh, yes, young I may have been, but I'd seen and heard enough of life to know that men did tire of women. Therefore, I saw it as advantageous that I was young enough for him to like it.

The visit to Netreg is vivid in some respects, dull in others. All I remember of the face of the woman who opened the door to our knock are the crow's feet etched around her eyes. Her hair, streaked with gray, is pulled harshly back into a matronly bun at the nape of her neck. I remember being taken to an inside room, a bedroom I think, although what makes me think that, I do not know. I dimly recall seeing some furniture in the room but when I close my eyes now and try to see then, the room is blurred, empty except for the thickset woman whose flesh sags every which way, like an aged wrestler's.

Neither do I recall whether she spoke to me in English or in Afrikaans. Indeed, did she say anything at all or did she make gestures; point and show me what to do? Did she smile? frown? or was her face barren of all expression? For whatever reason, all this has been banished from my mind.

What I do remember has never left my recall. On the other hand, what I have forgotten, I forgot with amazing swiftness: inside a week, and it was all gone. Moreover, it has remained safely tucked away. It doesn't haunt me. And for that, I am truly grateful.

What has stayed obstinately with me, like plaque to rotting teeth, are the sensations grooved into my heart, deep, deep inside my heart.

She had spread the newspapers on the floor. We were alone in the room, my mother and her *medem* had remained in the outer room. I remember a bowl of innocent-looking water, soapy water. She dipped her hands in it. Then she made me open my legs. Wide.

A wet hand touches me. Warm. I remember thinking, Oh, that water in the bowl must be warm, because of that. She forces a cold, smooth, slippery object into me. Although it is much smaller than a little boy's penis it snags, only for a second, however. Then coldly and stiffly it glides into me. Deep into me. I arch my back; expecting pain. My eyes are closed tight as a spoiled clam. I hear the grinding of my teeth. An elusive smell wafts softly up my nostrils.

Is this all? I begin to wonder. I begin to relax; the anticipated pain has not come. I start thinking this is one of those cases, where collectively memory multiplies the experience. I must have heard exaggerated tales, I tell myself, stories far from the truth. Correction comes swift, hard, and scorching; jogging the memory of my race.

This is what it must feel to swallow petrol and set a match into the mouth. My intestines are on fire. A raging fire that pushes and swells everything inside of me, puffing it up until I feel my tummy burst. I writhe, groaning. Tears wash my face. I am hot all over. Flames liquify my insides, filling me as they spread ever upward and outward and downward.

A terror-filled scream pierces my burning ears. A mad woman's scream? Or, a dying woman's?

The woman gives me a tablet. Thereafter, she calls the two people who'd brought me. While Mother helps me out of the house and toward the car, her kind employer reaches for her purse. Whether the money she gives the woman will be deducted from my mother's pay, I do not know. And I do not care. At that moment, I doubt I will ever care about anything at all again. I am convinced I am about to die. My legs confirm this; they have already died. I can't feel them. But the ton of lead they weigh slows me; that, I do feel. The awful heaviness makes the distance, a mere twelve meters at most, a torturous trek. I feel as if some powerful evil force has come to dwell inside my body and now, for each step I take, drags me back double the ground I've gained. A century later, we reach the car.

I am alone in the back. Ma is sitting in front with Mrs. Wilkins. I'm sprawled across the whole back seat, wide enough for three. My spine, too, has died. I can't sit up. My tummy, my thighs, and every other part of me, everything is on fire.

Soon, we are home. It is not quite dark yet. "Stand up straight and walk upright." We live in dread of our neighbors' vigorous tongues. Mother does not want to give them any encouragement. She does not want them to start any gossip. She is a member of the Catholic Mother's Guild, a prominent member. A scandal would shatter her reputation.

Late that night, an ambulance carried me to Peninsula Hospital. Later still that same night, with doctors in attendance, I lost my son, my blood.

That thieving day! My childhood gone. Forever. Gone, too, a special part of my life as a woman. Not because, years later, I would come to know that I would never bear a child. No. Not because I would never be able to have sex and enjoy it, because as a man's penis glides into me it triggers the memory of what glided out of me those many years ago. No. Nor is it the secret I carry, dark and fearful. The secret I fear will burst into full flower one day; explaining my love of washing babies—especially little boys. That is not what haunts me.

My friends know they can rely on me to look after their babies when I am not on duty. Yes, I went back to school, later on. Thanks to Sue, the feminist. She paid for my education and today I am a qualified midwife.

But she can never really buy me what I lost that day she took me to Netreg. No one can. And nothing can bring back the innocence I'd lost by the day we went there, when Mteteleli was supposed to pay *lobola* and make me his wife.

Fifteen years before, Mteteleli, then a boy of sixteen or so years old, had come to Cape Town as a migrant laborer.

Mother too has never been the same since that Sunday we went to the zones to get *lobola* from the father of the child I was carrying, the day Mother saw Mteteleli and recognized my father.

So, three weeks later to the day, I went to Netreg. It was Easter Sunday and I was almost fourteen years old.

CHARLES MUNGOSHI

is one of the most prolific and renowned novelists, poets, and playwrights of Zimbabwe. His opus includes nine books in English and Shona languages. In 1972 he published the book **Coming of a Dry Season,** *which was forbidden in Rhodesia. His novel,* **Waiting for the Rain,** *was published in England in 1975 and in 1976 he was awarded the Rhodesian Pen Prize. Only upon independence was the book published in Zimbabwe, in 1981, and became a textbook for schools and universities. Both books were translated into Hungarian, German, Bulgarian, and French. A collection of nine stories,* **Some Kinds of Wounds,** *was printed in 1980 and 1983. A collection of poems,* **The Milkman Does Not Only Deliver Milk: Selected Poems,** *was published in 1981.*

Charles Mungoshi's stories are widely anthologized.

His latest book, a collection of seventeen stories, is entitled **The Setting Sun and the Rolling World** *(1989).*

The prestigious African prize the Noma Award for 1992 was given to Charles Mungoshi for his book for children **One Day, Long Ago.** *It contains more stories from a Shona childhood.*

THE BROTHER

CHARLES MUNGOSHI

TENDAI FELT VERY EXCITED AS HE KNOCKED ON THE door. He was going to a secondary boarding school and he would be spending the last three days before schools opened with his eldest brother in the city. He knocked again. In his left hand he carried a paper bag full of food from the farm. There were two tins of peanut butter, one for him to take to school, and the other for his brother. There were cobs of green maize, some cucumbers and mangos. In the inside pocket of his jacket were his identity card and traveling papers, a list of the things that his brother would buy him for school, and a letter to his brother from his wife. The brother had just married and the wife would be expecting soon. She was at home helping with the farm work. They had taken her too early from her husband and she was worried that her husband would not be there when she went into labor.

At the third knock, the door opened. Magufu, Tendai's brother, stood in the doorway.

"Oh, it's you," he said. He didn't seem at all happy to see Tendai.

"Yes," Tendai answered, slightly put off.

"Come in."

They went into the house.

"I wasn't expecting you today. I thought you'd be coming tomorrow. Today isn't Sunday, is it?"

"No. Today is Saturday."

They sat on the sofas in the living room. There were some magazine pictures of naked women hung on the walls. For some reason, Tendai had expected to see some pictures of his brother's recent wedding. There were just those naked women pictures, a big portrait of his brother in dark glasses, like a black pop star, and some out-of-date calendars displaying more naked women.

It didn't feel like his brother's house at all. Not the brother who would drive the whole family to church every Sunday he was on leave.

Vaguely, Tendai expected some explanation.

"So?" Magufu was looking at him.

"So?" Tendai was startled. "What?"

"I thought you said you'd be coming on Sunday—tomorrow."

"Oh. Mother thought I should come today."

"So it's Mother, is it?"

Tendai didn't understand.

Magufu looked at his watch. "Look. I am going out to meet some people right now. I was just about to leave when you came in."

He pulled out a dollar. "You know where the shops are, don't you? Right where you dropped off the bus here. Get yourself something to eat. Everything you need—pots, pans, salt —is right in the kitchen. I won't be long." He was moving toward the door.

"I have brought some things—a letter from your wife— and . . ."

"I won't be long."

Magufu went out and Tendai heard his car driving away. All of a sudden Tendai felt he missed home very much.

Magufu didn't come back until Tendai was fast asleep, after midnight: with a woman.

Tendai had to get off the bed and spread out on the floor. He had not quite heard his brother's coming in and shaking him and telling him to take some blankets off the bed and spread out on the floor because he had been confused by having to be awakened in the middle of a dream into the nightmare of a glaringly lit room. Now, as he lay himself down and his head cleared, he realized that it was not his dream that had spilled into reality: the house *was* really full of people. There seemed to be a drinking party out there in the living room.

Tendai turned thrice before finding a comfortable position.

There were voices of men and women in the living room and they all seemed very happy because they were laughing and shouting and singing and now and then Tendai heard the noise of breaking glass.

His brother's voice seemed the loudest. Troubled by something he couldn't understand, Tendai drifted off into that uncharted world between sleep and wakefulness.

Later he woke up to the presence of someone in the room. He opened his eyes and saw his brother swaying in the doorway to the living room. There were still some low voices all over the house, otherwise there was a kind of tired quietness.

Tendai smelt perfume.

He looked round.

She was sitting on the bed. Magufu was swaying in the doorway, half turned, as if he was giving last orders to someone in the living room. Then he turned, switched on the light.

"Please," the woman pleaded, shielding her face with her hands. She was fully dressed, Tendai saw.

"Afraid of the light, huh?" Magufu laughed.

The woman didn't say anything. She kept her face in her hands. She wasn't a big woman. And she wasn't old either. From what he saw of her, sitting on the bed, her face covered and her head lowered, Tendai felt that she was younger than his brother's wife.

"A night mover, heh?" Magufu was laughing. He began to sing and shuffle on the floor, singing something about women of the night who shun the light, and shuffling in a drunkard's dance.

"Please. The light is killing my eyes," the woman pleaded. She had a girl's voice, an abused girl's voice.

"The light kills their eyes," Magufu danced toward the switch. The room flipped into darkness.

"Feel better? Feel safe?" Magufu asked, already half turning the words into song.

He shut the door and shuffled toward the bed.

There was the sound of the outside door opening and someone with good-humored drunken violence came in shouting.

"Magufu! Hey, Magufu!"

The whole house woke up—laughing and shouting.

"Who's that?" Magufu shouted, swaying near the bed. He stroked the girl's head.

"It's Sam!" called a voice from the sitting room.

"Oh, Sammy boy!"

"Wake up you louts! Wake up! Where's Magufu? I say— what's this? An hotel or brothel? My! My! My! Hey, Magufu! Wake up and tell me what you think you have got here!"

"Get out, idiot!" Magufu shouted.

"Who is calling me idiot? Huh? Where is the unnamable obscenity that's calling me . . ."

"Oh, Sam! Watch out. There're broken bottles on the floor."

"Sam. Oh, Sam."

"Where have you been, Sam?"

"Good old Sam."

"One of these days they are going to drag you out of Mukuvisi with a long knife in your back!"

"Hey, Magufu!"

"Sam's here, Magufu."

"Where's that black fart Magufu? Asleep is he? I'll teach him to . . . hey, Magufu!"

"Magufu your mother! Can't you fellows have respect for an honest, tired, hardworking man?" Magufu shouted.

"Won't you please tell them to keep quiet?" the girl said.

"Hey, Sam! Sam! The missus says you oafs shut up!" Magufu laughed.

"So you are there, are you? I'll teach you to leave a brother . . ." Sam was banging on the door. "Open up!"

"Please, Magufu . . ." the girl pleaded.

"Sam's all right. Hey, Sam, you are all right, aren't you?"

"Open up in there or I'll . . ."

"Respect, Sam! Respect!" Magufu shouted, laughing.

The banging stopped. In a semisober voice Sam said, "Respect, eh? You said respect, did you, Mag?"

"You heard me, idiot!"

"But look," Sam hissed, "you can't do this to me, you know. It's not fair."

"What's not fair?"

"Where the hell did you go? You nearly got me killed, you know."

"Killed?"

"Damnit, Magufu. They are right out here in the van! And do they want to see you! Oh boy, oh boy, oh boy."

"What are you talking about?"

"You know what I am talking about, you black this-and-that. And you know damn well that there isn't going to be any peace if you-know-who finds out that you have been knowing-what an unknown-who . . ."

Magufu sat up. "You mean . . . ?"

"Yes. I mean she is here and you know what that means." Magufu whistled.

"Sam."

"Yes, ass?"

"Do our skin a favor?"

"And my reputation?"

"You know what your reputation is worth you this-and-that. Now, listen. Do us a real big favor."

"You mean she is that you-know-what?"

"I wouldn't be asking you if she weren't, would I?"

Sam whistled. "You know, Mag."

"Come on."

"You'll get us all killed one of these days. You-know-who is really in one of her foul weather moods."

"Sam?"

"Yes, ass?"

"We are tired. We want to sleep."

Sam whistled. "Mag?"

"Uh—huh?"

"Is it worth breakfast with . . ."

There was a loud car horn blast outside.

"Get going, Sam, before . . ."

"I am on my way. See you at farting time!"

Sam went out shouting, "So all you I-don't-know-what-to-call-you don't know where that idiot Magufu is, huh?"

"Go on, Sam. We told you he isn't here, didn't we?" a voice in the sitting room shouted after Sam.

A minute later they all heard the sound of a car angrily starting and driving off with three short blasts of the horn.

"Good old Sam," Magufu said.

There was the sound of a bolt being shot home.

"You seem to have very good friends," the girl said. She was still sitting on the bed.

"Come on. You aren't going to spend all night sitting there, are you?" Magufu was undressing in the dark.

Dimly, Tendai saw the girl standing up and beginning to take off her dress. Tendai looked away.

The bed creaked as Magufu got into the blankets.

"Come on. What are you standing there for?"

"Who is this on the floor?"

"He doesn't bite. Come into bed."

"My things."

"What about them?"

"Where shall I put them?"

"Oh, damnit! Hang them on your nose and come right into bed."

"I can't put them on the floor—it's the only pair I have."

"You want me to take you right back where I took you from?"

"Please, I just . . ."

"You want me to take you back there?"

"Please, Magufu," she giggled and threw her things on top of Tendai.

Tendai heard her climbing into bed.

"I said take off *everything!*"

"Oh, please. I can't go to bed completely naked, you know." She gave a short nervous laugh. "It's only my pants."

"Take the damn stink off!"

The girl gasped. She got out of bed.

"All right. If that's how you like it. All right. If—there!"

The thing landed in Tendai's face. A smell of sweat and very strong perfume. Tendai quickly removed it.

"Good. Now come into bed."

She didn't move.

"Sheila! Sheila!"

The girl didn't answer.

"Do you hear me, Sheila?" Magufu's voice was thickening with anger.

Then slowly, terribly, Tendai realized that the girl was crying, trying hard to suppress violent sobs.

"Sheila, what's wrong?"

She didn't answer.

"Sheila! Sheila!"

"Yes?" Her voice was broken because of the crying.

"Don't you want?"

"I—I—don't . . ." She sobbed.

"Come on, Sheila. Tell me, what's wrong?"

"Nothing."

"Nothing?"

She didn't answer.

"I don't understand. I just don't understand." Magufu half rose in bed and leaned toward Sheila. He put his arm round her shoulders. She stiffened, caught her breath: "Don't."

"But why?" Magufu's voice was menacing.

"I didn't want to drink," Sheila said.

"Are you ill or something?"

"No."

"But . . ."

"Please, Magufu. You won't beat me, will you?"

"Why would I want to do that?"

"If you find out that I am a big disappointment."

"What do you mean?" Magufu's voice was very dark with suspicion.

Sheila didn't answer.

"Look, Sheila. I am not playing games anymore. What's bothering you?"

The girl seemed to think for a long time, then said, "All right then. I don't care. All right. Oh, it's all right."

She crawled into bed beside Magufu.

"Hell, you're so small," Magufu whispered.

The girl didn't answer. She seemed to be crying.

"What's wrong, Sheila? You ill or something?"

"I am all right."

"No. You are not all right at all. You are shivering like a kitten out of water."

Sheila didn't answer.

There was a long silence, then later on, as if she were being smothered, Sheila protested. "Please, Magufu. No. Please. No. No. No."

"Why?"

"I—just—can't—"

"Why?"

She didn't answer.

"Why, Sheila? I thought you loved me."

"It's not that."

"What is it then?"

She was quiet for some time, then said, "Promise me you won't be angry."

"Oh, come on, Sheila."

She thought for some time, then asked, "You are married aren't you?"

"No."

"True?"

"What the hell."

"I have got to know, you know."

"And if I am?"

"But *are* you?"

"Look. I don't see where this is getting us."

"You are getting angry."

"What's all this mystery talk about? I thought you under-stood when we left that place together."

"Understood what?"

"That you were coming home with me."

"I was drunk. You got me drunk."

"So what?"

"I haven't been drunk before."

"You would have had to start someday."

"No. I don't think so. You tricked me."

"Oh, come on, Sheila."

"You tricked me and now you say you love me but you won't tell me whether you have got a wife or not."

"I don't see what my wife has got to do with this."

"So you *are* married?"

"Oh, hell."

"Where is your wife?"

"Come on, Sheila."

"Does she know you trick people and when they don't know who they are and what they are doing anymore you drag them home to bed and tell them to strip to the skin?"

"Look, Sheila . . ."

"And who is that Sam?"

"A friend."

"What was he talking about?"

"Look, Sheila . . ."

"What was he talking about?"

"Look. If you're going to spend all night talking I am going to sleep, okay?"

"Why have you brought me here, Magufu?"

"You came on your own."

"Did I?"

Magufu didn't answer.

"Where are my sisters, Magufu. You brought me here to-gether with my sisters, didn't you? Where are they?"

Magufu didn't answer.

"Where are they, Magufu?"

"Look. Your sisters went out with some men and now shut up and let me go to sleep, will you?"

"They went with some men . . . did they say where they were going?"

"Sheila, you want me to take you back?"

"Where did they go?"

"I don't know."

"How did I come to be here without my sisters? You have got a wife haven't you? And you let my sisters go away without me. Do you always do this?"

"Do what?"

"Drug people's drinks and when they . . ."

The slap was like the sharp crack of close thunder.

Sheila didn't scream. She held her breath as if someone had pushed her head underwater, then she gasped.

"Take me home," she said, gasping. "I want to go back home. Please take me back home." She was quickly getting out of bed and Magufu was holding her back and then she began to shout and scream and Magufu was telling her to shut up and there were two more short, sharp slaps and Tendai realized they were fighting. They were now both on the floor and rolling toward him.

Tendai quickly got dressed and opened the door into the sitting room. In the dim light from the street Tendai could make out shapes of people sleeping on the sofas. There was deep gut-tural snoring. The place reeked with the stench of beer. The whole room seemed full of sleeping people.

Tendai opened the door and went out into the street. He leaned his head against a lamppost.

Then slowly, all the bile he had been resisting gathered into a tight burning knot inside his chest.

He hit the pole again and again till his knuckles were sore. He hit the pole again and again till he was sweating.

Then he began to walk along the street.

There was the sharp smell of flowers from the trees lining the street. The leaves reflected the yellow light. The location was sunk in a drunken stupor, with the slightest hint of the stench of urine, stale vomit and human sweat. There was a low hum which told Tendai that even in sleep the township was very much alive, dangerously alive, but he didn't care.

There was a little hill at the end of the street. There was a church on the hill.

He found the heavy dark doors of the church closed. Through a window he saw that it was very dark inside the church.

He walked round the church into the trees at the back.

He lay down on a flat rock under the trees and looked at the lights of the town on the other side of the hill. He found the garish brilliance of the city hurting his eyes and he looked into the deep moving darkness of the leaves of the trees above him. He closed his eyes and soon lost himself in the smell of the flowers and the darkness of the leaves. Something warm and comfortable moved into the center of his belly and he felt very safe. He didn't care for the stories they told about township thugs and *tsotsis*.

He heard the sound of the leaves calmly soughing in the slight wind on the hill, and he slept, carrying with him the play of dull light and deep shadow in the leaves above him.

He woke up at the milkman's bell just a little before sunrise. His body was stiff and numb from sleeping on the hard rock. He stretched and yawned and felt his muscles and joints cracking. The city lights and streetlights looked very weak in the eye of the coming sun.

His brother's house wasn't in his mind as he got down from the hill, so he walked round the location which at this early Sunday hour seemed to belong to children armed with loaves of bread wrapped in newspaper and the morning's paper.

When the streets began to fill up with older people looking sick and threatening from the heavy night, Tendai made his way to his brother's house.

There was a VW van parked in front of the house. Through the window Tendai saw a man lying between two women on a blanket on the floor of the van. They were fast asleep in their clothes. Tendai quickly looked away and passed on.

He tried the door and found it unlocked. He entered. There were two couples sleeping on the sofas in the sitting room. Empty beer bottles were scattered all over the floor. There were broken bottles and cigarette ends and ash swimming in dark splotches and puddles of beer. The air was heavy with the smell of beer, tobacco smoke and something else that could have only come from the sleepers.

Tendai went into the kitchen where he found two women sleeping in each other's arms, their mouths wide open and saliva trickling from the corners. They lay on a dirty tarpaulin without blankets. A black pot lay on its side in a puddle of dirty water and there were lumps of *sadza* at their feet. Close to it was a plate with the remains of meal in it. On a little stand at the women's heads, right below the kitchen window, was a paraffin stove with a dirty pan on it. There were onion skins and pink stains in the pan. The lower end of the curtain had been burnt.

Tendai felt sick from the complex smell in the kitchen. He went out. He hadn't realized that women could outsnore men.

The door to his brother's bedroom was closed. Tendai didn't

bother to find out whether it was locked or not. No one had stirred since he came in, and as he was about to go out one of the women stirred and sleepily said, "Turn your lavatory mouth the other side." The man didn't hear her and the woman turned away from the man and went back to sleep with slight sleepy moans and groans.

Tendai walked to the back of the house where he began to shoot imaginary villains and prodigal brothers with a shotgun as he had seen in Western films. The villains were too many for one man. They crawled out of holes and dropped down from trees and he was glad to forget them as he watched the breath-taking thing that was the sun rising: so close, so big, weak and vulnerable and glowing without hurting his eyes. Tendai felt that the sun was very friendly and lovely as it rose, it only got angry as it grew older and climbed higher in the sky. He felt sorry for it. It couldn't help it.

He was so lost in himself, getting restless and angrier as the sun got higher and forbade him to look it in the face, that he didn't realize that they were all up in the house behind him.

A man came round the back and startled him with his "Oh." Tendai looked at him. The man's eyes were puffed up and bloodshot, his lips very thick with scales of skin and corn beer. He winked and grinned, shook his head and, as he passed water against the wall of the house, said, "What a night" in a voice that sounded like gravel being unloaded.

There was a girl washing pots and plates at an outside sink at the next house. Tendai saw her giggling and pretending to be busy with the washing.

"Ohiyo—ouhgh! What a drunken terrible fanta—stic night," the man said, stretching and rubbing his eyes and trying to stop the yawn.

"Your fly," Tendai said, worried, looking quickly at the girl across at the other house.

"Oh, thanks," the man said zipping it up, then: "Hey!" The girl looked up at them. The man made come-here signs with his finger, making exaggerated motions of opening and closing his fly.

The girl stared.

"Want a sausage?" the man called in a loud whisper.

The girl giggled and went back to her pots.

"Good tail end, eh?" the man said to Tendai, winking and nodding to the girl.

Tendai left him and went round to the front of the house.

When he entered the sitting room all eyes turned toward him, including his brother's. But no one said anything. They were playing cards at a long low coffee table in the center of the room.

There were three men and two women playing and two more women who were sitting close together, sometimes watching the game, sometimes talking to themselves. They looked as if they didn't belong to the group, Tendai felt. They talked in very low voices, between themselves. Tendai recognized them as the women who had been sleeping in the kitchen.

There was an empty chair at the other end of the room. Tendai took it and went to sit by the window. He looked out.

They were playing seriously, tiredly but goodhumoredly, like people who have been together for such a long time that they need not discuss it. Except the two women who were not playing. One was tall and thin in a used sort of way and the other one was ugly, plump and pouting. They seemed to be disagreeing in a secret sort of way.

"Where have you been, Tendai?"

It was like a gunshot in a quiet room. Tendai looked round from the window. His brother was not looking at him. He had the pack in his hands and was dealing the cards. All the others had their heads turned toward Tendai.

"Haven't you got a mouth?" Magufu said loudly.

"I have been out."

"Where?"

"Just around."

"Don't give me the lip."

"Oh, leave him alone," one of the playing women said. She was pretty and brightly brittle. She said, "Is that your little brother?"

Tendai didn't like her voice. It was too high and brittle. Magufu didn't answer her.

"I said don't give me the lip, do you hear?"

"Yes."

"You can do that sort of thing to Mother and Father but I am paying your fees and responsible for you from now on. Do you hear me?"

"Kick it under, Magufu," one of the men said. He wore dark glasses and a thick beard. He didn't look as if he had been part of last night.

"I said do you hear me, Tendai?" Magufu wasn't looking at him.

"Yes," Tendai said in a small voice.

"Come on, Magufu," the bearded man said. "Talk to him later."

"I bloody well can talk to him anytime I damn well want and if it's now, it is now and who the hell is going to tell me not to?"

There was a terrible silence. Magufu had the cards in his hands. He slapped them hard on the table.

Everyone was looking down at the table.

"I said who the hell is going to tell me not to?"

No one answered.

"Magufu," the bearded man touched Magufu's shoulder. Magufu violently shook the man's hand off. The man shrugged his shoulders. He looked round at the others. They lowered their eyes.

"Let's go, Dan," one of the playing women said. She was small but hard and old. She had her hand on the knee of the third man, short, nervous-looking and frightened.

They stood up and left without saying good-bye.

The two women who were not playing looked at each other, said something to each other and stared at the men.

"Don't frighten the child," the woman with the brittle voice said. She looked at Tendai, smiled, then looked round the room and suddenly shouted: "Where is Sam? Did any of you see where Sam's gone?" She stood up.

"Sit down, Martha," the bearded man said. The two women by themselves giggled to themselves.

"Where is Sam?"

Martha's voice was shrill. "Did either of you see where Sam has gone?" She looked at the two women giggling between themselves. They didn't answer her.

"Am I talking to . . ."

"What's the trouble, Martha?" Sam entered. He came up to Martha and put his hands round her waist and pecked her on both cheeks. Martha closed her eyes and sighed, sinking back into her seat.

The two women laughed.

Martha looked at them hard and they shut up.

The bearded man smiled at Sam and Martha, absently taking the cards up. He began to shuffle them.

Magufu put his face in his hands and planted his elbows on the table.

"Where have you been, darling?" Martha asked Sam picking at something invisible on his chin.

"Selling sausages, darling," Sam kissed her but she quickly pulled away.

"Selling what?"

"Sausages," Sam said lazily and tried to kiss her again. She slapped him hard on the cheek: "I don't like that, ever! Do you hear me Sam? Don't ever bring the sausage joke with me!"

"Oh dear, oh dear," Sam said. "But they are in great demand." He winked at the giggling women. They squealed brightly and clapped their right hands together in a popular greeting gesture.

"Oh, Sam!" said the tall one.

"You kill me!" said the plump one.

Martha swiveled round and glared at them. "Get out!" She hissed. "Get out right now and don't ever let me see your dirty little tails again!"

Sam put his hand round her shoulders. She put her left hand round his neck. Sam winked at the two women. And they laughed into their hands, their heads down on their knees.

The bearded man smiled.

"Sam is my man and if either of you think you can repeat last night's scene with him you are getting out of town right now!"

"Oh, shut up, Martha!" Magufu roared, pulling his face out of his hands and glaring at her. Everyone looked at him, surprised, except the bearded man who was quietly shuffling the cards as if he wasn't there.

Sam looked at Magufu, suddenly very concerned and worried, then, just as suddenly, his face dissolved into its mischievous hangover.

Martha had stiffened, looking into Sam's face, hanging from his neck as if she were going to drown. Now, Sam looked down into her eyes and kissed them shut. They began to play, whimpering like ecstatic puppies. The two women looked elsewhere, very serious.

Magufu returned his face into the cave of his hands.

The bearded man began to play a game they called solo.

"Tendai," Magufu called, quietly, without taking his face out of his hands.

"Yes?"

"Did you see my letter?"

"Your letter?"

"I wrote a letter to Father. Didn't he say anything to you about it?"

"No."

"Are you sure?"

"Did it concern me?"

"Yes."

"He might have decided to keep it to himself. Was it about anything you wanted me to do?"

"It was about money."

"Money?"

"Your fees—damnit—haven't you got ears?"

Tendai said nothing. The others were careful not to look at Magufu.

"Didn't your father give you money for this term's fees?"

"No. He just gave me bus fare to town, some pocket money and told me you'd fix the rest."

"Including school uniform, toothpaste, soap, towels—and—?"

"Yes."

There was a silence.

The bearded man was trying very very hard to concentrate on his cards.

The two women kept whispering into each other's ear now and again, looking away from each other, apparently disappointed, and constantly watching the closed door into Magufu's bedroom.

Sam had leaned back in his seat, his face turned up to the

roof, his right hand absentmindedly tap-tapping Martha's right shoulder as if he were trying to put her to sleep. Martha had gathered all her upper self on Sam's chest, eyes closed, left hand round Sam's neck and the right moving up and down, across and back his chest, inside his open shirt.

It was a tense moment.

The bearded man quietly reached inside his jacket and pulled out a bottle of brandy. He put it on the table and pushed it across to Magufu, and went to his cards without looking or talking to Magufu.

Suddenly Sam brightened and leaned across Martha: "Aaah! The little blighter that's going to kill us all. And I thought we didn't have a single sip round the place. Good old Sando. How do you manage to pull out these wonders when everyone has begun to think the world is dead?"

Martha opened her eyes and said, "What is it?" She followed Sam's eyes and saw the bottle. She sat up suddenly, "Salvation at last!" She tried to reach for it but Sando held back her hand. She looked surprised, "But why?"

"No," Sando said quietly, firmly.

"Why not?" Martha shrilled.

"Because no," Sando said.

"Oh, come on, Sando. Don't be hard on your poor old friends. We'll soon be dead anyway, why the Censorship Board?"

Magufu was looking at the bottle from above his fingers with only his eyes, the rest of the face still covered.

The two women nudged each other and looked at the bottle and then at the others. They looked as if they were watching the opening moves in a boxing match.

"Huh—Brother Sando?" Sam pleaded.

Sando was back at his cards. Whenever he turned round, the dark glasses were in Tendai's way. He would have liked to see the man's eyes. The man's firm calmness was beginning to frighten Tendai a little, in an exciting kind of way.

"Brother Sando? Do you hear me? It's your wee little brother Sam out here. There is dry dust in my throat and a chill in my belly, Brother Sando?"

Sando went on playing solo.

"Brother Sando, please!" Martha croaked. She was licking her lips and there was a big cordlike vein bulging out from below her ear down across her neck into the little cavity where the neck disappeared into the chest.

Magufu was still looking at the bottle.

The women were waiting, excitedly, a little afraid perhaps.

"Brother Sando!" Sam and Martha said together.

Sando quietly laid down a card on top of another and said, "You vultures are a real hard boil in the innermost softest part of my ass's heart, you hear that?" He was very motionless, looking at the cards, but not playing. There was a slight tremor in the hands that held the cards.

Martha wriggled into some impossibly warmer and hidden place on Sam's chest moaning to herself. Sam swallowed and said, "No harm meant, Brother Sando," and his eyes suddenly dropped out of his face into some inner cave inside his arid belly.

The women waited.

Slowly Sando turned toward Magufu.

He looked at him hard and long from behind his dark glasses.

"Oh, damn you, Sando! To hell with you, Sando! Do you hear me, Sando? I said to hell with you and keep going don't you ever turn back because—" his hand trembling, reaching for the bottle. Suddenly Sando's hand flashed out and locked round Magufu's wrist in a grip that made both their arms shake.

Sweat broke over Magufu's face.

"All right, Sando," he whispered hoarsely. Sando let go Magufu's hand.

"Get us a jar of water, Sonbigy," Sando called over his shoulder to Tendai.

Tendai went out to get the water.

"It's all your fault, Sando," Magufu was saying, his face hidden in his hands again. "I told you I don't want to touch the stuff anymore. What are you doing to me, Sando?"

"Nothing that you aren't doing to yourself."

"Oh no!" Magufu was sobbing.

The plump woman whispered, "Let's go, auntie."

"And Sheila? We just can't leave her here alone with—with—"

Sando was looking at them. Their eyes clashed on the closed door to Magufu's bedroom.

Tendai brought in the jug of water.

"Get us some glasses, Sonnyboy."

Tendai went into the kitchen to fetch the glasses.

"Your brother is very sick, Sonnybig," Sando told Tendai as he handed him the glasses. "Every Sunday morning I have to come here very early to keep him company." Sando was pouring little measures into four glasses. "Tell you a secret, Sonnyboy? Without me your brother would have killed himself. You saw me hold back his hand there? He would have taken that stuff straight and dry without a blink."

Sando was adding water into the glasses. "Don't you ever try it, Sonnyboy. This stuff is a killer. And don't ever try it alone. Share it with friends. Don't transfer your troubles to it thinking it will burn them. It will only create more trouble."

Sando was handing the glasses round to the others. "It's a real chariot of fire that takes you—in the opposite direction. Ever read the Bible, Sonnyboy?"

"Yes."

"So you know about the Chariot of Fire?"

"Yes."

"Here is one but harnessed to the devil's horses."

Sando was screwing the lid back onto the bottle. He didn't give the two women any of the brandy.

"I am trying very hard to make your brother stop taking this stuff. It is bad for his health, and lately it's been very very bad for his work."

Sando sipped from his glass.

Sam and Martha did the same.

Magufu stared at his as if he didn't want to drink. His fingers were tightly curled in his face.

"You see, Sonnybig. This stuff is very bad for your brother. In the beginning it gave him a name and earned him admirers right and left in the drinking community. But now it's losing him friends fast, money faster and his health and sanity fastest. You understand all this, don't you?"

"Yes."

"No, you don't. Not now, later maybe, but not today. This stuff, my friend, taken dry and straight at the rate you drink water in a day, completely wipes out any sense of self, shame, pride or dignity, wrong or right out of some people's minds. It also causes blackouts, the shaking of hands, sleepiness, loss of memory and a queer hating and avoiding of people, especially those dearest to one's heart. Conversely it breaks the loved ones' hearts into so many tiny pieces and throws them as far apart as heaven and hell."

Magufu stealthily reached for his glass.

"Easy, Magufu, easy on it. Just a tiny wee sip to wet your tongue . . . that's right. Now, put it back . . . good."

"It is very important that you understand what's happening to your brother right now. It's a secret between you and me.

Don't tell your father or mother. You still have an expanding heart. You can accommodate almost anything if you try hard enough.

"Parents are a different thing altogether. They think they have seen the worst and now their hearts are built into little concrete squares that have no more room for expansion. If you tell them what I have told you about your brother you will only kill them. They haven't been taught to break the little concrete squares and make more room for emergencies like these."

"Aren't we going to have something to eat here?" Martha asked. Her glass was empty.

"So, Sonnybig brother, don't let me ever hear that you have been playing over this song to Ma and Pa back home or I'll break your neck, right?"

"Yes."

"It's not fair on your brother here and all of us his friends, right?"

"Yes."

"One day, if you live long enough, you will learn that in this life you can only talk of certain things and leave out certain others about other people."

Magufu put his glass down on the table. It was empty.

"Tendai," he said. His fingers were now locked together between his knees with the elbows resting on the knees.

"Yes."

"I am going to give you a letter to Father."

"Yes."

"When are you wanted at school?"

"On Wednesday."

"Today is Sunday morning. If you take the three p.m. bus you will be home before six. You will put up at home tonight and take the early morning bus back to town tomorrow—so around eleven you should be here. Tuesday I'll take a day off to do your shopping and you will take the Tuesday afternoon bus to school . . ."

"Aah, Sheila!"

"Sheila!"

The two women shouted together. Everyone looked up.

Sheila closed the door to Magufu's bedroom and came to sit between the two women.

"Hallo Sheila babe!" Sam shouted. His glass, too, was now empty. Only Sando seemed not to be drinking. He was concentrating on the game of solo.

Martha kept dangerously quiet but looking at Sheila with such a bright brittle look that one expected to hear the sharp breaking of glass anytime.

"And how is our Sheila?" Sam said.

"Let's go, Sam," Martha stood up.

"Come on, Martha."

"Come on yourself. What are we hanging round here for anyway? No food, no beer, no music. Come on, let's go." She was tugging at Sam's shirt sleeve.

Sam looked up at her, narrowed his eyes and said, "You know something, Martha?"

"No? What? Come on, let's get out of here."

"One of these very lovely days, Martha . . ."

"What is it?"

"Aren't you interested?"

"I am but hurry it up."

"Sit down first," Sam was smiling brightly at Martha.

Sando was looking at them.

Magufu was staring at his empty glass.

The two women were looking at Martha with open contempt. Sheila was looking for something in her handbag. She hadn't smiled or said anything since she came in.

"What is it, Sam?" Martha said, putting her hand round

Sam's neck and kissing him on the mouth with a bright brittle look at Sheila.

Sheila wasn't looking at them at all.

"Oh, I forgot to say hello, Sheila," Martha said. "Hello, Sheila!" she shrilled across the room and began to titter hysterically.

"Hello, Martha," Sheila said, looking up and smiling sadly at Martha and going back to searching for what she could never seem to find in her handbag.

"Isn't Sheila beautiful, darling?" Martha told Sam, kissing him on the mouth again.

"Not as beautiful as you are, my own dearest darling," Sam said, turning his mouth away from Martha's kisses, "and listen, darling. Remember what I said?"

"Yes. You said one of these lovely days . . . isn't that what you said?"

"Yes, exactly. You know you are very intelligent, Martha."

"Come on, Sam," Magufu said. He wasn't looking at them. "Not in front of the . . ."

". . . and you are very very bright and I love you so much that . . ."

"Cut it, Sam!" Magufu shouted.

Sando was looking at them and not playing solo anymore.

". . . one of these fine lovely days I'll tan your hide so black and ram your teeth right back your mouth so they will be smiling north when you are going south!"

"Sam!"

Magufu's shout was too late. Martha was lying back on the sofa, her mouth looking as if she were eating raw liver. She looked too surprised to say anything.

Tendai saw Martha's lips swelling. He looked out through the window, his eyes filled with tears.

Martha didn't get up where she lay. She was very still. She turned over on her belly to hide her fast-swelling lips.

"Don't mess up that seat. Go and wash!" Sam told her roughly, yanking her up by the scruff of the neck.

"Leave her now, Sam," Sando said. "She is all right now."

Sam dropped her and she lay without a sound or making the slightest movement.

Sando poured brandy into three glasses. He added water and gave Sam and Magufu theirs. He emptied his in one gulp. Sheila and the two women were looking at them.

Sam downed his and winked at the women. "Hi, Sheila!" He smiled. Sheila looked away and the women giggled and then burst into loud laughter.

Magufu was studying his glass, not yet touched, in both his hands.

Suddenly, Sheila spoke.

Her voice was very different from last night, Tendai felt. It was soft, low and lost, and it was worse than Martha's lips suddenly changing into overblown lungs.

"I had forgotten," she said to her two friends, her sisters of last night—"I had forgotten that it's my birthday today."

They all stared at her.

"How old are you now, Sheila?" Sam asked.

"Fifteen."

Suddenly the room was very quiet, everyone listening to but not looking at her.

"I had promised Connie and Rudo a party at our house. Now they will come and find I am not there."

Silence.

"You drank too much last night," the tall woman said unkindly.

"I was tricked. And you encouraged it." She searched in her bag. "I had never tasted a drop of beer or spirits all my life until last night. And you sat there while they poured that—what do you call it?—hot stuff into my Coke." She pulled her woman's things out of the bag. "Now, if only I can get those aspirins I hope by the time I get home nobody won't notice a thing." She turned her bag upside down and shook it. Nothing dropped. "Will just have to keep a mile's distance away from Father, though. No toothpaste will ever get this stink out of my mouth." She stuffed her things back into the bag. She looked up straight at Magufu, "No aspirins or anything for a headache in this house heh? Magufu?" She was smiling at him. Sam looked at her, at Magufu, then back at her and lowered his head, hiding something behind a forced cough.

"No. Nothing." Magufu shook his head and quickly brought his hand to his mouth, tilted his head far back and knocked out the drink without making a single sound down his throat. The two women looked at each other in amazement. He banged the glass on the table and shivered throughout his whole body.

Sando was now very involved in his game.

"I am hungry. Is there anything to eat in here?" Sheila asked.

Magufu shook his head.

The women giggled.

"Or milk," Sheila said. "Haven't you got any milk—fresh milk?"

"Get her a bottle of milk, Sonnybig," Sando said, tossing a coin toward Tendai.

"Thank you very much," Sheila said. "And—and Sonnybig —is that your real name? Anyway, no matter—Sonnybig—you are Magufu's brother aren't you? You are the one who was sleeping on the floor in there last night, aren't you? I remember that part—what I can't remember is the earlier part after everything was reeling and the lights were killing my eyes—anyway you,

Sonnybig, please get me some aspirin if there is any change. Is that all right, mister—if there is any change?"

"Get her some aspirins and a bottle of milk, Sonnyboy," Sando said.

Sheila giggled, "Sonnybig, Sonnyboy. Can't ever trust boys with too many names." She put her head on her knees and was still.

Everyone looked at her.

"Let's have a game of Crazy Eight," Sam suggested.

Sando dealt the cards and they began to play.

"Let's go, auntie," the plump woman said.

"Let's wait for Sheila's milk and pills."

After drinking the milk Sheila rushed outside and was violently sick.

She came back and rinsed her mouth thoroughly with water, then she swallowed her aspirins.

"You promised to take us back to Hartley, remember?" She was talking to Magufu.

"Oh, did I?"

"Yes. And you promised me four dollars last night after you hit me and I agreed to do what you wanted me to do."

Sam looked up. His mouth dropped. Magufu looked at the cards that were becoming smudged in his sweaty hands.

"Your turn, Magufu. Play," Sando said. Magufu played.

"I think you have forgotten what I said," he told Sheila.

"No. I haven't. Didn't he say that he would bring us back when we refused to drive out here with him last evening, auntie?"

"You promised," the tall woman said.

"You have to get us back," the plump one said.

"Please, Magufu," Sheila said. "Forget the four dollars for last night but please take us back to Hartley."

Magufu scratched his chin.

"Well—petrol. I haven't got any petrol. Have you got any petrol in the van, Sam?"

"Not enough to get us to Hartley and back."

"You can buy petrol, can't you?" Sheila asked.

"Yes—but—"

"Forget it, girls," Sando said, "we are all broke."

The women looked at each other.

Sheila put her head in her hands. When she looked up there were tears in her eyes.

"Look, Magufu. I said forget the four dollars you promised me when you thought I wouldn't give you what you wanted. Forget about driving and get a lift home."

"Well—let me see. One dollar? Sorry. Can't help you."

"But, Magufu—just a dollar?"

"Honestly I don't—"

"Borrow from your friends then."

"These are my friends and they too are broke."

"Please."

She was trying very hard not to spill any tears. "One night is all right. I can always tell Father we stayed up late at Rudo's place and her parents asked me to spend the night—but two nights? Have heart, heh, Magufu?"

Then she did a terrible thing. She went down on her knees and, her hands on Magufu's knees, looked directly into his eyes.

"Have heart, huh? I did what you wanted. Came all the way from Hartley with you, let you put brandy in my Coke, danced with you, came here and spent the night with you—my first night ever—and you can't do a little thing like giving me a dollar to see me home to my folks, huh, Magufu?"

There was a silence. One of the calendars flapped against the wall.

"Sonnybig?" Sando said.

"Yes?"

"You said Father gave you some pocket money didn't he?"

"Yes."

"You still have it?"

"Yes."

"Could I borrow a dollar? You got more than a dollar haven't you?"

"Yes."

"Can you get home and back on the remainder?"

"Not quite."

"Well—you can use part of the fees Father will give you—"

"The fees? But I am supposed to get fees from brother Magufu here."

"Your brother hasn't got any money. That's why you are going back home today. You are going to collect school fees and money for your school clothing from Father. Now, lend us that dollar and I shall give it and any money you will have used on the way back to you tomorrow evening."

Tendai handed Sheila the dollar.

"Thank you very much again," Sheila said. "Well bye, Magufu."

She didn't even say good-bye to her "sisters" as she went out. The men went back to their game and later the two women also left without saying good-bye to anyone. Only a funeral party could break up this way.

Tendai went into his brother's bedroom to collect his jacket. The bed hadn't been made and there were some bloodstains on the crumpled sheets and right on the floor was a ball of crumpled newspaper with more blood on it. Tendai saw the letter from his brother's wife on the bedside stand where he had put it the day before, still unopened. He grabbed his jacket and went out.

"I am going now," he told his brother without breaking his stride toward the door to the street.

"Hey, Tendai!" Magufu called.

Tendai turned his head. Magufu was smiling. "If you have just a little surplus of the money you really need—you see—we haven't got anything to eat here and—"

"I just have enough to get home on," and he turned on his heel and fled from that house. He felt very desolate.

Later on he would forget some details of those people in his brother's house that day but he would always remember that something very violent had been done to him and that is when he had begun not to care very much for his brother Magufu . . . except that they had the same parents.

WILLIAM (BLOKE) MODISANE

was born in 1924 in Johannesburg and brought up in the slums of Sophiatown, which was later on destroyed. For years he worked in bookshops and as a jazz critic for the newspaper **Golden City Post.** *He fled from South Africa in 1959 and lived in England and Germany where he died in 1986.*

Modisane was a versatile intellectual: playwright, journalist, chronicler, actor. Theater was his chief interest, and he took part in many plays broadcast on BBC and starred in various movies.

In 1963 he published the autobiographical book **Blame Me on History** *which was immediately banned in South Africa and which was posthumously published in the States by Simon & Schuster in 1990.*

His short stories are included in many anthologies.

THE DIGNITY
OF BEGGING

WILLIAM (BLOKE) MODISANE

THE MAGISTRATE RAISES HIS EYES ABOVE THE DOCUMENTS and plunges them like daggers into my heart. His blue eyes are keen: my heart pounds like the bass of a boogie-woogie.

"I'm sick to death of you . . . heartily sick. There's not a native beggar on the streets whose full story I don't know," the Magistrate says. "I've watched some of you grow up. There isn't one I haven't tried to rehabilitate many times. Some I was forced to send to gaol, but they always come back . . . they come back to the goose that lays the golden egg."

These are fighting words. The Magistrate sounds as though he's going to put us away for a few weeks. My only regret is that Richard Serurubele has to share my fate. If only the Magistrate knew that he is not a parasite like the rest of us, that he's what is called an exploited beggar. He was crippled by an automobile accident, and since then his parents have made capital out of it. They use him to beg so they can balance the family budget. They never show him the comfort of love. Relentlessly they drive him, like an animal that has to work for its keep and feed. He is twenty-one. Dragging one foot along, he is an abject sight who had all the sadness of the world in his face. He looks many times older than my mother-in-law.

"You beggars make it difficult for me to do my duty, and in spite of my failure to rehabilitate you, I always believe in giving you another chance . . . A fresh start, you might call it.

"But I'm almost certain that you'll be back here in a few days."

The Magistrate is getting soft, I can see my freedom at a distance of an arm's stretch. Here is my chance to put on my act. A look of deep compunction and a few well-chosen words can do the trick. I clear my throat and squeeze out a tear or two.

"Your Honor, most of us beg because we've been ostracized by our families; they treat us as though we were lepers," I say, wiping off a tear. "They want us to look up to them for all the things we need. They never encourage us to earn our own keep. Nobody wants to employ us, people are more willing to offer us alms, rather than give us jobs. All they do is show us pity . . . We don't want to be pitied, we want to be given a chance to prove that we're as good as anybody else."

I can see from the silence in the court that everybody is deceived . . . Everybody is filled with a sense of self-reproach. The Magistrate is as mute as the undertaker's parlor. I can read pity on the faces of all the people in the court; perhaps the most pathetic is my own. I am magnificent . . . an answer to every film director's dream. I know I have said enough . . . enough to let us out, that is.

"I understand you have matriculated, your name is Nathaniel, isn't it?" He turns a page of the report prepared by a worker in the Non-European Affairs Department. "Yes, here we are, Nathaniel Mokgomare, the department recommends that you be sent to a place where you will be taught some useful trade. I want you to report to Room 14 at the department's building tomorrow morning."

This is not what I had bargained for; my brilliant idea has boomeranged. Why must I take a job when I can earn twice a normal wage begging? After all, what will horses do if I take a job. I *must* uphold the dignity of begging. Professional ethics forbid all beggars from working.

"As for you, Richard Serurubele, I'll let you go this time, but mark my words: the next time you appear before me, I'll have you sent to the Bantu Refuge. Now get out of here, both of you."

If the Magistrate had seen the big grin on my face as we leave the court, he would have thrown my deformed carcass in gaol and deliberately lost the key. He does not see it though.

With the exception of a few loose ends everything has gone according to schedule, but my friend Serurubele is just about the most miserable man on earth. The trouble with him is he lacks imagination, but then of course, not everybody is as bright as I am. He always seems to be looking at the dull side of life, a vice coupled with an appalling brand of honesty most bishops would swear didn't exist.

"One of these days, I'm going to kill myself," Serurubele says. "I can't go on like this, I'm tired of living off other people. Why did this have to happen to me? Tell me, Nathan. Why?"

How this man expects me to answer a question like this is beyond me. For one unguarded moment I almost tell him to send his Maker a telegram and ask Him all about it, but my gentler nature sees the harm such an answer might do.

"I don't know," I say, abruptly. "Things like this just happen; it's not in us to question why. Nature has a way of doing things, but even then she gives something in return . . . at least I think so . . . But how should I know, anyway?"

This is the one time I cannot find something concrete to say; I want to show him that there is compensation for his disability, but I just cannot lay my hands on it. This, I remember, is what made me leave home.

I left because my parents did not understand. They almost made a neurotic out of me; but today I wonder if it wasn't my own sensitivity which gave their actions then their seemingly absurd proportions. They seemed afraid to walk about freely;

everybody sat down as if the house were full of cripples. I was treated like a babe in arms. All the things I wanted were brought to me, I was not even allowed to get myself water to drink. This excessive kindness gradually began to irritate me . . . It became a constant reminder that I didn't belong, that I was an invalid. It then became apparent that they would soon put the food into my mouth which they had already chewed for me, and push it down my throat. These thoughts of inadequacy drove me from home.

A new life opened for me. I got myself a wife, two bouncing boys and a property at Pampoenfontein, also a room at Sophiatown complete with piano. Within two years I had begged well over a few hundred pounds. The money had been used wisely. Only one problem confronts me now, I want enough money to provide for my old age . . . The two boys are also to be considered.

"For Christ's sake, Nathaniel," Serurubele says, "what's wrong with you. Why are you always so wrapped up in your thoughts . . . this is where I stay, remember?"

I say good-bye to him and go to my room. After having something to eat I settle down to some hard thinking. There are all sorts of insurances and societies, unions and what have you, which protect workers. Why not a beggars' union? I could rally all the beggars of the city into one union with some professional name like The United Beggars' Union, into whose funds every beggar would contribute ten shillings a week. In the city of Johannesburg alone, there are over a hundred beggars and if they could all be talked over, a capital of about two thousand four hundred pounds could be realized in one year.

What a brilliant idea . . . an inspiration of genius. Sometimes I feel depressed that the world has not had the vision to realize the potentialities of my genius . . . possibly it cannot accommodate Einstein and myself in the same generation. Anyway, so much for that.

I could promise to offer each a bonus of ten pounds a year. That would be smart . . . No beggar could resist such an offer. Maybe I should promise to buy each a property somewhere cheap, say, buy one property a year for the needy ones like Serurubele, equip him with third-rate tools and interest him in turning out junk that nobody will care to give a second look at. The scheme would be costly, but at least it would go far in enlisting their confidence. Only one would get the property; the others would wait patiently until I get religion.

The following morning I'm at Room 14 bright and early. A white man with a bored expression on his face is sitting behind a big mahogany desk. I tell him my name. He takes some paper and writes on it. He tells me to go to the address written on the paper.

The faint showers that were falling outside have become heavier, and as I go out I say something nasty about the weather. A brilliant idea strikes me as a well-dressed lady is walking toward me. She looks like a mobile gold mine ready to be tapped . . . in fact, I can almost see the gold nuggets in her teeth. I put on a gloomy face, bend lower than usual and let my deformed carcass shiver. She stops and looks at me as if she's responsible for my deformity.

"Why, you poor boy, you're freezing to death," she says, with melodrama. "Here, go buy yourself something to eat."

I feel the half-crown piece in my hand and give her the usual line of how the good Lord will bless her, and send her tons and tons of luck: but from the way she's dressed, she appears to have had more than her share of luck.

I play this trick all the way to the address I'm given, and by the time I get there, I count well over ten half crowns. Not bad,

I say to myself; at this rate I can become the richest and most famous beggar in the city. To think the department wants to pin me behind a desk! The idea is criminal, to say the least.

One of these days when I'm on my annual leave, I hope to write a book on begging, something like a treatise on the subject. It will be written with sensitivity and charm, brimful with sketches from life, and profusely illustrated with colored photographs, with easy-to-follow rules on the noblest and oldest occupation in the world: begging! It will be a textbook for all aspiring beggars, young and old, who will reap a wealth of knowledge from my personal experience and genius. In fact, it will be the only one of its kind in world literature. Even millionaires will take up begging as a pastime to color their humdrum existence.

It will naturally begin with a history of the art from its ancient crudity of maiming children as a preparation in their education, right up to the contemporary age of beggars who are driven to the city in the latest American cars . . . beggars with a bank balance big enough to impress the Receiver of Revenue. I can almost see it on the best-seller list for several months. This reverie almost causes me to lose my way.

I find the place and go in. My heart just misses a beat when I see the large number of people inside. Some, if not most, are deformed monstrosities like myself. What could be sweeter? I can see my plan taking shape.

The man in charge starts explaining the elementary principles of the typewriter. I pretend to be interested and ask many unnecessary questions, but intelligent enough to impress him. By five o'clock I'm running over the keyboard like a brilliant amateur.

On my way home I go via Serurubele's corner. He is still there and looking as miserable as ever. I suggest that we go home. I lure him to my room and when we get there I begin playing a certain tarantella like Rubinstein, only my rendering is in A flat Major. Either my piano recital is good or my friend just loves bad sounds.

"You can have a house like this and everything that goes with it; it's yours for the taking. Why beg for other people when you can do it for yourself?"

"I've got to help with the rent and the food," he says. "How do you think I'm going to get a house like this? I can't just wish for it."

"You don't have to, you must plan and work for it like I did. I have a plan that will give it to you in less than a year . . . Listen."

I then start explaining to him about the society with particular emphasis on the good it will do to all beggars. I see his teeth sparkling behind thick lips. I put him in charge of organizing them for our first meeting.

Last night I dreamt I was at the race course and I saw the winning double as plain as I see my twisted leg. I raid my savings in the room and make my way to Turfontein. When I get there I start scouting around for policemen. None are about and a soothing satisfaction comes with the realization that I shall not bother myself with police badges. I put a pound win on two and seven, a double in the first leg. As I'm making my bet, a man with eyes as big and lethargic as an owl's is standing next to me and beaming like a blushing groom.

I'm too nervous to watch the race, so I decide to walk about and appreciate the scenery. Suddenly I feel as though someone is staring at me. I turn round and look straight at Miss Gallovidian, a welfare worker, who has the uncanny habit of showing up at the most unexpected places. I don't need a fortune-teller to tell me I'm in trouble. She has a notorious record of having safely deposited more than twelve beggars in the Refuge. My only chance is to get out of here before she can find a beefy police-man. I'm walking to the gate when I hear people talking about two and seven. I even forget the trouble Miss Gallovidian is going to bring me. I run as fast as a man with a twisted leg can to the Bookie. Only six tickets were sold, the loudspeaker was saying, only I'm not interested.

As the Bookie is handing me the money Blushing Groom seems even happier than I am. His crooked teeth, which are dulled by tobacco, click every time the Bookie counts a hun-dred. His greasy lips are watering while a pair of bloodshot eyes are blinking with a dull brilliance. It hurts my eyes to look at him. I have hardly put the money in my pocket, when Grue-some pats me on the back and says, nice and loud: "We make it!"

I must have been a fool not to have been wise as to why Blushing Groom was acting the perfect chaperon.

"That's fine," I say. "What have *we* made?"

"Don't be bashful," he says, "we caught the richest double. Come, this calls for a celebration." He extends a hand, and all the time he's smiling as if his wife has given birth to quadruplets.

"Look, pal," I say. "It's a good try. I couldn't have done better myself. This is the perfect setup, isn't it? Well, I've got news for you: I caught that double alone, I don't know you and I don't care to. Go get yourself another piece of cheese . . . I'm not that easy."

This ape suddenly stops smiling and looks at me like I had the plague. His broad, flat nose starts puffing out steam like an angry Spanish bull (only I'm not in the mood to make fancy passes like a toreador). All in all, he looks positively fierce, like the animal in the simile.

"Six hundred and seventy pounds is a lot of money," he shouts. "Nobody's going to cheat me out of my share. You being a cripple . . ."

"Shut up!" I yell. "Never call me that again, you . . . You!" I swing a right cross to his face, but this ape is smart. He blocks it and lands a hard one on my chin. I rock back and land flat on my sitters, while jungle tomtoms beat out a solid conga in my head. After a while my head clears and I get up, burning with rage. If I only had the strength, I would tear this ape apart.

Blushing Groom has put on quite a show; we have a good audience. Some white folk are threatening to beat his brains out . . . I sincerely hope they do.

Suddenly I see a police badge jostling its way through. This is no place for me! I dash and start zigzagging through the people. A junior confusion starts, with everybody trying to give way. I run a few minutes, stumble and fall on my face. The policeman bends down and grabs me firmly by the arm and whispers: "Look, John, let's not have trouble. Come along quietly and everything will be just fine."

Under these circumstances I have no choice but to submit. My mother always told me never to resist arrest, let alone striking a uniformed officer of the law. Me and my money part company after Blushing Groom had preferred charges. My submission causes me to spend a not-so-glorious weekend at the Bantu Refuge. My transfer there being arranged by the thoughtful sergeant in the charge office, who out of pure love could not have me thrown in with hardened criminals . . . what with the place filled with housebreakers, extortioners, professional pickpockets and a generous assortment of other unsavory characters. Frankly, I hoped he would mind his own business. I might even have started a craps game and made me some money.

"I am almost certain that you will be back here in a few days," the Magistrate had said. Somebody ought to tell him he has a great future . . . reading palms. He looks at me and a grin spreads over his pancakelike face. This place must be short of Magistrates; why has it got to be the same one all the time?

"Beggars who play the horses are a dangerous nuisance. They misuse kindness that is shown to them."

Just my luck: now I have to listen to a lecture on morals. The Magistrate looks pleased with himself, and I don't like it, Miss Gallovidian looks at me and smiles like a proud victress. She probably expects a promotion for this. I'm called on to the stand.

Some man with a thin face asks me to raise my right hand and swear to tell the truth. After saying my piece, the prosecutor starts questioning me as if he's promised thirty percent of Blushing Groom's cut. After his session with me, he calls Blushing Groom to the stand.

"Do you know this man?" the prosecutor says.

"No, sir."

"How was it then you put up ten shillings to bet the horses with him?"

"I was losing all morning when I decided to try somebody's guesses. I met him, and we started talking."

"Did anybody see you talking to him?"

"I don't know, but somebody must have."

"Then what happened?"

"I asked him if he had a tip. He said he had one straight from the horse's mouth . . . A sure thing, he said. I then asked him if I could put up ten shillings. He agreed. I was afraid to make the bet, so I gave him the money and walked over to the Bookie's stand with him where he placed a pound win on two and seven."

"Why were you afraid to make the bet?"

"I thought he was luckier than I was . . . besides, I had been losing all morning."

"Why did you strike him?"

"He was trying to cheat me out of my share, and tried to hit me when he couldn't."

The Magistrate looks at me with something like contempt in his eyes. I won't have to put on a show for him this time. I might just as well kiss half my money good-bye. Blushing Groom's story is watertight.

"I'm thoroughly disappointed with you," the Magistrate says. "I didn't know you were a thief too. I don't believe you could have made that bet alone; beggars haven't got so much money. I believe his story, things like this do happen. The money will be shared equally between the two of you."

"I don't believe you could have made that bet alone." What a cheek! I'll have that hobo know I make more money in one week than he does in a month. I don't believe you . . . Good God!

I feel like committing mass murder as the court hands Blushing Groom three hundred and thirty-five pounds of my money. This prehistoric beast has a swell racket. A few more jobs like this and he can retire and buy himself a villa on the Riviera.

Blushing Groom is magnificent, inspiring awe. He is completely uncompromising, thoroughly unscrupulous, without qualms or a conscience. He has wholly realized the separateness of good and evil and attained a purity in evil worthy of honest appraisal. He would not allow himself to be swayed from cheating me by my being a cripple. If I were allowed to choose a brother, he would be my only choice.

I take my share of the money and clear out before the Magistrate and Miss Gallovidian cook up another charge against me. On my way home I find it difficult to resist the temptation of stopping at some busy corner and doing my stuff. I might make up for some of the money, but I just happen to be wearing my best and have been a beggar long enough to know that people don't give money away to beggars who are dressed better than they. People who give alms to beggars do so to establish their superiority over the receiver, and like I said: I'm not an apprentice beggar.

When I get home I find a letter from my wife.

Our son, Tommy, is sick. Please come home . . .

I become afraid and anxious for my Tommy, and even the kind words of my outsize landlady fail to move me.

I had to wait for something like this to show me the folly of my ways. A man's place is next to his wife and family. I had hoped that someday I would be able to provide my boys with a decent education, to grow them like normal boys, not just sons of a helpless cripple . . . to find a place for them in the sun. I might be a big shot beggar but as a husband and father, I stink.

"If I should not see my friend Serurubele, will you . . ."

"Yes, I'll explain to him. I'll always have your room for you if you should ever want it again."

Deep down I know that I will want it again. I have three hundred and thirty-five reasons why I should. Blushing Groom and the gullible public of Johannesburg will live in my mind for ever . . . I have to come back. I owe it to the profession.

WILLIAM SAIDI,

though a Zambian, was born and educated in the then Southern Rhodesia, now Zimbabwe. He worked as a journalist for Zambia Daily Mail and Times of Zambia. In 1964 he cofounded the New Writers Group of Zambia, the first organization for creative writers in Zambia.

William Saidi has been publishing his short stories in newspapers and literary periodicals. His stories are included in the book Voice of Zambia, *an anthology of Zambian short stories.*

THE GARDEN
OF EVIL

WILLIAM SAIDI

MR. PARKER SAID, *"WENA SKELEM, WENA,"*★ SPEAKING IN
kitchen kaffir.

Old Mwanza smiled his ancient smile. He surmised that Mr.
Parker was complimenting him. His withered chest filled with
pride. Mr. Parker was not generous with his praise. He was an
inspector in the Northern Rhodesia Police.

"Ya, wena skelem wena Mwanza," Mr. Parker said again.

He was surveying with a lordly contentment the garden of
vegetables. The dark rich greenness of the cabbages and the
bright luscious greenness of the lettuce were mouth-watering.
Everything exuded a health, a vitality and a delicious aliveness
which rejuvenated Old Mwanza's tired faith in life.

Mr. Parker smiled at Old Mwanza. That too was a rarity and
a bonus. Mr. Parker had false teeth. They were unnaturally almost obscenely white. To most Africans, they constituted an
unfathomable curiosity, to be ogled at until the mystery was
unraveled. Mr. Parker hated the experience.

Old Mwanza had discovered Mr. Parker's toothlessness on a
day that was to prove portentous for both men.

Mr. Parker's wife and three children had flown to Durban,
Natal, in the Union of South Africa. They had gone for a weekend holiday with Mr. Parker's parents who lived there in the
luxury of seaside retirement. Mr. Parker saw them off at Lusaka

★ *"You are dangerous, you."*

airport that morning and returned to the house with an evil, vengeful glint in his eye.

Mwanza worked steadily in the garden, wondering idly when his daughter would visit him from her home in Chilenje African township. Her last visit had been an elixir for Old Mwanza. She had brought her first-born child, two weeks old, his first grandchild. Old Mwanza gazed in lachrymose gratitude and amazement at the little cherubic face, its eyes closed softly and its fresh lips parted slightly. His daughter kept reminding him how much like him the little boy looked.

"Let your husband hear you say that and you will be sorry," he admonished her gently.

As he worked, with one ear cocked for outlandish noises from the huge house, he waited for the explosion. It was uncanny, he thought. Mr. Parker's wife and children were away. The cook had taken the day off and so had the South African born nanny. Mr. Parker and Old Mwanza had the entire house and the vast garden and orchard to themselves. There was a tranquillity about the place, a tranquillity which Old Mwanza knew to be unnatural and transient.

It came two hours later.

*"Mwanza, you skelem! Buya lapa! Buya lapa! You You bobojan!"**

He heard the shout clearly from behind the huge closed windows of the bedroom. Mr. Parker had a stentorian voice to match his police inspector's physique.

In his weak, reedy voice, Mwanza replied, *"Mina buya, Bwana!"*†

He could feel the tendons in his neck standing out with the exertion.

"Mina buya, Bwana!" He quickened his normally lugubri-

---

* *"Mwanza, you dangerous animal! Come here! Come here! You baboon!"*
† *"I am coming, Master!"*

ous, tortured pace. You are not a young man anymore and re-member that stupid foot of yours, he reminded himself unneces-sarily, as he hurried into the house.

In the bedroom, with its luxurious white furniture and ex-pensive lace curtains, he found Mr. Parker lying cadaverously in the massive double bed with the snow-white eider down. His face was a bizarre study in drunken idiocy. The lips were slack and there were no teeth. The skin on the face was a flaming pink and the eyes appeared opaque and wild. Mr. Parker had no clothes on except a pair of white tennis shorts.

Old Mwanza walked fretfully into the room, his bare feet sinking dangerously into the thick pile of the carpet. He waited. At last Mr. Parker stirred.

"Yes, *Bwana? Mina buyile.*"* Old Mwanza spoke in a tremu-lous whisper.

"Mwanza, *wena yazi lo skelem ena kona lapa township? Lapa Matelo, na lapa Chilenje? Wena yazi lo skelem?* Those little bas-tards, those little half-educated bastards! *Ena fun bulala lo Mazungu, wena yazi? Ena funa bulala lo Mazungu.*† The stupid idiots!"

Old Mwanza had the weird sensation that this was a mono-logue. He kept his peace. Most white people in Northern Rho-desia spoke thus at this time. In Southern Rhodesia and Nyasa-land, on the borders, the Africans were reported to be speaking of getting rid of the white people too. Mr. Parker had himself spoken like this before, even when he was sober. So Old Mwanza concluded benevolently that the viciousness came from the drink.

His discovery of Mr. Parker's toothlessness was a secret tri-umph for Old Mwanza. He was older and had all his teeth. It

---

* *"Yes, sir? I have come."*
† *"Mwanza, you know those dangerous animals in Matero and Chilenje African townships? They want to kill all white people."*

was true that he could not chew with the same efficiency as before, but he still had his teeth. Mr. Parker's misfortune (to Old Mwanza it was something to be utterly ashamed of, like losing your toes in a war) made him—Mr. Parker—vulnerable, mortal, weak and susceptible to all human frailties. For Old Mwanza, it was an astounding revelation.

Mr. Parker's speech had not been entirely shorn of its military thunder. Yet to Old Mwanza there was something comical about it. He concluded sagely that people with false teeth had no business trying to speak without them.

"Where are my teeth, Mwanza? *Upi lo* teeth *kamina? Upi Upi!*" Old Mwanza cast his tired eyes around the opulently furnished bedroom and wondered mischievously what would happen if the teeth, by some miracle, disappeared forever. His amusement was short-lived. The family had two cars and three servants, including the nanny, whom Old Mwanza had wooed in vain. The family always ate well, their dinner table invariably replete with fresh fruit, apart from the other victuals. To Old Mwanza, any European family which could afford fresh apples and oranges (not even from their own orchard) for dessert had to be rich.

The teeth were in a glass of water on a small table next to the bed. Old Mwanza cleared his throat to suppress laughter.

Loudly, he exclaimed dramatically, *"Bwana Bwana!"* with a shaking finger, he pointed to the glass, in which the dentures floated calmly.

Mr. Parker looked at the glass in amazement and laughed with exaggerated gusto, his rubbery lips stretched taut to reveal the barren pink gums in the darkened cave of his mouth. Old Mwanza felt laughter bubbling in his throat, but experience restrained him. To laugh with your master presumed equality. It could spell the end of a good job.

Mr. Parker walked regally along the smooth paths which

separated the symmetrically arranged beds. Haughtily polite cau-
liflower looked with tolerant disdain at the lowly, peasant-look-
ing cabbage. That perennial garden vegetable, the asparagus,
looked with suspicion at the green virility of the spinach, while
the juicy tomato, its eyes closed coyly, pleaded not to be bothered by the ungainly beet.

Old Mwanza thought Mr. Parker had at last begun to recognize the incredible beauty and aliveness of the garden. For years,
he and the garden had lived a separate existence from the rest of
the household. Even the cook, who marched neatly into the
garden to cut vegetables for the pot, was an alien here. Mrs.
Parker and the children? For all the attention they paid to the
garden, it was nothing but a plaything for the eccentric, senile
African gardener. It was Old Mwanza's kingdom, his own little
garden of Eden. He knew every plant like the master of a castle
knows his servants. Sometimes he would speak to them and a
strange sensation would assail him, that they responded famil-
iarly. Mr. Parker had not bought a hose or sprinkler for watering
the garden. By tacit arrangement, Old Mwanza had devised his
own ingenious irrigation system. This consisted of two cans
fashioned crudely from two discarded four-gallon paraffin tins.
These were suspended on a thick wooden pole placed horizon-
tally on his shoulders. Old Mwanza did not know the pesticides
by name. He could read or write after a fashion and only in his
mother tongue, Nsenga, a derivative of the more widely spoken
Nyamja of the Eastern Province. He approached both writing
and reading with acute trepidation and performed them only
when his life or job depended on it.

Today, Mr. Parker walked in the garden as if he too wanted
to be close to the plants. The prospect filled Old Mwanza with
foreboding. He treasured his attachment to the garden to the
point of being insanely possessive and jealous.

"There is no garden boy like you, my boy. You are . . .

how old . . . about sixty? Yet, you are . . . you are just fantastic.''

When Mr. Parker spoke to him in straight English, Old Mwanza felt humbled. It signified Mr. Parker's profound depth of feeling in what he was saying. That he believed that Old Mwanza had only a vague notion of what he was saying probably made him feel a martyr in the cause of better understanding between Europeans and Africans in the three troubled territories which constituted the ill-fated federation of Rhodesia and Nyasaland at the time.

Mr. Parker walked back into his house, leaving Old Mwanza to speculate anxiously on whether his daughter would visit him again. He lived in the servants' quarters which were concealed from general view by a high wall between it and the big house. He had a bedroom and a kitchen to himself. The other half of the semidetached house was occupied by the cook, who was married.

Old Mwanza rarely ventured into the townships now. He had lived there all his life, raising his children with the same haphazard devotion that any other African paterfamilias raised their offspring in that detribalized maze.

During those sprightly days, Old Mwanza had worked as an office messenger, flitting from office building to office building on his bicycle, delivering letters, buying sandwiches and cold drinks and performing other menial errands for the Europeans. He enjoyed the social life too. Even his wife had enjoyed it, though she always went to the local church on Sundays. They lived in Matero, the African township on the outskirts of Lusaka. At weekends, he and his wife joined friends and neighbors in orgies of senseless drinking and singing. His wife recounted the events to the Catholic priest every Sunday. Old Mwanza became something of a local bon vivant until his wife clipped his wings. His ardor for the hedonistic life evaporated quite suddenly when she threatened to leave him unless he reformed. Abruptly, maturity came and without ever consciously acknowledging the fact, he recognized the essential truth that life did not finally constitute a series of liaisons with women of easy virtue. Then he joined friends who had boasted that there was adventure, fame and fortune to be made in the army. He went to Malaya and spent most of his time cooking. For all his relative security among the foul-smelling cabbages and beans, the Japanese had almost blown off his foot. It ended up with three toes, happily for Old Mwanza, including the big one. When he returned, wiser but frightened of life, they gave him a medal and he gravitated almost inevitably to a night watchman's job. The foot gave him frightening moments and he changed to gardening. He had almost no hope and soon after his discovery that he and Nature wanted the same things he was more or less settled spiritually. His war experiences helped. They earned him the kind of respect that acted as a powerful talisman. He had fought on the side of RIGHT. In truth, he had only a hazy recollection of his days in the jungle of Malaya. After the Japanese had nearly blown off his foot, the whole experience became something of a living, waking nightmare.

As a gardener, he developed a liaison with Nature, an affinity which his first employer suspected had something to do with primitive witchcraft. In Mr. Parker's garden, Old Mwanza found his metier.

Often, he would sit up in bed, unable to sleep. Memories of his wife, memories of his halcyon days in Matero, memories of the cordite-filled days in Malaya would come flooding into his mind. His head would throb and reverberate and there would be explosions of a thousand cannons, their roar deafening. He would get up and walk into the quiet darkness of the night. In the distance he would hear the noise of barking dogs. In Chilenje township, they would be barking, not here in the European suburb of Woodlands, where the dogs were trained to bark only when there was an intruder. Mr. Parker had a basenji dog, which Old Mwanza had been told never barked. He had never heard it bark and had been told by Mrs. Parker that the basenji was a rare dog. It was so intelligent that it was almost human, she said. It was probably the only one of its kind in Northern Rhodesia, she claimed breathlessly. Old Mwanza, who had been raised entirely in the city where respect for dogs was only incidental, did not believe her. A dog was a dog.

In the darkness, knowing that the barkless dog would be watching his every move from its kennel near the house, Old Mwanza would walk into the garden, his nostrils distending as he savored the fresh smell of the vegetables. He would close his eyes and try to think of the object of all his love, past and present. He would see the image of his wife. He would think of his wife and the garden, the garden and his wife, his wife and the garden, until the two would blend into one individual unity. He would return to his bed, his disturbed soul somehow satiated. On the periphery of his consciousness, he would hear the cook and his wife trying once more to explore the chemical impurity which was preventing them from having a child.

His daughter came the following Saturday afternoon. Old Mwanza was ecstatic. She brought him a cooked chicken swimming in curry soup. As she warmed it on his primus stove in the little kitchen, he cradled the boy in his lap. His daughter was a short, chubby woman who had the cheeks and watery smile of her mother. She smiled often, a sexy smile, which Old Mwanza knew to have been one of the attributes which had drawn him, mothlike, to her mother. She was a healthy woman and he hoped fervently that her husband, a young man who worked for the government, was her equal. There was love between father and daughter.

Old Mwanza held the boy in his arm and watched with

tenderness as his daughter prepared the chicken. She worked with the same effortless dexterity that he had loved in his wife. When she had cooked the *nshima,* they sat down to eat, talking quietly with familiar laughter and smiles, about their lives and about the boys.

"Jeremiah was at our house yesterday."

The daughter spoke with an imperceptible shake of her head, a nascent choke in her voice.

"What is it this time?" Old Mwanza squeaked with accustomed fright.

"He said you should not go on working. He says Mr. Parker is an evil man. He says things are going to be different soon. He says you fought for nothing in Malaya, now you are growing vegetables for nothing. He says you should be ashamed of yourself."

"This is an old story. An old story. He is young. How is Obadiah? He is older. He understands how these things are. Have you seen him recently?"

"No, Father, I have not seen him recently. He lives in Chibolya. You know what type of people live there. Criminals and prostitutes."

"Is he a criminal too? He was always very quiet. How does he feel? Mr. Parker says I am nearly sixty years old now. I cannot return to the village. I would not survive. My people have forgotten me. I have forgotten them too."

Father and daughter were silent. Old Mwanza enjoyed the chicken with much licking of the fingers. He wished they could leave some of it for the next day. He would hold a small party and invite the South African nanny. It could be the catalyst.

"Father, you know that something terrible is going to happen. Not to you. Something terrible is going to happen in the country. In the townships, they are talking wildly."

"Of what, my dear child?"

"Of things. Obadiah and Jeremiah, they may be different. But they say you should go to the village. They are always talking wildly."

"Of what?"

"Of the white people."

"What of the white people?"

The woman placed the plates softly into a dish of water. Her face was impassive, her voice steady and her demeanor unhurried. Only the wet smile was missing.

"They say they are evil. They say we should get rid of the evil."

Old Mwanza laughed nervously, trying to put derision to the laughter. His daughter turned abruptly to look at him in exasperation. The expression touched her face briefly, like a passing shadow. She was still his daughter.

"This is what Obadiah and Jeremiah are saying? My own children. They are mad." He laughed again, reflectively. "No they are just little children. Just children. The white man is evil? Who gave us Light? Who gave us God? Obadiah, he was a prophet. He called upon doom on Edom and predicted triumph for Israel in the Judgment. Jeremiah. He was a prophet too. A great prophet who was imprisoned for warning of doom. Your mother chose those names. She also chose yours, Esther. She loved God, your mother. All these things, who brought them?"

The woman was silent, sitting cross-legged on the floor, one big breast's dark teat in the mouth of her sleeping infant.

In a sudden, querulous voice, Old Mwanza exploded. "I am not a village boy. My people have forgotten me. We are strangers. You understand?"

The woman looked at her baby, serenely sucking on the teat. She nodded noncommittally. Old Mwanza was perplexed. "You understand, don't you? You are the oldest. You understand."

"Yes," she said, not looking at him. Old Mwanza shook his head in uncomprehending despair.

"No, Father. They are just wild, Obadiah and Jeremiah. They are just wild. They are wild to talk of driving out the white people. Forget about them, Father."

She rose, her practiced arms transferring the baby from her lap to back in one swift, fluid movement. Her breast, the milk dripping slowly from it, hung in embarrassment from her bosom. Old Mwanza did not look at her, his gaze examining in dawning consternation the uneven floor of the little room. He was a man to whom the Truth had been dramatically exposed as something less than pure, something foul and filthy, something he now looked at with deepening suspicion and mounting revulsion.

They talked on about known innocents, about truths that could be perceived, fathomed and comprehended at one uncomplicated glance. She talked about her husband, the great job he was doing for the government. He talked briefly about his garden, about his wife, her mother, and soon they lapsed into an embarrassed, tense silence, as each remembered the tender moments with the departed woman. Old Mwanza shook his head, as if to acknowledge his senile failure to grasp the true meaning of the new life.

That evening, after his daughter had left, he strolled through his kingdom, speaking quietly to his subjects, questioning them about Life and its lost meaning. He had asked his daughter to prevail on the two boys to visit him the next weekend. He loved the garden. Mr. Parker's relevance was receding. Neither he nor his family cared much for it. It was the only thing that mattered now, not Mr. Parker, not his wife, not his children.

He stood still and closed his eyes. His two sons came into focus. They were there, two short, powerfully built, younger replicas of himself, with the chubby smile of their mother and the primitive physique of their father during his heyday. They were dark, with short kinky hair which never seemed to grow to its natural length. Hard to comb. They were two good, good-looking boys. They were unmarried.

He smiled. Probably still sowing their wild oats. He remembered his predilection for the company of girls, many girls, different girls. If his wife had not threatened him so earnestly, if he had not grown up so suddenly, he would still be as wild. They were good boys, considerate and loving. When he returned from the war and found his wife sick, they cared for her while he searched for a new niche in a changed society.

They hadn't berated him for his purposeless absence. They should have, he realized with new insight. It had been a waste of manhood. He did not fight for anything that he knew or understood. The people of Malaya were small, but they had not called him to help their jungle war. He had always done what the white man asked of him. Even in the garden? Not the garden. He loved the garden. He did what he and Nature wanted done. Not Mr. Parker. He hoped fervently that his children would understand.

*"Mwanza? Wena kona lo skopo. Wena yazi lo Mazungu en kona skopo maningi."**

Old Mwanza knew that the white people were more than just ordinarily clever. People who could invent the airplane had to be extra clever. He did not need reminding. He did not need reminders of their unhuman cleverness. Mr. Parker said he, Old Mwanza, was also clever. That was because he did not believe, as did those fools in the townships, that he had even an iota of the cleverness of the white man, that he could conceivably devise anything, ANYTHING at all, that could rival anything that the white man had already created. The knowledge that he was

---

* *"Mwanza? You have brains. You know that the white people have a lot of brains."*

clever because of his recognition of the white man's superior cleverness warmed him.

They were walking in the garden. Most of their conversations, most of their intimate exchanges, took place here. It was their common denominator. In the garden, Mwanza thought he was king. Mr. Parker did not, could not know it, but Old Mwanza watched his every move, lest he stepped on the vegetables. Old Mwanza did not know how he would react if he had.

Mr. Parker talked on in kitchen kaffir, reminding Old Mwanza that those stupid agitators in the townships were going to be punished most severely. It was explained that the authorities were preparing for the rascals. They had guns which spat smoke and some which spat real bullets. Did not Old Mwanza remember those guns? Hadn't he used such guns in the war in Malaya, when he fought for justice and freedom? Oh, yes, Old Mwanza remembered them. Yes, didn't that mean that they would kill some of the Africans?

Of course, it did, but didn't Old Mwanza realize that if the authorities did not kill the agitators, they (the agitators) would kill innocent white people and perhaps innocent Africans, good Africans as well, such as Old Mwanza himself? Oh, was that the problem. The assurance gave him a real sense of security. Yes, people like Old Mwanza and himself, Mr. Parker, had to protect themselves (with the aid of the authorities) against the agitators who were nightly preparing to kill them.

In his bed that night, Old Mwanza trembled in indescribable terror. It hurt his atrophying limbs to know that death—his, Mr. Parker's or his children's—was in the air, that it could visit any of them now. People who walked innocently during the day, even the cook and the nanny, were plotting to kill, or had someone else plotting to kill them. There was a war on. It was nothing like the terrible business in Malaya, but it was there.

The next morning, Old Mwanza sought out the cook. They

rarely spoke, the cook believing that his status precluded any obligation to speak politely to the gardener and the nanny. He was a thin, mustachioed young man who kept himself scrupulously clean, in a strange narcissistic way. The smell of an anti-B.O. soap floated above him like an invisible halo. He took a bath two times a day, forcing his naturally slovenly wife to do the same. Old Mwanza had long wondered why he suspected that the man's fastidious care of his body explained more easily than any witchcraft the couple's childlessness.

The kitchen window was high above the ground. Old Mwanza walked slowly from his garden and stood some distance from the window, speaking loudly and looking up at the cook, who was busy rinsing something in the sink.

"What do you make of all this wild talk in the townships?"

"What wild talk, old one?" he asked crossly.

"About what they are going to do to the white people, like Mr. Parker and his family?"

"Oh, that." The Oracle in him, flattered, opened up with haughty condescension. "It is much stupid talk. It is these people, who think they are educated. They want to chase away the white people. I laugh at them. No, I spit on them."

"So you think they are wild too?"

"Of course, they are wild." He leaned toward the window and spoke in a conspiratorial tone. "Can you imagine anyone being cleverer than the white man, than Mr. Parker?"

"I am happy that you think it is all wild talk."

"It is wild talk. You know, it is the hyenas, making all that noise when they cannot fight." They laughed. Old Mwanza walked back to his kingdom, his crooked step firm and confident.

"You are my children. I have always taught you the right way to behave. I want to teach you again today."

The two boys, casting furtive glances at the door, listened. Their eyes were impatient, darting from the door to the old man, from the uneven floor to the corrugated iron roof and back to the old man. Old Mwanza spoke with paternal authority and the assurance of one who is conscious of the infallibility of his advance. He sat in the one chair in the room and they sat cross-legged on the floor. They had arrived after he had retired. He had not heard their footsteps or any sound. He had not even heard the gate opening and wondered how they could come into the yard without alerting the deadly, silent basenji. They could only have been allowed in by Mr. Parker himself. After all, they were his children.

"This foolishness must stop. I told your sister. It is impossible for me to return home. I am too old. There is nothing for me there. Mr. Parker is not an evil man. All white people are not evil. What do you know about evil?"

Obadiah spoke. He was only slightly taller than his brother, though they appeared to be identical twins. They were dressed in uniformly threadbare nondescript clothes and the odor of stale sweat filled the room.

"Father, if Mr. Parker were not here, what would you do?" he asked nonchalantly, already preparing his follow-up question.

"Well . . . I . . . would . . . what do you mean, if Mr. Parker were not here?"

"What he means is, if we are able to arrange for Mr. Parker's removal, would you go home, even to confront strangers?" Jeremiah spoke with the same sangfroid.

Old Mwanza laughed, his spirit buoyed by Mr. Parker's assurances.

"I have heard the wild talk in the townships. It is like hyenas. Just loud talk. Your people think you are cleverer than the white people? Ha ha ha ha! You wait. They are preparing to deal with you. They have guns that spit smoke and fire."

"We know all about that, Father. We are also prepared. The point is, would you like us to remove Mr. Parker so that you can go home?"

"Now listen. Go back to the townships and talk to your sister. She knows these things. More than you do. She will advise you. Stop all the nonsense."

"Father," Obadiah said as they stood up languidly, their eyes still searching the room, catlike, "she is with us. Her husband is helping us. She told us to urge you to leave. She said she could not say so to you herself."

Old Mwanza wept when they had gone. Again, he saw his Truth being soiled, abused, dirtied and muddied. He walked silently into his garden, enveloped in a stygian darkness of uncertainty. He spoke to the vegetables, and discovered with shame that no one, not his daughter, his sons, not his vegetables, listened to him anymore. In the far-off distance, he heard raucous, derisive laughter. He walked back to his house, his aching shoulders hunched, his head bowed, his mouth slack. People who appeared vaguely familiar seemed to be laughing at him.

In the night, he heard little that he could later associate with the bloody violence to which he was to be introduced. It was three days after his sons' visit, Old Mwanza could not reconcile himself to the truth, which was that his Truth had been mutilated and trampled underfoot by creepy, crawling monsters who said they were his progeny and bore no resemblance to him. He gazed for long minutes at Mr. Parker, even as he spoke while they strolled leisurely in his garden. He had forgotten his tragic toothlessness. Mr. Parker was a pitiable man. All the truth that Old Mwanza had gleaned from him, which Old Mwanza had embraced as universal truth, was being challenged. Old Mwanza tried to cling to his belief in Mr. Parker's invincibility.

Indeed, until the very last moment, until that apocalyptic moment, when his eyes saw what had to be seen, he still retained a residual faith in the power of Mr. Parker, in his cleverness and the cleverness of his race.

Absently, Old Mwanza wondered once more how the boys had neutralized the great basenji. He had felt the sleep creeping slowly upon him, like a thief for he had not wanted to sleep, being possessed of a presentiment once more.

They came to the door of his house, called him out in whispers and shepherded him to the main house respectfully, two sons taking their doubting father to a scene that would furnish incontrovertible testimony of their maturity.

The three children and Mrs. Parker were tied with pieces of torn bedsheets. They were tied so tightly that a uniform dull and deadly purpleness was spreading slowing up to their faces, as the flow of blood appeared to be slowing down. They were all on the huge four-poster double bed with the white eider down. They stared with long-gazed eyes at Mr. Parker who was on the carpet. Old Mwanza saw Mr. Parker's head split neatly in half, the short, sharp-bladed ax up to its hilt in the crown of his head. Mr. Parker was in his white tennis shorts. He was on his back and stared with blank, terrified, unbelieving eyes at the ceiling.

Old Mwanza looked from the inert body to his sons. He screamed a meaningless scream. He was screaming incoherently at his sons. Then he started to scream his wife's name. There was terror, disbelief and supplication in the voice. It was the mendicant wail of a recalcitrant child, begging its mother for forgiveness.

"You will return home now?" Jeremiah did not boast. He spoke with emotion.

"No! No! No! What about the garden? What about the garden? Will you give me a garden?"

He rushed at them, his fingers talons, tearing at their faces, wanting to obliterate their existence, as he had brought it into being.

They grabbed him easily and led him out of the house.

As they approached the gate, the old man's meager belongings fashioned into a crude bundle on the shoulders of Obadiah, powerful searchlights lit up the house and the whole yard. The basenji stood victoriously in front of the lights. They heard the familiar, commandingly insolent voice of a white police officer: *"Wena, funa ifa? Kabanga wena kumbuka tina dhlala kupela? Tina kona lo makulu gun. Makulu steleki."**

There was a white man in pajamas whom Old Mwanza recognized as the man who lived at the next house. His eyes returned to the barkless dog, which Mrs. Parker had said was incredibly intelligent.

His two sons released him and retreated into the darkness behind them. He heard the roar of the powerful guns. He hit the ground as they had taught him in Malaya. He thought of the garden.

He wondered if the white police officer would shoot a man who spoke to vegetables in the dead of night.

---

* *"You want to die? Perhaps you think we are just playing? We have very big guns. Very big."*

A. R. GURNAH

A Tanzanian writer, A. R. GURNAH was born in 1948. He has published his stories in the Nigerian literary periodical Okike. In 1987 he published his book Memory of Departure and in 1988 Pilgrim's Way. Soon after in 1990 he appeared again on the literary scene with the book Dottie.

BOSSY

A. R. GURNAH

A LONG TIME AGO THAT WAS, SITTING ON THE BARNACLED pier, swinging our legs through the air. Princess Margaret pier in the long shadow of the afternoon, watching the sea beneath us frothing with arms and legs and flashing teeth. A long story I told him, urbane and wise, a fabric of lies. I told him of a man who stood by the sea and peed, and how his pee was continuous without end. Like the tongue of infinite length, all coiled up in a man's insides. On Princess Margaret pier we watched Ferej eat up the water like a shark. The water choppy and bright on the day he won the schools championship. On Princess Margaret pier after a day in 1956 when the good princess laid foot on our humble land. On the other side were four guns, riveted into the concrete and facing the sea. Ceremonial firecrackers to bid the princess welcome.

The letter had arrived that morning, a dirty scrap to shatter my self-inflicted peace. Karim's name was written clearly on the back of the air mail form, and all the remaining space was covered with handwritten HAPPY NEW YEAR wishes.

31st December 73.

Dear Haji,

(O Pilgrim to the Promised Land)

I am sitting inside our office, or to be more precise our storeroom, being entertained by the sounds of the sawing, planing, sanding and drilling machines. Together with the rhythmic tapping of hammers on nails, all this combines to form a unique masterpiece at the eleventh hour of the year. The prevailing atmosphere has nothing to do with my writing to you, but just to deliver that presently I am indentured to a cyclops by name Rahman whose cave this Wood-Works is. I guess you will be surprised to hear that I am also concubined to his daughter.

You may also be surprised to hear that today I am celebrating my first "Go West Young Man" anniversary. It is only twenty miles west, but you know how big that distance really is. Exactly a year ago, on a Sunday afternoon, myself along with some other freedom lovers were preparing to act and follow that great genius, master and generator of electricity, the organizer and pilot of our expedition, Captain General Jabir Dumas (also well known as Hamlet of ST 9 fame). Between you and me, I learned the identity of the mastermind too late to retreat, just when the sail was being hoisted in fact. But before we could wave fond good-bye to the dear homeland, forever verdant and green, we were tackled by a wandering varantia. It needed a hefty bribe to fix him. We had a hazardous journey, during which it was apparent that our Hamlet did not know southerly from a handsaw. However, we landed on a beach which turned out to be some eighty miles north of our destination. Once we'd landed, the journey was smooth and easy, and I shall remain content to say that we arrived here tired but in one piece. So much for the forced adventure.

What has been happening to you over the last year? Your silence seems to grow deeper with time. Your last letter contained only one line, and I did not even understand it. Are you still working or have you found a University place yet? Write and tell me how you are doing, buddy. I want to hear about all those females who are keeping you busy. Send me a snapshot if you can. I want to see if you have got any fatter.

I have been continuing with my studies in evening classes. It's damned hard work getting back from the mill and going straight to college. As you might guess, I am not doing very well. I have to attend every evening. I start work at seven in the morning which doesn't leave much time for studying at home. Still, nothing ventured: I have become very interested in the poetry of the French Symbolists, but as you know it's not easy to get books here. If you see anything along those lines, I would be very grateful if you would send it to me. Refund by pigeon-post. You know, I miss all those conversations we used to have. There's no one here to talk to, not seriously anyway. People just want to talk about who has been caught fiddling with government funds.

A lot of the pals from home are here now. Hassan was caught trying to escape with some Goan girls in a ngarawa. They were kept for a few days, then released, nobody knows why. Hassan somehow managed to find another way of escaping and he too is here now. The Barrister has gone to a University in Boston to do Intentional Chemistry. Don't ask me, that's what he said. I met his brother recently and he told me that our Barrister is paid a lot of dollars by the American government, who are also paying his fees. So I am thinking of applying to Uncle Sam too.

Did you have a nice Christmas? It was very quiet here except Bachu got drunk and started calling our island leader "ham-neck." Poor fellow got kicked out of his office for calling his boss a donkey. Incidentally, do you remember Amina Marehemu Rashid's sister? She must have been about ten when you left. She is now a prostitute. No more room. Write soon and don't forget the snap. Regards from all the pals.

Yours,
Karim.

Gleeful tally sheet of past misdeeds. A time there was . . . but we ended it all with a careless selfishness. Now a fool with a poor style can make fun of your sister. He wants me to send him books of the French Symbolists because he can't get them out there. You missed the worst, Rashid. You missed the worst, my Bossy. Your sister appears as a footnote and not a tear shed for her. You too, you and I, we would have watched while a neighbor turned beggar and sold his daughter for shark meat. And we too would have laughed. All they taught us was how to be meek while they rode roughshod. You and I, we had something . . . In this cold and often hostile place I often think of you. It was a morning in December that I first wept for you. But by then that heartless land had turned your blood to dust.

It was a beautiful morning in December, bone dry and hot. We went to borrow a boat to go sailing because we were bored with being on holiday with nothing to do. He went one way, I went the other. He got a boat. I didn't.

—This is your captain speaking, he said, assuming command.

When he saw that I wasn't going to argue, he suggested that we go and find somebody else to go with us. At that very minute a fellow called Yunis appeared and we struggled into the outrigger and pushed off before he could come and talk to us.

Yunis was nicknamed Wire because it was quite obvious that he had some wires disconnected in his head. He was harmless enough but he had allowed this idiocy of his to go to his head. A little guiltily I watched him standing on Ras Matengo looking our way. He was probably used to people running away from him.

Before I got to know Rashid well, Wire and I used to spend a lot of time together. He told me about his crazy projects and I told him about mine. He was going to build a ship and sail it himself. He possessed several manuals on shipbuilding and navigation. The people at the shipping control office knew him well and called him captain to please him. Wire never seemed to listen when you talked to him and even little children could bully him. I saw a little boy of six pee in his mouth once while he was lying in the shade of a tree. Without saying a word, Wire had stood up and left. The adults watching had laughed and patted the boy on the back. I have seen Wire walking past a group of youths lathering at the mouth with fear. But under the line of trees by the dockside, very few people bothered us. We started a club the two of us. It was really a prisoner of war camp. I was a major and he was, of course, a captain. I boasted to him about how well I was doing at school and he lied to me about his father's estates in India.

His father lived in one of the houses my father owned. It was supposed to be a shop and apparently was at one time a thriving shop. But as far as I can remember, all it ever had were boxes of rusty nails and showcases with old fishing hooks and twine. If anybody stopped to buy anything from the shop, Wire's father would ask them to lend him some money. He went to the mosque every day, five times a day, and always asked somebody for money. He did the rounds of his neighbors and asked them for money. He went to the welfare office and asked them for money. I don't know if he made any money from all this, but I know he never paid my father any rent. He was thin and small and the skin on his cheeks was leathery and flabby. His jaw was sunken because he had no teeth left. Wire told me that he had large estates in India but he did not have enough money for the journey back home. Wire would build a ship and take his family back home. In the meantime his father tried to persuade him to take a job, but Wire always refused on the grounds that then he would not be able to continue with his maritime studies.

I watched him standing at the water's edge on Ras Matengo and remembered the times we used to sit under the line of trees and eat rotten fruit and stolen biscuits. My parents were worried then, they thought I too had a screw missing. I watched the idiot standing at the brink, watching us sailing to his father's estates in India.

Rashid was laughing, saying what a close call that was. In full sight of the beach Rashid began to imitate Wire's mad mannerisms. He folded his legs under him and rocked his trunk backward and forward in a steady rhythm. Wire used to do that when he was young, for hours on end. He was watching us with a smile. He smiled and waved and turned to go.

—What did you do that for? I said to Rashid.

He ignored me and peeled his shirt off. I think he was ashamed of my former friendship with Wire.

—Let's get cracking, he said, if you want to get to the island and back in time for dinner.

Bossy was in his element. I knew nothing about boats and he was an expert. He was also a champion swimmer, a national record holder over 400 meters. He was a footballer with a future and a very useful slow left-arm bowler. He was fair-skinned and handsome and wore a wristwatch with a silver strap. It was given to him by the English Club for taking seven of their wickets for twenty-three runs. To begin with I was proud to be his friend, but over the years we have got to know each other and he has stopped bossing me around.

My God, it hurts to talk like this, as if what has happened has not happened. Bossy and I walked the streets in tandem. We wrote love letters to Hakim and signed them Carol and watched him strut and preen and boast of a secret admirer. We even arranged meetings between him and "Carol" and always canceled them at the last minute. Bossy and I spent many dark hours by the cricket ground talking about the future and the past.

On that day in December we set off for Prison Island. The island had been used briefly by the British as a jail. There was now only the perimeter of the camp left. It was a beautiful island, with gently rolling hills and underground springs bubbling into streams. It was off bounds to visitors but nobody took any notice.

The sail on the outrigger caught the breeze and we slipped over the water with only a faint tearing sound. The sea was calm and blue under the morning light, and Rashid started to sing. He sang very badly and did it to provoke laughter more than anything else. He turned to look back toward land. I remember that because then he turned round to me and said didn't it look beautiful from here. It was calm and peaceful and the breeze was just enough to keep the boat moving and us cool. But there was something else. You felt that somehow you had got away from a suffocating room and you were now running free in an open field. The water was cool, as you might imagine water to be, not like the lukewarm water out of a tap. It was the town that looked unreal, like a quaint model in a builder's office. Out here it did not matter that the trousers did not fit, that your skin was fair or dark. There were no smelly alleys to walk through, no slippery ditches to cross, no fanatical and self-righteous elders to humiliate you. There were not even women to taunt you with their bodies beyond your reach.

• • •

—I can't just leave Mama and Amina, said Rashid.

His father had died a couple of years previously. In the Msikiti Mdogo I had stood at a distance and watched him calmly performing the duties of a bereaved son. He walked around among the mourners, accepting the condolences of neighbors and strangers with a dry face. I wished he would shed a few tears, for his own sake. It doesn't look good when a sixteen-year-old can go to his father's funeral with a dry face. Afterward he said that he did not cry because he had felt nothing inside. He had wanted to feel sad that his father had died but instead has felt only responsibility. He said his father had been cruel and distant to him ever since he could remember. And now he was really quite relieved that the old bastard had died. I said you can't hold that sort of thing against a dead man. So he smiled his tolerant big brother smile at me and asked who he should hold it against then. I told him that a dead man needed our prayers and he said that prayers would not do that old fucker any good at all. He said the angels of hell must be rubbing their hands at the prospect of his arrival. I said it didn't seem right to talk about your father like that. He said I did not understand because I had a kind father who cared about me and took an interest in me. I said it still didn't seem right to want him to go to hell. He was silent for a long while, then told me that there was no hell. And here I told him that he was wrong.

—I can't just leave them on their own, he said. What will they do? What will they do on their own?

—You won't be gone forever, I said. You'll be back to care for them.

—Mama is getting old, he said. What's the use of me going away somewhere for five or six years to become a forestry officer only to come back and find that my mother is dead and my sister is a whore.

—Don't bullshit, Bossy, I said.

—Okay, he said, maybe I'm not painting it too bright.

I told him that his tone reminded me of Mundhir's painting of the Black Sea.

Ancient perambulator of a seaward elitat. Velvet blue waist-coats and dark green metal rims waving from the steamer. Buibui on a waterborne outing with a crowd of ragamuffin to serve the sweetmeat. Out for the day with muscular chaperones and camera-clicking siblings.

At the island.

Improvised louver in the bush for temporary lordosis with bent knees.

Hasty dunking on the treacherously sandbanked beach to wash the crumbs away and depart for the crumbling fortress of a bygone empire.

Bygone by name.

Over the remains Bossy read the Psalm of Life and lingered meaningfully over dust to dust and sang Rule Brittania with an emotional choke. Lest there be any mistaking his intention, he waved two fingers in benediction.

Deadwood remnants at the camp of the trivial offender against the crown. At the word of command the salvo blew the cheeks apart. That will teach the silly bugger to pay his taxes next time.

Deadwood remnants of pillar post contumelia in thatch-wood alcoves in Indonesian plan.

Over the water turned to dust and a musical lyre was found by the British Archaeological Expedition to the Eastern Coast of Africa in 1929 to clinch the theory of an Indonesian invasion plan. Fragments of skull found by Blunt KCMG at the lip of the gully to suggest human life before the beginning of time. As counted from the eighth millennium B.C. Before that do not apply.

In Blunt Gully Bossy louvered again and nearly choked from the smell.

In a grotto of palms choked with weeds and wild tomatoes we discovered an underground town. We were not welcome and hurried from fierce mandibles until weakened by fatigue and hunger we collapsed under a mango tree which we immediately named Out of Town.

Pungent leaf mold and rotting humus and ripe mangoes oozing on the ground. Bossy bigboots was voted upstairs to wheedle bounty for the starving vanguard of a civilizing race. Mangoes on the ground in torpid contentment, oozing like dysentery in harmony with the flies. The captain returned with phosphates in his eyes, the bounty of a discordant piebald crow. We sank to our knees in humiliating penance and fought for mangoes with the flies. God was on our side.

Bossy bigboots brushed the dirt off his booty while hygiene rang through my skull.

I held Hunger in Abeyance and warned Bossy that by Avarice he was undone.

O Mummy in my heart, I prayed, if ever I needed you it is now. Tell me truly, O Fount of Hygiene, will I sooner die of Hunger or of Dysentery. O Wiper of my Arse, I have heeded your word through Thick and Thin generally speaking, but now a Text sirens through my guts to throw Caution to the winds. Could it be the Serpent, viper vile, that so flatters me to eat against your word? To a thicket I slunk and guilty rash gorged of the forbidden fruit. Earth trembled from her entrails but I took no thought content to eat my fill.

Faint rumble pinpoint umbilical cord, distant flutter in the heart. I knelt down waiting for the thunder to strike, and Bossy looked on with pagan amazement. Mother Hygiene restrained her hand. We left that pernicious grotto myself restrained and chastened, Bossy exultant and full.

To the waterfall.

It seemed then that there ought to be a watermill as a sign of progress and evidence of an ancient Indonesian culture. Feet in the pool at the bottom, kicking the water in adolescent delight. We drank the water at our feet, walked to the slimy rocks midpool like rising crustaceans covered with slime. We posed for a photo to show the folks back home hand on hip. This rock we named Bygone My Arse.

As we sat under that rippling fall, I gazed in wonder at what the old voyagers must have seen. In this same place an Indonesian sultan must have stood with the power of the human gaze to tear holes through nature's incomprehensible veil. Bear thee up Bossy and trust the power of thy unflinching gaze. How many men had stood where you and I then stood and saw nothing of what we saw? We were God's chosen few . . . and we sat by the brimming pool and saw world without end in our humble reflections . . . in foolish daydream pretense. The words of dead past masters ringing anvils to stiffen our self-esteem.

But soon it was time to leave the haven of that waterfall encampment for the final leg of our journey. Bossy took the lead while I patrolled the rear. As I watched him cut his way through the thicket I wondered again at the destiny that the Almighty had arranged for us. But come what may, I knew that we had done our share in fulfilling the burden of our race. Notwithstanding. Around.

We got back to the beach where we had left the outrigger and went in for a swim. At least Bossy did while I stood in water waist deep and washed the grime off my body.

—Don't show off, I shouted to him.

He waved back, turned to face the beach and came in at a sprint. I told him he was a bighead and he just grinned contentedly. We sat on the beach to dry off and he told me that he could swim back to town quicker than I could sail the boat back. He was always boasting like that and I just said yeah.

—You don't believe me? he asked.

—I believe you, Bossy, I said. Now stop mucking around.

It was getting late in the afternoon and I suggested that we make our way back. We turned the boat round and pushed it out to sea. I jumped into it first and helped Bossy in. As soon as we'd hoisted the sail, Bossy stood up, said good-bye and jumped overboard.

—See you in town, he said, grinning in the water.

I shouted to him not to be stupid but he was already on his way.

Suddenly a fierce squall filled out the sail and I struggled for the tiller. The wind was blowing the boat across the island and away from the town. I tried to turn the tiller and nearly overturned. I sat horrified while the boat sped along like a frenzied animal. I thought of lowering the sail but as soon as I let go of the tiller, the sail flapped savagely and I had to grab the tiller to steady the boat again. I cursed that bloody fool and his showing off. He would have known what to do. We were still going across the island and I could see me being blown out to sea and dying a violent death at the jaws of a shark or something. We passed the island, the boat and I, and we were still going in the wrong direction. Then just as suddenly as it had started the wind died away. I rushed for the sail and lowered it.

I could not find him. I called for him, yelled out for him, screamed for him. I tried to turn the boat round to go back to the island, but as soon as I put up the sail the wind filled it out and took me in the opposite direction. I didn't know what to do.

You left me, Bossy. You played your games once too often.

Bossy, what happened to you?

Bossy, you left me.

Bossy, what happened to you?

Bossy, I sat in that boat frightened to death that you might be in trouble but there was nothing I could do. The boat was too big for me, the water was too deep for me and you were nowhere in sight, Bossy. I called for you and all the time, Bossy, I was moving away from you. Bossy O Bossy, my Boosy, you wanted to make me feel a fool while you swam to land and I felt like a fool but where did you go, Bossy? I did all I could with that boat but I could not turn it back to you. You would have admired its power, Bossy, you would have admired its power, even while you laughed at me you would have admired its power. I tried all I could . . . What else is there to say? I turned the boat round once but I lost control and had to lower the sail. When I put it up the wind took me away from you again.

Bossy, what happened to you?

I tried all I could.

I stayed there and called out for you and called and cried out for you.

Then I thought that maybe I was just being a fool, that you were safe and well and on your way back to the town. Then I thought that maybe I would never make it back to the town myself and I was angry at what you had done, Bossy, and I stood up in the boat and called you names for running off and leaving me like that.

And all the time I was sailing farther away from you.

And all the time I knew that I had lost you.

I called you a bastard for making me feel such pain. And all the time I knew that you had left me.

I made it back to land. I don't know how.

You missed the worst, Bossy.

That night I landed at Mbweni and walked the three miles to town. I did not get past the golf course. I was beaten by men with sticks and stones and they told me the day had come. They beat me and said this was the day when all Arabs would get theirs. They beat me and the blood was pouring off my face and I don't remember. I came to on the beach by the golf course. There was the sound of gunfire in the air. I did not recognize it at first, it sounded like children playing with pop guns. I struggled along the beach bleeding and weak. I got as far as Shangani before I was stopped by some wild men with *pangas* and guns and they said I was *askari* from the barracks and they wanted to shoot me. They said they had overrun the barracks and the Prime Minister had surrendered and they had beaten the fuck out of him. They said the day had come and all the Arabs would get theirs. They said the sultan had already run away to the ship off the harbor and if they were to get hold of him they would whip his *kikoi* off and fuck his arse before stuffing it full of dynamite. They said I deserved to die for being an Arab, they said anybody who was no good must be an Arab. They said where did you get those cuts if you weren't at the barracks? They said it was all over and what was I shaking like that about. They said this fellow is a weakling; shall we fuck him first before we put a bullet in him? They said we have not time and they said kill him now before the others get to the rich houses. They said if we don't hurry all the best stuff will be gone and all the good women will be ruined. They said don't waste a bullet on him, here let me show him my steel. Here they said, hold this . . . but I was too tired and weak and they beat me and urinated on me and left me lying senseless on the beach.

You missed the worst, Bossy.

TOLOLWA MARTI MOLLEL

was born in Tanzania. His stories have been broadcast on the BBC and published in many literary journals, such as the Nigerian literary periodical Okike. Mr. Mollel is a teacher of drama at the University of Alberta, Edmonton, Canada.

A NIGHT OUT

TOLOLWA MARTI MOLLEL

FOR A LONG MOMENT, MIKA SAT AWKWARDLY, WITHOUT his usual self-assurance, despite the alcohol singing in his veins. But suddenly feeling a fool for his unease, he cleared his throat, a trifle too loudly, and ventured: "What's your name?"

"Mama Tumanini." (Mother of Tumaini)

She did not lift her eyes but went on busying herself with putting the child to sleep on the mat on the floor. Quite unexpectedly, the child began to cough, a violent, racking outburst that threw his little body into spasms.

Mika leaned forward and felt the child. His brow was damp and hot with fever. "Has he had treatment?" he asked, relieved to find something neutral to say.

She replied, "There isn't an aspirin to be had at the dispensary."

Under the mother's soothing, the child Tumaini eventually lay still, asleep, his breath rasping in and out. Mama Tumaini wrapped herself in a *khanga,* then lit a mosquito coil. Smoke rose in spiral, spreading over to the mat. The child stirred and sneezed. The mother, squatting, gently patted him to sleep.

"God grant you health, my little one," she murmured, "God grant you health and strength, good little mama's soldier!"

"Why soldier . . . ?" Mika asked, rather pointlessly.

"Yes, soldiers don't starve, or get sick." She spoke with such toneless simplicity, it could have been a child talking.

"Yes, they don't starve," Mika said, "they get killed!"

"Better to die than this nameless misery of ours," she shot back. "Better a quick clean bullet in the head than this slow dying and burning from hunger and disease!"

"Oh, soldiers starve too, you know, when there is nothing to eat . . ." Mika said hard-heartedly.

But she was sunk deep in her thoughts, she might not have heard. Then, as if to herself, alone in the room, she said, "Tumaini's father was a soldier . . ."

"Was . . . ?" went Mika.

". . . a real bull of a man he was, with none to equal him. Life was easier then, with him around. He was like a father to me, to my mother, to all of us. Now living has become such a task. You have to struggle for each small thing. Everything, everything, you have to pay for in blood, if you can find it! If Tumaini's father were around still . . ." She seemed almost on the point of bursting into tears, but she didn't.

"Why, is he dead?" Mika asked, but purely out of curiosity, his voice too loud and untouched by the woman's dull sorrow.

"I don't want to talk, don't ask me, please . . ." she pleaded, then she began to cry and said through her tears, "He went off to Uganda, to war. He might be alive, he might be dead . . ."

Mika said nothing. The child Tumaini was still again, his mother's hand on him, still patting, absently. At last Mama Tumaini straightened up and turned off the small tin lamp in the room. In the dark, she submitted herself, silently, dutifully, and professionally. But, afterward, when Mika rolled his body off her, there wasn't the usual feeling of having conquered; though fully sated, he lay back less than happy, vaguely unsettled, the labored breathing from the mat adding to his sense of deflation.

He did not know when he finally fell asleep and woke up with the panic of one who does not know where he is. It was

not until he felt Mama Tumaini's body by his side that he remembered where he was.

He got out of bed and lit a cigarette. The coil had burnt out
and mosquitoes buzzed angrily. He sat frowning in the dark,
something troubling him, though he didn't know what. Suddenly he was aware of the silence in the room.

Mouth dry and head faintly throbbing, he got up putting
out his cigarette, and went to the mat. There was no sound from
the child and in the darkness he could only make out a mute,
still haze, but he dared not strike a match to light the lamp. He
put his hand out toward the child, and his eyes, gradually used to
the dark, gazed down fascinated at the little body, lifeless and
cold to his touch, its form now becoming distinct under the first
stabs of dawnlight.

Mama Tumaini stirred, mumbled something, then went
back to sleep. Mika waited until her breathing grew deep and
even again before he sat on the bed, gingerly, and lit another
cigarette, his mind busy.

Then, moving softly, he picked up his clothes from the floor
where he had dumped them in a drunken pile. Dressed, he
paused awhile, his eyes involuntarily seeking the child's body.
No, he must leave immediately, he urged himself. It wouldn't
do to get caught in the mourning and the funeral ceremonies.
There was no point and it would delay him further. And anyway, he found himself thinking, what was the child to him, or
the mother for that matter? Mechanically, he took out his wallet,
peeled off several notes, and with no attempt to make out the
amount, placed the money on a stool by the bed, and set the
lamp on it as weight.

The door squeaked as he unbolted it. He paused, his heart
pounding, his ear strained toward the bed.

Mama Tumaini stirred. "You're going already?" she asked
him.

"Yes," he answered.

"This early?"

"You know that transport is a problem, and I have to travel today."

Come what may, he just had to get out today, and try and make it to Dar es Salaam by nightfall. For two days now, he had been sunk in this dreary little town, because petrol shortage had crippled transportation and inundated the small town with stranded travelers. It was to get away from the sweating hordes hopelessly milling all over the town in search of transport that on the previous day he had decided on an evening of entertainment and action. Drink had appealed to him as just the antidote he needed for his despondence. But the search for beer, which he preferred, was doomed from the start. There had been no beer in town, he was told at the first bar he stopped in, since the day the beer truck went crashing over a bridge leading into town. The truck was still there, a useless wreck of scrap metal. Mika did not want to believe this although he suspected it was probably the truth. He would have given his little finger for a drop of beer, and he went all over town, which didn't take long as there was little of it besides the bus stop.

A couple of depressing, dusty, narrow lanes made up the backbone of the town and beyond that was only a patchwork of slums. But he had no luck whatever in his search and had to make do with the local pombe which was in abundance. He had little stomach for local stuff, but even though he imbibed it slowly and grudgingly, gradually the booze took hold and he felt some of his despair lift. He even felt cheerful enough to join a group of local drinkers at a nearby table. But just as the evening seemed to be taking off, he suddenly found himself abandoned, his fellow drinkers having left for other bars or their homes. He had left too, and gone stumbling through the night. He would never remember how he ended up in Mama Tumaini's place, or why he decided he could not spend the night alone in his bed in the room he had rented at the lodging house. Funny, he thought aimlessly, paying for a room then sleeping elsewhere; wasteful, he concluded grimly.

Mama Tumaini was talking. "Even so," she said, "won't you wait for me to make you a cup of tea at least, to start you off?" That was the last thing he wanted, her getting up and finding out about the baby. He had to get away first. "No, no," he said quickly, "my things are at the lodging house, I've to get ready. I'll eat somewhere."

"Suit yourself," she said, turning over. Then faintly, almost inaudibly, as if it was an afterthought, she wished him a safe journey.

He thanked her, then limply, guiltily, he mumbled, "Your money . . . I've put the money . . . your money . . . on the stool." But she might have gone back to sleep or she might have had enough of him, as she made no response.

Mika opened the door and walked away in quick, tense steps, as light broke out over the rooftops and wisps of smoke from the early morning cooking lazed over the slums, announcing the start of another day.

NNADAZIE F. INYAMA

*was born in Nigeria in 1946 where he completed his
schooling, graduating with a degree in English in 1974
and then obtaining M.A. and Ph.D. degrees in England
in 1978 and 1981, respectively. He is now working as a
senior lecturer in English at the University of Nigeria.*

*Since 1980 Inyama has been publishing critical essays
and short stories, mainly in the Nigerian literary journal*
Okike.

HOT DAYS, LONG NIGHTS

NNADAZIE F. INYAMA

FROM SUNUP IN THE GREAT CITY OF AKASSA, A CENTRAL noise would hit the visitor's ears, no matter where he stood. In the mornings, a person standing a mile away from the source of this noise could break it into different notes, some rising high, others trailing off. In the afternoon, as the heat intensified and breathed down in waves on people, the noise and the varying notes would acquire a rhythmic harmony, no longer high, or low, but coming in waves like wind, as if some force had finally fused the noise into one heavy, almost hypnotizing blanket of sound.

If one walked toward the source of this noise, ever present, ever constant in its pattern of development, he would discover it to be the great Akassa City Market, where men and spirits alike meet, and where all things imaginable, from trinkets to human spare parts, are sold. In the morning, when the market has many different voices, the traders would be opening their sheds and setting up their goods. From the countryside lorries laden with food, and bearing the hardy producers of these goods, would be arriving, powerful engines revving as the drivers maneuvered for parking space. The noise of the morning would also be that of market mammies, arguing and quarreling as they bid and outbid each other for goods. "Dis woman, why you always coming for something I price? You no see another place?" they would ask in the central dialect of the city. And, "Customer, if you no sell this thing to me today I no-go happy. Okay, I go put two shillings on what I price, if you no 'gree, fin' anoder person."

And the men who pull handcarts and wheelbarrows, by no means pleased by these delays, would stand and wait for the haggling to end and the goods to be lifted into their carts and barrows and wheeled, with great curses, into various parts of the market. Their impatience is understandable. The morning is boom time in Akassa market.

In the mornings, the traders, especially the mammies, usually stood out behind their wares, because the sun would not be high and hot yet, and call on everyone who passed to take a look at their goods. They knew that anyone who came to the market in the morning had not come for mere sight-seeing. The traders would watch out particularly for the up-country people. They were easy to spot. They clutched their handbags to themselves and frowned sternly at any person who so much as involuntarily rubbed his body against theirs. They knew the city to be full of notorious pickpockets and bag snatchers.

If a trader talked one such up-country man into his stall, his day had started off well. He could keep the up-country man there and fetch for him all the things he wanted to buy that morning, making great profits in the process.

There were also budding merchants, carrying penny-grouped wares, mostly groundnuts, kolanuts and akara, and screaming these goods at people, so that even if one didn't buy they had the satisfaction of giving him a little displeasure with their shrill voices.

The Tinkers Row, an all-male zone, was distinctive for many reasons. The men worked always with their shirts off because they sweated easily, even in the morning. The Tinkers Row contributed powerfully to the noise from Akassa city market as hammer went resolutely against metal. It was not often that sophisticated city wives came there. But up-country wives did, and when they concluded a deal they would step aside and dip their hands into their loincloths to extract the money from some secret receptacle, paying almost the same amount of money for the tin pot as it would have cost them to buy the shiny *English-made* ones they left somewhere else, suspecting that they would cost very much more. The men would look discreetly away when this operation was on, and wink at each other, knowing that a good sale had been made.

The Tinkers Row was never a quiet zone. Even in the midday when the sun had forced most traders to semidazed retirement into their stalls and the mammy's temper was no longer long with late shoppers, and her voice no longer cajoling, the tinkers would go at their work with unabated vigor, noise and sweat. And it was at this time that their voices rose in song. They always sang. Songs of hard work, of joy and of sorrow. Bawdy songs too, of the young madam who did her buying on the bed hidden behind the handsome trader's goods; of maids who took madam's husband. They also would sing popular record hits, adding their own touches—salt and pepper—to suit their own humors. It was not always that they sang together. But often they did, going at a currently popular song with amazing gusto and laughing together when they hit a funny line in the song.

Abafa and Akori occupied shed 4 on the Tinkers Row, and Oga Dako occupied "Double" shed 2. Dako was the master craftsman of this trade and he was the president of the A.C.M.T.U., the Akassa City Market Tinkers Union, for every trade in the market had a union for the protection of its interests. But it was not for this only that everyone called him Oga. It was more because many of the tinkers in this place had learned their trade from him, and even those who had "freed" from his tutorship would come to him from time to time to learn some new intricate way of fashioning metal, for Oga Dako had creativity flowing through his hands. He was a rather quiet man, speaking as little as possible; and even after more than twenty years in Akassa, he still didn't know most parts of the city. He never joined in the songs, but when a song was particularly sweet he would be seen nodding his head in time to it. But that was as far as his participation went.

Abafa and Akori owned one work shed together. They were the most traveled, for, according to them, they had seen most of the world together. They had spent years in such romantic and far-off places as Accra-Ghana, Santa-Isabell and Matadi-Congo and numerous other places. Ah! They had seen the world and known happy times. They came home, they told everybody, because a man couldn't spend his life wandering all over the face of the earth. And Abafa was home also because his "brother" would soon come back from "oversea." He was learning to be a doctor. The rest of the people in the Tinkers Row would see him one day "enjoying" in his brother's car and they would open their eyes wide and ask, "Is that not Abafa who was here with us yesterday?" And he would laugh and tell them "Na so the world be." And he would elaborate so much on his coming prosperity that people would lose interest and get impatient.

Abafa and Akori did not sing with the rest of the people in the Row. They sang strange songs—songs they said they learned in the strange lands they had visited and lived in. They would wait till there was a pause in the singing of their neighbors, then they would break into their own songs. Often, there was no uniformity in the words and this discord made the songs more meaningless and pointless to their neighbors. But the two would insist that they were singing the same thing, only the hearers were unfamiliar with the language. The other men tolerated these things and would at times set them off on one or other story of great doings in far-off places, real or imagined.

Oga Dako, you remember, never took any great interest in these songs, except to nod his head like a lizard from time to time. It was, therefore, a great surprise to everyone when he asked Abafa and Akori the meaning of the song they were sing- ing at that particular moment. The interruption from Oga Dako was so unexpected that everyone stopped work for a time. Per- haps, this particular song, new and even more meaningless to the ears, had annoyed him. But no one could tell, because his face was as calm and dignified as always, and as befitted the president of a union.

"Ah . . . em . . . Oga," said Abafa, "is song we learn for Sombrerro."

"Which country dat one dey now?"

"Ah, Oga," said Akori, "Sombrerro no be country. Is a nightclub for Saida Layout. 'E dey for Akassa here." Oga Dako was inwardly irritated by the relish with which Akori gave this piece of knowledge. He seemed to be finding great joy in expos- ing their ignorance of Akassa, in addition to their lack of knowl- edge of other lands, like Matadi-Congo and Younde . . .

"If de Sombrerro, or whatever you call it dey for dis town, why you dey sing for dat kin' language?

"Abi dem no fit sing for we language?"

"No be so, sir," Abafa put in. "De band is not call Som- brerro. De band is from Ghana and dem name be De Seven Aces. Dem come new for de town and na for Sombrerro dem dey."

"Is dat so?" asked Dako, a very faint note of interest in his voice. This seemed to put Abafa on the path to new great tales.

"We go dere every night to enjoy and . . ."

"Every night? Abi de thing is for free?" asked Dako in disbe- lief.

"No be so, Oga. You pay only four shillings at de gate . . ."

"You pay four shillings every night to learn dis kin' song?"

• • •

Oga Dako was as surprised as the other men who were listening to this conversation with almost total attention. And they wondered, how could these two be going to the nightclub every night and paying four shillings? Dako knew that they were among the least productive of the tinkers, producing more noise than finished wares. It was impossible to reconcile what they earned in a week with such a rate of spending. It would be ungenerous to say that they must be stealing, so it meant that they were lying.

But Abafa, completely insensitive to the surprise he had created, went on, "Like yonder night we been drink with Honorable Alakeda. Me I drink four bottle of beer. Is good to know de big men . . ."

"What do you mean?" asked Dako. He knew Hon. Alakeda, everybody knew Hon. Alakeda, the flamboyant member of parliament for Akassa South. How could these two be drinking with him at a club? His face mirrored the disgust he felt at these two storytellers.

"Nothing we no go hear for dis place!" someone exclaimed. The roars of laughter that greeted this statement in no way embarrassed Akori. "Plenty big men come dere every night. All de big politician use to come wit' dem girl frien'. Dey always buy beer for all de people inside de club. You know, de politicians always campaigning for vote."

Dako and the other people were not convinced, but they let the matter be. Abafa and Akori did not seem to care whether they were believed or not, they went at their songs with greater gusto, ignoring the laughter that was all round them.

It was Saturday evening. Oga Dako was feeling very satisfied. The Ministry of Welfare had paid him one hundred and sixty pounds for a contract. This was no small money and it would justify some kind of celebration. Apart from the mandatory two pounds he would pay the Umuachara Abroadian Union, because they had helped him win the contract, the rest of the money was his. And it was no small money! But how was he to celebrate? His social engagements in all his years in Akassa ended with monthly attendances of the Abroadian Union meetings. He was unfamiliar with places of enjoyment. Then, he remembered Sombrerro. Had not Abafa and his friend said that it was a place for enjoyment? The more he thought about it the more excited he became. Yes, he would go there and "make big man" for once. Perhaps he would meet Abafa and Akori, if what they said was true, and buy beer for them. One hundred and sixty pounds was no small money, he told himself again.

Soon he was dressed, in baggy trousers, a great John White pair of shoes, a coat he had worn only once since he bought it, being mostly unable to overcome his shy nature—and topped off with a hat of the type called "London Opinion." When he emerged in the street his confidence in his appearance as a "big man" was reinforced by the numerous "good evening sirs" he received from people.

Then he remembered that he did not know the exact location of the club, except that Abafa had said that it was at the Saida Layout. He decided to take a taxi, and was soon on his way. In ten minutes he arrived. The driver charged him one shilling above the normal fare, and Dako obligingly paid. This evening he would play big.

The club was a large house. An electric sign proclaimed its name. From inside it poured forth the sharp blare of trumpets and the thunderous beat of drums and the clash of cymbals. The people inside cheered uproariously. Outside, on the paved front of the building there was a crowd of Akassa's less affluent class, made up mostly of youths who had run to the city from the villages. They did odd jobs in the daytime, pushing barrows, selling hemp, carrying loads on their heads and at night seeking out places such as this and getting into mischief. Dako knew that many of them owned no rooms to sleep in and would make themselves comfortable at night in motor parks or abandoned kiosks and cars. They knew who played what songs and knew all the dance styles. A fight was often a part of the evening's fare.

Whenever a car arrived they rushed up to identify who was in it and would emit jeers or applause, depending on how they rated the man. All this was exciting, but Dako felt frightened. His confidence sank appreciably. This was a new environment, something he did not know existed in Akassa. He hesitated, and one mind asked him to call the taxi back and go back to his house. But the car was already far away. Someone from the crowd said, "You no wan' enter again?" Dako was lucky because at this time most of them were dancing. Only a few had noticed his arrival, otherwise this hesitation, brief as it was, would have earned him very cruel taunts. They would have minutely analyzed his mode of dress and made him feel like one clothed in straw. He walked to the door of the club, as solidly as he could muster courage. He was surprised when they informed him that a ticket cost six shillings. When he asked if it was not four shillings they laughed and said, "Four shillings? Who say is four shillings? Is always six shillings." This rebuke was almost making him ashamed as he fumbled in his pocket and brought out his money. They made way for him and he escaped into the room. He thought, "Abafa and Akori lied to me."

The room was large, one end of it was full of tables, the other half was the dancing area. A few people were sitting and drinking, the tables were packed with bottles, full and empty. He wondered why the empty bottles were not carried away. The dance floor was full. The couples, either because of limited space, or out of desire, held themselves in so close a manner that Dako was shocked. These people were not just dancing, he thought, seeing for the first time another side of the city.

As he stood and watched these things, a woman walked up and put her hand around Dako's shoulder.

"Dance?" she asked. He woke with a shudder. He looked at the woman, so young, and she smiled alluringly at him. Dako disengaged her hand and said, "No, I just arrive. I wan' to sit down."

"Okay," she said, and guided him to a table. He sat down and she said, "You want drink, not so? How many bottles?" Dako looked at the other tables. Filled up with bottles. It would be shameful to stay without beer on his table; it would also be shameful if he did not ask for many bottles like those who were drinking on the other tables. He did not like beer, it always tasted bitter. He always drank cola when he went to Union meeting. But he would buy the beer and let the bottles be on his table. He would open one, pour some into a cup and just let it stay there.

"Bring four," he said to her. She stretched out her hand for the money. He gave it to her and she went off, turning and twisting her buttocks. Soon she was back, the four bottles in a tray. She also had two glasses. A man was following her along, a half-filled tumbler in his hand. She sat down and the man sat on the next chair. She opened the bottles and poured into the two glasses. The man who had followed her turned to Dako.

"I been watching you since you enter. I think I see you for de conference last Thursday?" Dako said he was not at any conference. He was the president of the Metal Workers' Union. He asked the man to drink. The woman smiled. She knew the man and his ways of getting free drinks.

There was no conversation between them. Dako watched them drinking away his money. If he had not come to make "big man," he would have been very bitter. He wished that Abafa and Akori would appear now; then, at least, some people he knew would be gaining from his money. Except that they had told him all those lies and he had come here. The band, for instance, sang in his own language. And, nobody was buying any free drinks for people, except perhaps himself. Everyone went and bought his own beer and sat down and kept drinking it, offering none to his neighbor. As for the big men, the few who looked like truly "big men" were the most distant. So where were the big men who turned magic beer taps for Abafa and Akori? And now these people were drinking his beer so fast, especially the woman. He had always heard of such women, but he had never been to a place like this to see one.

Then the music ended. The dancers clapped and made their way to their seats. The response from outside was a thunderous roar. They wanted more, and any break was greeted with shouts and curses for more. Then they rushed to the windows, pressing their faces on the glass panes, eager to see what was going on inside. Dako looked at the windows. At one of the windows he could see the face of Abafa staring unmistakably at him. Then when their eyes met, Abafa dodged out. Dako was sure of whom he had seen. Should he go and bring him in? That would embarrass the poor fellow, especially after all those stories at the Tinkers Row. And if he was with Akori that would drag Dako into great expenses. Dako took another look at the window as the band struck up again. This time Abafa was not alone. He was engaged in a heated argument with Akori, glancing in his direction from time to time, perhaps trying to settle whether it was him or not. He turned his face away, ignoring them and giving them no chance to know, as they could not see his face properly now. Soon they tired of their argument and went off to the crowd of dancers outside.

Dako got up and headed straight for the door. The woman was surprised at this unexpected movement. She shouted after him, "You no wan' go wit me?" He had no ears for such things. He only wanted to escape now, after discovering

Abafa and Akori. He felt slightly guilty for having known their secret.

Outside, the scene was as rowdy as when he arrived. There were circles around people "demonstrating" the "latest" dance styles, and the smell of dust and cheap cigarettes and marijuana smoke produced a suffocating pungency. There was a departing taxi and Dako gratefully hailed it. Soon he was going away to where he belonged and where he felt most at home.

Monday morning, Akassa market was shouting in its many voices and the sun gave promise of a hot day. At the Tinkers Row the men had already taken off their shirts. The lorries bellowed like cattle in a wild fury. The tinkers were again beating metal with a post weekend vigor. From his shed Dako watched Abafa and Akori. He saw that they were giving him frequent, uneasy glances.

Finally, unable to contain himself, Abafa said, "Oga, you been go to 'Sombrerro' last Saturday night?" Dako did not expect the question. But, he was also not surprised that it was asked. Should he say "yes," and cut away the foundations of their stories? Their make-believe world? He thought about it in a quick moment and said, "No. I don' know de place at all."

"You see?" Akori said in apparent triumph. "Oga no go there at all. I tell you say dat person no fit be Oga his self."

Abafa, deflated, said, "People use to resemble too much. 'E get person we see dere dat night. He look like you. But we no look proper. De dance too hot dat time." But he was reassured. Nobody knew yet where they did their dancing and drinking. They wouldn't even wait for midday to come before they were again singing unintelligible songs. Dako watched them, unable to even make himself angry or spiteful. If they chose this kind of illusion to tide them over life's hardness, why should he destroy it for them?

SEMBÈNE OUSMANE

was born in 1923 in Senegal. He is equally famous as a writer and a movie director. His literary work serves him as a starting point for his movies: La Noire de . . . (The Black Girl from . . .), Le Mandat (The Money Order), Xala. *His movie* The Money Order *won an award at the Venice Film Festival.*

Ousmane's career was a rich one. He was a fisherman, mason, mechanic, dockworker. As a writer he is very prolific: in 1956 he published his first novel Le Docker Noir (The Black Docker), *followed by* O Pays, Mon Beau Peuple (O Country, My Beautiful People, *1957),* Les Bouts de Bois de Dieu (God's Bits of Wood, *1960),* L'Harmattan *(1964), a collection of short stories* Voltaïque (Tribal Scars and Other Stories, *1962),* Le Mandat et Vehi Ciosane (The Money Order and White Genesis, *1969),* Xala *(1973),* Le Dernier de l'Empire (The Last of the Empire, *1981—in two volumes).*

Ousmane's stories figure in many African anthologies.

HER THREE DAYS

SEMBÈNE OUSMANE

Translated by Len Ortzen

SHE RAISED HER HAGGARD FACE, AND HER FARAWAY LOOK ranged beyond the muddle of roofs, some tiled, others of thatch or galvanized iron; the wide fronds of the twin coconut palms were swaying slowly in the breeze, and in her mind she could hear their faint rustling. Noumbe was thinking of "her three days." Three days for her alone, when she would have her husband Mustapha to herself . . . It was a long time since she had felt such emotion. To have Mustapha! The thought comforted her. She had heart trouble and still felt some pain, but she had been dosing herself for the past two days, taking more medicine than was prescribed. It was a nice syrup that just slipped down, and she felt the beneficial effects at once. She blinked; her eyes were like two worn buttonholes, with lashes that were like frayed thread, in little clusters of fives and threes; the whites were the color of old ivory.

"What's the matter, Noumbe?" asked Aida, her next-door neighbor, who was sitting at the door of her room.

"Nothing," she answered, and went on cutting up the slice of raw meat, helped by her youngest daughter.

"Ah, it's your three days," exclaimed Aida, whose words held a meaning that she could not elaborate on while the little girl was present. She went on: "You're looking fine enough to prevent a holy man from saying his prayers properly!"

"Aida, be careful what you say," she protested, a little annoyed.

But it was true; Noumbe had plaited her hair and put henna on her hands and feet. And that morning she had got the children up early to give her room a thorough clean. She was not old, but one pregnancy after another—and she had five children—and her heart trouble had aged her before her time.

"Go and ask Laity to give you five francs' worth of salt and twenty francs' worth of oil," Noumbe said to the girl. "Tell him I sent you. I'll pay for them as soon as your father is here, at midday." She looked disapprovingly at the cut-up meat in the bottom of the bowl.

The child went off with the empty bottle and Noumbe got to her feet. She was thin and of average height. She went into her one-room shack, which was sparsely furnished; there was a bed with a white cover, and in one corner stood a table with pieces of china on display. The walls were covered with enlargements and photos of friends and strangers framed in passe-partout.

When she came out again she took the Moorish stove and set about lighting it.

Her daughter had returned from her errand.

"He gave them to you?" asked Noumbe.

"Yes, Mother."

A woman came across the compound to her. "Noumbe, I can see that you're preparing a delicious dish."

"Yes," she replied. "It's my three days. I want to revive the feasts of the old days, so that his palate will retain the taste of the dish for many moons, and he'll forget the cooking of his other wives."

"Ah-ha! So that his palate is eager for dishes to come," said the woman, who was having a good look at the ingredients.

"I'm feeling in good form," said Noumbe, with some pride

in her voice. She grasped the woman's hand and passed it over her loins.

"*Thieh, souya dome!* I hope you can say the same tomorrow morning . . ."

The woman clapped her hands; as if it were a signal or an invitation, other women came across, one with a metal jar, another with a saucepan, which they beat while the woman sang:

> "*Sope dousa rafetaïl,*
> *Sopa nala dousa rafetail*
> *Sa yahi n'diguela.*"
> (Worship of you is not for your beauty,
> I worship you not for your beauty
> But for your backbone.)

In a few moments, they improvised a wild dance to this chorus. At the end, panting and perspiring, they burst out laughing. Then one of them stepped into Noumbe's room and called the others.

"Let's take away the bed! Because tonight they'll wreck it!"

"She's right. Tomorrow this room will be . . ."

Each woman contributed an earthy comment which set them all laughing hilariously. Then they remembered they had work to do, and brought their amusement to an end; each went back to her family occupations.

Noumbe had joined in the laughter; she knew this boisterous "ragging" was the custom in the compound. No one escaped it. Besides, she was an exceptional case, as they all knew. She had a heart condition and her husband had quite openly neglected her. Mustapha had not been to see her for a fortnight. All this time she had been hoping that he would come, if only for a moment. When she went to the clinic for mothers and children she compelled her youngest daughter to stay at home, so that—thus did her mind work—if her husband turned up the child could detain him until she returned. She ought to have gone to the clinic again this day, but she had spent what little money she possessed on preparing for Mustapha. She did not want her husband to esteem her less than his other wives, or to think her meaner. She did not neglect her duty as a mother, but her wifely duty came first—at certain times.

She imagined what the next three days would be like; already her "three days" filled her whole horizon. She forgot her illness and her baby's ailments. She had thought about these three days in a thousand different ways. Mustapha would not leave before the Monday morning. In her mind she could see Mustapha and his henchmen crowding into her room, and could hear their suggestive jokes. "If she had been a perfect wife . . ." She laughed to herself. "Why shouldn't it always be like that for every woman—to have a husband of one's own?" She wondered why not.

The morning passed at its usual pace, the shadows of the coconut palms and the people growing steadily shorter. As midday approached, the housewives busied themselves with the meal. In the compound each one stood near her door, ready to welcome her man. The kids were playing around, and their mothers' calls to them crossed in the air. Noumbe gave her children a quick meal and sent them out again. She sat waiting for Mustapha to arrive at any moment . . . he wouldn't be much longer now.

An hour passed, and the men began going back to work. Soon the compound was empty of the male element; the women, after a long siesta, joined one another under the coconut palms and the sounds of their gossiping gradually increased.

Noumbe, weary of waiting, had finally given up keeping a lookout. Dressed in her mauve velvet, she had been on the watch since before midday. She had eaten no solid food, consoling herself with the thought that Mustapha would appear at any moment. Now she fought back the pangs of hunger by telling herself that in the past Mustapha had a habit of arriving late. In those days, this lateness was pleasant. Without admitting it to herself, those moments (which had hung terribly heavy) had been very sweet; they prolonged the sensual pleasure of anticipation. Although those minutes had been sometimes shot through with doubts and fears (often, very often, the thought of her coming disgrace had assailed her; for Mustapha, who had taken two wives before her, had just married another), they had not been too hard to bear. She realized that those demanding minutes were the price she had to pay for Mustapha's presence. Then she began to reckon up the score, in small ways, against the *veudieux,* the other wives. One washed his *boubous* when it was another wife's turn, or kept him long into the night; another sometimes held him in her embrace a whole day, knowing quite well that she was preventing Mustapha from carrying out his marital duty elsewhere.

She sulked as she waited; Mustapha had not been near her for a fortnight. All these bitter thoughts brought her up against reality: four months ago Mustapha had married a younger woman. This sudden realization of the facts sent a pain to her heart, a pain of anguish. The additional pain did not prevent her heart from functioning normally, rather was it like a sick person whose sleep banishes pain but who once awake again finds his suffering is as bad as ever, and pays for the relief by a redoubling of pain.

She took three spoonfuls of her medicine instead of the two prescribed, and felt a little better in herself.

She called her youngest daughter. "Tell Mactar I want him."

The girl ran off and soon returned with her eldest brother. "Go and fetch your father," Noumbe told him.

"Where, Mother?"

"Where? Oh, on the main square or at one of your other mothers'."

"But I've been to the main square already, and he wasn't there."

"Well, go and have another look. Perhaps he's there now."

The boy looked up at his mother, then dropped his head again and reluctantly turned to go.

"When your father has finished eating, I'll give you what's left. It's meat. Now be quick, Mactar."

It was scorching hot and the clouds were riding high. Mactar was back after an hour. He had not found his father. Noumbe went and joined the group of women. They were chattering about this and that; one of them asked (just for the sake of asking), "Noumbe, has your uncle (darling) arrived?" "Not yet," she replied, then hastened to add, "Oh, he won't be long now. He knows it's my three days." She deliberately changed the conversation in order to avoid a long discussion about the other three wives. But all the time she was longing to go and find Mustapha. She was being robbed of her three days. And the other wives knew it. Her hours alone with Mustapha were being snatched from her. The thought of his being with one of the other wives, who was feeding him and opening his waistcloth when she ought to be doing all that, who was enjoying those hours which were hers by right, so numbed Noumbe that it was impossible for her to react. The idea that Mustapha might have been admitted to hospital or taken to a police station never entered her head.

She knew how to make tasty little dishes for Mustapha which cost him nothing. She never asked him for money. Indeed, hadn't she got herself into debt so that he would be more comfortable and have better meals at her place? And in the past, when Mustapha sometimes arrived unexpectedly—this was soon after he had married her—hadn't she hastened to make succulent dishes for him? All her friends knew this.

A comforting thought coursed through her and sent these aggressive and vindictive reflections to sleep. She told herself that Mustapha was bound to come to her this evening. The certainty of his presence stripped her mind of the too cruel thought that the time of her disfavor was approaching; this thought had been as much a burden to her as a heavy weight dragging a drowning man to the bottom. When all the bad, unfavorable thoughts besetting her had been dispersed, like piles of rubbish on wasteland swept by a flood, the future seemed brighter, and she joined in the conversation of the women with childish enthusiasm, unable to hide her pleasure and her hopes. It was like something in a parcel; questioning eyes wondered what was inside, but she alone knew and enjoyed the secret, drawing an agreeable strength from it. She took an active part in the talking and brought her wit into play. All this vivacity sprang from the joyful conviction that Mustapha would arrive this evening very hungry and be hers alone.

In the far distance, high above the treetops, a long trail of dark gray clouds tinged with red was hiding the sun. The time for the *tacousane,* the afternoon prayer, was drawing near. One by one, the women withdrew to their rooms, and the shadows of the trees grew longer, wider and darker.

Night fell; a dark, starry night.

Noumbe cooked some rice for the children. They clamored in vain for some of the meat. Noumbe was stern and unyielding: "The meat is for your father. He didn't eat at midday." When she had fed the children, she washed herself again to get rid of the smell of cooking and touched up her toilette, rubbing oil on her hands, feet and legs to make the henna more brilliant. She intended to remain by her door, and sat down on the bench; the incense smelt strongly, filling the whole room. She was facing the entrance to the compound and could see the other women's husbands coming in.

But for her there was no one.

She began to feel tired again. Her heart was troubling her, and she had a fit of coughing. Her inside seemed to be on fire. Knowing that she would not be going to the dispensary during her "three days," in order to economize, she went and got some wood ash which she mixed with water and drank. It did not taste very nice, but it would make the medicine last longer, and the drink checked and soothed the burning within her for a while. She was tormenting herself with the thoughts passing through her mind. Where can he be? With the first wife? No, she's quite old. The second then? Everyone knew that she was out of favor with Mustapha. The third wife was herself. So he must be with the fourth. There were puckers of uncertainty and doubt in the answers she gave herself. She kept putting back the time to go to bed, like a lover who does not give up waiting when the time of the rendezvous is long past, but with an absurd and stupid hope waits still longer, self-torture and the heavy minutes chaining him to the spot. At each step Noumbe took, she stopped and mentally explored the town, prying into each house inhabited by one of the other wives. Eventually she went indoors.

So that she would not be caught unawares by Mustapha nor lose the advantages which her makeup and good clothes gave her, she lay down on the bed fully dressed and alert. She had turned down the lamp as far as possible, so the room was dimly lit. But she fell asleep despite exerting great strength of mind to remain awake and saying repeatedly to herself, "I shall wait for him." To make sure that she would be standing there expectantly when he crossed the threshold, she had bolted the door. Thus she would be the devoted wife, always ready to serve her husband, having got up at once and appearing as elegant as if it were broad daylight. She had even thought of making a gesture as she stood there, of passing her hands casually over her hips so that Mustapha would hear the clinking of the beads she had strung round her waist and be incited to look at her from head to foot.

Morning came, but there was no Mustapha.

When the children awoke they asked if their father had come. The oldest of them, Mactar, a promising lad, was quick to spot that his mother had not made the bed, that the bowl containing the stew was still in the same place, by a dish of rice, and the loaf of bread on the table was untouched. The children got a taste of their mother's anger. The youngest, Amadou, took a long time over dressing. Noumbe hurried them up and sent the youngest girl to Laity's to buy five francs' worth of ground coffee. The children's breakfast was warmed-up rice with a meager sprinkling of gravy from the previous day's stew. Then she gave them their wings, as the saying goes, letting them all out except the youngest daughter. Noumbe inspected the bottle of medicine and saw that she had taken a lot of it; there were only three spoonfuls left. She gave herself half a spoonful and made up for the rest with her mixture of ashes and water. After that she felt calmer.

"Why, Noumbe, you must have got up bright and early this morning, to be so dressed up. Are you going off on a long journey?"

It was Aida, her next-door neighbor, who was surprised to see her dressed in such a manner, especially for a woman who was having "her three days." Then Aida realized what had happened and tried to rectify her mistake.

"Oh, I see he hasn't come yet. They're all the same, these men!"

"He'll be here this morning, Aida." Noumbe bridled, ready to defend her man. But it was rather her own worth she was defending, wanting to conceal what an awful time she had spent. It had been a broken night's sleep, listening to harmless sounds which she had taken for Mustapha's footsteps, and this had left its mark on her already haggard face.

"I'm sure he will! I'm sure he will!" exclaimed Aida, well aware of this comedy that all the women played in turn.

"Mustapha is such a kind man, and so noble in his attitude," added another woman, rubbing it in.

"If he weren't, he wouldn't be my master," said Noumbe, feeling flattered by this description of Mustapha.

The news soon spread round the compound that Mustapha had slept elsewhere during Noumbe's three days. The other women pitied her. It was against all the rules for Mustapha to spend a night elsewhere. Polygamy had its laws, which should be respected. A sense of decency and common dignity restrained a wife from keeping the husband day and night when his whole person and everything connected with him belonged to another wife during "her three days." The game, however, was not without its underhand tricks that one wife played on another; for instance, to wear out the man and hand him over when he was incapable of performing his conjugal duties. When women criticized the practice of polygamy they always found that the wives were to blame, especially those who openly dared to play a dirty trick. The man was whitewashed. He was a weakling who always ended by falling into the enticing traps set for him by women. Satisfied with this conclusion, Noumbe's neighbors made common cause with her and turned to abusing Mustapha's fourth wife.

Noumbe made some coffee—she never had any herself, because of her heart. She consoled herself with the thought that Mustapha would find more things at her place. The bread had gone stale; she would buy some more when he arrived.

The hours dragged by again, long hours of waiting which

became harder to bear as the day progressed. She wished she knew where he was . . . The thought obsessed her, and her eyes became glazed and searching. Every time she heard a man's voice she straightened up quickly. Her heart was paining her more and more, but the physical pain was separate from the mental one; they never came together, alternating in a way that reminded her of the acrobatic feat of a man riding two speeding horses.

At about four o'clock Noumbe was surprised to see Mustapha's second wife appear at the door. She had come to see if Mustapha was there, knowing that it was Noumbe's three days. She did not tell Noumbe the reason for her wishing to see Mustapha, despite being pressed. So Noumbe concluded that it was largely due to jealousy, and was pleased that the other wife could see how clean and tidy her room was, and what a display of fine things she had, all of which could hardly fail to make the other think that Mustapha had been (and still was) very generous to her, Noumbe. During the rambling conversation her heart thumped ominously, but she bore up and held off taking any medicine.

Noumbe remembered only too well that when she was newly married she had usurped the second wife's three days. At that time she had been the youngest wife. Mustapha had not let a day pass without coming to see her. Although not completely certain, she believed she had conceived her third child during this wife's three days. The latter's presence now and remarks that she let drop made Noumbe realize that she was no longer the favorite. This revelation, and the polite, amiable tone and her visitor's eagerness to inquire after her children's health and her own, to praise her superior choice of household utensils, her taste in clothes, the cleanliness of the room and the lingering fragrance of the incense, all this was like a stab in cold blood, a cruel reminder of the perfidy of words and the hypocrisy of rivals; and all part of the world of women. This observation did not get her anywhere, except to arouse a desire to escape from the circle of polygamy and to cause her to ask herself—it was a moment of mental aberration really—"Why do we allow ourselves to be men's playthings?"

The other wife complimented her and insisted that Noumbe's children should go and spend a few days with her own children (in this she was sincere). By accepting in principle, Noumbe was weaving her own waistcloth of hypocrisy. It was all to make the most of herself, to set tongues wagging so that she would lose none of her respectability and rank. The other wife casually added—before she forgot, as she said—that she wanted to see Mustapha, and if mischief makers told Noumbe that "their" husband had been to see her during Noumbe's three days, Noumbe shouldn't think ill of her, and she would rather have seen him here to tell him what she had to say. To save face, Noumbe dared not ask her when she had last seen Mustapha. The other would have replied with a smile, "The last morning of my three days, of course. I've only come here because it's urgent." And Noumbe would have looked embarrassed and put on an air of innocence. "No, that isn't what I meant. I just wondered if you had happened to meet him by chance."

Neither of them would have lost face. It was all that remained to them. They were not lying, to their way of thinking. Each had been desired and spoilt for a time; then the man, like a gorged vulture, had left them on one side and the venom of chagrin at having been mere playthings had entered their hearts. They quite understood, it was all quite clear to them, that they could sink no lower; so they clung to what was left to them, that is to say, to saving what dignity remained to them by false words and gaining advantages at the expense of the other. They did not indulge in this game for the sake of it. This falseness contained all that remained of the flame of dignity. No one was taken in, certainly not themselves. Each knew that the other was lying, but neither could bring herself to further humiliation, for it would be the final crushing blow.

The other wife left. Noumbe almost propelled her to the door, then stood there thoughtful for a few moments. Noumbe understood the reason for the other's visit. She had come to get her own back. Noumbe felt absolutely sure that Mustapha was with his latest wife. The visit meant in fact: "You stole those days from me because I am older than you. Now a younger woman than you is avenging me. Try as you might to make everything nice and pleasant for him, you have to toe the line with the rest of us now, you old carcass. He's slept with some-one else—and he will again."

The second day passed like the first, but was more dreadful. She ate no proper food, just enough to stave off the pangs of hunger.

It was Sunday morning and all the men were at home; they nosed about in one room and another, some of them cradling their youngest in their arms, others playing with the older children. The draughts players had gathered in one place, the card-players in another. There was a friendly atmosphere in the compound, with bursts of happy laughter and sounds of guttural voices, while the women busied themselves with the housework.

Aida went to see Noumbe to console her, and said without much conviction, "He'll probably come today. Men always seem to have something to do at the last minute. It's Sunday today, so he'll be here."

"Aida, Mustapha doesn't work," Noumbe pointed out, hard-eyed. She gave a cough. "I've been waiting for him now for two days and nights! When it's my three days I think the least he could do is to be here—at night, anyway. I might die . . ."

"Do you want me to go and look for him?"

"No."

She had thought "yes." It was the way in which Aida had made the offer that embarrassed her. Of course she would like her to! Last night, when everyone had gone to bed, she had started out and covered quite some distance before turning back. The flame of her dignity had been fanned on the way. She did not want to abase herself still further by going to claim a man who seemed to have no desire to see her. She had lain awake until dawn, thinking it all over and telling herself that her marriage to Mustapha was at an end, that she would divorce him. But this morning there was a tiny flicker of hope in her heart: "Mustapha will come, all the same. This is my last night."

She borrowed a thousand francs from Aida, who readily lent her the money. And she followed the advice to send the children off again, to Mustapha's fourth wife.

"Tell him that I must see him at once, I'm not well!"

She hurried off to the little market nearby and bought a chicken and several other things. Her eyes were feverishly, joyfully bright as she carefully added seasoning to the dish she prepared. The appetizing smell of her cooking was wafted out to the compound and its Sunday atmosphere. She swept the room again, shut the door and windows, but the heady scent of the incense escaped through the cracks between the planks.

The children returned from their errand.

"Is he ill?" she asked them.

"No, Mother. He's going to come. We found him with some of his friends at Voulimata's (the fourth wife). He asked about you."

"And that's all he said?"

"Yes, Mother."

"Don't come indoors. Here's ten francs. Go and play somewhere else."

A delicious warm feeling spread over her. "He was going to come." Ever since Friday she had been harboring spiteful words to throw in his face. He would beat her, of course . . . But never mind. Now she found it would be useless to utter those words. Instead she would do everything possible to make up for the lost days. She was happy, much too happy to bear a grudge against him, now that she knew he was coming—he might even be on the way with his henchmen. The only means of getting her own back was to cook a big meal . . . then he would stay in bed.

She finished preparing the meal, had a bath and went on to the rest of her toilette. She did her hair again, put antimony on her lower lip, eyebrows and lashes, then dressed in a white starched blouse and a hand-woven waistcloth, and inspected her hands and feet. She was quite satisfied with her appearance.

But the waiting became prolonged.

No one in the compound spoke to her for fear of hurting her feelings. She had sat down outside the door, facing the entrance to the compound, and the other inhabitants avoided meeting her sorrowful gaze. Her tears overflowed the brim of her eyes like a swollen river its banks; she tried to hold them back, but in vain. She was eating her heart out.

The sound of a distant tom-tom was being carried on the wind. Time passed over her, like the seasons over monuments. Twilight came and darkness fell.

On the table were three plates in a row, one for each day.

"I've come to keep you company," declared Aida as she entered the room. Noumbe was sitting on the foot of the bed—she had fled from the silence of the others. "You mustn't get worked up about it," went on Aida. "Every woman goes through it. Of course it's not nice! But I don't think he'll be long now."

Noumbe raised a moist face and bit her lips nervously. Aida saw that she had made up her mind not to say anything.

Everything was shrouded in darkness; no light came from her room. After supper, the children had refrained from playing their noisy games.

Just when adults were beginning to feel sleepy and going to bed, into the compound walked Mustapha, escorted by two of his lieutenants. He was clad entirely in white. He greeted the people still about in an oily manner, then invited his companions into Noumbe's hut.

She had not stirred.

"Wife, where's the lamp?"

"Where you left it this morning when you went out."

"How are you?" inquired Mustapha when he had lit the lamp. He went and sat down on the bed, and motioned to the two men to take the bench.

"God be praised," Noumbe replied to his polite inquiry. Her thin face seemed relaxed and the angry lines had disappeared.

"And the children?"

"They're well, praise be to God."

"Our wife isn't very talkative this evening," put in one of the men.

"I'm quite well, though."

"Your heart isn't playing you up now?" asked Mustapha, not unkindly.

"No, it's quite steady," she answered.

"God be praised! Mustapha, we'll be off," said the man, uncomfortable at Noumbe's cold manner.

"Wait," said Mustapha, and turned to Noumbe. "Wife, are we eating tonight or tomorrow?"

"Did you leave me something when you went out this morning?"

"What? That's not the way to answer."

"No, uncle (darling). I'm just asking . . . Isn't it right?"

Mustapha realized that Noumbe was mocking him and trying to humiliate him in front of his men.

"You do like your little joke. Don't you know it's your three days?"

"Oh, uncle, I'm sorry, I'd quite forgotten. What an unworthy wife I am!" she exclaimed, looking straight at Mustapha.

"You're making fun of me!"

"Oh, uncle, I shouldn't dare! What, I? And who would help me into Paradise, if not my worthy husband? Oh, I would never poke fun at you, neither in this world nor the next."

"Anyone would think so."

"Who?" she asked.

"You might have stood up when I came in, to begin with . . ."

"Oh, uncle, forgive me. I'm out of my mind with joy at seeing you again. But whose fault is that, uncle?"

"And just what are these three plates for?" said Mustapha with annoyance.

"These three plates?" She looked at him, a malicious smile on her lips. "Nothing. Or rather, my three days. Nothing that would interest you. Is there anything here that interests you . . . uncle?"

As if moved by a common impulse, the three men stood up.

Noumbe deliberately knocked over one of the plates. "Oh, uncle, forgive me . . ." Then she broke the other two plates. Her eyes had gone red; suddenly a pain stabbed at her heart, she bent double, and as she fell to the floor gave a loud groan which roused the whole compound.

Some women came hurrying in. "What's the matter with her?"

"Nothing . . . only her heart. Look what she's done, the silly woman. One of these days her jealousy will suffocate her. I haven't been to see her—only two days, and she cries her eyes out. Give her some ash and she'll be all right," gabbled Mustapha, and went off.

"Now these hussies have got their associations, they think they're going to run the country," said one of his men.

"Have you heard that at Bamako they passed a resolution condemning polygamy?" added the other. "Heaven preserve us from having only one wife."

"They can go out to work then," pronounced Mustapha as he left the compound.

Aida and some of the women lifted Noumbe onto the bed. She was groaning. They got her to take some of her mixture of ash and water . . .

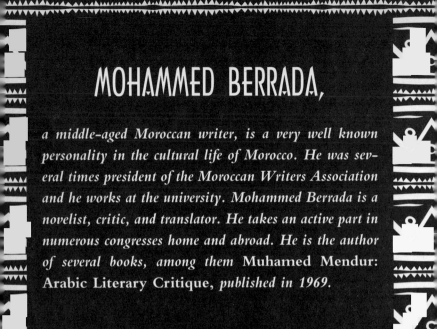

MOHAMMED BERRADA,

a middle-aged Moroccan writer, is a very well known personality in the cultural life of Morocco. He was several times president of the Moroccan Writers Association and he works at the university. Mohammed Berrada is a novelist, critic, and translator. He takes an active part in numerous congresses home and abroad. He is the author of several books, among them Muhamed Mendur: Arabic Literary Critique, published in 1969.

A LIFE IN DETAIL

MOHAMMED BERRADA

Translated by Alice Copple-Tošić

IT IS ALREADY QUITE LATE WHEN WE WAKE UP, WE stretch in bed, our body softens. This new day promises to be like the others preceding it. We rest the back of our neck on the head of the bed; our face has a troubled look. A bleak pallor spreads most indubitably over our face. We have already taken our case to the doctor, he nodded his head as he said, "You are not the only ones to experience this . . . All those who meditate and dream, all those who are dissatisfied, are familiar with these symptoms."

We remember that a doctor (perhaps it was this very same one) has already given this same answer to one of the friends of our friends when he complained of digestion troubles and acute gastritis.

"Is there a cure for it, Doctor?"

"I will prescribe some very effective pills, but above all, I advise optimism . . . The moment you awake in the morning, rummage through your memory in search of a funny story or an amusing event, and laugh heartily, then jump out of bed and put on whatever air comes to mind (even the most disagreeable voices are allowed)."

We decide to try out the doctor's advice and rummage through the recesses of our mind in search of a story that can make us laugh before breakfast . . . Ah . . . We have found one. It is the story of our neighbor, the foreign woman, who, although she has a car of her own, amuses herself from time to time and takes a taxi home. When she reaches the door of the building, she pretends to have forgotten her wallet at home and asks the taxi driver to wait for her while she goes to fetch the fare, then she disappears . . . and does not return. The poor man honks his horn at length, all the tenants of the building rush to their windows wondering who has brought on this situation . . . Not knowing the apartment of his passenger, the taxi driver loses hope and leaves while the hussy shakes with laughter in her room. Ha, ha, ha!!! We laugh until we cry and secretly thank our malicious neighbor, then we jump out of bed and into another new day of our summer holiday.

We linger for a long time in front of the crammed shelves of our library. Most of the books have not been read, we have always put off reading them until the appropriate moment appeared. Our hand reaches toward a volume with a red binding. The author, Mohammed Ben Abdallah Al Mouakit, lived in Marrakech forty years ago: his book is entitled *Alrihla Al Marrakchiya, Aw Mirat Al Massaoui Al Waqtiya (Sojourn in Marrakech or Mirror of Fleeting Misfortunes)* or there is *Esseif Al Massloul A la Al Muridh an Sunnat Ar-Rassoul (The Sword Hanging over the Head of Those Who Turn Away from the Traditions of the Prophet).*

". . . Then Sheikh Abdel Hadi continued: the examiner and the examinee lived in the tenth century, thus in our own epoch, as dark as the black night, whose leaders oppress their peoples, devour their flesh and drink their blood, gobble their bones and suck the marrow. They leave people neither the world nor religion; they have monopolized the world, and distorted religion. We have seen it with our own eyes and by no means imagined . . ."

Abou Zeid asked, "God help you, does he wish to live in this place in spite of his powerlessness in the face of injustice?"

Reading brings no relief, the past seems to be the present, the present seems past, reason roars at the impossible and refuses to admit that "the sun is blind." We think that the cause of all the pain could be boredom, friendships of many years, the exploration of the depths, shrinking illusions, fading dreams, an attachment to the future, lack of interest in what is established. Let us therefore exert patience; let us live the present in detail and daily routine.

Our guest at lunch is a close relative, he is pushing sixty. He learned the Koran when he was a small child, tried all different types of professions, then finally ended up as a muezzin.★ A widower who lost his wife a year ago, he chose a new fiancée from among his relatives (it is hardly fitting to be an unmarried muezzin) but preferred to postpone the marriage until he returned from his *hadj*.†

Schemers made moves during his absence, the woman found another husband and left him forsaken . . . He is still in search of a spouse . . .

"Thank God, everything is going well. We praise him at any rate. How is your health, work? All right, don't ever forget to pray for us. How is our young "El Azri," is he a conscientious worker? Ask him, he will tell you; as far as I am concerned, I don't think he works enough. You are wrong, my son . . . If you would only follow the example of your uncle "Abder-Rahmane.""

And since these words reawakened a sad memory in us, we asked, "The one who drowned?"

"Yes . . . the martyr . . . for according to the Hadith‡ those who are burned, drowned and buried alive are considered to be martyrs."

★ The crier who calls the faithful to prayer.
† Pilgrimage to Mecca.
‡ Traditions arising from the prophet Muhammad.

Now he addresses "El Azri" who does not seem to be much concerned since he is so used to hearing all forms of advice and instruction. "At the age of eighteen your uncle Abder-Rahmane already excelled in all the sciences."

The child interrupts him with a smile. "I'm only seventeen."

A delicate intervention proves necessary.

"Your head is as empty as a jackass's skull . . . You should listen to what you're told . . . the future is yours. You will be the one to lose out if you don't follow our advice . . . Do you think all you have to do is bend down to pick up your bread . . . You shouldn't think that the moon is made of green cheese."

El Hadj continued: "Abder-Rahmane—may his God keep his soul—excelled in all the sciences . . . his handwriting was one of the loveliest. He was employed in Dar el Makhzen, he already wore the caftan and turban when still quite young . . . He was a good swimmer, a dashing young man . . . A fakir from Sousse noticed him while visiting us, he was fascinated by his intelligence and the extent of his knowledge, particularly when he found out that he knew el Damiti by heart. He therefore wanted to protect him from the evil eye of humans and jinni, and transcribed an amulet that he asked him to pin to his caftan."

To show our pretended interest, we feel it worth remarking, "And he drowned in spite of this amulet?"

"It was destiny. Returning to Sale from Rabat, he crossed the Bouregreg wadi in a small boat. Once he reached the other side, he took off his turban, made the ritual ablutions, said the midday prayer and then left. After several dozen steps, he felt like taking a swim, so he retraced his steps, undressed and entered the water . . ."

As the first time, the child interrupts with a smile. "Did they swim naked in those days?"

The question seems reasonable to us, but the situation requires a different demeanor, we shoot him a glance, clap our hands and make superhuman efforts not to burst out laughing.

"No, they had loincloths . . . That day he had forgotten his amulet in another caftan, his swimming skill was of no avail, the sea swallowed him up forever. Thus died Abder-Rahmane and we, we lose ourselves in the science of our world and that of the hereafter."

The discussion wears out before the end of the meal. We observe the man chewing carefully. What other subject could we take up? We try to remember the stories and tales that he has recited to us countless times . . . It would suffice to mention just one of them and he would launch once more into relating these tales that we have heard so many times. We could say perhaps: the people of that time were quite right to acclaim their king and chant, "Glory and fortune to Moulay Abdelaziz." He would then recount the maneuvers and battles led by Sultan Moulay Abdelaziz against certain tribes and, threading his way through the story, would reach the era of Bouhmara and the arrival of the French . . . But this subject is very dull and we prefer to question him about his private life. What does he do after the call to prayer? He has stopped smoking "kif" since his return from Mecca, he has still not found a new wife, so how does he spend his time? Does he imagine he is dead? His relations with his surroundings seem very limited, he receives information, swears to keep it a secret and concludes by saying, "God puts to the test and chooses."

The child eats heartily, perhaps he is not thinking about anything? He is interested in his surroundings in a purely mechanical manner. He has tasted the pleasure of smoking in secret, of running after the neighbor girls, he is crazy about soccer . . . He expresses the desire to go to Europe during his summer vacation, even on foot (making the pilgrimage all the more meritorious). And us? We think of the sheikh and the child, we try to guess what could be on their minds. We ask ourselves about their relations with their environs, but afterward? The siesta. And then? Take a stroll and breathe in a bit of fresh air, what next? Telephone a friend, meet her, chat, get fired up, let our instincts break loose, then find boredom once more and take leave of each other. Join friends, talk about everything, criticize, approve, denounce, then see our enthusiasm decline before the magnitude of our powerlessness. We rush into the street once more. Feel desire mounting once again through the bouncing of the round and curved parts of women's bodies. We asked our married friends each time if their wives replaced all those of their sex? The answer was invariably: Not at all, no one desires other men's wives more than married men, even when they claim to love their spouses. We then tried to understand and rationalize these facts: there is not a single doubt that this is due to mingling, exciting advertising, makeup, high heels and . . . what else?

We were saying this to him but he interrupted severely: "Rubbish . . . With love we can overcome the obsession with sex."

"Then where is love?"

"Ah . . . . so you are one of these pessimists . . . I will tell you about my case (obviously the story is completely innocuous . . . They wanted to marry her to an old man, she threatened suicide, they swore to love each other until death . . . etc.).

Fine, he will never understand us, there is no use in citing Freud: "I am beginning to believe that there are four partners in every sexual act."

We exaggerate, the moment subdues us and imprisons us. Obsession with sex is not all that threatens us and fascinates us. There is also obsession with crime, with suicide, with alcohol and with revolution. The other forms of obsession are less attractive because they do not destroy routine. And writing?

He is quiet, does not offer any reply and starts to finger his chaplet. Abdel-basset says to him, "Master, we have always known you to be endowed with a quick flair to disarm the most brilliant orators and dazzle the best minds . . . You stimulate us morning and evening with your lectures that captivate the heart and refresh the soul . . . what is therefore the matter?"

In the evening, the same sluggishness overcomes us, but the melancholy is still too somber to chase it away, we think of administering this memorable medical prescription, but we hesitate, the doctor has indicated quite precisely that it is to be taken in the morning and not the evening . . . We are going to take a stroll through the streets, scrutinize the faces, perhaps it is there that we will discover the remedy. We walk for a long time: the cafés are full, bottles of beer are emptied in the blink of an eye, laughter rises, the tapping of the flippers is continuous . . . nonetheless, our melancholy is clinging. Cars pass, the buses are packed and slow, the movie theaters display posters of their heroes . . .

It seems to us that all those around us are fleeing, we are tempted to stop them and shout in their faces, "You are running away," but the idea seems idiotic and unfounded. We therefore wonder: Is there no way out? We return home to write down this life that we are living by well-rationed portions.

ALI DEB,

the Tunisian poet, was born in 1941. Apart from a collection of poems he published some studies, short stories, plays, and had a lot of broadcasts on the Tunisian radio. He works as a professor of a secondary school and is a member of the board of directors of the Tunisian Writers' Union.

THE THREE-PIECE SUIT

ALI DEB

Translated by Alice Copple-Tošić

THIS MONTH, FOR THE FIRST TIME, THE HOUSEHOLD BUD-
get has been met and . . . even left me a little supplement
. . . I don't know why, I went against my habits and bought
myself an elegant three-piece suit, tailored in a magnificent English fabric of lovely sky-blue—the color of sunlit days—in
which the tailor's skill was displayed so well that one would say
we were born together, one for the other . . . The buttons
sparkling in the sun were like stars on the shoulder of a sailor
swollen with courage. The spinning sensation that its price
aroused did not last long, and I said to myself as I straightened
my head and shoulders, "Tell me how you dress, and I'll say who
you are."

I made my way without hesitation toward the largest café on
the main street. As expected, my friends made a fuss over me,
touching, feeling and dusting me with their fingers. I strutted,
proud as a peacock, then I took out a package of paper handker-
chiefs and cigarettes and offered them to eager hands. "Usually I
don't smoke, but they are truly fine, what a pleasure!" exclaimed
one of them.

I murmured: "Ordinary cigarettes are infested with tar and
nicotine."

Naturally I paid for the drinks and left a fat tip for the waiter who gave me his best compliments. There was glib talk of the rise in prices and the high cost of living.

At this point one of them murmured into my ear, "What kind of shirt and tie are these?" Then he led me to a shop that was celebrated for the high quality of its merchandise and for its voraciousness. His good taste and affability were such that my pockets were emptied and it was only with great difficulty that I managed to pay the ticket home.

For one whole week, I concentrated on straightening out my accounts and forced myself to exactitude and strict austerity. I was thus obliged to forgo luxury and excess such as eggs and butter. I also reduced by half my consumption of meat and cigarettes and pretended to lack the time for entertainment with my friends. . . . I managed somehow or other to put my accounts back in order, while still not forgetting to trim my mustache, smooth my face with a close shave and spray myself with aftershave.

There I was, strolling about, puffed up with pride, on the main street, taking care to pass by the women's soaks since their tastes are more refined and assured and their eyes are sharper . . . I heard as though a murmur in my ear, "The flaw is in your shoes"? I turned and noticed a light blush on the face of a young girl. I counted the age of my shoes on my fingers. Goodness, how quickly the months had flown by. "Only a pair of shoes stands between me and perfection!" I chose a pair on Liberty Avenue, then returned to my friends. They directed their entire repertoire of flattering expressions my way and I was literally overcome by a delicious peace that was only troubled by the price of a cup of coffee. I almost proposed another spot in which to drink it but gave up, this café was better suited to my attire. My only recourse was a long but discreet sigh.

On the way home, the weather took a sudden turn and fine

little drops fell on my oh-so-proud nose. "Abominable sky," and I bought an umbrella that saved me, in spite of its poor quality.

On Barcelona Square, I was accosted by young beggars. Their sullen faces, extended hands and supplications surrounded me to the point of suffocation. There were three of them, I handed fifty millimes to each one and, rid of their harassment, I gave a sigh of relief, but their leader came after me, repeating, "You're worth much more," showing the coin to all the passersby. I bought his silence for double the amount . . .

I walked prudently, taking the sidewalk, avoiding the dust on cars and jostling pedestrians. I fled the crowd and buses and never forgot to polish my shoes and iron my shirts carefully, often using the fire to dry them faster. The January cold suddenly came to mind and I anticipated the need to buy a coat and change my suit when winter had passed. Should I hold out my hand for a loan or draw directly from the company's cash box? Finally, I got on the train. I breathed in the fetid breath of the passengers. I leaned on the armrest of a seat; a lady grumbled and said to her neighbor, "They're even contesting our second-class seats." So I slipped into the first class where a seat and a supplementary fee of some consequence awaited me. I went into the local supermarket. It had been quite some time since I had taken care of my shopping. Upon seeing me, a neighbor literally shrieked for joy, shook my hand and then, raising his flat voice, asked me for a loan that I would have naturally refused him if I had not been wearing my suit.

I bought several items and held them in my arms against my chest. The salesgirl greeted me and unhooked a suitable basket. I had no other alternative but to deposit my purchases inside, and since the proper sort of people, my sort, buy without consideration for the price, I did not even bother to look at the cash register total. When I had returned home, my blood pressure was at its peak, my head was literally boiling, my tongue was twisted and my chest heaving. I no longer saw where I walked or where I threw my jacket, vest and trousers. I clenched my teeth and gritted them as I cursed the traps of this century and the folly of fools. I finally went back to being my old self and since that day no one has troubled me anymore.

MOHAMMED MOULESSEHOUL

is an Algerian writer, imbued by the oral tradition and theater of his people.

The collection of six stories entitled **Houria** was published in 1984 with Entreprise Nationale du Livre, Algeria.

THE WICKED TONGUE

MOHAMMED MOULESSEHOUL

Translated by Christina Zorić

SHE RESEMBLED ALL THE WOMEN IN THE VILLAGE.

She had neither a third eye between her brows, nor four arms. Not beautiful and not ugly, men said she was all right. In the middle of a crowd, she attracted no more attention than the neighboring women. If you didn't know her, you would never doubt her.

She seemed modest and clean. Her physiognomy gave no hint of any dark secret and betrayed nothing spiteful. She sported an affable smile that put the timid at ease.

In the beginning, she was respected.

Women called her: "Sister Mimouna."

Children: "Auntie."

Men greeted her courteously when she passed their way.

She even served as a model of behavior in her day. Husbands never stopped holding her up as an example to their wives: "You disgrace your home, can't you behave decently, like your seida Mimouna? Why do you always have to drive me out of my mind? Oh God, why have you given me this unbearable creature for my lifelong companion, when all she knows how to do is vex and exasperate me? What intolerable thing have I done to be condemned to drag around such a woman, like a convict his ball and chain?"

Mimouna took meticulous care of herself. She washed every

day, wore clean dresses and could not bear the slightest stain on her veil. Her gestures, her words, her comportment, bespoke a great sense of measure, a sterling quality of reserve.

Women envied her.

Men envied her husband.

But all that was before.

Now, things had taken a different turn. Mimouna had become a different woman. People avoided her. They accorded her not even a passing glance. At the fountain, the women would move away when she approached, returning to fill their jugs only after she had departed.

Everywhere she encountered nothing but contempt and animosity.

At the *djemaa,* men fell silent when she passed by, averting their eyes. Some, unable to contain their disgust, railed against her.

"Scum!"

"If I were her, I'd go and hide my shame at the bottom of a grave."

"She'd poison the earth with her sins."

"Why don't they run her out of town? She'll finish by uprooting our trees, drying up our rivers, making our fields crack open, dispersing our neighbors and emptying our village. Our walls tremble with disgust when she touches them. Our most intrepid dogs flee from her. Even the sun in our sky is niggardly and seems to swerve widely to avoid our houses."

Mimouna hid her face behind her veil. Every word made her stumble, every sentence wrenched her heart. She fled, only to find the same hatred everywhere.

What had happened? What disgrace followed this woman?

Mimouna was the tenth child of a humble family numbering fifteen. Nine boys and six girls. The house, while not a palace, was spacious, and the food sufficient, despite the mediocrity of its quality. The father worked for a rich *kaid* who owned two hundred head of sheep and three fields of corn.

In Hassi Taha, the seasons quietly took their meandering course. Feast days were an event. Charlatans found nourishment among these small people until their next customers. Sometimes, a troubadour, surrounded by a flock of ragamuffin children, would break the monotony of the mornings, and except for the *kaid*'s occasional outbursts of rage, time passed like a slow Sunday stroll.

At the time, Mimouna was a young headstrong girl, as frisky as a gazelle. She played with girls her own age, went bathing with the most brazen and foraging with the most audacious. No one held it against her. She could also be useful. She went shopping for her mother, took care of others, collected wood for the fire, washed the dishes and, when her brothers were away, took meals to her father who worked in the distant fields.

After a few years, she succeeded, through her work and her conduct, to win over her closest neighbors.

"This little one would make a good wife for my son," some of the women murmured. Active and enterprising, wise and chaste, what else could one ask for?

Flattered, her mother smiled at the overtures made by her companions, saying: "Come, come now. She's still just a grasshopper."

Another woman would add: "My little cricket would be proud of her."

At fifteen, she was already being coveted by boys. She had only to cross her doorstep, and their eyes would be riveted on her. She was not very pretty, but her lissomeness and many other qualities were impressive. Her couscous and sweets were renowned. Moreover, she liked cleanliness and order.

Mothers homed in on her.

"Mimouna would be the joy of my house. She's an angel

and my son is a lion cub. Their union would be a blessing, and their children unrivaled."

"Mimouna is capable of taming a bull. Tayeb, my nephew, is a real devil. Wine and bad company are relentlessly dragging him to bottomless depths. Your daughter could put him back on the right track."

"Sister, your virgin deserves everything because she is capable of giving everything. Give her to me and I will be more than generous. It's a happy prospect for all of you. I know lots of families that would like to be in your place. I hope you realize, my dear, the place you could hold by joining the biggest and richest family in the region: the family of the *kaid,* Othman Ben Othman. Furthermore, my son is a handsome man. He has been educated like the Roumis. He comes from the city. He still reads books as thick as this, books which talk about things that neither you nor the imam could manage to understand. I will even go so far as to say that, with his charm and his eloquence, my son has captivated Michele, Captain Desmarnes's daughter."

Some were timid, with nothing more to offer than a piece of their heart.

Others were haughty and garrulous, promising a thousand moons for one night of lies.

They were easy to recognize. The former, with their baskets of sweets and their heads bowed. The latter, with their bright scarves, little slippers, gold bracelets running up their arms and, above all, their imperial way of sizing up the poor.

The mother knew only how to listen.

She consulted the father.

He stood stunned in front of the procession passing through his house. He retreated into a corner and meditated at length. He wanted happiness for his daughter and had to consider everything before taking any decision. He started by discarding the families that were too rich. He had served them all his life and knew only too well what went on behind their deceptive facades. He knew that these people were bad players: they placed too much on temporary life, the flash of gold making them forget the accounts being kept by eternity. With them, girls like Mimouna withered young and subsisted on contempt and leftovers.

He said finally: "My dear wife, we have a conscience so as to avoid the bad and seek the good. When it happens that we must choose, then we must reflect upon it. Marriage is a grave decision. It has the aftertaste of a verdict. To make a mistake would be a crime which would haunt us to our graves. If you are in agreement with me, this is what I'll tell the drunkards who see my daughter as their remedy: 'He who turns his back on the affairs of life cannot defend himself; to hide in the fog of oblivion is to risk losing one's way forever. Wine is a mirage of false promises; man can define himself only in reality. My daughter is not crazy to forgive sins or rectify wrongs. She is but a woman. And a woman is more fragile than a man . . .' I will reply to the *kaid*'s family: 'Let those who see their opulence as a magic wand know that the world can be bought, but love, never . . .' Our daughter is neither an object for sale nor a decorative piece of furniture. Boudjemaa is a simple man, a perfect Moslem. His gaze is clear and honest. He is not rich, but he is well off. His father is the imam, the renown of his faith graces every mosque. His mother is kindness itself; for her honesty has the magnitude of miracles . . . Stand up, my wife. Go see your daughter and speak to her of Boudjemaa. She will know how to understand you better than she would me."

The ululating shook the terrace.

The knife gleamed on the stone before slitting the throats of seven sheep.

The guests invaded the main house and its outbuildings.

The *ghaita* wailed and the drummers beat in rhythm.

When the bride appeared, decked out in her prettiest dress, cries of admiration rang out. Supported by her mother, who was crimson with pride, Mimouna walked slowly, her eyes lowered.

All the women sang:

> "Belle, belle is my gazelle
> With the light of day on her cheeks,
> The sparkle of the moon in each tooth.
> Belle, belle is my gazelle
> She is the jewel of all women
> And the mad dream of all men."

Outside, the men thronged around the dishes laden with couscous, grapes and pieces of meat. They ate, laughing. One song followed another, the crowd applauded until the palms of their hands were raw. The *berrah,* dressed with finesse and imagination, surpassed himself with taunts and scathing gibes at the expense of his audience.

On an esplanade, splendid horsemen performed a fantasia. They could be seen urging on their swift mounts in a cloud of dust, their burnooses flying in the wind of the race. The loud shot was answered by the powerful ululation of the women perched on the terraces.

Sid er-Jem did not flag. He deserved his praiseworthy nickname "The Wind." He blew into his immense *ghaita,* the way the storm blows on the islands. He moved his head to the beat, pretending not to notice the admiration of the listeners. Beads of sweat formed on his protruding forehead, his eyes bulged with the effort and his chubby face was afire, threatening to explode when his cheeks puffed up.

He was seated on two thick pillows, surrounded by his illustrious orchestra: two rawboned men, as mysterious as fakirs, one banging his *derbouka* with zeal, the other beating his drum with dignity. Enthroned slightly in front was the most celebrated singer in the entire Grand Rif, an immense plate overflowing with honey within reach. He had one hand on his ear and his neck painfully strained by the dissonant yelling which the people, in their exultation, interpreted otherwise.

Sometimes, unable to resist the temptation, Sid er-Jem whispered to him: "Can I have a drop of that honey that smells so good?"

And the singer would reply disdainfully: "What for? I think your saliva lubricates your monstrous sound box well enough."

"I just want to taste it. It smells so good!"

"But you, you don't sing. Come on now, you can't enjoy such a privilege. Honey is for preserving the voice . . ."

"Just a little drop."

"Out of the question. Blow your *ghaita,* Sid er-Jem, and spare my ears a language that is as boring as it is insipid. Don't you see that by your deplorable conduct you are mocking the pure soul of the artist, who is such a rarity in this day and age? Listen to your *ghaita* and you will hear it reproach you for such a lack of scruples."

Thereupon, the scowling singer, not without a certain deliberateness, sucked his fingers which were dripping with the "sacred" nectar.

The festivities intensified with nightfall. The young groom arrived on his dazzling white steed, escorted by some twenty close friends. He went straight in to the virgin. Outside, the singing and dancing were relentless. The noise died down for an instant. A gunshot! Everybody looked up . . . Ululation . . . The virgin had become a woman!

The celebration died down with the first light of dawn. The guests began going home. Mimouna's mother, her eyes puffy with fatigue, tried to smile at the congratulations. The father, ever arrogant, regretfully watched the rise of the sun and fall of his own reign. His sons lay sprawled out here and there, exhausted.

The band collected its instruments and prepared to move on to fresh glories. The singer deemed it necessary to have one last lick of the honey plate, smacked his lips and arranged his fez. Sid er-Jem, who twice had vomited into his *ghaita* because he had wolfed down too much, dipped his buzzing head in a basin of water, giving sound to uncontrollable "ahs."

Slowly the *haouch* was emptied of people and the father wished to lie down for a bit.

Thus passed Mimouna's marriage, in the utmost joy.

Mimouna started off her married life in happiness. Her husband pampered her. He was a traveling tradesman and never failed to bring her back a present from every trip. Harmony reigned in their home, and the neighbors tried to follow their example.

"Look at how they live, man. We're wrong to bicker, when they know how to savor every moment of life."

"Know, woman, that your bellowing penetrates the walls of our hut and know that behind these walls Boudjemaa and his wife are laughing and loving."

Mimouna cropped up in conversations all the time. She kept house like no other, was the pride of her family, and her reputation won tribute all around. And from the height of her pedestal, she raised and raised her head, losing it in the clouds. In the face of so much praise, she learned to despise first other women, and then her own circle.

"Mansourah," she told a neighbor, "is a real pest. She never stops bending our ears with her bragging. What on earth does her husband do, then?"

"Well! Her husband has no authority over her. He's ineffectual. She leads him around by the nose."

And Mimouna: "I hate men who make themselves their wives' slaves."

"Some women are terrible."

"Certainly not! There are no terrible women; there are only naive men. A slap in the face; what am I saying? A frown and the terrible tigress becomes a docile, loving cat."

The days rolled by, the weeks and the seasons, and Mimouna turned into a perfidious tongue. The ease and especially the efficacy of slander enthralled her. She thought that in it she had found the best way to preserve her superiority and pitilessly crush her rivals. She came to denigrate the whole world. Nothing found favor in her eyes. The woman watching a man pass by was soon drowned in Mimouna's venom. The woman who dared to oppose her or proved to be more beautiful or intelligent than she was finished.

The treacherous tongue without end, without borders, lashed, tore, smeared, bit, darted in every direction, like a ravaging tentacle. It sowed doubt in families. Men became suspicious, women fearful and distrustful. Neighbors avoided talking or lingering outside. They watched each other like clay dogs and pointed deadly fingers at one another. The bedouin smells were smothered under the stench of the plots. People began to drink too much coffee, eat too little, sleep badly, mistreat their children for no apparent reason. Everybody became increasingly short-tempered and a catastrophe would develop out of nothing.

Mimouna glowed, burning like a torch in a night of reprisals. She succeeded at each blow . . . In one month, four broken homes. First the *qadi*'s; Mimouna claimed to have surprised his wife with a stranger in the fields. Humiliated, the *qadi* did not seek to understand. He chased off his wife with a gun. Then Mimouna laid into the home of a peasant. The third woman barely escaped her husband's knife. And the fourth, a delightful creature whom everybody revered, threw herself down a well.

The village discarded its burnoose of respectability and confidence to don the black cape of infamy. Women cloistered themselves at home to avoid the possibility of scandal. But this was no protection against the viper's tongue.

Mimouna babbled, talked, lied. Without drawing a breath. She armed each word with a merciless poisoned barb. She wanted to be the only perfect woman around, the only unsullied woman . . .

The only one!

By besmirching everyone else. Even the men!

She went so far as to accuse a poor impotent old man of attempted rape: "I was filling my jugs when he came out from behind the Big Boulder. I thought he was thirsty and wanted to drink some water. I stepped aside. Without any warning, he pounced on me and tried to rip off my clothes . . . Thank God, I managed to slip through his grasp."

After this story, Boudjemaa saw red. He grabbed his gun and went in search of the old man. He found him in the fellow's orchard and, without asking for an explanation, fired a bullet straight at his head.

The old man's body was discovered and taken home. He was mourned for a long time. Women tore at their cheeks with their nails. Young men dispersed into the night, each to shed the tears of his sorrow in a corner where nobody would disturb him.

At sunrise, the body was moved to the mosque. The cortege accompanying Sid Ali was impressive. The deceased had spent all his life preaching the five pillars of Islam, loving his neighbors with a religious love. His tragic demise weighed heavily on many hearts.

"She's always the one to unveil the wrong, to have seen it all, heard it all," somebody in the crowd muttered. "She's always the one to discover what the rest of us haven't even noticed. First the *qadi*'s wife, who was said to be as pure as the luminescence of the mosque. Then the incredible blah-blah about the poor Badrah who, to escape opprobrium, threw herself down a well. And the peasant's wife, whose sole crime was that she was too beautiful for the taste of some. And all the others, all the others . . ."

"She's either an infallible seer or an unforgivable shrew."

"The latter name suits her like a caftan."

People talked about Mimouna.

Sid Ali was buried. In the heavy silence that precedes a storm.

"That will not be the end of it!" raged El-Haddi.

El-Haddi was Sid Ali's eldest son. He assembled all his close relations, his brothers, cousins and sons-in-law, in the deceased's house. He sat where the old man had sat when he was alive.

"I have gathered you here today to seek out the truth, the whole truth in all its stark nudity. And if this nudity is indecent, if it risks obsessing us till the end of our days, that's too bad. After all, it is the truth. And who can escape the truth?"

"You propose, we will approve, great brother."

El-Haddi rose and invited his people to follow him.

They headed straight for the mosque.

"My children, my children," cried the imam. "I understand and share your distress, but I will not tolerate fighting in our village."

"You see yourself that we're not carrying arms. All we ask is that you call a meeting of the Council of Elders."

An hour later, the entire Council of Elders was in the mosque.

After a brief speech, the Sherif, a high-spirited centenarian, turned the floor over to El-Haddi.

"In the name of Allah the clement and merciful . . . My

brothers, first let me start by apologizing for having taken you away from your work, but I am sure that anything to do with the community is close to your hearts. We have assembled in the house of God to learn the truth. Nothing but the truth. For some time now, our village has been living a veritable nightmare. Slander has come into currency. Many of our homes have disintegrated, many of our nearest and dearest have distanced themselves from us. I think the time has come to rediscover peace and harmony. We must now decide the fate of our village. Shall we let doubt and suspicion continue to consume us? Shall we continue to see future scandals in our wives, future orphans in our children? Let us start learning now, today, to confront matters with greater determination and conviction."

There was a rumble of approval.

El-Haddi added: "We shall summon the person who was at the origin of all these anomalies, all this ill feeling. And we shall leave it to the imam to enlighten us. He is not the wisest among you, or the fairest. He has simply promised me to take care of the matter."

Mimouna arrived, her husband and mother at her side.

"My daughter," declared the Sherif, "we are going to unravel an enigma. I ask you to be calm."

"I don't understand."

"Have a little patience. You will answer a few questions. It will be very simple."

He asked her mother and Boudjemaa to join the *djemaa,* then he sat Mimouna on a red carpet and blindfolded her.

The imam appeared, carrying a book. He placed it in front of the woman and whispered to her: "Touch . . . touch . . ."

Hesitant, Mimouna let a nervous hand fall on a thick cover, fingered the pages and fearfully withdrew her hand.

"What is it, my daughter?"

"It's . . . it's a book."

"Correct! It is a book, the sacred Koran."

Mimouna felt a chill in her heart. Her face suddenly became ugly and pallid. She started biting her lips.

"Relax, my daughter," whispered the imam. "You have nothing to fear of Allah if you are innocent. Allah punishes only the guilty."

"I don't understand, *sidi.*"

"It's simple enough. You will place your hand on the Koran and recite three times the *el-Baqara surah.* Then, you will say this: 'God Almighty, I aver before you that I have not slandered to doom the innocent to a shameful future, and if I have lied, make my body burn in this same mosque so that in my pyre everybody present here may see the fate that awaits sinful creatures.' "

Mimouna perspired.

She ventured: "And . . . and then?"

"Then, it will be for God to act. If you have told the truth, nothing will happen to you. But if you have not . . ."

"If I have not . . ."

The imam deemed it wise not to reveal anything.

Terrified, Mimouna tried to get up and run. But her legs refused to obey her. She seemed immobilized. Her teeth chattering, she began reciting the *el-Baqara surah.* Her face broke out in a cold sweat. Her ears quivered, her heart pounded, she felt faint. Gasping for breath, she faltered, and the verses became entangled before coming out in a stream of gibberish.

The silence terrified her.

Suddenly, she exploded. She tore off the blindfold, threw herself onto the carpet and screamed: "Mercy! I lied . . . I am cursed. Mercy!"

She was seized by a violent attack of hysterics.

El-Haddi rose and, pointing at the woman, said: "She lied. My father was innocent."

Then, addressing Boudjemaa, he said: "Do you understand, man? You unjustly killed an innocent man."

El-Haddi added: "This evening, after the *el-icha* prayer. At the very scene of your crime . . . I'll be waiting for you!"

Upon uttering these words he ordered his relatives and friends to follow him out.

Boudjemaa spent the day in his house where Mimouna would never step foot again. He prepared lunch himself for his two little ones. At dusk, he lay them down on the straw mattress, told them lovely legends about the Brave and the Good, about the Poor who become sultans for having dared to speak the truth, about Truth who was hated by a wicked queen named Lie, because Truth was more beautiful than she. He told them, too, the sad tale of the Innocents who invariably pay for those who are really guilty, and that of a gnome named Justice who always managed to vanquish a cyclops that was as big as a mountain and as strong as destiny, and whose name was Falsity . . .

The two children dropped off into a sleep full of dreams and light.

Boudjemaa prayed.

Then he took down his gun, kissed the little ones who smiled like angels, turned off the oil lamp and went out.

The night was clear and the air soft.

Boudjemaa knew that his weapon was not loaded. He walked knowingly toward a death he deemed to be just. He never even thought of defending himself.

On his way, he came across his wife. She was waiting for him under a cactus. She stood up. With his hand he signaled for her to stay where she was and passed by without stopping.

Mimouna slumped onto the ground, sobbing.

El-Haddi was already waiting for him in the orchard. Only his *gandura* rustled in the evening breeze.

Boudjemaa stopped and lifted his unloaded rifle to his shoulder.

Sid Ali's son did the same with his gun.

A shot roared out and bounced off the mountains before losing itself in infinity.

Not a cry arose.

Boudjemaa lowered his weapon. His chest was burning. Blood flowed from his mouth. He turned on his heels and moved away.

"Allah is the Greatest!" murmured El-Haddi.

His gaze vacant, his legs uncertain, Boudjemaa advanced unsteadily. In the distance a jackal imitated the world and its false dog silhouette was clearly outlined at the top of the rock.

Boudjemaa tried to quicken his step. He hoped to reach his house where his children were afraid of the dark. But his strength was fading quickly. Blood trickled from his wound. He felt no pain. He just seemed to be drowsy. He felt light, very light.

Mimouna rose to her feet upon seeing her husband return. He passed by without noticing her. She held her arms out to the distraught man who was about to die, but she dared not approach him.

Boudjemaa kept walking. Like a blind man. With only his instinct to guide him. He thought he recognized his house. His weapon slipped from his hand. He shivered; he was terribly cold.

Suddenly he fell, the full length of him . . .

Mimouna was rejected by everybody. No one wanted to hear of her anymore. Her children were taken over by their uncles. She lived among the rocks, like a ghost, covered in rags and shame. And the kids learned to pelt her with pebbles, to chase her across the gorge, shouting: "Mimouna, *settoute!* Mimouna, you insult! Mimouna, *settoute!"*

She fled aimlessly from her pain, her body hurting, her head bleeding. In her solitude, she roamed grumbling incomprehensibly, occasionally stooping to pick a herb or an edible root.

I. N. C. ANIEBO

was born in 1939 in Nigeria. He joined the Nigerian Army in 1959 and during the civil war he fought on the Biafran side and was discharged from the Nigerian Army in 1971. He then went to the University of California and read English and History. At present I. N. C. Aniebo is a lecturer in the University of Port Harcourt, Nigeria.

I. N. C. Aniebo published the novel **The Anonymity of Sacrifice** *in 1974 and* **The Journey Within** *in 1978. His collection of twenty-two short stories, entitled* **Of Wives, Talismans and the Dead,** *appeared in 1983.*

FOUR DIMENSIONS

I. N. C. ANIEBO

"HACK HER TO PIECES! SHE MUST NOT BE BORN AGAIN," cried the Third Priest in a rasping voice.

"Throw her pieces to the four winds. Let them be blown to the ends of the earth so that even her *chi* cannot find them," the Second Priest intoned.

"Who are we that we should sit in final judgment over her?" asked the First Priest, shaking his white head sorrowfully.

"We are the appointed judges of Ajala, our great Mother Earth. This woman sinned against *her* and should not be returned to her," answered the Second Priest contemptuously.

"We were appointed to judge mortals not spirits," countered the First Priest. "Therefore let us be merciful. The woman has sinned, it is true, but her sins have been washed away by her death." His mellow, slow voice calmed the acolytes whose hysterical chanting now became a low dirge.

"You are the First, the anointed head," said the Third Priest. "But let my dissension be recorded. Not all sins can be washed away by death alone, else there would be no evil or tormented spirits and all mortals dying would automatically be washed pure and reborn. But the spirit of sinners must sojourn in Hades, to be tormented and to wander around for some time with hopes of being born again. One of the greatest punishments that can be meted out to a mortal or spirit is to be left wandering without hope. This woman's sin cannot be washed away by death, not even by letting her spirit wander for some time. It is better she be cut to pieces so that she can never be born again and her spirit will wander endlessly."

"So let it be, O First," chanted the Second Priest.

"No! It shall not be. Let it not be said we stretched our mortal hand into a world we know nothing of. Let the spirits judge the spirits and the mortals, mortals. Therefore, let the spirit of the dead woman wander for a while and not endlessly. We will bury her with the honors befitting a noble woman, with chalk and camwood markings on her face and body; with a root of the Iroko and spittle of the tortoise mixed into a potion to anoint her belly and her *okike* stringed across the top of the two tallest palm trees in the village and not untied till it has either been shot down or eight days have elapsed; with the mat woven from the *ute* that grows on the banks of the sacred stream. I, the First, have passed judgment. We will now wait for Mother Ajala to declare her wishes."

There was a hushed silence. Even the acolytes with their heavily chalked faces and foam-specked mouths controlled their moaning.

Presently the rays of the full moon cut through the foliage of the giant age-old trees surrounding Ajala's shrine and fell on the circular sacrificial stone on which lay the naked body of the dead young woman. Ranged round her were the three squatting priests who waited, their closely shaven heads bent, to learn the wishes of their goddess, but their minds could not concentrate on the same thing for a very long time. And as time rolled inexorably by, lengthened by the silence of the surrounding forest, their thoughts veered away to . . .

She had walked into his house that afternoon two years ago, her three multicolored beads sitting so becomingly on her slim, dark waist. On her beautiful lips was the smile he knew so well, the teasing smile that could set the muddy blood of an old man on fire. Without touching her breasts, he knew her nipples were hard because of the way they stood out, and round them, as always, were two concentric circles of *uli*.

"Okwomma," she greeted him.

"My child," he answered, controlling, with difficulty, the trembling of the lips and hands that often assailed him in her presence.

She sat down on the opposite *ngidi* (mud bed), not the way women always sat with legs stretched out together in front of them, but in her own exciting way—legs drawn up and hands hugging her knees as if she were cold.

"I just thought I should come by and greet you, Third Priest," she said in her low, husky voice, her eyes modestly lowered.

"You did well, my child. Had your beloved father been alive, he would have approved. But why didn't you go to the Afo Ezinma today?"

"I had nothing to sell, Third Priest. And besides, Mother and the other wives were going, so I decided to stay at home to look after the children and cook dinner."

He grunted and brought out his old black clay pipe and leaf tobacco from his soot-covered raffia bag which had been handed down to him from his grandfather. With superfluous concentration, he began to fill his pipe. He had often discovered that a smoke quieted his blood, and took his mind away from mundane thoughts, particularly the one that bothered him at that moment.

The sound of children playing in the heat haze of the afternoon, the bark of lean, dirty dogs, the occasional squawks of frightened chickens taking cover from the sharp claws of a diving hawk and the bleating of goats emphasized the absence of all the able-bodied men and women in the village who had gone to the Afo market in Ezinma, five miles away.

His pipe lighted, he leaned back on the red mud wall and sucked a grateful lungful. "Don't you like my staying at home?" asked Maruma.

"Why do you ask, child?"

"Because you grunted after I explained why I stayed."

"I was filling my pipe."

"You hadn't brought out your pipe then." She had dropped the formal manner of addressing the priests of Ajala, and her legs were now curled up under her.

"No, my child," said the Third Priest slowly. "I don't dislike your staying home. In fact, I like it."

"I knew you would, Third Priest."

As if caught unawares, he puffed away nervously at his dying pipe. He had been staring at her for some time, figuring what *it* would be like. Now he bent forward and rearranged the smoldering wood of the fire between them. Deftly, he picked up a glowing charcoal with his fingers and put it into the bowl of his pipe. He drew hard at the pipe, his large Adam's apple moving rhythmically up and down, and now and again he pressed the charcoal in with his index finger. Before long, he was enveloped in pungent smoke.

"I don't like the smell of your tobacco."

"Why, child? It smells good to me."

"Don't call me a child. I'm a full-grown woman."

He removed his pipe and stared at her. Her long slim legs were now stretched out in front of her, thus exposing her wide hips, flat belly and large bosom, and on her lips played that smile —innocent, teasing and inviting, all at the same time.

"Yes, you're right," he said slowly. "I'm sorry . . ."

"It's all right," she hastily assured him. She had begun to

feel uneasy and afraid she might not be able to control the emotion she was stirring up. Those looks of his were not the looks of a priest, and she had felt his eyes mauling her. "It's all right, Third Priest," she said, recalling that he was, at a mere thirty-five, the youngest of the three and had become a priest by inheritance, and not by personal achievement or remarkable holiness.

She stood up, tall and straight, luscious and desirable, a woman at eighteen, conscious and proud of her bloom.

"I'm going to prepare lunch for the children." The flesh was strong, but the will weak.

He, too, was standing.

Without looking, she could see the cloth *ugbolo* tied between his legs in the form of pants, striving and straining to contain the stirring of life down there. She could also feel, without touching, the heat radiating from his hard-packed, bare body, and the fire between them accentuating it. She swallowed hard in an effort to clear the impending clogging of her throat, and her other self wondered why she felt as she did, why she had become hypersensitive to every nuance in the environment. She had been in this situation with him before and had come out of it unscathed, having enjoyed every minute of it, but . . .

"Maruma, look at me." It was the first time ever he had called her by name.

Their eyes met, and she thought she saw lightning flashes crisscrossing between them.

He thought the same too, or willed it, and in one bound, he was by her side and the next carried her into his bedroom. Her cry rent the air as he threw her onto the bamboo bed. He tore at his *ugbolo* with feverish, erratic fingers—but he couldn't undo it!

Her next cry cut across his befogged brain like a whiplash. She had called on the protection of Ajala and she must, therefore, remain inviolate or he would be damned. He wrung his hands in fury, cursing silently the day he was born and his inherent fear of this goddess whom he served and was bonded to serve to the end. With glazed eyes, he watched her get off the bed and walk through the low door to freedom. His bird had flown again, after having walked into his den. Cursed be her *chi!*

And as Maruma stepped into the hot sun she began to shiver as one suffering from the ague.

His son had rushed into the hut that evening holding his stomach, and through his fingers he could see red seeping through, leaving a well-emblazoned trail. His heart sank when he knew instinctively what it was.

"Nwobi, what happened? Who did that to you? Tell me, tell me!"

The boy collapsed on the *ngidi* moaning, his handsome face a picture of pain and wonder. "Maruma, Maruma stabbed me, stabbed me in the stomach." He fainted.

Maruma, that she-devil, thought the Second Priest as he dressed his son's wound. Thanks to Ajala, it was not a very deep one, but still an ugly sight. Nwobi must have jumped back as she struck since his flesh had a "torn" look.

"Oh, Ajala, what shall we do to this vixen before she destroys all our young men?"

With his knowledge of the herbs, the Second Priest brought his son back to the land of the living in four days—one Ibo week —and during that period he often wished he were not Ajala's priest so that he could take vengeance on Maruma, though she was the Chief's daughter and, like everyone in the village, Ajala's child.

The shepherd could not scatter his flock; if he did, he would be many more times damned!

And what was more, no one should ever know that his son had been worsted in a fight with a girl!

It took another three days before the Second Priest could get his son to tell him how it had all happened. Had the boy's mother been alive, he would have known sooner, but then her death had made it possible for him to prepare for the priesthood.

Nwobi had recounted the events in his singsong high tone.

Three days before the incident, Maruma had asked him to escort her to the farm to pull up some cassava tubers. He had accepted with alacrity, for even though he was three years older, she could twist him round her finger. So much did he love her!

The day was hovering between the end of the afternoon and the beginning of the evening when they set out to the cassava farms two miles away. Maruma led, in her loping gait, her body swaying and undulating in a way all her own, and her graceful long neck straight, carrying the head on which balanced an elongated rectangular basket.

"Why do you have to get this cassava tonight?" Nwobi had asked diffidently.

"Because I couldn't do it earlier, and besides we're having many guests on *Nkwo* day."

"What of your other sisters? Surely, they could have escorted you."

"How can the blind lead the blind? They're afraid of the dark as much as I. But with you here . . ."

Pulling up the cassava tubers was easy as they had been planted on slightly sandy soil and soon their basket was full.

In a nearby stream, they washed and chopped the cassava into six-inch lengths and immersed them in a big pot full of water berthed at the edge. By the time they finished they were hot and dirty.

"Let's have a dip before we go," suggested Maruma. They waded to the bathing area downstream. "Do you know that my pots of cassava ferment faster than all those here? Mine take only two days while the others take from three onward."

"It seems you have the devil heating the bottom of your pots."

"Maybe. Father says the devil loves beautiful women!"

They did not dally at the stream, but it became completely dark before they were halfway home.

"Nwobi, may I hold your hand? I can't see well in the dark." In this way they proceeded another hundred yards. "Why don't we wait till the moon comes up?"

"What will your mother say when we come home very late?"

"I'm too old to be lost or kidnapped!"

She put down the basket and he the little hoe and matchet and they sat close together by the edge of the path. As time passed, she leaned on him more and more, her arms encircling his waist. Once, perhaps to kill an ant, she slapped her right thigh hard and while replacing her hand round his waist, she touched the stirring life. She did not seem shocked but rather fascinated by it, for pushing aside his *ugbolo,* his only article of clothing, she touched it many more times, wonderingly, like a child given a new toy. Sometimes she enclosed it softly in her palm, feeling the urgency, the tautness and the throb of life.

And oh, how hard he tried to get into her! But when he seemed to succeed, she would cry out in pain, withdrawing as if he were a leper, and so he contented himself with touching until his dam burst . . .

He did not see her, even though he constantly patrolled the approaches to her home throughout the next day, till the day of the incident. He had been looking for the holes dug by the *ewi* (big rat) when on parting a shrub . . . she was a few feet away, her back toward him. She was trying to break a small coil of brass bangle and was so engrossed in it—he could see the straining muscles of her back—she did not hear him approach.

He did not disturb her, else she might break the perfect

picture she created with the setting sun flooding her naked back with golden tears, and making her beads glint.

She must have succeeded, and with legs placed wide apart, she bent down and began digging up the earth with the broken bangle.

He could stand by no longer, and was soon trying to thrust himself into her, but she was swifter. With a little cry, she swiveled round and . . . the pain . . . the pain and the blood . . .

"The she-devil!" muttered the Second Priest, his lined face a picture of hatred and anger.

"No, Father, she isn't! She is an *angel*. It was my fault . . ."

That was eight years ago, and Nwobi was fifteen then.

The news had spread like an epidemic.

The First Priest was sick, sick unto death. Not even his fellow priests, nor the doctors, could tell what was wrong with him, except that the symptoms were high fever, coughing and lack of appetite. There was no close relative to nurse him, either. He had taken to the priesthood at a very young age, and did not marry, even though he was the only surviving male child of his household. Many times, people had advised him to leave the priesthood and get married but he had refused.

"I was called by Ajala to serve her!" he always answered. "Perhaps if I'm devoted to her, completely and without guile, I may be able to expiate the sins of my family and stop the curse on them spreading to their daughters and their children."

But now it seemed his services to Ajala were coming to an end.

"Ovuegbe," greeted Maruma one afternoon.

"My child," said the First Priest in a barely audible whisper. He was lying on his back and looked very emaciated; one could almost smell death in his smoke-filled room.

"I've come to nurse you back to health."

He managed a thin, wry smile, "My child . . . you talk as if you're Ajala herself. Those who can have tried and failed. I'm resigned to death. Already I can hear the knocking on the wall."

She sat down on the edge of the *ngidi*. "Please don't say that." She brushed away the tears that filled her eyes. "I can't let you die. You're the only person I've got since Father died."

The priest's long silence frightened Maruma. She was about to panic, when he started one of his coughing spasms that often left him exhausted and breathless. After he recovered he said: "Don't bother, my child. Your intention is noble. But it's too late."

"Even if it is, please promise you won't give up hope of being well again. Just promise me that and I'll be satisfied."

His reply took a long time in coming and when it did, she had to bend forward to hear. "Nobody likes to die, my child," and he fell into a coma.

She immediately set to work cleaning the house. She washed the cooking pots and clay plates, swept the compound that was beginning to resemble the abode of a dead man, littered with fallen leaves and refuse of many days. The firewood and water would last her for that day.

From the moment she had entered the First Priest's house, Maruma felt she knew what was really wrong with him, because her father had suffered the same illness at regular intervals, and had allowed only her to prepare his medicine. After restoking the fire in the room where he lay, thus eliminating most of the smoke, she went out in search of herbs. With the optimism of youth, she cut several handfuls of lemon grass, leaves of lime including a few branches, dug up the yellow roots of *nkpologwu* and picked the kidney-shaped leaves of the *ejeje* shrub. Reaching home, she kindled a fire in the kitchen, and began to boil all that she had collected in a huge wide-mouthed pot. Next, she peeled yams with which to prepare a hot palm oil broth, and as it was getting dark, lit a palm-husk candle.

The First Priest had come out of his coma by the time she finished brewing the medicine and the broth.

"How do you feel, First Priest?" she asked, sitting down on the edge of his bed.

He did not answer but moved his head slowly from side to side.

"Will you be able to stand up?"

Again he moved his head.

Maruma went back to the kitchen and brought out the steaming pot of medicine, placing it as close as possible to the edge of the sick man's bed. She had decided to treat him where he was. From the wooden box on the alcove, she took out a thick cloth that looked like a bedspread. Gently she helped the First Priest to sit up in such a way that the pot of medicine was between his legs and then she covered him and the pot with the cloth. She removed the cloth a few minutes later when the First Priest started gasping for air, and noted with satisfaction his sweat-covered body. She rubbed him down with lukewarm water, fed him some spoonfuls of the broth she had prepared and put him to bed, covering him with every available mat and cloth. For the first time since his illness the First Priest slept through the night like one drugged.

Maruma continued her treatment for another two days making sure, however, that the First Priest drank a potion of the medicine, after she had rubbed him down.

On the morning of the third day, he woke up earlier than she. When she heard her name called in a sonorous voice that reminded her of the echoes of the mother of drums, Maruma was startled. Slowly she sat up, her face a mixture of happiness and relief.

"So you haven't gone yet?" the First Priest asked. She shook her head. She was unable to speak.

"How long have you been here?"

"Three days," her lips formed the words.

"What of your mother? Didn't she look for you? Oh, never mind. But why do you bother yourself with an old man like me?"

And she began to cry, all her pent-up feelings of relief, happiness, irritation and fatigue finding expression at last in a welter of tears.

Six months later, Maruma's husband of one month, Nwaobi, died suddenly after a few hours' illness. The rumor was that she poisoned him, but none could prove it. When, however, she went mad a few weeks afterward, the Second and Third Priests said Ajala had punished her for killing her husband. She was immediately ostracized and a hut was built for her at the edge of the bad bush. She lingered on in her madness and at the age of twenty fell off a coconut tree and died.

"I have heard the voice of Ajala," chanted the Third Priest.

In a dreadful crescendo, the acolytes burst into their wild song of the judgment; a song that could be heard miles away, and that warned the villagers of the presence of the great goddess in her shrine.

"I too have heard her command!" The Second Priest could not suppress his joy; at last, at last . . .

"Speak, Third Priest." There was deep sorrow in the First Priest's voice as he added, "And may the goddess hold you to ransom if you speak with a false tongue."

"You cannot scare me, First Priest. I heard the voice of our Mother loud and clear and her message is unmistakable. She said, 'Tell my First Priest I am displeased with his judgment for he has let himself be swayed by sentiments. It is true, this dead daughter of mine saved his life, but then a woman has more than one nature. It is the sum total of her natures that determines whether she is good or bad, and to know her natures you have to see her in four dimensions. I have thus listened to the four winds from the four directions; the winds that saw all her movements during her lifetime and I hereby pass judgment. My dead daughter was a bad woman! I therefore command that she be thrown into the bad bush, and a black goat sacrificed to cleanse the people who will take her there. I also command that on pain of death, none of my children now and in generations to come be given her name nor told of her.' Thus did Ajala command, First Priest."

"You have heard rightly, Third Priest. For I, too, heard the same. May you now seal the judgment, First Priest."

"So be it then, even though I do not think our merciful Mother would have passed such judgment on a poor girl who suffered greatly. Third Priest, heat the seal of judgment."

The Third Priest gathered dry leaves and a few sticks and soon made a fire in the stone hearth twenty yards from the sacrificial stone. The youngest acolyte, there were thirteen of them, handed him the brass seal of judgment, shaped in the form of *infinity* with a wooden handle attached to the center, which he heated until it was hot to the touch. He was about to pick it up when he heard a rumbling noise from above. He straightened up, peering into the thick canopy of leaves but he could detect nothing.

Meanwhile, the chanting had ceased, and there was a hush and a chill in the air, and the moon seemed to have lost much of its cold luster.

The rumbling noise increased in volume, and the First Priest, his voice sounding like a god's, asked, "What is delaying you, Third Priest? Shall we not seal the judgment you said Ajala passed through you?"

But the Third Priest seemed not to hear. He was intent on the commotion that seemed to be coming from the very heavens. He stood there petrified, his feet bound to the earth with cords of iron.

Then with a roar and a crash, a huge dead tree fell on him, crushing him into the earth.

". . . and may the goddess hold you to ransom if you speak with a false tongue."

DAMBUDZO MARECHERA

(1955–87) was born and educated in Rhodesia, now Zimbabwe. He was expelled from the Rhodesian university and awarded an Oxford scholarship.

A collection of short stories, **The House of Hunger,** *appeared in 1978 with Heinemann Educational Books, England, and in 1980 it was printed in Zimbabwe, too, upon its independence. The book was warmly acclaimed by critics and readers and was awarded the fiction prize of the newspaper* **Guardian** *in 1979. His second book,* **Black Sunlight,** *appeared in 1980, and* **Mindblast** *in 1984.*

Posthumously Marechera's texts were collected and a trust for printing his unpublished work (six novels, five plays, over a hundred poems, and several essays and reviews) was founded. The first volume, **The Black Insider,** *appeared in 1990.*

THOUGHT TRACKS IN THE SNOW

DAMBUDZO MARECHERA

THE SKIES HAD BEEN OVERCAST. MY AFFAIRS WERE GOING badly and I was as gloomy as the great gray clouds that hid the sun from view. I had been ill, a fever, and had had to put up with medicines and a great deal of curious attention from my landlady who had taken the position that my writing was certainly not doing me any good. It snowed heavily that Sunday night and I watched the thick white doves' feathers of it come sailing down and pile up everywhere. I could not sleep. A restless refrain was repeatedly flashing through my mind: "You're crazy, you're crazy, you're crazy." And great armfuls of it were snowing down onto the roofs, onto the roads, onto the pavements, snowing down into everything: "You're crazy, you're crazy, you're crazy."

The week before, I had finished typing out my novel and had sent it off and had thought that I would be free of it. But the thing was oppressing me and I was making the postman nervous and making myself ill all over. I had then pulled myself up sharply and started again, giving lessons to a pimply youth who was certainly not interested in the course he had signed up with me. He came from Nigeria, he said, and what did I think about the Rhodesian crisis and about white girls? And anytime I so much as hinted that we were supposed to be paying attention to his unwritten essay on William Blake he would shake his head in such a way that I felt quite uncomfortable. My sessions with him always turned out to be alcoholic bouts because he brought with him not the essays he ought to have done but bottles of spirit which invariably made us quite jolly and talkative about anything under the sun—as long as it was not anything to do with English literature. He had, he said, read my stories and found them quite indigestible. Why did I not write in my own language? he asked. Was I perhaps one of those Africans who despised their own roots? Shouldn't I be writing within our great tradition of oral literature rather than turning out pseudo-Kafka–Dostoyevsky stories? What did I do with myself when I was not working—did I have a girl? Did I know that I was a shit? No, he said, I did not quite mean that—I meant shit in its good earthy sense.

And outside, the wet snow piled up softly like things which a man has chosen to forget, things sailing down the sky and quietly gathering up inch by inch to bury me. I felt so hot I was unbearably cold. I felt so cold I could not stand the heat of it.

It seemed the teargas fumes were still choking me; the police dogs still biting chunks out of terrified students; the stones still crunching into fat white faces; and from every side the howling of sirens, the grinding run of boots, the upraised truncheon—in the instant before the jarring of bone beneath polished hardwood—arrested by the camera shutter opening and shutting. Thick smoke erupting over the rugby and cricket fields suddenly covered everything; when it cleared armed policemen and soldiers had herded the students onto the old cricket pitch and a long line of wire-meshed vans was taking groups of students to the emergency detention centers. A group of white students were cheering the police and jeering the prisoners; a Rhodesia Television cameraman was carefully recording everything. The huge Alsatians were licking their massive jaws at the long line of prisoners . . .

Thought tracks in the snow—shit!

As the plane burred into the night, leaving the Angolan coast and heading out into the void above the Atlantic, I suddenly remembered that I had, in the rude hurry of it all, left my spectacles behind. I was coming to England literally blind. The blurred shape of the other passengers was grimly glued to the screen where Clint Eastwood was once again shooting the shit out of his troubles. I was on my own, sipping a whiskey, and my head was roaring with a strange emptiness. What was it really that I had left behind me? My youth was a headache burring with the engines of a great hunger that was eating up the huge chunks of empty air. I think I knew then that before me were years of desperate loneliness, and the whiskey would be followed by other whiskeys, other self-destructive poisons; I had nothing but books inside my head, and they were burning me, burring with the engines of hope and illusion into the endless expanse of air. Who was I leaving behind? My own prematurely gray head still sat stubbornly upon my shoulders; my family did not know where I was or whether I was alive or dead. I do not think they would have cared one way or the other had they known that at that moment I was thousands of feet above the earth, hanging as it were in the emptiness which my dabbling with politics had created for me. I felt sick with everything, sick with the self-pity, sick with the Rhodesian crisis, sick!—and the whiskey was followed by other whiskeys and my old young man's face stared back at me from the little window. Would Oxford University be any different—was I so sure of myself then? Dawn broke as we flew over Biscayne Bay; and the fresh white dove's down of breast clouds looked from above like another revelation that would turn out, when eaten, to be stone rather than bread.

"I meant shit in its good earthy sense," the Nigerian repeated.

On the little table between us was the forgotten text of William Blake's *Songs of Innocence and Songs of Experience*.

A sudden knocking saved me from making any reply. I looked at my watch and knew immediately who it was who had come. When she came in and curled herself up on the rug by the fire and muttered something shocking about the weather, I could see the silent accusation in the Nigerian's eye, an accusation that suddenly turned into a challenge. I could see it was going to be one of those days again. My head was burring again with impotent anger, a sickening desperation which for once I dared to crash.

"It's time for my next lesson, so you must excuse me," I said breathlessly.

All my life I had never been able to control my breathing.

The Nigerian looked up sharply. He decided to let things go; and got up and left without another word. Rachel was staring into the fire; the way her shoulders were shaking I knew she had resolved to do something drastic.

"You finished it?"

Her voice was coiled round the steel wire of a taut self-control.

"Yes, I've sent it off to the publishers."

She had not turned round. My glass was unsteady in my hand.

"Aren't you going to say hello to me?"

I had not expected this.

I got up and put my hands on her shoulders but she twisted round suddenly and slapped me hard on my cheek. Good heavens—what was it that had happened to her face? I stood there, with my old man's gray head, and knew that I would always be slightly ridiculous.

She had turned back to the fire. Her shoulders—those small frail shoulders!—still shook. I sat down and refilled my glass and remembered quite bitterly the Nigerian's taunts. It was a poisonous comedy the two of them expected me to play.

"Don't you care I've been seeing him? Sleeping with him?" she asked suddenly.

But I was prepared. Though I knew the wound would hurt badly after she left, I was at that moment prepared for the knife thrust. Did she then really think so little of me?

"Rachel, it's your body, not mine, and you can do what you like with it," I said.

"You know what you are—a nigger jackass," she said.

"You don't have to remind me, Rachel," I said.

"A hypocrite."

I felt weak with the heady buzzing inside my head; teargas canisters were exploding around my leaping feet. I hurled a paving stone at an advancing policeman—

My glass had toppled over, spilling my spirit onto the floor.

"I just don't know why I married you," she said.

We had been married for two years but had slept together only for the first five days.

"Perhaps if we had had a child . . ." I hazarded.

She swung round, but the fire was still burning in her eyes. This is it, I thought.

"I am with child," she said softly.

She always lowered her voice when she delivered what she thought was a deadly sword thrust.

"And it's his child," she added.

I refilled my glass; emptied it; refilled it again.

"That Nigerian boy?"

"He isn't a boy," she said. "He's a man, a real man. Not an impotent bastard like you."

"I'd rather you left my mother out of this," I said, "but if you must drag her in, by all means do."

"I want a divorce."

"By all means get one, Rachel. I told you seventeen months ago that . . ."

"You really think you're superior to everybody, don't you?"

"Now, Rachel, you know that's not true."

"Don't Rachel me!"

Her screamed words struck the ceiling and bounced back onto the bookshelves.

I cleared my throat.

"You never really loved me," she said.

The note of self-pity in her voice—I recognized it in that far-off Rachel with whom I had tramped around North Wales and been immeasurably happy for five short days.

I nodded toward the decanter. And she silently, thoughtfully, made a drink for herself.

"Damn it, Charles, why—why?"

She was chewing her lower lip. And then, abruptly, she sat down on the arm of my chair.

"Why?" she repeated.

I said nothing. She was deliberately impulsive—playfully almost—when she chose to be.

"How long have you known?" she asked.

"Long enough not to hurt anymore," I said. The door was opening slowly.

I leaned forward to refill my glass and she circled my shoulders with her arm and with the other turned my face toward hers and kissed me. The door swung wide open and the Nigerian stormed into the room, cursing: "You bitch! You bloody bitch!"

"Charles!"

"Fucking white bitch!"

"Charles, don't just sit there—he's hurting me—your wife!"

I tried to duck but the truncheon struck the side of my head.

"Charles! I'm your wife!"

She was down there on the floor being mauled by an Alsatian. Another canister exploded on the wall behind me. Thick white choking gas engulfed me. I held down my breath and lunged at the uniformed figure. Somewhere in the background, my landlady was hovering about with a rolling pin.

I grappled with the Nigerian. He was still cursing: "Fucking Rhodesians—get independence first, then perhaps you'll learn how to fight!"

He was hurting me badly. I could feel the blood rushing out through my nose. Rachel was somewhere on the floor near the shattered glass case. The landlady cautiously crept up behind him and smashed the rolling pin on his great head. He slumped to the floor, out cold. I was trying to wipe the blood from my face and at the same time trying to congratulate the landlady on her timely appearance when a blinding flash of pain hurled me to the floor. When I regained my senses, the landlady was slapping my face and Rachel was coming in with a dish of steaming water and a towel. The Nigerian was nowhere in sight.

The landlady reached out for the towel, but Rachel said: "You've done quite enough as it is. You could have killed my husband, you know."

The landlady sighed like one who is used to being ill used: "It's my glasses. I couldn't see which one was the Nigerian and which one was him, you know. And I thought I may as well knock them both down, because I didn't know who it was I knocked down first. You know," said the landlady as she peered down at me.

My lips had stretched out in a tight smile; I was trying not to laugh.

The landlady picked up the dangerous rolling pin and said: "These are very handy, you know. When my husband came home drunk the other day . . ."

"That will be all, Mrs. Sutcliffe-Smith," Rachel said firmly.

The landlady winced; and strode out with great dignity.

Rachel stared down at me and—for the first time since those distant five days looked much older, I mean not much older, than the eighteen-year-old she was.

"It's still not late for an abortion," she said.

She wrung out the towel and wiped the blood streaming out of my nose.

"Did you hear what I said?"

"I'm having dinner with Michael—you remember him, don't you, from when you were training as a nurse?"

"The one with the stammer?"

I nodded.

I corrected myself: "We're having dinner with him tonight. He's the best doctor in Oxford. We'll mention it casually to him.

"Rachel," I added, "welcome home."

Thick white doves' feathers snowed down from the overcast skies. Would my novel be accepted? Would Rachel soon tire of me once again? I was still rather weak; but I knew that deep inside me I had said good-bye to Africa, forever. The illusory dawn of the white white snow gleamed with a desolate brightness. Christchurch struck four o'clock. Once more I paced up and down in my study and tried vainly to drive away the startling refrain that was, like a stuck record player, repeating itself over and over inside my head. When I looked out through the windows, hoping to retrace my life's footsteps, I saw that fresh armfuls of snow had covered up my thought tracks.

KEN LIPENGA

was born in southern Malawi, where he lived and entered the University of Malawi in 1971. He graduated in 1976 and stayed on at Chancellor College where he now teaches literature and language.

K. Lipenga is a versatile author. Apart from short stories he writes poems and critical reviews.

In 1981 Lipenga published the collection of short stories entitled **Waiting for a Turn,** *with Popular Publications, Malawi.*

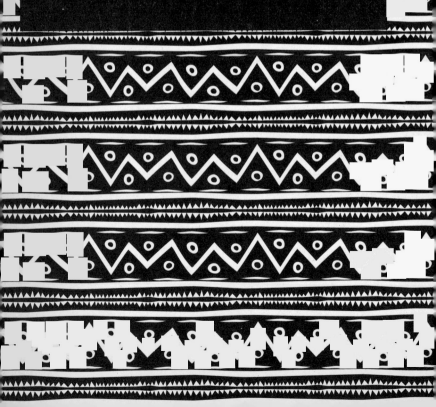

WAITING FOR A TURN

KEN LIPENGA

ALL ROADS LEAD TO SAPITWA. ALL TRAFFIC MOVES TO-ward Sapitwa. Rivers crisscross and point in different directions. But all rivers flow into Sapitwa pool. Tears of laughter and tears of sorrow flow into Sapitwa pool. All enemies meet and shake hands at Sapitwa.

I

There was no question that my Mbambande Tailoring Shop was the most successful in town. Everyone, from platformed young men and bewigged girls to respectable big shots, came to my shop for their clothes. Everyone who wanted the very latest fashion came to Mbambande. Wives refused dresses from their husbands unless they carried the "Mbambande" label. Girls ignored a young man unless they were convinced that his suit was from Mbambande. Children refused to go to school until *ababa* bought their school uniforms from Mbambande. Anything without the Mbambande label was old-fashioned. Fragile marriages collapsed beneath the weight of the "Mbambande" label. In short no one was anyone unless they were clothed by Mbambande Tailoring Shop. Such was my success.

All this was a pleasant surprise. There were times, I admit, when I felt genuinely alarmed at my success. For I had not expected anything of the sort when, a few months after leaving the university, I resigned from that insurance job. And here I must give you a little more detail.

I had resigned for two reasons. First, I could not understand why after spending years at the university, I found myself living from day to day, without the slightest sign that I would ever become rich. I am the get-rich-quick type and hadn't the patience to wait till I had crept through all the usual acrobatics that one must perform in order to get raises and rises. I also have a flighty temper, a weakness which wouldn't let me stand being bossed around by someone for the rest of my life.

I saved some money and resigned, planning to start a business of my own where I could boss myself and control the pace of my progress to the top. I chose tailoring. I don't quite know why. It may have to do with the fact that I had always been one for fashions in clothing. But at the time of my decision, I scarcely knew how to operate a sewing machine. I had to take a one-month course at one of the city tailoring shops. Thus I was in every way a novice in the business, and the success which soon came my way was a great surprise.

I think the hunchback appeared at about the time when I was approaching the peak of success and I needed more tailors. He came one morning, and before the day was over we all saw that he was exceptional. Exceptional in his skill and hard work. Give him a piece of cloth to be made into trousers and they would be ready within an hour. Get suspicious and look for faults and you would find none. Customers always went away satisfied. Oh, such a clever, fast tailor I had never seen before.

I was, of course, delighted; not only because his example infected the rest of my staff, but also because I felt his presence would make my business boom. I could already see rival firms withering away as I shot to the top.

Then came the shock. After a week Hunchback came to ask if he could live in the shop, as he could find no accommodation elsewhere. He was serious. But how could I allow this? My shop was on the city's main street, and to allow a hunchback, no matter how skilled and hardworking, to live there would be bad for business. Even without this problem the whole idea was unthinkable. So I said "No," as I am sure any other sane man would have done; but I also told him that I would look into the problem. He said nothing in reply.

The next morning Hunchback came in with his two wives and thirteen children. There was no word of explanation but it was clear that he had decided to move into the shop whether I liked it or not. The arrival of that army of children caused chaos; they roamed everywhere, pulling at the clothing, turning everything upside down, and causing panic and confusion among my tailors. Such rascals I had never seen before. But life is an unpleasant business, and I know such trials ought not surprise anyone. I found it all very painful.

I told Hunchback to leave. But he quietly refused to budge, and generally behaved as though he was only exercising a natural right. Well, I have already confessed that I am not a saint when it comes to keeping my temper on a leash. I kicked the hunchback with a heavy right boot, and, well, I swear I had never thought he was so light. My modest kick sent him clear into the street where he landed on his head, more or less.

I now seemed to be possessed by some evil spirit for I followed him and started clobbering him severely in front of all those people on the street. At this point his thirteen children, all of them very small and apparently of the same age, swarmed over me and started tearing at my clothes. And the people who had quickly gathered in a crowd gasped in amazement. They opened their mouths wide and although they did not say anything in particular I understood the message.

Hunchback, my exceptional tailor, disappeared with his two wives and thirteen children. Where he went, I knew not.

But immediately my business began to decline. It seemed that people generally disapproved of my beating up Hunchback. They also seemed to think that it would have done my business no harm at all to allow the hunchback and his family to live in my shop on Main Street.

I see no harm in begging to differ but, oh, why is life so unpleasant? People stopped coming to Mbambande Tailoring Shop and the ugliest things were said about me. People were earnestly warned off for fear of assault. Some ingenious fellow made the sudden discovery that we were not in fact good tailors at all, that my shop had from the start produced the lousiest tailoring in town. The news spread. Husbands pulled the Mbambande label from the clothes in their households for fear of having them burnt by angry wives. Girls scornfully ignored boys wearing Mbambande clothes. All around I saw smaller shops booming and growing. My tailors complained that their wives threatened to leave them unless they stopped working for "the murderer." The tailors proved how they loved their wives by dropping out one by one.

Darkness settled on my shop. The sewing machines began to rust; a ghostly silence crept in; spiders built empires in dark corners; lizards played on the walls; grass grew fast outside: Mbambande Tailoring Shop was no more.

My wife, an imaginative woman, began to wonder why there was no bread no margarine no meat no soap no this no that in the house. She then proceeded to conclude that I was squandering my money on other women, and even claimed that she knew I had been doing this all along.

I kicked my wife with my favorite right boot, and I had not thought she was so light. My modest kick sent her flying through the door; I followed and angrily beat her up. My children pulled at my clothes, and the people from the neighborhood, who had quickly gathered in a crowd, opened their mouths wide and although they said nothing specific I could see they were not on my side.

My imaginative wife disappeared with the children, took them to her people. Ah, life is an unpleasant business.

Well, there was no going back now. I went into the kitchen and smashed the china. I came out and smashed all the furniture in the lounge. It didn't help. I piled up all my clothing and blankets and set them on fire. The smoke filled my eyes with tears, I turned on the radio full blast, went into a corner of the bedroom, and cried like a six-year-old. That didn't help either, so I took the radio outside and set it on fire while the crowd watched. They watched me in silence, their mouths agape, and when they were satisfied that I had destroyed all several rushed off in a hurry. I knew where they were going.

But they couldn't make a fool of me, for I had already sized up the situation and made the inevitable decision. None in the crowd dared come near me.

I set out for the mountain.

II

I lifted my bruised limbs and turned round to look back. It had been a great climb. Looking back at the world was like looking down a deep well; everything seemed so infinite. I tried to recall a picture of life down there, to come to terms with it, and mark its place in time. But time vanished and desolation grew. I abandoned the effort and became myself again.

I turned to face my new landscape. So the rocky massif glimmering in heavenly silver before me was Sapitwa. School geography books had merely said this was the highest peak in the area, without suggesting any spiritual power. How thrilling it was! How elevating! What better site could I have chosen? Here on Sapitwa I was at the apex, here on Sapitwa I was (at least physically!) above mortals, and this thought made my blood surge with joy. I kept reminding myself that no other mortal had ever thought of this idea.

Long ago, when I was very young in the village, I asked my grandmother why she held the mountain in such reverence, indeed at times even worshiping it.

"Because, son," she said, "the spirits of the ancestors dwell there."

"Where exactly?"

She had laughed before she realized that I was serious.

"Near the top," she had answered.

"But why not on the very top itself, grandmother?"

"Because on the very top, son, dwell the Great Spirits themselves, guarding the Great Abyss."

Imagine! I had selected for the site of my deed the dwelling place of the Great Spirits themselves! I had not been thinking of the conversation with my grandmother when I made that inevitable decision. I only remembered it on arrival before the peak. I was thrilled at the idea of being received by sacred entities. It added a divine dimension to my plan. And this was what I had wanted: an original kind of departure, not something ready-made which you only had to put on when the time arrived. No, a ready-made life was to be rewarded with an original death.

From the landscape it was easy to guess where it must be, the East. There was something ominously inviting about the East, some mystical spell about this region which was associated with sunrise and the Magi. And that was only proper, for was not the leap itself a step toward spiritual renewal? Would not that simple act let me live in the world of the Great Spirits? I walked on toward the Abyss, oblivious to all but the spiritual ecstasy eating up my inside. Closer and closer to the Abyss I went, and all along I readied myself for the leap.

But from nowhere four hands suddenly grabbed my neck and arms. A dizzy spell pinned my soul to the ground; I felt like a grasshopper under an elephant's foot. I had feared at the start that I was being followed but had never expected anyone to come this far. I sank into delirium.

Hello my exceptional tailor hello my imaginative wife! Glad to see you two again! What can I do for you? I'll do the impossible for you. Just wait here a moment while I fetch the impossible. But why are your friends' mouths gaping? Why doesn't anything come out of those mouths? Why don't they say something?

My captors had given me some time to recover from the shock, for when I came to they were sitting patiently on a rock beside me. I looked at them, two heavy figures in a strange uniform, and my eyes begged for an explanation.

"Sorry, uncle," said one in a voice all its own. "We didn't mean to be rough with you. Only we thought you might need some help."

His voice was a hen's scratch on a healing wound: it provoked a nausea from the distant past which had somehow managed to pocket itself away. I felt insulted, extremely insulted. I mumbled something about privacy; something about rights to my own property; something about Hunchback being a man. But my voice failed, my will vanished when I realized that the two men did not follow what I was saying.

"Sorry, uncle," said the spokesman. "We don't understand what you are saying, but we don't believe we've anything to do with it. We only want to clear up a certain misunderstanding. I . . . er . . . I take it you're on your way to the Abyss?"

I nodded.

"Then please come this way. You must take your place in the queue . . . I take it you're aware of the queue?"

There was something hovering at the doorway of my mind which I struggled to pin down. The man's voice made me feel as if I was cutting a ludicrous figure in a crowd. I felt like a clown. I felt I was being laughed at. Someone had found that I was a clown and spread the news. It seemed that I was about to be the victim of some mysterious force.

"I take it you're aware of the queue?"

All roads lead to Sapitwa. All traffic roars toward Sapitwa. Rivers crisscross and point in different directions. But all rivers flow into the Sapitwa pool. Tears of laughter and tears of sorrow flow into Sapitwa pool. Blood sweat and tears flow into Sapitwa pool. The wind blows all fires toward Sapitwa. All roads lead to Sapitwa. Deadly enemies seal their mouths with the sap of the *kachere* tree and swear never to talk to each other. But all enemies meet and shake hands at Sapitwa.

In my head, pictures of a clever Hunchback shrouded in smoke.

"I take it you're aware of the queue."

It was a still, multicolored thread which disappeared into the distance on both sides, a silent river made of faces, black faces, brown faces, white faces, yellow faces, young faces, old faces, middle-aged faces, rich and poor faces looking bored, grim faces of businessmen and beggars, faces of red-eyed prostitutes and professors, faces of bus drivers, faces of drunken old women, faces of banana sellers, faces of international politicians, faces of spear-brandishing warriors, faces of mourning mothers side by side with faces of pilots of bomber planes, faces of convicted thieves, tired faces, happy faces, angry faces, frightened faces, faces, faces, faces; faces of all kinds, standing still in that endless line.

"You see," spokesman was saying, "you've to wait for all

these people in front of you. They came here before you. You mustn't jump the queue. It isn't proper. Quite against the rules here."

A mystical experience. We walked on.

"These people you see all came here long before you. Er . . . I wouldn't be wrong to assume that you too, uncle, are on the Quest . . . I mean for a . . . er . . . shall we call it a parting of your own?"

The feeling you get is of transparent nakedness, a feeling such as you experience in a dream where, walking around amid a crowd a short distance from your house, you discover that you are going about stark naked.

"In that case, as you can see, you have company. But we believe in being orderly here. Hence the queue. I take it you don't mind?"

Every particle of the experience hovered on the threshold, like a memory struggling to come clear.

"Good. I thought so. You see, uncle, the moment you appeared there, I knew you were one of us. You have company, you have company. I tell you, it used to be all chaos here, before things were organized. People fighting to get a place at the edge to leap to their end. Some even getting killed before they got a chance to die their chosen death. It was survival of the fittest then, crude brute behavior. That's why it was necessary to have a kind of system."

I think we walked for a year or so. I could not measure the time or distance. But in the end my captor said: "Aha, we're here at last, uncle. This is your place in the queue. Stay here, and wait for your turn."

III

I am still waiting. Been waiting all these years. Gray hairs have raided my head. My front teeth have dropped earthward. Sometimes I feel as if spiders had built empires in the dark corners of my head, and from time to time I think I hear lizards playing hide and seek in my inside. Yesterday I was amazed to see folds on my forehead. These days I avoid making journeys, and when I do I have to rely on my companion the stick. I know that soon I shall have to give up journeys altogether, for my eyes are losing faith.

I am still waiting. My turn has not yet come. They say it will, that we must keep waiting and not lose faith. Last year progress was made: I received The Initiation, and now have a new name. I am at last fit for the Great Abyss. The Great Spirits will receive me! Oh, how I long for the day!

There are many of us here on Sapitwa, and we get new arrivals every day, all on the Quest. If you look over the edge of the peak on the far side, so the young men tell me, you see countless humans clambering to reach the top. Most are young and are on the run for one reason or another. Sometimes I feel the brats ought to be sent back. Their reasons lack depth. But there's no choice, for these youngsters are a force on their own. Only a few months ago, they ganged up and threatened to reintroduce chaos at the Abyss.

I am told that the peaks surrounding Sapitwa are also filled with humans clambering on the Quest. So we are not the only ones after all. It's reassuring, though I don't quite know if the story is true. People can take advantage of your weak eyes and tell you all sorts of lies.

With the growing population here on Sapitwa we had to

reorganize ourselves into a kind of community, with leaders and representatives of this and that and the other. Last year came a priest who has been active in establishing a church and school too, because of the many children being born here as we wait our turn. A hospital has also been built and is proving very useful.

I don't know when my turn will come, but I'm certain that more years will pass. While I wait I have found something to fill my time. Over the years it has become necessary to have tailors here on Sapitwa, and my skill was naturally called upon. So, well, I'm not ashamed to say that I have opened a tailoring shop. On the door of my tailoring shop a Sapitwa artist has painted in crude letters: "New Mbambande Tailoring Shop." I have a number of tailors working for me, and among them are two or three who worked for me in the old shop. They came here too. Isn't life a mysterious affair? I have, however, been particularly careful to avoid tailors of the hunchback kind. It is a simple business precaution.

IBRAHIM ABDEL MEGID,

the Egyptian writer, was born in 1946. He published his first novel in 1979 entitled **During the 67th Summer.** *Afterward he published some other novels, among which were* **The Night of Passion and Blood, The Fisherman and the Pigeon,** *and the collection of stories* **Small Contemplations Around a Big Wall.**

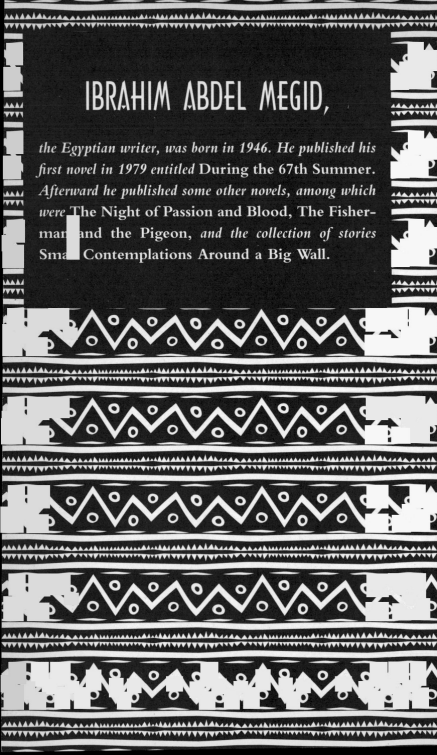

THE OTHER CITY

IBRAHIM ABDEL MEGID

Translated by Alice Copple-Tošić

THE DOOR OF THE AIRCRAFT OPENED AND I BEHELD the silence . . . It is a very rare occasion to feel the freshness of air-conditioning on your back while the sun is already bathing your chest and face and you have not yet passed through the door of the aircraft. A hand pushed me lightly from behind and I had to take the first step.

I had barely let go of the little ladder and brushed the ground when I had the sensation of creating, together with the ground and space, a single and indistinguishable object, empty and hot.

I had to walk the distance that separated me from the airport terminal. The airport was small, one single little dark yellow airplane was parked in the distance. The American flag was drawn on its flank; underneath, I read in English "United States Air Force."

Soldiers with sunburnt faces were standing by the terminal door. One of them yelled, "Men in the line to your right, women to the left." Through the window I noted, in a corner of the terminal, a circular conveyor belt just above the ground and I knew that my suitcase would arrive on it.

"Come forward 'young man,'" yelled one of the soldiers to me.

Those in front of me were already in the terminal . . . I must have fallen asleep on my feet, in the line.

"Have you forgotten me?"

I was confused and almost apologized but I said, "Not at all, I was waiting for you."

"Wait for me, we'll leave the airport together."

The baggage began to arrive . . . I deserted him to approach the conveyer belt. What was it about this young man that put me off?

I picked up my little red suitcase and placed it in front of one of the customs agents, all of whom seemed very young to me; looking at their faces and bodies, they could have scarcely been over eighteen. I opened it rapidly, he searched it just as rapidly. I had barely closed it when he ordered me to open it again.

"What's that, books?"

"That's a medical journal, *Your Doctor.*"

"It's forbidden."

We looked each other in the eye. I could find no rejoinder.

"What is it with these Egyptians, why do they love to read so much?" he asked in a loud voice. I remained silent. Should I say that "Farouk"—the one who'd gotten me the job contract—had asked me to bring him this special issue on "Maternity and Birth," or should I say that I was not familiar with the laws of the country?

"Pass . . ." he said in a nonchalant voice; he closed the suitcase with one hand, leaving the journal inside. I walked away without believing it and saw Farouk smiling at me through the window . . .

"Didn't I say that you'd forgotten me?"

This time I was very embarrassed. It was the second time that Abed had surprised me like this. I was sitting in the car next to Farouk, while he spoke to me through the open window, almost sticking in his long face with narrow eyes and thick eyebrows, clearly knit in the middle. I shook off my confusion and introduced him to Farouk who said, as he started the car, "Hello, Abed. We've already met."

"Yes—is he really a relative of yours? He's awfully shy."

"It's his first trip outside of Egypt, he'll show up at work tomorrow."

Farouk spoke without even bothering to look at Abed who had put his head all the way through the open window. I could almost feel his breath and didn't know which of the two to look at. But Abed left and I said to Farouk: "Why didn't you offer him a ride?"

"He has his own car."

"But he's just come in from Cairo with me!"

"Don't upset yourself about others."

I felt as if I didn't understand a thing and chose to keep quiet. I decided to become a child again, a blank page holding all the colors, a polished mirror reflecting things and making them slide without leaving a trace. The air was hot and stifling . . .

The Japanese Datsun darted onto the long narrow road bordered with endless sand. Farouk drove at a reckless speed. The road was empty, true enough, but I had never been in a car that raced that fast. Farouk put a cassette in the tape deck and I heard the voice of Mohammed Abdo singing "La Turiddin al-Rasail" (You don't answer).

"Here's your enterprise," he said as he caught sight of several shacks scattered on the side of the road. Two children were playing in front of the shacks. A car speeding even faster than ours passed us on the right. I jumped. Farouk smiled and said: "Everyone's wild about speed here and everyone passes on the wrong side . . ."

I retreated into my contemplations and thought about Abed . . . As is usually the case in an airplane, when two people find themselves accidentally sitting in neighboring seats, conversation is inevitable. He worked for the same enterprise that had just employed me and had spent his annual holiday in Cairo. He offered me his place to stay my first night, I answered that I had a relative in the small town, then he told me that lodgings were expensive, that the enterprise had its own residence but that it had been invaded by Asian workers and beds were only available on rare occasions. He questioned me at length about my origins, my previous job, how I had gotten the job contract, my future plans, if I was married or single and many other things besides; his questions really bothered me but I said to myself that perhaps he was only trying to be helpful.

"I see that you were very late at the airport."

"Your Doctor . . . They said it was forbidden."

Farouk said: "It's of no more use."

I smiled. "So you've become a father."

He stepped on the gas. "It's more like I became single, I divorced."

The small town appeared and then disappeared again; Farouk had branched off to the right and taken a road that ringed it at some distance. Next to the road I saw a block of low houses, the majority of them single story, unlike most of the residences in town that I had briefly glimpsed that had seemed relatively tall. The car jolted along the poorly paved alleys. Many cars were parked in front of the narrow iron doors of the houses. "In this place, every alley is a real car show," said Farouk, who had certainly noticed how engrossed I was in the different types of cars.

"It's been less than a year since you got married," I remarked.

"She wanted to buy a plot of land in her village," he replied, "and I wanted to buy another in mine."

I didn't understand. The rare times that I had met Farouk, he hadn't appeared nervous or cantankerous. Actually, he was my mother's cousin. Barely five years ago—the year I graduated from the university—he had suddenly appeared in our life, maintaining that he had been posted by the Civil Department of Bridges and Highways as an engineer in Alexandria and that it was an opportunity to come and visit us. My mother mentioned the names of several of her relatives in the village; he told her that they were all dead. He interrupted his visits for a period of one year and then reappeared, reproaching me for not having gone to visit him and my mother had said he was right; I didn't want to say that it was difficult to develop strong ties with a relative who appeared suddenly when I was already an adolescent and, in actual fact, I'm not acquainted with our village, I wasn't born there and have never visited it. The strangest thing is that Farouk disappeared again after two or three visits; I don't know how my mother learned that he was in Saudi Arabia or what induced him to write me, offering to help me travel. I hesitated at length, but I had to accept.

I said: "You could have postponed this acquisition."

"Why shouldn't a wife obey her husband?"

I was silent, but he continued.

"I gave her three thousand pounds; that's what the marriage cost me. I'll make up for it and find a much better match." He was quiet for a moment. "Here's my house. A doctor and a teacher lodge with me."

The cold shower is truly a divine invention. I would have preferred to be left alone, to myself, but they insisted that I sit with them and take part in a spirited game of backgammon. I disliked the house at first glance. Two rooms on either side of a large interior courtyard, the bathroom and kitchen at the end. Farouk said that the house had been modeled after Arabic architecture but in my opinion it was only an arrangement of concrete cubes. Two of the rooms were narrow and their windows looked onto the courtyard and not the street, which was more restful perhaps but the tiny windows looked like those in a prison cell . . . Under the cold shower, I heard the dice move, the clicking of the counters, the applause and laughs; I thought of sneaking quickly to my room which Farouk had furnished with a plastic collapsible closet, a single bed and an electric fan, but they surprised me and pronounced in unison, "No one sleeps before midnight here, it's the law of nature . . ." I joined their group. I noted during the short trip from the bathroom to where they sat that my chest and legs were already sweating.

It was almost night and the atmosphere hadn't changed. The air was so heavy and stagnant that it could have been cut into pieces and held in your hand!

"Do you have any rials [Saudi money]?" began the doctor who, I was to learn later, was named Wajih.

The question shocked me, and it was the teacher who replied; I learned later that his name was Said. "We play for money."

I sat at the place they had made for me next to them. Someone knocked at the door. Farouk hurried to answer it. Abed's face appeared behind the door that Farouk held half-open. I got up to greet him.

"One of the beds in the enterprise residence has been vacated, if you want to take it I can reserve it for you!" said Abed.

I would have liked to open the door wider and invite him in, but Farouk held the door ajar and his body almost completely blocked the opening. He spoke before I could say a word: "We'll see about that tomorrow."

"I had quite a time finding your house; I dropped by the enterprise by chance and learned that a Pakistani had died and that his place was free. I thought it was a good opportunity and that I should let you know about it." Abed spoke in a very friendly voice; I stood there, embarrassed.

Farouk said: "Thank you."

Abed answered: "Don't let it slip through your fingers!" and then he left.

Farouk closed the door and returned to his seat. I remained standing for several moments and then followed him.

"I'll lend my cousin five rials," he said.

I made no comment.

"Don't be afraid, whatever you lose you'll win back, that's the rule in this game," said Dr. Wajih.

I did not reply.

"We're just killing time," said Farouk.

I made no remark.

"Each game is worth ten rials; we note the wins and losses in this notebook," said Said, the teacher.

I continued to remain silent.

"At the end of the month, the winner repays the loser the money he's lost, and we start all over again," said the doctor.

We were all silent for several moments and he continued: "You must certainly wonder what is the purpose of all this since each one is certain of recovering his money?"

I didn't reply. He then said enigmatically: "To tell the truth, we don't even know ourselves . . ."

NDELEY MOKOSO

is a Cameroonian author with a varied career: he was a journalist, industrialist, and politician. From this rich experience he gained a good knowledge of the West African society which he artfully weaves into his very short stories. His collection of thirteen stories was published in 1987 under the title **Man Pass Man and Other Stories**.

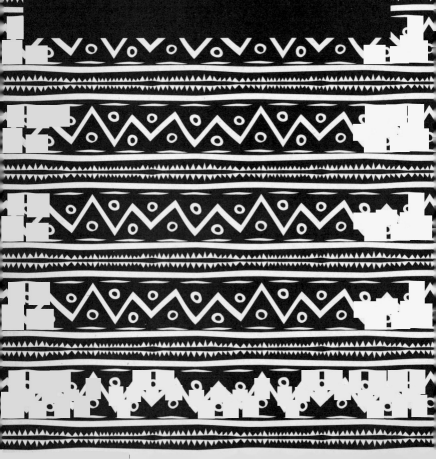

GOD
OF MEME

NDELEY MOKOSO

THE VILLAGERS NAMED THE FESTIVAL THE "VISITATION."
A festival handed down by their grandfathers and great-great-grandfathers before them. Once a year, they assembled on the banks of the Mungo River, to pay homage and sing praises to the "god" of the river.

They had trekked for miles, men, women and children. Among the throng were members of the man-crocodile cult, identified by woven strands of crocodile hide worn around their right ankles.

Members of the cult were held in great respect and awe. There were the stories of the fanatic adherence to the cult by its members; its survival under the ruthlessness of the early German administrators, and its near demise as a result of the persuasions and organized campaigns by the Christian missionaries.

The crowd retreated as members of the cult trooped down the riverbank; two of them carrying a bleating he-goat for the sacrifice, another followed with a machete. The ceremony was brief. The goat was tethered on to a stake driven into the ground. They then surrounded the goat—all of them. The tallest of them raised the machete high above his head, then brought it down—one stroke that severed the head from the body. The blood-spattered carcass was flung deep into the river.

Then the drumming, singing and clapping started, with members of the cult performing a jig peculiar only to their group. One of their members had worked himself into a frenzy as the tempo of the drumming increased and dropped heavily on the ground. His colleagues quickly cordoned off the area, rallying round him as he lay sprawled on the ground, quite relaxed, his chest heaving slowly. The rest continued in hilarious mood, stamping their feet as the drums throbbed louder and louder.

From the opposite bank of the river came a loud snort, then the snout, the large protruding eyes, the head and the long scaly body.

The crowd yelled in ecstacy and prayed in unison—

> *"Lord of the river*
> *Thy might we acknowledge*
> *Protect us from the evil one*
> *Fill the bellies of our women with babies*
> *And provide the rich harvest to feed them*
> *Long may you reign"*

The crocodile waddled up the opposite bank and opened its mouth in greeting, displaying two long rows of gleaming white teeth. The crowd roared and cheered hysterically as it later submerged, retrieved the carcass, thrashed its tail and glided slowly downstream and out of sight.

The crocodiles in this river were docile beasts—domesticated, to be more exact. They could be identified, talked to and stroked lovingly. I myself had witnessed a startling and weird incident while taking a trip by canoe to one of the villages. We had come across what appeared to be a log of timber. The canoe man had tried to maneuver his craft on course, when a member of the cult, who happened to be traveling with us, ordered him to drop anchor. He announced, rather jokingly, that a friend of his had blocked our course. He then stood up, waved his hands in salute and called: "Lokindo . . . lokindo . . . Masengo, your colleague, salutes you. Pray let us proceed." A few yams were thrown overboard, and what had appeared to the rest of us as a log of timber turned out to be a live crocodile. It thrashed its tail, submerged and gave us right of way.

Many a time, the crocodiles lay basking in the sun on the muddy bank while men, women and children swam and bathed with no concern whatsoever regarding their safety. They all knew the animals were harmless—human beings in crocodile form. The story goes, however, that a certain German administrator, named Von Schnieder, had been killed by a crocodile. That he was the only victim seized from a group of five. The rest were unharmed. They said it was a reprisal for his brutality and other acts of callousness against the natives. They said he had caused ten identified members of the man-crocodile cult to be shot.

The natives around had been summoned forcibly at gunpoint to witness what was classified as a punitive measure. In a specially prepared arena, the condemned men were made to climb on trees and a game hunting exercise began. White soldiers armed with rifles brought them down one by one—a spectacle that was intended to shock the natives into submission. Those who showed signs of sympathy or wept for executed relatives or friends were stripped and whipped with horse whips. Von Schnieder's corpse was never found.

But the "god" of the river was now aging. He had lost his youthful skill and speed that had earlier characterized the quick dispatch of his victims. He had been content with lying in wait for forest animals—antelopes and other small game which came down regularly for a drink. Many a time he had succeeded in flailing them with his powerful scaly tail, so powerful that it crushed the victim into a battered shuddering heap. The strong jaws and claws retracted into the body which was then dragged virtually underwater and drowned.

Today, he had watched a small herd of antelopes cropping the grass, anxious for water, but, for some reason he did not know, afraid to approach the river. He moved slowly. Only the tip of the snout and the large bulging eyes above water.

Two young antelopes ventured down the river's edge. They seemed to have sensed the danger, for they suddenly stopped drinking, raised their heads and cocked their ears. Now, he must take his time. A lot depended on this particular kill—he had been some days without food. He made a desperate dash for the nearest antelope. His timing was faulty, and he had just missed his victim by inches. The animals gave the alarm and the whole herd stampeded to the safety of the forest.

Farther up the river, a little footpath zigzagged to the river-bank. The local people simply called the place "Small Beach." Here, everyone to and from the village had to be taken across by canoe. It was market day, a very busy day for the canoe man. Women with baskets of cocoyams and plantains strapped on their backs stood waiting for their turn. Today, they were growing rather impatient and angry—the canoe man had arbitrarily raised the toll by two pence.

The "god" of the river watched these goings and comings with renewed interest. Not that he was doing so for the first time. Today he was hungrier than usual; really hungry and the urge to survive had put him in a different frame of mind. He wondered what human flesh tasted like. "Must be horrible," he thought as he tried to work out how best he would set about it. It was a strange feeling that touched his very heart, but the urge to survive was uppermost.

Five more persons had arrived—three women carrying baskets of cassava on their heads and two petty traders on bicycles. Two of the women were first taken across, the third had emptied her basket of cassava and started peeling them. The two men with the bicycles were ferried across too, and finally the broad-breasted woman, who had by now finished peeling her cassava. After taking her across, the canoe man settled down to his breakfast of koki and plantain. After the meal, he walked down to the river to rinse his mouth and wash his hands.

There was no one in sight. The crocodile moved closer. "Now, I must take my time," he thought. Another false movement meant another day without food. He wanted it to be a clean business. None of his subjects should witness such an atrocity. The "god" of the river was becoming a man-eater.

The man washed his hands, scooped out the water in the boat and checked the mooring rope. Satisfied that all was well, he walked a few paces from the water's edge and sat down for a brief rest before his customers arrived for the return trip.

The crocodile moved stealthily closer. He was not sure whether the man's gaze was fixed on the river. It became clear, as he drew closer, that the man was dozing. Then he struck. It was quick work, delivered with the right timing and precision. Only a sharp, muffled scream. The powerful jaws locked on the man's shoulder like a vise and dragged him to the bottom of the river. The now limp body coughed and kicked desperately until it choked and lay still.

The villagers found the bloody trail. The canoe still lay moored. They could not believe their eyes! It had never happened before! They could not understand it at all, and no one dared accuse the "god" of the river of such an atrocity!

And so the "god" of the river's blood lust continued with unabated fury. The baby left by the mother to wander while she did her laundry had disappeared. Villagers paddling down river in canoes laden with cocoyams and plantains had been chased by the crocodile. At first, the smell of human blood had sickened and frightened him. Now it had a sweetness that caused him pangs of desire to kill again and again.

The next victim was Water-boy, the laborer who carried

water from the river to the Estate Manager's house up the hill. Once again, it was a successful operation. Only Water-boy's empty bucket was found. There again were the signs the unseen and merciless enemy had left behind—a bloody trail which ended by the riverbank.

Following this latest incident, David Jones, the Estate Manager, had received a delegation of the Workers' Trade Union. They demanded that some drastic action be taken to safeguard the lives of its members. They had given the Manager ten days to show what was described as some positive measures, failing which the Union would take any action it deemed fit. It was clear to the five-man delegation that the Manager was equally concerned about the recent threat on the peaceful and orderly existence of his little community. He realized that he would have to pay large sums of money under the Workmen's Compensation Ordinance if the crocodile's blood lust continued.

David Jones had discussed the matter with the local Administrative Officer, suggesting that the man-crocodile cult be banned. He had argued that the crocodile was a menace and its continued existence not conducive to public peace and safety. He was aware that crocodiles were protected under the Wild Life Preservation Ordinance, but there was the proviso which stated that if such protected game threatened the peaceful and orderly existence of the community, thereby constituting a danger to life and property, it could be destroyed in the public interest.

This is why David Jones had shot at the beast when it killed his dog before his very eyes. The livid flash and the explosion had brought down groups of scared and angry villagers, all members of the cult to the riverbank. They had protested vehemently and explained that the recent happenings were the wrath of the "god" of the river. The spokesman pointed out that the tendency had been for certain persons to ignore the laid down taboos with regard to the river. They had continued to shout across the river; they had continued to wash the soot off cooking pots and "bitter leaf" in the river. All these actions were regarded and accepted as gross disrespect for the "god" of the river. His recent attempt to kill the "god" of the river was an affront and a desecration—an act which was likely to cause a breach of the peace. They wanted an assurance that the "god" of the river would not be threatened or molested. "You will be taken away like the other white man before you, if you persist," they warned him.

The meeting ended in uproar. The Manager accused the group of blackmail, asked them out of his office and threatened to call the police. That settled it. They shook their fists and cursed as they backed away. They swore they would "call" the rain. And the rain came a few hours after the meeting. It rained as it had never rained before. The river began to rise, and twenty-four hours later the young rubber trees were standing in three feet of water. Reports soon came in about the two wooden bridges which had been swept away by the floods. Effective supervision of the estate was now impossible. The rain-makers too had joined the vicious circle.

At the meeting convened by the District Officer to agree to a line of action, the District Clerk, a local man who had made good, sat tight-lipped throughout the discussions. He looked greatly terrified when opinion weighed in favor of shooting the crocodile. He had pleaded in tears that such an act would completely disrupt the communal life of his people. He expressed the fear that he would be killed by a crocodile if it was known that he had connived with the administration in taking such a decision. His fears were allayed. He was promised protection against any possible reprisals or molestation.

But the meeting had not ended when a court messenger arrived with the sad news of yet another victim—a little girl aged ten. Something had to be done at once. The man-eater was to be destroyed and the activities of the cult banned. That was the consensus. Orders were given for four policemen with crack shots to be issued with four rounds of ammunition each. They were to report to headquarters for briefing. A Land Rover equipped with radio communication equipment, tear gas and handcuffs was requisitioned in case there was mob resistance. The little force then left, led by the Administrative Officer and the Police Commissioner.

The road was steep all the way and rugged. There were several flooded stretches and time and again the auxiliary gears had to be engaged. After half an hour the Land Rover chugged to a halt. They had come to the end of the motorable road. The rest of the journey had to be done on foot, through a bush track —a distance of about two miles. The forest was thick, and sometimes it was dark as the dense foliage cut off most of the light.

It was about midday when they arrived at a clearing. The vegetation was less dense. There were plantain and cocoyam farms all over and in the distance there was rising smoke. Another ten minutes trek brought them to the village. It was like every other village in the district—a tight cluster of bamboo huts covered with thatch. There was a large crowd at one end. People were talking in low tones and over the hum of voices came the traditional wailing so common at village funerals.

The crowd moved back slowly as the group arrived. There, on a rough wooden bed, lay the mangled remains of the ten-year-old girl. The body had been found with the face torn off and the guts scooped.

A slight rustle commenced among the audience as the policemen unshouldered their rifles. Then there was silence as the voice of authority spoke. "This is a very sad thing," the District Officer began. "Very sad, very bad thing," he emphasized, picking his words slowly. "This thing cannot be allowed to go on. People cannot continue to live in fear. Government has an obligation to protect its citizens. This animal is a menace, and it is the Government's determination that it be destroyed." He stopped and watched the reaction of the crowd. Then he went on. "I want three powerful men to pull us up the river in a boat." There was silence. "Are there no volunteers? I will give you three minutes to decide. Thereafter I will take whatever action I deem fit."

The villagers stood their ground. None of them wished to be involved in what they considered a conspiracy against the "god" of the river. The Administrative Officer looked at his watch and raised his hand. "You, you and you," he pointed to three stocky, broad-chested villagers. "March these fellows down the river." The policemen stepped forward, their guns held menacingly. The terrified men meekly and resignedly did a "quick march" as ordered.

One man in the crowd eyed the Administrative Officer owlishly. He began reciting an unintelligible litany of woe, followed by an unending flood of bitter invective. The man was simply known as Tata Maloba, a surly old man aged about sixty. "And what's the meaning of this?" he screamed, his look glowering— contempt mingled with respect. "I've come to shoot the rogue of a crocodile and nothing will stop me. I don't even care if it is your own." He looked determined. The old man threw himself on the ground begging. He would never molest or kill anyone, ever again. He was bluntly told that it was now too late and that his confession could not help him.

Tata Maloba's crocodile lay basking peacefully as a result of the previous day's heavy meal, when the plop-plop of dipping paddles came to him; then the voices of men. His first instinct was to slip away unobserved. But it was too late; the men in the boat had seen him.

Corporal Doh, the man with the best shot, stood up. He withdrew the bolt of his rifle, slid a round into the breech and signed himself. His breathing deepened with nervous excitement as he raised the rifle high in the port, its butt pressing into his armpit. Then he pulled the trigger. He heard the explosion and the short screech of the bullet which smashed into the animal's head. Then followed three other explosions in quick succession as the other men raked him again and again.

The river took on a deeper brown hue as the crocodile in the throes of death thrashed and churned the muddy waters. It took some time to die, making noises that were really human, with eyes full of hate watching the men in the boat as it died.

Back in the village, a small crowd gathered as Tata Maloba collapsed, screaming and clutching at his head, crying: "I've been shot . . . I've been shot . . . I'm dying . . ." And he died soon after. The postmortem indeed proved that he had died from gunshot wounds. The corpse was riddled all over by bullets.

KEN SARO-WIWA

was born in Nigeria in 1941 and studied at the University of Ibadan. He has taught in Nigeria's universities, served in government at cabinet level, and is currently a businessman. He has traveled extensively worldwide.

Saro-Wiwa's first collection of short stories, A Forest of Flowers *(1987), was short-listed for the Commonwealth Writers Prize. His other works are entitled* Sozaboy: A Novel in Rotten English *(1985),* Basi and Company: A Modern African Folktale *(1987), and* Prisoners of Jebs *(1988).*

His collection of poems is entitled Songs in a Time of War *(1985).*

Saro-Wiwa writes children's books, too: Tambari, Tambari in Dukana, Mr. B, Mr. B Again, Mr. B Goes to Lagos, The Transistor Radio.

His play Basi and Company *became a long-running television comedy series, broadcast in eighty episodes. Afterward Saro-Wiwa wrote another play:* Four Farcical Plays *(1989).*

On a Darkling Plain: An Account of the Nigerian Civil War *is a book of general history.*

Adaku and Other Stories *appeared in 1989.* Pita Dumbrok's Prison, *a novel, appeared in 1991, as well as* The Singing Anthill, *an Ogoni folk tale.*

He is at present the president of the Association of Nigerian Authors.

AFRICA KILLS HER SUN

KEN SARO-WIWA

Dear Zole,

You'll be surprised, no doubt, to receive this letter. But I couldn't leave your beautiful world without saying good-bye to you who are condemned to live in it. I know that some might consider my gesture somewhat pathetic, as my colleagues, Sazan and Jimba, do, our finest moments having been achieved two or three weeks ago. However, for me, this letter is a celebration, a final act of love, a quality which, in spite of my career, in spite of tomorrow morning, I do possess in abundance, and cherish. For I've always treasured the many moments of pleasure we spent together in our youth when the world was new and fishes flew in golden ponds. In the love we then shared have I found happiness, a true resting place, a shelter from the many storms that have buffeted my brief life. Whenever I've been most alone, whenever I've been torn by conflict and pain, I've turned to that love for the resolution which has sustained and seen me through. This may surprise you, considering that this love was never consummated and that you may possibly have forgotten me, not having seen me these ten years gone. I still remember you, have always remembered you, and it's logical that in the night before tomorrow, I should write you to ask a small favor of you. But more importantly, the knowledge that I have unburdened myself to you will make tomorrow morning's event as pleasant and desirable to me as to the thousands of spectators who will witness it.

I know this will get to you because the prison guard's been heavily bribed to deliver it. He should rightly be with us before the firing squad tomorrow. But he's condemned, like most others, to live, to play out his assigned role in your hell of a world. I see him burning out his dull, uncomprehending life, doing his menial job for a pittance and a bribe for the next so many years. I pity his ignorance and cannot envy his complacency. Tomorrow morning, with this letter and our bribe in his pocket, he'll call us out, Sazan, Jimba and I. As usual, he'll have all our names mixed up: he always calls Sazan "Sajim" and Jimba "Samba." But that won't matter. We'll obey him, and as we walk to our death, we'll laugh at his gaucherie, his plain stupidity. As we laughed at that other thief, the High Court Judge.

You must've seen that in the papers too. We saw it, thanks to our bribe-taking friend, the prison guard, who sent us a copy of the newspaper in which it was reported. Were it not in an unfeeling nation, among a people inured to evil and taking sadistic pleasure in the loss of life, some questions might have been asked. No doubt, many will ask the questions, but they will do it in the safety and comfort of their homes, over the interminable bottles of beer, uncomprehendingly watching their boring, cheap television programs, the rejects of Europe and America, imported to fill their vacuity. They will salve their conscience with more bottles of beer, wash the answers down their gullets and pass question, conscience and answer out as waste into their open sewers choking with concentrated filth and murk. And they will forget.

I bet, though, the High Court Judge himself will never

forget. He must remember it the rest of his life. Because I watched him closely that first morning. And I can't describe the shock and disbelief which I saw registered on his face. His spectacles fell to his table and it was with difficulty he regained composure. It must have been the first time in all his experience that he found persons arraigned on a charge for which the punishment upon conviction is death, entering a plea of guilty and demanding that they be sentenced and shot without further delay.

Sazan, Jimba and I had rehearsed it carefully. During the months we'd been remanded in prison custody while the prosecutors prepared their case, we'd agreed we weren't going to allow a long trial, or any possibility that they might impose differing sentences upon us: freeing one, sentencing another to life imprisonment and the third to death by firing squad.

Nor did we want to give the lawyers in their funny, black, funeral robes an opportunity to clown around, making arguments for pleasure, engaging in worthless casuistry. No. We voted for death. After all, we were armed robbers, bandits. We knew it. We didn't want to give the law a chance to prove itself the proverbial ass. We were being honest to ourselves, to our vocation, to our country and to mankind.

"Sentence us to death immediately and send us before the firing squad without further delay," we yelled in unison. The Judge, after he had recovered from his initial shock, asked us to be taken away that day, "for disturbing my court." I suppose he wanted to see if we'd sleep things over and change our plea. We didn't. When they brought us back the next day, we said the same thing in louder voice. We said we had robbed and killed. We were guilty. Cool. The Judge was bound hand and foot and did what he had to. We'd forced him to be honest to his vocation, to the laws of the country

and to the course of justice. It was no mean achievement.
The court hall was stunned; our guards were utterly amazed as
we walked out of court, smiling. "Hardened criminals,"
"Bandits," I heard them say as we trooped out of the court.
One spectator actually spat at us as we walked into the waiting
Black Maria!

And now that I've confessed to banditry, you'll ask why I
did it? I'll answer that question by retelling the story of the
young, beautiful prostitute I met in St. Pauli in Hamburg
when our ship berthed there years back. I've told my friends
the story several times. I did ask her, after the event, why she
was in that place? She replied that some girls chose to be
secretaries in offices, others to be nurses. She had chosen
prostitution as a career. Cool. I was struck by her candor. And
she set me thinking. Was I in the merchant navy by choice or
because it was the first job that presented itself to me when I
left school? When we returned home, I skipped ship, thanks
to the prostitute of St. Pauli, and took a situation as a clerk in
the Ministry of Defense.

It was there I came face-to-face with the open looting of
the national treasury, the manner of which I cannot describe
without arousing in myself the deepest, basest emotions.
Everyone was busy at it and there was no one to complain to.
Everyone to whom I complained said to me: "If you can't
beat them, join them." I was not about to join anyone; I
wanted to beat them and took it upon myself to wage a war
against them. In no time they had gotten rid of me. Dismissed
me. I had no option but to join them then. I had to make a
choice. I became an armed robber, a bandit. It was my
choice, my answer. And I don't regret it.

Did I know it was dangerous? Some girls are secretaries,
others choose to be prostitutes. Some men choose to be

soldiers and policemen, others doctors and lawyers; I chose to
be a robber. Every occupation has its hazards. A taxi driver
may meet his death on the road; a businessman may die in an
air crash; a robber dies before a firing squad. It's no big deal.
If you ask me, the death I've chosen is possibly more
dramatic, more qualitative, more eloquent than dying in bed
of a ruptured liver from overindulgence in alcohol. Yes? But
robbery is antisocial, you say? A proven determination to
break the law. I don't want to provide an alibi. But just you
think of the many men and women who are busy breaking or
bending the law in all coasts and climes. Look for a copy of
The Guardian of 19th September. That is the edition in which
our plea to the Judge was reported. You'll find there the story
of the Government official who stole over seven million naira.
Seven million. Cool. He was antisocial, right? How many of
his type d'you know? And how many more go undetected? I
say, if my avocation was antisocial, I'm in good company. And
that company consists of Presidents of countries, transnational
organizations, public servants high and low, men and women.
The only difference is that while I'm prepared to pay the
price for it all, the others are not. See?

    I'm not asking for your understanding or sympathy. I need
neither, not now nor hereafter. I'm saying it as it is. Right?
Cool. I expect you'll say that armed robbery should be the
special preserve of the scum of society. That no man of my
education has any business being a bandit. To that I'll answer
that it's about time well-endowed and well-trained people
took to it. They'll bring to the profession a romantic quality,
a proficiency which will ultimately conduce to the benefit of
society. No, I'm not mad. Truly. Time was when the running
and ruining of African nations was in the hands of half-literate
politicians. Today, well-endowed and better trained people
have taken over the task. And look how well they're doing it.

So that even upon that score, my conscience sleeps easy. Understand?

Talking about sleep, you should see Sazan and Jimba on the cold, hard prison floor, snoring away as if life itself depends on a good snore. It's impossible, seeing them this way, to believe that they'll be facing the firing squad tomorrow. They're men of courage. Worthy lieutenants. It's a pity their abilities will be lost to society forever, come tomorrow morning. Sazan would have made a good Army General anyday, possibly a President of our country in the mold of Idi Amin or Bokassa. The Europeans and Americans would have found in him a useful ally in the progressive degradation of Africa. Jimba'd have made an excellent Inspector-General of Police, so versed is he in the ways of the Police! You know, of course, that Sazan is a dismissed Sergeant of our nation's proud army. And Jimba was once a Corporal in the Police Force. When we met, we had similar reasons for pooling our talents. And a great team we did make. Now here we all are in the death cell of a maximum security prison and they snoring away the last hours of their lives on the cold, smelly floor. It's exhilarating to find them so disdainful of life. Their style is the stuff of which history is made. In another time and in another country, they'd be Sir Francis Drake, Cortes or Sir Walter Raleigh. They'd have made empires and earned national honors. But here, our life is one big disaster, an endless tragedy. Heroism is not in our star. We are millipedes crawling on the floor of a dank, wet forest. So Sazan and Jimba will die unsung. See?

One thing, though. We swore never to kill. And we never did. Indeed, we didn't take part in the particular "operation" for which we were held, Sazan, Jimba and I. That operation would've gone quite well if the Superintendent of Police had fulfilled his part of the bargain. Because he was in it with us.

The Police are involved in every single robbery that happens.
They know the entire gang, the gangs. We'd not succeed if
we didn't collaborate with them. Sazan, Jimba and I were the
bosses. We didn't go out on "operations." The boys normally
did. And they were out on that occasion. The Superintendent
of Police was supposed to keep away the police escorts from
the vehicle carrying workers' salaries that day. For some
reason, he failed to do so. And the policeman shot at our
boys. The boys responded and shot and killed him and the
Security Company guards. The boys got the money alright.
But the killing was contrary to our agreement with the Police.
We had to pay. The Police won't stand any of their men
being killed. They took all the money from us and then they
went after the boys. We said no. The boys had acted on
orders. We volunteered to take their place. The Police took us
in and made a lot of public noises about it. The boys, I know,
will make their decisions later. I don't know what will happen
to the Superintendent of Police. But he'll have to look to
himself. So, if that is any comfort to you, you may rest in the
knowledge that I spilt no blood. No, I wouldn't. Nor have I
kept the loot. Somehow, whatever we took from people—the
rich ones—always was shared by the gang who were almost
always on the bread line. Sazan, Jimba and I are not wealthy.

Many will therefore accuse us of recklessness, or of being
careless with our lives. And well they might. I think I speak
for my sleeping comrades when I say we went into our career
because we didn't see any basic difference between what we
were doing and what most others are doing throughout the
land today. In every facet of our lives—in politics, in
commerce and in the professions—robbery is the base line.
And it's been so from time. In the early days, our forebears
sold their kinsmen into slavery for minor items such as beads,

mirrors, alcohol and tobacco. These days, the tune is the same, only the articles have changed into cars, transistor radios and bank accounts. Nothing else has changed, and nothing will change in the foreseeable future. But that's the problem of those of you who will live beyond tomorrow, Zole.

The cock crows now and I know dawn is about to break. I'm not speaking figuratively. In the cell here, the darkness is still all-pervasive, except for the flickering light of the candle by which I write. Sazan and Jimba remain fast asleep. So is the prison guard. He sleeps all night and is no trouble to us. We could, if we wanted, escape from here, so lax are the guards. But we consider that unnecessary, as what is going to happen later this morning is welcome relief from burdens too heavy to bear. It's the guard and you the living who are in prison, the ultimate prison from which you cannot escape because you do not know that you are incarcerated. Your happiness is the happiness of ignorance and your ignorance is it that keeps you in the prison, which is your life. As this night dissolves into day, Sazan, Jimba and I shall be free. Sazan and Jimba will have left nothing behind. I shall leave at least this letter, which, please, keep for posterity.

Zole, do I rant? Do I pour out myself to you in bitter tones? Do not lay it to the fact that I'm about to be shot by firing squad. On second thoughts, you could, you know. After all, seeing death so clearly before me might possibly have made me more perspicacious? And yet, I've always seen these things clearly in my mind's eye. I never did speak about them, never discussed them. I preferred to let them weigh me down. See?

So, then, in a few hours we shall be called out. We shall clamber with others into the miserable lorry which they still call the Black Maria. Notice how everything miserable is associated with us. Black Sheep. Black Maria. Black Death. Black Leg. The Black Hole of Calcutta. The Black Maria will take us to the Beach or to the Stadium. I bet it will be the Stadium. I'd prefer the Beach. So at least to see the ocean once more. For I've still this fond regard for the sea which dates from my time in the Merchant Navy. I love its wide expanse, its anonymity, its strength, its unfathomable depth. And maybe after shooting us, they might decide to throw our bodies into the ocean. We'd then be eaten up by sharks which would in turn be caught by Japanese and Russian fishermen, be refrigerated, packaged in cartons and sold to Indian merchants and then for a handsome profit to our people. That way, I'd have helped keep people alive a bit longer. But they won't do us that favor. I'm sure they'll take us to the Stadium. To provide a true spectacle for the fun-loving unemployed. To keep them out of trouble. To keep them from thinking. To keep them laughing. And dancing.

We'll be there in the dirty clothes which we now wear. We've not had any of our things washed this past month. They will tie us to the stakes, as though that were necessary. For even if we were minded to escape, where'd we run to? I expect they'll also want to blindfold us. Sazan and Jimba have said they'll not allow themselves to be blindfolded. I agree with them. I should want to see my executors, stare the nozzles of their guns bravely in the face, see the open sky, the sun, daylight. See and hear my countrymen as they cheer us to our death. To liberation and freedom.

The Stadium will fill to capacity. And many will not find a place. They will climb trees and hang about the balconies of surrounding houses to get a clear view of us. To enjoy the free show. Cool.

And then the priest will come to us, either to pray or to

ask if we have any last wishes. Sazan says he will ask for a cigarette. I'm sure they'll give it to him. I can see him puffing hard at it before the bullets cut him down. He says he's going to enjoy that cigarette more than anything he's had in life. Jimba says he'll maintain a sullen silence as a mark of his contempt. I'm going to yell at the priest. I will say, "Go to hell, you hypocrite, fornicator and adulterer." I will yell at the top of my voice in the hope that the spectators will hear me. How I wish there'd be a microphone that will reverberate through the Stadium, nay, through the country as a whole! Then the laugh should be on the priest and those who sent him!

The priest will pray for our souls. But it's not us he should be praying for. He should pray for the living, for those whose lives are a daily torment. Between his prayer and when the shots ring out, there will be dead silence. The silence of the graveyard. The transition between life and death. And it shall be seen that the distinction between them both is narrow, as the neck of a calabash. The divide between us breathing like everyone else in the Stadium and us as meat for worms is, oh, so slim, it makes life a walking death! But I should be glad to be rid of the world, of a meaningless existence that grows more dreary by the day. I should miss Sazan and Jimba, though. It'll be a shame to see these elegant gentlemen cut down and destroyed. And I'll miss you, too, my dear girl. But that will be of no consequence to the spectators.

They will troop out of the Stadium, clamber down the trees and the balconies of the houses, as though they'd just returned from another football match. They will march to their ratholes on empty stomachs, with tales enough to fill a Saturday evening. Miserable wretches!

The men who shall have eased us out of life will then untie our bodies and dump them into a lorry and thence to some open general grave. That must be a most distasteful task. I'd not do it for a million dollars. Yet some miserable fellows will do it for a miserable salary at the end of the month. A salary which will not feed them and their families till the next payday. A salary which they will have to augment with a bribe, if they are to keep body and soul together. I say, I do feel sorry for them. See?

The newspapers will faithfully record the fact of our shooting. If they have space, they'll probably carry a photograph of us to garnish your breakfasts.

I remember once long ago reading in a newspaper of a man whose one request to the priest was that he be buried along with his walking stick—his faithful companion over the years. He was pictured slumping in death, devotedly clutching his beloved walking stick. True friendship, that. Well, Zole, if ever you see such a photograph of me, make a cutting. Give it to a sculptor and ask him to make a stone sculpture of me as I appear in the photograph. He must make as faithful a representation of me as possible. I must be hard of feature and relentless in aspect. I have a small sum of money in the bank and have already instructed the bank to pay it to you for the purpose of the sculpture I have spoken about . . .

Time is running out, Zole. Sazan and Jimba are awake now. And they're surprised I haven't slept all night. Sazan says I ought at least to have done myself the favor of sound sleep on my last night on earth. I ask him if I'm not going to sleep soundly, eternally, in a few hours? This, I argue, should be our most wakeful night. Sazan doesn't appreciate that. Nor does Jimba. They stand up, yawn, stretch and rub their eyes. Then they sit down, crowding round me. They ask me to read out to them what I've written. I can't do that, I tell

them. It's a love letter. And they burst out laughing. A love
letter! And at the point of death! Sazan says I'm gone crazy.
Jimba says he's sure I'm afraid of death and looks hard and
long at me to justify his suspicion. I say I'm neither crazy nor
afraid of death. I'm just telling my childhood girlfriend how I
feel this special night. And sending her on an important
errand. Jimba says I never told them I had a girlfriend. I reply
that she was not important before this moment.

I haven't even seen her in ten years, I repeat. The really
compelling need to write her is that on this very special night,
I have felt a need to be close to a living being, someone who
can relate to others why we did what we did in and out of
court.

Sazan says he agrees completely with me. He says he too
would like to write his thoughts down. Do I have some paper
to lend him? I say no. Besides, time is up. Day has dawned
and I haven't even finished my letter. Do they mind leaving
me to myself for a few minutes? I'd very much like to end the
letter, envelope it and pass it on to the prison guard before he
rouses himself fully from sleep and remembers to assume his
official, harsh role.

They're nice chaps, are Jimba and Sazan. Sazan says to tell
my girl not to bear any children because it's pointless bringing
new life into the harsh life of her world. Jimba says to ask my
girl to shed him a tear if she can so honor a complete
stranger. They both chuckle and withdraw to a corner of the
cell and I'm left alone to end my letter.

Now, I was telling you about my statue. My corpse will
not be available to you. You will make a grave for me,
nonetheless. And place the statue on the gravestone. And now
I come to what I consider the most important part of this
letter. My epitaph.

I have thought a lot about it, you know. Really. What

d'you say about a robber shot in a stadium before a cheering crowd? That he was a good man who strayed? That he deserved his end? That he was a scallywag? A ragamuffin? A murderer whose punishment was not heavy enough? "Here lies X who was shot in public by firing squad for robbing a van and shooting the guards in broad daylight. He serves as an example to all thieves and would-be thieves!"

Who'd care for such an epitaph? They'd probably think it was a joke. No. That wouldn't carry. I'll settle for something different. Something plain and commonsensical. Or something truly cryptic and worthy of a man shot by choice in public by firing squad.

Not that I care. To die the way I'm going to die in the next hour or two is really nothing to worry about. I'm in excellent company. I should find myself recorded in the annals of our history. A history of violence, of murder, of disregard for life. Pleasure in inflicting pain—sadism. Is that the word for it? It's a world I should be pleased to leave. But not without an epitaph.

I recall, many years ago as a young child, reading in a newspaper of an African leader who stood on the grave of a dead lieutenant and through his tears said: "Africa kills her sons." I don't know what he meant by that, and though I've thought about it long enough, I've not been able to unravel the full mystery of those words. Now, today, this moment, they come flooding back to me. And I want to borrow from him. I'd like you to put this on my gravestone, as my epitaph: "Africa Kills Her Sun." A good epitaph, eh? Cryptic. Definite. A stroke of genius, I should say. I'm sure you'll agree with me. "Africa Kills Her Sun!" That's why she's been described as the Dark Continent? Yes?

So, now, dear girl, I'm done. My heart is light as the daylight which seeps stealthily into our dark cell. I hear the prison guard jangle his keys, put them into the keyhole. Soon he'll turn it and call us out. Our time is up. My time here expires and I must send you all my love. Good-bye.

Yours for ever,

Bana

ALIFA RIFAAT,

a middle-aged Egyptian author, writing in Arabic, spent a lot of time in the countryside with her husband, who is a policeman, and three children. Therefrom she drew her topics for two collections of short stories. Out of them the book entitled Distant View of a Minaret, *consisting of fifteen stories, was published in 1983 in English.*

Her stories are often anthologized.

AT THE TIME OF THE JASMINE

ALIFA RIFAAT

Translated by Denys Johnson-Davies

HE LEANED HIS HEAD AGAINST THE BACKREST OF THE SEAT as the all-station train to Upper Egypt took him joltingly along, producing a doleful rhythm on the rails.

With his handkerchief he wiped his face, removing the specks of sand. Even so the view before his eyes remained blurred, the telegraph poles intermingling with the spectral forms of date palms that broke up into misty phantoms that were soon erased, leaving the yellow surface of sky to others which no sooner made their appearance than they vanished with the same speed.

He caught sight of some young boys plunging naked into the long winding cleft of the Ibrahimiyya Canal, cooling themselves in its shallow waters, while the sun's heat grew stronger, carrying with it what little breeze there was and turning it into a scorching inferno.

Time was at a standstill, stifling his breathing. He began toying wearily with his black tie as he glanced distractedly at the platforms of the small stations the train was passing by, amused at seeing the hefty men proudly clasping their guns slung on their shoulders, and the women spread out on the platform, their children carried close to them, while alongside them lay the cages of chickens they would be trading in the markets.

The cable he had received that morning lay in his jacket pocket.

"Your father Hagg Aballah Shalabi has died. Respect for the dead demands speedy burial."

The words fell heavy as gravel in his throat, despite the fact that for a long time his father had, for him, been like someone already dead—ever since the day he had sent him away to the English school in Maadi some time after his mother's death.

Every morning his mother would place the silver ewer before him and he would rush off to where his father would be sitting at the edge of the prayer mat, his sleeves rolled up and his hands stretched out above the little silver basin, and he would pour the water over them slowly and carefully, in his eyes an expression of admiration for his father as he made his ablutions; then he would pour the water over his feet from which he had removed his socks. He couldn't remember ever having opposed his father in anything, not even when he had carried him out to where the men were and had put him on Antar's back, laughing and boasting jubilantly: "My son Hassan's a real man, a bold horseman—riding's in his blood."

He hadn't been scared that day and hadn't looked up toward the window from which his mother surreptitiously gazed down on him, the kohl mixing in her eyes with tears of pity. He had merely let his short legs hang down the warm flanks and, taking the end of his galabia between his teeth, had clung with both hands to the long hair of the mane. Antar had rushed off with him, crossing the intersecting banked-up tracks round the village, and had brought him back, prancing about amid the admiring cries of the men.

Even when Muntaha, the sweet, shy girl with the thick black pigtails, had come to the house with her red box in her howdah on top of the camel from the neighboring hamlet, and his father had carried her and put her into his bed where his mother used previously to sleep, even Muntaha he had loved. He would cling to her bright-colored, scented dress as she went about the house, finding companionship in her from the loneliness he suffered after his mother had left him.

During the time away from home spent with foreign tutors his childhood quickly died, his love for his father froze and he himself became a sophisticated man not greatly concerned with emotions, subordinating everything to rational standards and to convention. The nostalgia within himself for his village Behbesheen was lost with the passing of the days, and the nights erased from his mind the memory of its rich pastures.

When he grew up he did his duty by visiting the place whenever his father was blessed with another child lest it be said of him that he was annoyed about brothers and sisters sharing with him his father's lands. Once he had opened his own accountancy office his visits grew less owing to his being taken up with business and then came to an end when he married his Turkish colleague Louga Hanem Toubchi. That day he had sent his father a cable reading: "Am getting married tonight."

His father received the news with silence, and when he was blessed with a daughter he again informed his father of the good news. The father contented himself by replying with a cable which said: "Call her Jasmine."

As the days passed his wife turned into a person who was always grumbling, afflicted by the arrogance of her countrymen. He bore her patiently until the day when she shouted at him: "I am Louga Hanem Toubchi—is my name to become Madame Shalabi?"

"Go back to them," he told her with frightening calm.

Taking her daughter, she had gone to the Toubchi household in Zamalek and he had stayed on in his flat in the center of Cairo, not worried about being on his own. He let her be, thinking to break her obstinacy, but she only grew more stub-

born and did not return. After this he did not think of visiting
the village owing to his having become wrapped up in his work.
Today, after the death of his father, his link with the rest of his
relations would no doubt be cut and he would remain without
roots.

The train stopped at Boush, his village's main township, so
he took up his suitcase in which he had, together with his pajamas, thrust the shroud he had bought before leaving Cairo. Duty
demanded that he should bring with him a shroud that was in
keeping with his father's position in the village. People would
think badly of him if he didn't bring some white and green silk
and a cashmere shawl and lay on a fine funeral night. In his
pocket was a large sum he had drawn out from his savings at the
bank to be spent on doing what was expected of him.

As he got down from the train he was seized by the hands of
men come to convey their condolences. Faraghalli, who used as
a child to steal with a fish hook the chickens of Madame Car-
mel, wife of the Health clerk, and who had now become a
spokesman for the peasants, wrapped him round in an embrace
inside his rich *aba* as he muttered: "May God give you strength
to bear this loss, Mr. Hassan."

He muttered some vague words in answer, then his hand was
seized by the strong grasp of Sheikh Hammad, his father's over-
seer, as he passed him Antar's reins with the words: "It's very
hot, men, and it would be wrong of us to leave the dead man till
midday."

Hassan jumped onto Antar's back, proudly sitting upright in
order to assure Sheikh Hammad that a soft hand had nothing to
do with being a real man. The sun was sending down its scorching vertical shafts onto his bare head. The men were pressing
their mounts forward, having let down the ends of their turbans
to protect them from the blazing heat. He himself lifted up the
morning newspaper over his head as he used to do in Cairo,

then lowered it again to his side when he saw the line of girls from the jasmine factory standing and staring at him as he passed between them.

The blast of hot air brought with it the aroma of jasmine, whose pervasive smell clung to the flying specks of sand, penetrating deeply into men's chests so that, in time, all the people of the district suffered from a chronic cough—and no sooner had things quietened down than the next season had made its appearance.

By staying in Cairo he had escaped the malady but now, breathing in the aroma, he began to cough badly. With the coughing his eyes watered, until they became reddened and puffy, while Antar took him along the banked-up tracks between the fields and then came to a stop in front of the stone wall surrounding the house.

"The burial permit is ready," said Sheikh Hammad, "and the sheikhs are here."

As soon as he entered voices were raised in wailing from the women seated on the ground, who were covering their heads with earth.

His young brother came forward carrying the silver basin and ewer for him to make his ablutions, his face bearing the same dull dismay he himself had been afflicted with the day his mother had died.

He patted his shoulder consolingly, then made his ablutions and entered the dead man's room. His legs began shaking suddenly as he advanced toward the brass bed where his father's body lay. He drew back the end of the sheet covering the face and the flies buzzed, then settled again. Staring at his father's face, he muttered through dry lips: "Peace be upon you and the mercy of Allah."

Then he pressed them to the cold forehead. Though incapable of returning the salutation, the dead man had certainly heard him. Crystal tears glinted in his eyes, putting the walls out of focus and setting dancing before his eyes the framed Qur'anic verse in large Kufic calligraphy that stood over the bed: "Make ready for them such force and tethered horses as you are able— Allah the Great has spoken aright."

The voices of the sheikhs grew louder as they recited the most beautiful names of Allah. Sheikh Abdul Maqsoud the corpse-washer came forward and drew off the white galabia and undid, from round the waist, the black snake-skin belt that the Hagg used to wear, a snake he had shot after it had for long struck terror in Behbesheen.

Sheikh Abdul Maqsoud turned the belt over in his hands, his deep-set eyes gleaming with joy; he then took hold of the dead man's hand and pulled the large gold ring off it: all this had now become his, a contribution of alms made to him by the family in memory of the dead man. He then raised the rigid body with his assistant and laid it down on the wooden plank set over the large brass bowl.

He handed the brass cup to Hassan and advanced the container of pure water toward him, saying: "Take hold of yourself, my son, otherwise your tears will make the water impure."

With steady hand Hassan poured the water over the head and body which Sheikh Abdul Maqsoud was rubbing down with soap.

When the voices began reciting the Qur'an they performed the rites of ablution on the dead man, then dried the body. They tore the winding sheets with a shrill screech that jolted Hassan's nerves. He took control of himself as they stitched up the pieces of cloth and wrapped them round the body, tying them securely at the legs and on top of the head. They spread the bed covering in the wooden bier and laid the body on it, then covered it over with the cashmere shawl.

Sheikh Hammad entered and took the brass bedstead to

pieces, while the women's voices rose loud with wailing. The brass bedstead had been set up ever since Hagg Aballah's first marriage; Hassan's mother had breathed her last in it, and to it he had brought Muntaha in marriage and in it she had had his other children. But with the death of the master of the house the bedstead must be done away with and not set up again till after the period of mourning.

Hassan gave a sharp cough as the aroma of incense inflamed the sensitivity of his nose and the tears flowed copiously from his eyes. Stolidly, he passed the handkerchief over his face and went forward to take up one of the front shafts of the bier with Sheikh Hammad, who took the other, the rear ones being taken by two faithful retainers. Resting it on their shoulders, they went out into the courtyard.

Owais, the man in charge of the livestock, threw a young water buffalo to the ground in front of the bier and ran Hamid the butcher's knife over its throat and the blood spilt out on the hot, burning sands in a sacrifice to the dead man.

The men trod across the pool of blood as they bore the bier to the other side of the stone wall and the funeral cortege arranged itself in ranks behind them.

They hurried along with the bier as they fervently uttered, in hoarse voices, the formula of the unity of Allah: there is no god but Allah. The women hastened behind them, clad in the *shagga* that hung down over their bodies like a tent, allowing nothing to show but the gleam of their eyes.

The sun had passed the center point in the sky but still sent down its searing rays into the sands so that its heat penetrated stingingly through their sandals.

They passed along the winding village lanes till they came down to where the only mosque stood, in the middle of the road that led to the other hill where the ruins of graves lay in ranks at the foot of the mountain.

Casting off their sandals, they took the dead man in and placed him in the *mihrab*. Seven times they uttered the words "Allah is greatest," then said the funeral prayers, after which they again took up the bier and hurried along with it to the cemetery. The gravedigger had prepared the grave, opening the mouth and removing the earth from the entrance and collecting up the bones of the former inhabitants and tying them up in their decaying shrouds and placing them against the inner wall painted with lime; then he scattered the soft sand mixed with henna, in preparation for laying down the new corpse.

The coffin grew heavier on its bearers as they hurried along, panting hard, their shoulders almost twisted from their bodies; it was as though the dead man was resisting the grave in terror, so that, as they advanced, the front of the bier turned them in the direction of the houses and they progressed with sideways steps. The stalks of maize in the basins of cultivated land gave out, behind red sparks discharged from the sharp blade of the sun, a white vapor that made their eyes smart. Having reached the opening, they put down the bier in front of it.

Sheikh Hammad placed a small pair of scissors in Hassan's hand, saying between his teeth: "Come along, man, do your duty. Snip the shroud or it will be stolen by those dirty thieves of gravediggers. I swear by the Almighty if one of them falls into my hands I'll hang him on the tree alongside the mosque."

Then he spat on the ground to show his disgust.

Hassan took the scissors and went down behind the corpse into the darkness of the grave.

The sound of the Qur'an reciters grew louder, speeding up their recitation, as though they had another appointment.

A lizard passed between his feet, then disappeared into the darkness. He squatted down on his knees alongside his father and stretched out his hand with the scissors and began cutting the shroud, careful not to touch the dead flesh. The gravedigger patted him on the shoulder as he muttered: "Come along, man —may the Lord give him protection."

He got to his feet and walked backward behind him, as he gave his salutations to the dead man and then came out into the sunlight. He stood among the men till the gravedigger had completed his task and had piled the earth against the entrance and poured water over it, then watered the nearby cactus with what was left.

The sun was now suspended over the peak of the mountain, and it cast forth red shafts of light that made long shadows, depicting vague specters. The tombs looked similar to the scattered houses in the dusky light of sunset.

Someone called out: "Say that Allah is One!"

In a deep voice they all muttered fervently: "There is no god but Allah."

"Everyone thereon passes away," quoted the gravedigger, "and there remains your Lord's face possessed of majesty and splendor."

"That which Allah has said is the truth," they all called out.

Stealthily Hassan passed some money to the gravedigger and set about returning, with the crowd following him, to the courtyard of the house.

The men seated themselves on the cane chairs that had been set out in rows with the kerosene lamps above their heads; each time the Qur'an reciter finished a chapter, cups of coffee were handed round. They would listen fervently, rocking to the rhythm, until the reciter concluded by reciting the Fatiha. By this time it was midnight, and the men spread out the palms of their hands, then passed them over their faces in supplication.

Giving Hassan a sideways look, Sheikh Hammad said: "May Allah have mercy upon him, he was a loving father to everybody, and the greatest horseman in the whole district."

Faraghalli answered him: "There are plenty of horsemen

about, man. What was special about him was that he could put his ear to the ground and say 'So-and-so's going along such-and-such a track and he'll be arriving after such-and-such a time' and his words would ring true as a gold guinea."

Hassan lowered his head in silence. Perhaps these men knew his father better than he did. Was it in fact he himself who was responsible for the estrangement between himself and his father? He took out a wad of notes from his pocket and thrust them into Sheikh Hammad's hand.

"Spend them on what's required—tonight's at my expense."

Confused by Hassan's generosity, Sheikh Hammad exclaimed: "What nobility—May the Lord bless you."

Trays with bowls of broth ranged round with pieces of boiled meat were set up on the low tables, and Hassan rose to invite the men, while he himself ate a little with difficulty, waiting till everyone had dispersed and the pressure lamps had been put out.

Entering the house, he walked in loneliness through its rooms, passing among the women squatting on the mats, clad in black. From the ground there rose a black tent that moved toward him; from two tiny slits there looked out at him two eyes which he recognized as those of Muntaha, his father's wife. She held out her hand with a key, muttering in a voice choked by weeping: "The Hagg Aballah handed over to me the key of the cupboard in trust for me to give to you."

"Be strong," he muttered, taking the key from her.

"Strength is with Allah."

He went to the cupboard he had known since childhood. As he did so his eyes fell for an instant on the glistening water on the floor, left over after the dead man had been washed.

His hand came across a large bundle of notes, also a piece of paper on which was recorded the names of those who were to benefit from the sum of money. His gaze came to rest on the name of his daughter Jasmine mentioned among those to inherit. The words became blurred and he sat down on the edge of the mattress that had been laid out on the ground for him to sleep on instead of the bed that had been dismantled and some of whose pieces were leaning in the corner against the wall. He placed his head between his hands and the papers between his outstretched legs. The smell of the jasmine whose flowers were opening in the night like white stars was wafted in to him by the breeze. He had said "Call her Jasmine." He had loved her and had mentioned her among his own children in his will. He had no doubt thought about her and had perhaps sometimes longed to see her. Why had he not asked to meet her? More than once he'd said to Louga Hanem, before the final break: "We must take a train to the country so my father can see my child." She would put her elegant nose in the air and he would keep silent. Too often he kept silent. Once, during one of the rare times they met, his father had said: "Next year, my son, we'll make the pilgrimage together," and he had burst into childish laughter.

The years had passed and a life had come to an end and the wish had not been fulfilled. He smiled sadly at the memory, beset by a feeling of bafflement. The days had robbed the two of them and they had not gone. They hadn't even seen enough of each other, and a sensation of yearning for his father exploded suddenly in his breast. Which of them was to blame?

He woke up from his thoughts to the echoing howling of the mountain wolves. Had the grave robber done it? Had he left the opening of the grave unclosed after him?

The blood rose up into his neck, as he choked with grief and anger and he let his body fall back as though struck by a blow from the Hagg's famous staff. He had never in fact suffered it. When he was young it was enough for Hagg Aballah to wave it in his face and shout "The rod's for the insubordinate," for his weak body to tremble under the imaginary blows.

"Father, you gave me a real beating tonight."

The winds whistled forlornly through the branches of the date palms, then silence reigned while the jasmine buds carefully folded themselves against the rapidly spreading rays of the sun. The cooing of pigeons rose from the dovecotes on top of the houses.

Sheikh Hammad's voice called from outside: "Mr. Hassan, the commissioner has sent the Jeep to take you to the station—there's half an hour till the train goes."

Awwad entered carrying the basin and ewer, and in his wake Muntaha, her hair disheveled and in her nightgown, carrying a tray of breakfast.

He went out to the car. As he got into it he waved at the men who had gathered, then it moved off, leaving behind it a whirlpool of dust that enveloped the children who had risen from sleep and collected at the sound of the car and were now trying to catch up as, with the ends of their galabias in their teeth, they ran along on their thin brown legs.

OSSIE O. ENEKWE

was born in 1942 in Nigeria where he graduated at the University of Nigeria in 1971. In 1982 he got his Ph.D. from Columbia University. In 1977 Enekwe published the collection of poems entitled Broken Pots *and a novel* Come Thunder *in 1984.* Marching to Kilimanjaro *is the title of his newest collection of poems (1992).* Igbo Masks: The Oneness of Ritual and Theatre *(dramatic theory) was published in 1987.*

Enekwe's fiction and poetry have been featured in several U.S. literary journals, and in Okike, *the Nigerian literary periodical.*

A member of the editorial board of Okike: An African Journal of New Writing *since 1978, Enekwe is the current editor of the journal, based at the University of Nigeria, Nsukka, where he teaches dramatic arts and creative writing. He was founding editor of* Omabe: Poetry from Nsukka *(1972) and the* Columbia Reader *(1974).*

A founding member of the Association of Nigerian Authors, Enekwe was its national vice president (1988–91).

THE
LAST BATTLE

OSSIE O. ENEKWE

IT WAS ABOUT 7:30 P.M. IN UZOLLA SECTOR.

Noise of battle completely swallowed the whole front. The battle line was one vast furnace as Federal and Secessionist guns roared and thundered like a thousand wounded monsters. Flashes of fire lit the jungle as shells burst into fragments, swept away in all directions, carrying with them dust and rocks, branches torn from trees and pieces of flesh and bone.

It was in this circumstance that young Lt. Joseph Umeh, formerly of the Suicide Squad, arrived at the 30th Brigade Camp at Emele-uzo. He was angry to be sent there. His request to be transferred to the rear had been rejected and he was now being sent to another hot sector.

"To another hot sector," he murmured, biting his lower lip with his front teeth, "I must be told whether I alone caused this war. How can I be moving from sector to sector like an armored car, whereas other officers, those that have godfathers, remain at the rear attending parties."

He had felt like this, disillusioned and angry, since he received the deployment signal. He had almost gone mad. Something would have happened to him if he had not been restrained by some of his fellow officers. He had wanted to march to his C.O. and tell him to "go to blazes." He would have ripped open his fading battle shirt and shown him the scar of a ferret wound spreading from his navel down to his groin. He would have shown him his buttocks too. And then said to him: Sir, have you ever heard the whistling of a bullet? But his fellow officers had restrained him. No doubt he would have ended up in a court-martial which might have cost him his life.

And to top it all, he had also to carry his kit on his head and hitchhike a distance of about fifteen miles to Uzolla sector. What an affront! His C.O. had refused to assign a vehicle to him because he was no longer his "responsibility." They would not even allow him to take his batman with him because of "scarcity of men." So he had to carry his kit on his head to the front.

So, Lt. Joe Umeh was like a battered old pugilist. He had joined the Rebel Army because he wanted to cut a figure. His bravery in battle was not all as a result of his belief, but something inside him, a capacity for hard labor and an obsessive desire to excel. Many of his kind had kissed the dust and rotted in hundreds of fields. But, he was lucky. Since the start of the shooting, he had taken part in twenty battles. There were some he knew who got killed in their first battles. Before every battle he never expected to return alive, but God was very kind to him.

It seemed he would never die. After each battle, he came out full of praises. Once he had single-handedly wrecked a ferret car which he had trapped in a ditch. The proper name for him should have been the "forest fox." But, his mates and followers called him "Atila." He was tall and heavy, but his face and manners were gentle. He smiled often, even when he was angry.

God was kind to Lt. Umeh, but his fellow human beings were hostile. In spite of all his exploits, he had been passed over again and again for promotion. Maybe it was because he was a stammerer or because he did not curry favor with his superiors. It could have been both. It could also be because his face was ugly (not from nature, but from the handiwork of a bullet which had hit him between his right eye and his nose). He was lucky though. The bullet had traveled very far before it hit him and buried itself two inches deep. The doctors had pulled it off quickly. So within four weeks he was again battle-worthy.

The 30 Brigade Camp in which he found himself was dark and cold as a mortuary. There was a tiny arrow of light sticking out of some place. So he walked toward it. It turned out to be a batcher. He halted and listened and then tapped on the bamboo door. After about ten seconds, he heard boots approaching the door. When the door swung open, the light of a lamp hit his face and he was looking up at a soldier. Lt. Umeh said, "Good evening. I am Lt. Umeh recently deployed here. Can I see the Adjutant?"

The soldier stepped back into the room and said, "Come in . . . I am Captain Ofili, the Adjutant. I am pleased to meet you."

"Thank you."

"How did you come?"

"On foot."

"Hah, you must be tired."

"Yes, I am really exhausted."

Captain Ofili led the way to the end of the hall. Lt. Umeh noticed that he had a slight limp. He was happy to see a man who had got a battle scar, like himself.

Captain Ofili said, "Lt. Umeh, we have no food in the camp. But, we have some palm wine. Let me get you some."

"It's okay, sir."

Captain Ofili indicated a low bench by the corner and asked Umeh to sit down. There was a cupboard full of files by the corner, too. Ofili opened it and brought out a bottle of palm wine and a tumbler which he handed over to Umeh. Umeh filled the glass, drank half of it and looking up at Ofili asked, "When do I meet the C.O.?"

"Not this night. He lives five miles away. But he will be here tomorrow morning."

Umeh sighed. "When did the present operation begin?"

"Exactly at 18:00 hours. It has always been like that here. We have lost over eighty men since the present ops. Over ten officers have died since the last twenty days."

"This is a disastrous war," said Umeh, full of premonition. "We are doing the impossible, like throwing pebbles at a man armed with a spear."

"And on top of that, hunger," added Ofili.

There was a long pause during which the two men reflected. Presently, Ofili said, "Umeh, come along, let me take you to my room. I suppose you want to sleep?"

"Yes," said Umeh, "I need to sleep. I am dog tired."

Ofili limped along, leading the way, across the dark field of the camp. Soon, they approached a collection of batchers. Ofili tapped on the door of one of them. A young private opened the door.

When he was seated Ofili said, "Umeh, we are glad to have you here." But Umeh kept mum. "We have heard of your exploits."

Umeh sighed and said, "But, you have not heard of my problems."

"Everybody has problems."

But Umeh said, getting a trifle angry, "I don't care about other people's problems."

Ofili was surprised. He asked, "What is wrong?"

"I have two fat bullets inside my buttocks, but that doesn't qualify me for a transfer to the rear. I am among those who have to die so that the mighty lords may live and enjoy."

"Yes, I understand. I too have a crippled knee. But couldn't the doctors remove your bullets?"

"How could they? No. The bullets went into corners where

they cannot be tampered with. They won't come out unless my bones are split like firewood. And yet I do not deserve to be given rear duty." Lt. Umeh was getting more infuriated as he spoke.

"Now look," he said, unbuttoning his khaki shirt and loosening his belt, "this is a ferret wound I got at Onitsha sector."

Captain Ofili shrugged his shoulders when he saw the scar. He did not say anything. It was amazing that somebody could have had such a wound and remain alive.

Umeh continued: "So you can see . . . I have been moving from sector to sector collecting bullet wounds and being stitched all the time like a punching bag."

Captain Ofili sighed and said, "Hah, if one were to worry about the injustices inflicted on us little men, the war would have ended a long time ago."

There was silence for about five minutes. Captain Ofili indicated the bed and said, "Umeh, you better sleep. I go back to the office. I'll remain there until I hear reports from the battle."

Umeh asked, "What of the other officers?"

"They are all taking part in the ops. And if we lose them, only two officers will be left in the Brigade—you and me."

"Why?" asked Umeh in amazement.

"We have been expecting several officers from the DHQ. But, none has arrived. Good night."

Captain Ofili wanted to get away fast. His conversation with Umeh did not cheer him. When a hero loses faith, his admirers go dumb.

Later in the night, remnants of the attackers from the 32 Brigade staggered back into the camp. Of the one hundred and twenty attacking force only forty returned. The two officers who led them had been torn to pieces trying to charge a Federal position. The report, though shocking, was not altogether disheartening for there were several reports of cold-blooded bravery. There was the story of a young private who charged a machine-gun crew with an empty rifle. It was only the lack of ammunition that brought them defeat, claimed the survivors.

The next morning, during parade, the C.O. drove up in his Land Rover. There was a hush as the six soldiers on escort jumped out onto the field and spread out, brandishing automatic rifles. It was as if the whole camp was full of enemy troops. The escorts stood in a horseshoe formation behind him. The Adjutant limped toward him and saluted. The C.O. got the report of the last operation and asked, "Have the Infantry officers deployed here arrived?"

"Only one, sir."

"His name?"

"Lt. Joe Umeh, sir."

"Dismiss the parade and bring him to me."

In the office, the C.O. congratulated Lt. Umeh on his previous exploits and explained his plans, one of which was to launch an attack on the Federal positions the same night. He told him, "As soon as the objective is secured, at least five hundred troops will arrive from other sectors to help. Lt. Umeh . . . I'll allow you to draw your plans and choose your men. You have ample ammo."

"Yessir."

"Any questions?"

"Yessir. Please, can I have some automatic rifles for my men?"

"There are no automatic rifles . . . As you were."

"Yessir."

Lt. Umeh walked across the wide school field toward the old school hall where the privates were being rested. Some of them were sitting on the grass in front of the building and breaking palm kernels which they chewed and swallowed hurriedly in order to numb the hunger which was gnawing their maws all the time.

Some of them were naked, stark naked. Some had tattered rags around their hips. The outlines of their ribs were clearly discernible on the dark skins.

When they saw him striding toward them, they got to their feet like tired dogs and began to scuttle back into the hall. Lt. Umeh smiled—a wan, painful smile. He was not surprised. These boys were like waifs waiting for extermination. These boys were afraid of the world. The world had treated them badly. They were full of bitterness: an inexpressible feeling was eating deep into their hearts. They were the boys who won and lost battles. When they were well led by good officers, they fought. If not they ran. They were used to being kept at a camp for rest which was meant to keep them available for new attacks. And so they were afraid of new officers, new signals and new movements.

Lt. Umeh walked on as if he was not interested in them. He strode into the hall and saw many of them lying on the bare floor among little heaps of kernel husks. They stood up with great effort and saluted, "Mon sarp."

"Good evening, my brothers," he said. "Wey the sergeant?"

"Here, sir," said a tall boy who had no visible sign of his rank.

"Okay, I want everybody outside immediately."

"Yessum."

Lt. Umeh stood there and watched them shuffle along like people who had never drilled before. Only two or three of them had boots on. But those boots were worn to the sole.

Outside, they stood in lines and waited for him. Lt. Umeh marched forward and said, "I be Lt. Umeh. I don fight for every sector, but I never die. And I no go die. Those wey follow me, no go die. I don come make I come help you people here. Make you no fear. Everything go be alright. You go get plenty wakis. Stand by . . . Rest and sleep. Biafra, Kwenu! . . . Biafra Kwenu! . . ."

There were only fragmentary sounds of "yah."

Lt. Umeh said, "Make una sing me one song."

There was silence for about thirty seconds. Then the sergeant began, *"Enyi Biafra le le, Enyi Biafra le le le,"* expecting the boys to reecho the second line. There were only tired responses, but he kept on singing. Singing painfully.

> *"Remember nu Chuma Nzeogwu*
> *Chuma Nzeogwu bu nwa Biafra, Enyi.*
> *Remember nu Willie Archibong*
> *Willie Archibong bu nwa Biafra, Enyi."*

The singing continued for a few more minutes and died.

Lt. Umeh was now incredibly downhearted. His head was full of voices speaking to him at the same time. He went back and lay on the bed till midnight.

At 5 a.m. Lt. Umeh was at the battle line with the boys. With the light they would see the Federal positions and attack immediately. That was the plan. The Federal side would not be expecting them so soon after the previous day's disaster. It was going to be a surprise attack.

The boys were armed with bolt-action rifles which they called "cock-and-shoot." They had six bullets apiece. Lt. Umeh, since his last encounter with the C.O., had been very taciturn. But these boys had never fought under him and so could not tell that he had changed.

His position was about five hundred yards to the enemy trenches. He was looking up at them from a valley. He said to the boys, "You no go fire until I command." "Yessir," they murmured with fear in their hearts. At six, he said, "Advance."

When they marched about a hundred yards he pulled a dirty white handkerchief from his pocket, stuck it to his bayonet and said, "Make una drop your guns. Raise your hands. We are surrounded." They obeyed easily enough.

From where they lay with their guns at the ready, Federal troops watched in amazement as the platoon marched toward them with their hands raised over their heads.

ADEWALE MAJA-PEARCE

was born in 1953. His first collection of short stories is entitled Loyalties and Other Stories *(1987) and his travelogue:* In My Father's Country *(1987).* In 1990 he published The Heinemann Book of African Poetry in English—*a chronological representation of excellence in African poetry over the last thirty years,* and in 1992 A Mask Dancing: Nigerian Novelists of the English. How Many Miles to Babylon? *(1990) and* Who's Afraid of Wole Soyinka? *(1991) are his latest books. At present he is editor for Africa of the journal* Index on Censorship.

CIVIL WAR
I–VII

ADEWALE MAJA-PEARCE

I

WE WERE SPLIT UP INTO GROUPS OF TWO AND ASSIGNED A hut each. Our Commander said: "Be ready at 05:30 hours," and with that we turned in.

In our hut a woman lay on a mat and an old man squatted on the ground beside her. He stopped talking and stood up to meet us. His skin seemed to be stretched across his bones.

"Welcome, gentlemen, welcome," he said. He turned to the woman, who had not stirred.

"Can't you see that we have guests? Stand up and attend to them," he said. The woman, who was young, got up silently and backed into a corner. She watched us with frightened eyes. She was clutching a bundle.

The old man raised his hands: "It is little enough, gentlemen, but it is yours. Will you take tea?"

"Don't bother," I said.

"Old man, where are your troops hiding?" my companion said.

"Troops?"

"Yes, your troops. Where are they hiding?"

The old man laughed.

"Do you think I am joking?" my companion said. He removed his revolver from the holster and held it in his palm. "Where are they?" he asked.

"Gone," the old man said, "those of them that are alive."

"I don't believe you. I think they are hiding in the forest. They are waiting for us to sleep."

The woman made a sound.

"They are waiting for us, I can feel it," my companion said. "Light a candle, I know that you want to trick us."

"But . . ." the old man began.

"Light a candle I say, don't you hear me?" He waved the revolver in the old man's direction. The woman began whimpering and would have screamed but I looked at her and shook my head.

When the candle was lit I went over to my companion. "Take it easy," I whispered. "Remember that we have sentries posted all around. If anything happens they will alert us. Let's get some sleep, we've been marching all day, and tomorrow it'll be the same." He looked at me mistrustfully. "You can take the mat," I said.

He looked at the woman, who had not moved.

"Come here," he said. She opened her mouth to say something but no words came. Only her eyes expressed her terror.

"Are you deaf?" the old man said to her. She got to her feet.

"Show me," my companion demanded, indicating the bundle. She began whimpering as before and tightened her hold on it. He slapped her hand across the face and snatched it from her. Wrapped in the cloth was a tiny child.

"It's dead," he said. "Doesn't she know?"

The old man shrugged. I went out.

When I returned my companion and the woman were lying together on the mat. The old man was squatting against the far wall. I stretched out across the entrance and fell asleep.

I woke up when it was still dark. I heard a noise from the mat. As my eyes became accustomed to the darkness I peered over to where the old man was. He was in the same position, staring at the couple. I closed my eyes.

In the morning we marched out. We were a pathetic bunch. We had been fighting continually for weeks and we were exhausted. All day long the insects swarmed around us and the sun beat down on us. What little food we had would not last us much longer.

Those who were wounded had to take care of themselves. By evening time some of them had fallen behind. We did not expect to see them again.

When we finally camped our Commander said: "According to my calculations we should be near the town of O___. With any luck we will be there the day after tomorrow. Try and get as much rest as you can. I myself will take the first watch."

Suddenly my companion shouted: "I don't believe you, Captain, it is all lies you are telling us." I ran toward him as he started to unbuckle his revolver but before I could reach him I heard a single shot and he fell. When I got to him he was already dead. The bullet had entered his skull and lodged in his brain.

I waited until everyone was asleep and then started out. When I thought I had traveled far enough I switched on the torch. The forest was full of sounds, and every moment I expected to be my last.

When I reached the village I sought out the hut. At the entrance I paused. I heard the familiar voice of the old man. He was speaking in a low voice in a language I couldn't understand. I entered.

"Who is there?" he asked, turning to me. I shone the torch on my face and then back at them. The woman was lying on the mat, clutching her bundle.

"You've come back," he said.

"To . . . to see if I could do anything for you," I said.

"Have you any food?" he asked.

"No, but I have some money." I held out some notes; it was all I had. He spat on the ground.

"What will that do for us?" he said.

"I don't know," I said.

"Then go back to your people, you can do nothing for us," he said. He turned his back on me and bent over the woman and continued his monologue in his unfamiliar language. I stood there for a while before I left.

II

For three days we had been wandering about in the bush, tired, hungry, and sick. Outside the town of O___ we had been surprised by a patrol of Federal troops and only a handful of us had managed to escape. Now we were without supplies, and if we did not soon find food and shelter we would perish.

There were a dozen of us, with half as many rifles between us and hardly any ammunition. We had no choice but to press on and hope.

It was the nights that were the worst. After a long day's march we would be exhausted but unable to sleep. The wounded among us would begin to moan, low and steady at first but, as the night wore on, louder and more insistent, the only sound in that vast tropical stillness. And as if that wasn't enough we would be assailed by mosquitoes, thousands of them, attracted no doubt by the smell of human blood. By the morning of the fourth day I knew something had to be done.

There was only one man I fully trusted. He was the only other with some experience of warfare. I called him over.

"Joshua, we must go west, back to the town of O___," I said.

He nodded.

"Can we do it in a day, do you think?"

"Only if we get rid of the sick," he said.

He had understood me perfectly. The war had knocked all the sentimentality out of him, which is why I liked him.

"Round up the fit ones and take them away," I said. "I will do what must be done and catch up with you."

He made as if to go, but hesitated.

"What's the matter?" I asked.

"Let me be the one to do it, Captain. They are my people, it will make it easier for them."

I agreed. There were four who would be left. One was a boy of fourteen. He had been shot in the leg and gangrene had set in. Without medical help he would have died anyway.

So I set off with the remainder. Although no one spoke I knew what they were thinking, but I also knew they were relieved not to have been the ones to have had to make the choice.

That night we arrived back at the town. We split up into groups of two and made for a house where we knew we would be welcome. The Federal troops were all over but we managed to make it without incident.

The house we gathered at was owned by an old man whose sons had fought under my command, and he was pleased to see us. While his daughter served us he gave us a rundown of the movement, size, and distribution of the enemy.

In the morning I was the first to wake. Dawn was only just breaking but I felt refreshed. Somewhere in the depths of a dream an idea had presented itself to me and I went off in search of Joshua. He was stretched out on a mat in the corner of the living room. His throat had been cut with a sharp instrument and the blood had congealed without spilling. Which of my men had done it? Or had they all conspired? Had they been called upon to avenge the blood of their brothers?

III

After six months' heavy fighting they liberated the city of N___ from the rebels. Death and disease had cut their original force by half and they had almost run out of ammunition. A relief force was on its way to take over and they were recalled to barracks, a journey of almost six hundred miles.

The last night in the city they spent celebrating. Oluwaju lost count of how many beers he'd had after the first couple of hours. He went from one bar to the next until, sometime after midnight, he found himself in a nightclub with three companions.

Because he had money in his pocket he was immediately surrounded by women. He ordered drinks all round and danced. This went on until he passed out. When he woke up it was morning and he was in bed with a young woman.

"Where are we?" he asked.

"In my room, don't you remember?"

"Did you drag me all the way here yourself?"

"How could I? You walked."

His head was throbbing. He saw his trousers hanging from a nail on the back of the door.

"Where is my money," he demanded, searching through the pockets.

"I didn't touch your money," she said.

"You lie," he said. "I couldn't have spent it all."

She shrugged. "As you like," she said, and began to dress. Furious, he grabbed her shoulder and slapped her face.

"You are a liar," he repeated.

She looked at him without fear. "Are you happy now?" she said and went out.

When she returned she handed him a cup of tea and sat on the bed. Her mouth was sore from where he had hit her because she drank hesitantly, the rim of the cup barely touching her lips. Then there was a knock on the door and an old woman entered. She was lame in one leg and carried a stick.

"You have a visitor," she said when she saw him.

"Yes, Mama."

The old woman went away.

"Does she live with you?" Oluwaju asked.

"Yes."

"Tell her to come back, I have to be going," he said.

"Wait," she said suddenly, clutching his arm. "I want to go with you."

"How do you know where I'm going?"

"You and your friends were talking."

He laughed. "How can I take you and your mother? You're crazy. And what will you do in Lagos? Do you know anybody there?"

"I am young, I know how to survive. I can't stay here any longer. Please, take me. If I stay here I don't know what will happen to me. Before this war started I had a good job and I lived in a house with my family. Just look at me now," she said.

"I'm sorry," he said, "but it's out of the question. Even if I wanted to my Captain wouldn't allow it. And then there's your mother, she's an old lady . . ."

"My mother would stay here," she said.

"You would leave her here!"

"Of course," she said, and added: "The journey alone would kill her."

"And what will become of her?"

"She hasn't long to live," she said. When she saw the look he gave her she said: "So you think it is bad of me, eh? What do you know of my suffering? Did I ask for this stupid war? Did I? The things I have to do to eat . . ."

"I'm sorry," he repeated.

"Now it's you who lie," she said. "If you were really sorry you would help me." She was working herself up; in a moment she would be hysterical. He grabbed his shirt and fled, and as he emerged into the street he heard her calling after him.

IV

Look, let me tell you at once: he was not a bad man. In the three years I spent fighting I saw worse men, believe me. If I tell you some of the things our men did you will call me a liar to my face.

The day before it happened he saved my life. If it wasn't for him I wouldn't be here today. You think I'm joking? Let me tell you. It was like this. We were advancing on the village of O____. It was nearly dark and we were tired and hungry. All I wanted was to lie down and go to sleep, even in that bush. I didn't care about the war or anything, I just wanted to be left in peace, you understand me?

Okay, so our Captain told us that we had to capture the village that night. Well, what could we do? We had to obey. Orders were orders: let me see the man who would have said otherwise. As I told you, night was approaching. He and I and two others were told to go on ahead and scout around. All of a sudden there was a shot and I was hit. Then you know what happened? The other two ran away. Only he remained. He placed himself in front of me and opened fire in the direction from which the shot had come. There was a scream and then silence.

Time passed. We heard our men some distance behind us. The next thing I knew he lifted me up on his shoulder, and then I passed out.

When I woke up I was lying on a mat in a hut. There was a candle beside me and he was bending over me.

"How are you feeling?" he asked.

"I'm fine," I said.

"Good," he said, then, in a whisper: "Listen, I saw a woman. You know how it is. If you think you will be alright here by yourself I won't be more than an hour at most."

"Go ahead," I said.

I fell asleep. I was woken by a sound while it was still dark. It was him: he had returned. I waited for him to settle down before I spoke.

"Was it good?" I asked him.

"Not bad," he said and lit a cigarette. There was something wrong with the way he said it, but I did not press him: after all, it was his own business.

When I woke in the morning he was not there. I heard a commotion outside. People were shouting. I could not make out what they were saying and I was too weak to go and see for myself.

Later in the day our Captain came to see how I was. I asked him what was happening.

"There was a murder here last night. One of the men from the village was killed, and his wife says one of our own men did it. She has identified him."

He didn't have to tell me; I knew who it was.

"What are you going to do with him?" I asked. He

shrugged and turned to go. At that moment I felt sorry for him: I could see how troubled he was.

"Listen and you will hear," he said, and left.

I waited. An hour later I heard the order and half a dozen rifles go off in unison.

Well, such is war. It changes a man. As you see me so I am not the same person I was before this wretched business started: in those days I was only a kid. But bear witness now: never again will I do it. You can trust me on that.

V

The boy hid behind the old shed and watched the soldiers march into the village, and when the last of them had gone past he ran across the yard and into his hut.

"Mama," he called, excited. The woman looked up from the stove before which she was squatting. There was a baby tied on her back.

"Come and eat your food," she said.

"Mama, the soldiers have come," the boy said.

"Sit down and eat, I say," the woman said. The baby started crying. She untied it, sat on the bed, and gave it her breast.

"And when you have finished don't let me hear that you were playing among them," she said.

"Yes, Mama."

"They are not good people. They are the ones who killed your father and they wouldn't mind to kill us. How many were they?"

"Plenty," he said, "about a hundred. And they all carried rifles."

"You better not go out at all," she said.

"But . . ."

"But nothing. Do as I say, you want to get yourself killed? Don't you know that they take small boys like you into the bush?"

"Yes, Mama."

The day grew hotter until the heat was almost intolerable. The boy read some of his old schoolbooks and listened to the shouting and laughter of the soldiers. In the middle of the afternoon two of them came. One sat down while the other searched the room. It was the work of two minutes: after he had looked under the bed and inside the wardrobe there was nowhere else.

"Nothing, Captain."

"Where is your husband?" the Captain asked his mother.

"He's dead."

"How do you know?"

"I was told."

"By whom?"

"A friend whose husband was killed with him."

"How long ago was this?"

"About six months."

"Are there no men left in the village?"

"Only the old and wounded."

"Where have they all gone?"

"They are all dead."

"I don't believe you," he said. The boy saw how frightened his mother was, and he pitied and hated her for it.

"But it is true," she said.

"We have had reports that rebel troops were seen here less than a week ago."

"Who told you, it's a lie."

"So you say, but we were told about it from several of your own people."

"They only told you that to please you."

The Captain suddenly banged his clenched fist on the table. The boy saw his mother jump, and then try desperately to regain her composure.

"You know what we do to people who lie to us?" he shouted. His mother hung her head. Her hands were shaking by her side, and he saw that the Captain noticed it.

"Hey, you, come with me," the Captain said and stood up. His mother swung round and pulled him to her.

"Leave him, he is only a child," she pleaded. The Captain laughed.

"Do you think we are going to harm him?" He signaled to the other, who had all the while been standing to attention.

"I just want to have a little chat with him, that's all," he said.

The Captain took him around the village, all the while watching everything.

"It's women who bring all the trouble in this world," he said. "We men know how to speak the truth and get it over with, not so?"

"Yessah."

"Don't call me sir, my name is Baba. What is yours?"

"Christopher."

"Well, Christopher, won't you level with me, man to man, eh?" He stopped and looked at him and smiled. "Now, tell me, is it true that your father is dead?"

"Yes."

"You saw his body for yourself?"

"No, I was told."

The Captain put his hand on his shoulder. "Don't let it worry you, I can see that you are somebody who will go far in life. It's this wretched war that messes up our plans. Perhaps when it's over I'll see what I can do to arrange for you to get out of here and make something of yourself in the world."

The boy nodded. They resumed walking. Still the Captain never ceased his watching.

"How many of your troops were here last week?" he asked abruptly, peering toward the distant bushes.

"About thirty," the boy answered without thinking, and then he knew he had done wrong. The Captain stopped and looked at him. The smile had gone from his face. The boy felt fear.

"Were they armed?"

"I . . . I . . ."

"Answer me, boy!" he shouted. Terrified, the boy nodded.

"All of them?"

"Yes."

VI

There were ways in which he was absolutely fearless. The men under his command had the greatest respect for him, and there were many who thoughtlessly risked death at his word. He was the only Commander who lived like his men, and more. He took privileges for himself and always headed the scouting parties into enemy territory.

One day he walked straight into a contingent of Federal troops. It was not an ambush and they were as surprised as we, and only managed to get the better of us because there were more of them than there were of us. And they were better armed. At some points the fighting was literally hand-to-hand, but I knew we were done for.

"Let's get out of here," he shouted to me at the first opportunity and we fled. We lost ourselves in the jungle and never paused to look back. By the time we finally stopped our clothes were torn and we were bleeding all over.

"We'll rest here for a while," he said.

"Do you know where we are?" I asked.

"I think so, but I'm not sure." He looked up. Through the tops of the trees the sun dipped to the west.

"If we go that way we should come to the village of O____ by nightfall," he said, pointing in the opposite direction. "Let's hope the Federal troops don't get there before us."

"Are we the only survivors?" I asked.

"I suppose so. There was nothing we could have done. It's my fault, I made the mistake of underestimating their advance. I knew they were in the area but I didn't think they would have moved so fast."

"There's no point blaming yourself," I said.

"I know, I know, but I was responsible for the lives of those men and it weighs heavy on me. The usual precaution and it may not have happened," he said and stood up. "Anyway, first thing tomorrow we better try and find Okafor's men and join up with them until we get fresh orders."

We started off, traveling slower to keep up our strength. Several detours were necessary to avoid the worst of the undergrowth. Once I nearly stepped on a boa constrictor; as for the mosquitoes our sweat and blood seemed to attract them from miles around. At last, as the sun was starting to set, we came in sight of the village, just as he had predicted.

We approached with caution. About a hundred yards away, concealed by the bushes, we lay down and waited for darkness. A few women, children, and old men wandered about talking in low voices.

"That is the hut we will spend the night in," he said, pointing to one near us.

"Who does it belong to?"

"A woman I used to know when I was a child. We grew up

in the same neighborhood and then she married a man from here."

"Do you know her husband?"

"Yes. He's a good soldier."

"Where is he now?"

"Who knows? Fighting somewhere most probably."

From his shirt pocket he produced a crumpled cigarette and a match. He broke the cigarette in half and we smoked in silence.

"What were you doing before this war started?" he asked afterward.

"I was studying at the University."

"One of the lucky ones, eh? When I was fifteen I was supporting my family. I had six younger brothers and sisters and my father was a drunk. One day he disappeared and we were all a lot happier," he said.

The sun was now an orange glow on the horizon. In a moment it would be out of sight.

"Where is your family?" he asked.

"In Lagos. My father didn't waste any time. When he saw what was happening he packed up and took them all to safety."

"Why didn't you go with them?"

I shrugged. "It's not so easy to say. I was idealistic enough in those days to think that it was my duty to fight for what I believed in."

"And now?"

"I'm not sure any longer whether it's worth believing in anything. I've seen so much death and misery to think anything can be worth it."

He laughed. "You know what your trouble is," he said.

"What?"

"You think too much. Life has always given you a choice

whereas I have always had to survive from day to day the best way that I could."

The darkness was falling rapidly. A few stars had appeared in the sky.

"War is a peculiar thing," he said.

"How do you mean?"

"For example, it is only because of it that you and I met."

"We might have otherwise, you never know. The world is altogether a very strange place indeed. Sometimes, if I think about it long enough, I find it hard to believe that it's real, do you understand me? It's as if the whole thing is just a dream, a bad joke, and nothing really exists. I'm not saying it very well but do you see what I'm getting at?" I said, half-ashamed at my outburst.

"I already told you, you think too much," he said and laughed.

It was completely dark now. We had to wait until the moon had risen to give us enough light.

"All my family are dead," he suddenly said after what seemed like a long time.

"I'm sorry."

"They were traveling to my mother's town and the bus was blown up. There were no survivors. I heard about it many months later."

"I'm sorry," I said again.

After about an hour we decided to move. As we neared the village we heard voices but saw no one. We reached the hut and entered quickly.

"Who is there?" a woman's voice called.

"It is I, Chike. I have a friend with me."

"Wait," she said. I heard the rustle of clothes, and then she struck a match.

"Sit down," she said, indicating two chairs. By the light of the candle I saw that she was young. Her head was bare and she was wearing a faded cotton housecoat. She drew a curtain across the doorway. Then she gave us some bread and margarine and sat down on the bed.

When we finished eating she said: "There is a rumor that the Federal troops will be here by morning."

"I thought as much," he said. "We left them not twelve hours ago. Don't worry about them. What of you, how are you keeping?"

"Obi was killed, did you hear?"

"No, I didn't. When did it happen?"

"About six months ago. Thank God he saw his son before he died."

For the first time I noticed the child on the bed.

"Are they treating you well here?"

"As well as I can expect, but you know how it is. I married one of their sons but I am not one of them."

"Our people!" he said and shook his head.

"It's better if I blow the candle out so as not to attract attention," she said. She got up and took a mat from under the bed and handed it to me.

"Can you manage with this?" she asked me.

"Thank you," I said. I rolled it out in a corner and lay down and then realized how tired I was. Before I knew it I had dozed off.

The war had made me into a light sleeper. While it was still dark I was woken by voices from the bed.

"I am afraid to die," he was saying.

"We must all die when our time has come," she said.

"I don't have your faith. I don't believe in God anymore."

"You're suffering from strain, you don't know what you are saying. Try and sleep, it will be better in the morning."

"It won't be better in the morning, it will be the same . . . and the next day and the next."

There was a desperate quality to his voice. I had heard it so many times before. In most cases it turned out to be a premonition of death, but perhaps someone in that state just becomes careless. The baby stirred and began whimpering.

"Wait, I must feed it," she said. There was a movement and then I heard it suckling with short, greedy noises.

"Obi was strong, that is why you married him. I am weak," he said.

"No, you mustn't talk like that. You are only human."

I heard him sit up. And then I heard him crying.

"Come," she said, "come."

As the time passed he grew calmer. By now I could make out their forms, three shapes crouched together on the bed. She was sitting up, her back to the wall, while the baby suckled at one breast and the man at the other. And then I heard her own weeping, quieter, more restrained than his, and then I fell asleep again.

VII

What could I have done? There were five of them, and they were armed, and there was just her and me, tired, hungry, and demoralized. We were at their mercy, and they knew it. At best I could have gone for one of them, but that would only have been misplaced heroism, surely you can see that. Just look at the facts and tell me what you would have done. One move and they would have cut me down without a thought. As it was I could see that two of them had half a mind to put a bullet through me and have done with it. Who would have known? I would have just been another dead Biafran, so much the better!

It was like this. In the middle of the night our town was attacked. Our own soldiers ran away and we civilians were herded into the hotel. Sure I had listened to their propaganda, their promises that no genocide would be committed, but would you have believed them? Those Nigerian soldiers were wild, let me tell you, and to make matters worse they had uncovered a stash of palm wine and they were getting drunk. There was no telling what they would do. So I escaped. I ran into the forest and just kept on running until I dropped from exhaustion.

Toward morning I fell asleep. When I woke up there she was squatting on the ground beside me.

"What are you? How did you find me?" I asked her.

"I followed you," she said.

"I didn't hear you. Why didn't you call out to me?" I asked.

"I did not want to frighten you. Anyway, you would have told me to go back because I am a woman," she said.

"Who are your people?" I asked her.

"I am not from your town," she said. "I am from N___, but after we were attacked I and my family left with the others."

"Where is your family now?"

"I left them behind. They did not want to come with me. They said that they were tired of running," she said.

We started off. If we followed the sun I knew that we would reach the main road by nightfall, and from there we could follow it to the new capital. If we moved quickly the journey would take us about five days.

All that day we pushed forward. We were lucky that the rainy season was late otherwise it would have been impossible.

As it was, without a machete, we had a tough time getting through the worst of the undergrowth. I was surprised that she was able to keep up with me and did not once complain. My annoyance at her presence gradually gave way to pity, and then admiration. In the end I was grateful to have company.

Just before dark I called a halt. We found a clearing about half a mile from the road.

"The Red Cross people use that road," I said. "We may be lucky tomorrow and meet one of their trucks."

"And if we don't?"

"Then we will have to beg. There is a village about twenty miles farther on, they cannot refuse us."

We set about collecting wood, and when we had enough I set fire to it. I hoped there were no troops about, but I was more afraid of being attacked by animals. I could hear hyenas in the distance, and I knew it was our presence that they could smell.

I smoked my last cigarette, but on an empty stomach it made me dizzy.

"What is your name?" I asked her.

"Charity."

"Are your people Christians?"

"Yes."

"I don't believe in the white man's God," I said. She did not answer. She just squatted there and gazed at the fire.

"How old are you?" I asked.

"Eighteen," she said. A bat flew by overhead. It looked black against the purple sky.

"What were you doing before the war began?" I asked. She threw some more sticks on the fire. They crackled and sparked and lit up her face.

"Nothing. We were poor farmers. I helped my mother in the house," she said.

I put out my hand and touched her arm. "Come and lie

down with me," I said. She did so. I held her to me, and then
made love to her. She was a virgin.

We slept fitfully that night. Every now and then she would
get up and feed the fire, but it was the mosquitoes that kept us
awake. They buzzed round our ears and by the sound of them
they must have been monsters.

When day broke we set off again. The going was easier but
we had to remain on the alert all the while. In the middle of the
afternoon we heard a truck approach. We hid in the bushes but
when it passed us I saw that it was our own troops. We went
back on the road to listen for others. I was certain they were
heading for the capital and they might see their way to giving us
a ride. Sure enough another approached. I waved it down but it
wasn't until a Nigerian soldier jumped down that I realized I had
made a mistake.

So you see. You can't say that once I had hailed them down
we could have escaped. We were at their mercy. They took us
into the back of their truck and then one by one they raped her
while I was forced to watch. She screamed and fought and
begged, but what could she have done against them? And let me
tell you, I made myself deaf to her suffering, I did nothing, and
worse. When the ringleader had finished with her he looked at
me and smiled. Yes, he smiled at me, and I smiled back. I knew
he despised me, that he was saying, "Look at what I can do to
your woman in your presence and there is nothing you can do
about it"; and I was saying, "Do what you like with her, what is
she to me? She is only a woman, but please spare me." He knew
what I was thinking and he despised me even more. To him I
was less than a dog. When they finished they drove off and left us
there.

Now I ask you: Would you have done otherwise? Would
anybody else have done different? Only a fool would have tried
to stop them. Put yourself in my place for a moment and think

about it. It was a time of war, normal feelings and behavior no longer applied. For the next eighteen months I forgot all about it. When you are fighting for survival you forget everything except what concerns you at the present time. But it couldn't last forever, and sooner or later it had to end. I began to dream about her, and then I could think of nothing else. I remembered how I had smiled at the soldier and what had gone through my mind. Gradually I lost interest in everything. Women no longer attracted me and I did not care about my work or anything. Life seemed pointless and the struggle for survival a waste of time. I know now that it would have been better for me to have died then. Life has become pointless, do you understand what I am saying?

ACKNOWLEDGMENTS

Grateful acknowledgment is made to the following for permission to reprint their copyrighted material.

"Four Dimensions" by I. N. C. Aniebo, from *Of Wives, Talismans and the Dead*. Copyright © 1983 by I. N. C. Aniebo. Reprinted by permission of the author.

"Une Vie au Détail" by Mohammed Berrada, from the periodical *Lotus, Afro-Asian Writings,* Journal of Afro-Asian Writers Association, No. 59, 1988. Not copyrighted. (Translation by Alice Copple-Tošić.)

"A Child in the Bush of Ghosts" by Olympe Bhely-Quenum, from the Nigerian periodical *Okike*. Copyright © 1980 by *Okike*. Reprinted by permission of O. O. Enekwe, editor, on behalf of the author.

"Le Completveston" by Ali Deb, from the periodical *Lotus, Afro-Asian Writings,* Journal of Afro-Asian Writers Association, No. 59. 1988. Not copyrighted. (Translation by Alice Copple-Tošić.)

"The Last Battle" by O. O. Enekwe. Published by permission of the author.

"Bossy" by A. R. Gurnah, from the Nigerian literary periodical *Okike,* January 1979. Copyright © 1979 by *Okike*. Reprinted by permission of O. O. Enekwe, editor, on behalf of the author.

"Papa, Snake & I" by L. B. Honwana, from *We Killed Mangy Dog and Other Mozambique Stories*. Copyright © 1969 by Luis Bernardo Honwana. Reprinted by permission of AP Watt Ltd., literary agent, on behalf of the author.

"Hot Days, Long Nights" by Nnadazie F. Inyama, from the Nigerian literary periodical, *Okike*. Copyright © 1989 by *Okike*. Reprinted by permission of O. O. Enekwe, editor, on behalf of the author.

"Waiting for a Turn" by Ken Lipenga, from *Waiting for a Turn*. Copyright © 1981 by Popular Publications. Reprinted by permission of Popular Publications, Malawi.

"The Advance" by Henri Lopès, from the book *Tribaliks, Contemporary Congolese Stories*. Copyright © 1971 by Editions Cle, Yaounde. English language translation copyright © 1987 by Andrea Leskes. First published by Heinemann Educational Books Ltd. in the African Writers Series in 1987. Reprinted by permission of Andrea Leskes.

"It Was Easter Sunday the Day I Went to Netreg" by Sindiwe Magona, from *Living, Loving and Lying Awake at Night*. Copyright © 1991 by Sindiwe Magona. Reprinted by permission of the author.

"Civil War I–VII" by Adewale Maja-Pearce, from *Loyalties*. Copyright © 1986 by Adewale Maja-Pearce. Reprinted by permission of Longman Group Ltd., UK.

"Thought Tracks in the Snow" by Dambudzo Marechera, from *The House of Hunger*. Copyright © 1978 by Dambudzo Marechera. Reprinted by permission of Zimbabwe Publishing House (PVT) Ltd., Zimbabwe.

"L'Autre Ville" by Ibrahim Abdel Megid, from the periodical *Lotus,* Afro-Asian Writings, Journal of Afro-Asian Writers Association, No. 59, 1988. Not copyrighted. (Translation by Alice Copple-Tošić.)

ABOUT THE EDITOR

Nadežda Obradović is a critic and eminent scholar of African literature at the University of Belgrade in Yugoslavia. She is the editor of *Looking for a Rain God: An Anthology of Contemporary African Short Stories*.